# RESIDUAL SUGAR

## GELBERT FAMILY WINERY

FIVE FAMILIES VINEYARD ROMANCE

KELLY KAY

Published by Decorated Cast Publishing, LLC

✻ Created with Vellum

*For Nancy.*
*I'll be shocked if she reads it, but she'll be more shocked it was dedicated to her. Love you.*
*Thanks for ALWAYS being in my corner.*
*Xo*

## ALSO BY KELLY KAY

All books available on Kindle Unlimited*

### FIVE FAMILIES VINEYARD ROMANCES

Interconnected standalone by winery small town series exploring the lives and loves of five winery families.

### LaChappelle/Whittier Vineyard Trilogy

(Josh & Elle) *Enemies to Lovers*

*Crushing, Rootstock & Uncorked*

### Stafýlia Cellars Duet

(Tabi & Bax) *Friends to Lovers*

*Over A Barrel & Under The Bus*

### Gelbert Family Winery

*Meritage: An Unexpected Blend* (Nat & David)

*Secret Baby, Reformed Player, Single Dad*

*Residual Sugar*

(Becca & Brick) *Reverse Grumpy Sunshine, Forced Proximity, funny suspense*

### Pietro Family Estate

*Bottled Up*

(Poppy & Sal) *Mafia, Opposites Attract, Secret Life*

## Coming in 2024

### <u>Langerford Cellars</u>

*Complex Finish*

*Suspense and an epic second chance*

### <u>Prohibition Winery</u>

*Grand Cru*

*A series epilogue and a wedding that should have happened five babies ago*

(Pre-Orders are live)

BOSTON BROTHERS: a second chance series

Keep Paris

Keep Philly - a newsletter exclusive novella

Keep Vegas

Keep Tuscany - (pre-order live!) when life gives you lemons, make limoncello - A single dad, second chance with lots of pasta.

CHITOWN LOVE STORIES

**A Lyrical Romance Duet**

Shock Mount & Crossfade

**A Lyrical Spinoff Standalone**

Present Tense

CARRIAGE HOUSE CHRONICLES

Funny, steamy, standalone novellas

ChiTown spin offs

Follow Me - Now available

Sound Off

For the Rest of Us

Something Good

EVIE & KELLY'S HOLIDAY DISASTERS*

ROMCOM Holiday Novellas with Evie Alexander

**VOLUME ONE**

Cupid Calamity

Cookout Carnage

Christmas Chaos

*(Not in Kindle Unlimited)

# NOTE TO READERS

**Welcome back to Sonoma!**

As with all the winery books, this book can be read as a standalone but has all the winery folks involved. You don't need to know them ahead of time, or if you only know a book or two, or even just Tabi, you'll be more than fine.

If you want to read the entire series, it starts with Crushing and can currently be found in Kindle Unlimited and on Amazon.

There are lots of breadcrumbs leading up to this story for those who have lived in the world of the Five Families with me. But again, you don't need to know any of them to enjoy.

TRIGGER WARNINGS- there are several violent scenes off-page, and there are some deaths that occur off-page. There's some threatening violence on the page and the aftermath. And there's language and explicit sex, but you knew the last two.

THANK YOU.

Happy Reading.

Talk soon,
Kelly K

# Residual Sugar
## Five Families Vineyards Romances Book 7

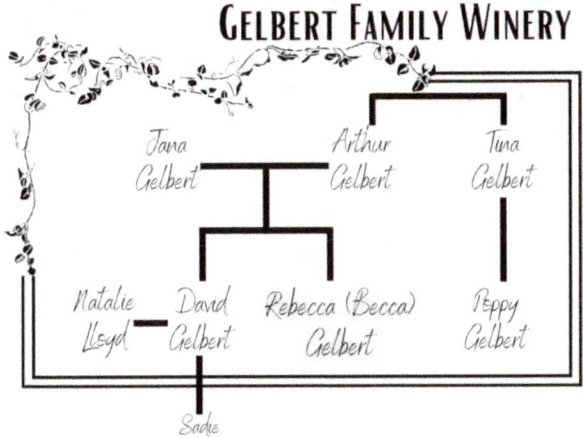

## GELBERT FAMILY WINERY

Jana Gelbert — Arthur Gelbert | Tina Gelbert

Natalie Lloyd — David Gelbert | Rebecca (Becca) Gelbert | Poppy Gelbert

Sadie

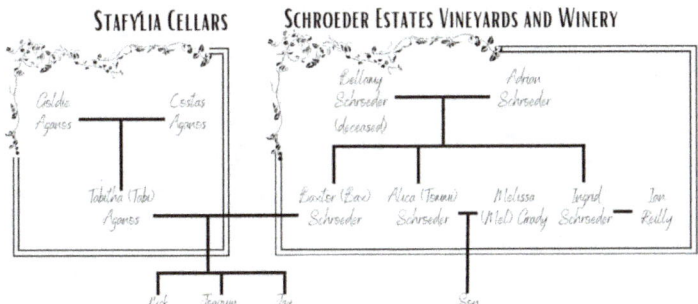

### STAFYLIA CELLARS

Ovidia Agonos — Cestas Agonos

Tabitha (Tabi) Agonos

Nick | Joaquin | Jay

### SCHROEDER ESTATES VINEYARDS AND WINERY

Bethany Schroeder (deceased) — Adrian Schroeder

Baxter (Bax) Schroeder | Alica (Teana) Schroeder | Melissa (Mel) Grady | Ingrid Schroeder — Ian Reilly

Stan

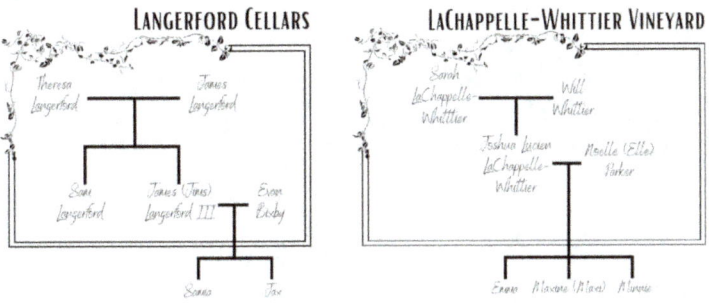

### LANGERFORD CELLARS

Theresa Langerford — James Langerford

Sean Langerford | James (Jones) Langerford III | Evan Busby

Sonia | Tori

### LACHAPPELLE-WHITTIER VINEYARD

Sarah LaChappelle-Whittier — Will Whittier

Joshua Lucian LaChappelle-Whittier — Noelle (Elle) Parker

Emma | Maxine (Max) | Minnie

# DEFINITION

### <u>Residual Sugar</u>
ri-ˈzi-jə-wəlˈ/shú-gər

A winemaking term, residual sugar (or RS) refers to the sugars left unfermented in a finished wine. It is measured by grams of sugar per liter (g/l).

The amount of residual sugar affects a wine's sweetness. It's rare for a wine to drop below 1 g/l, because some types of sugar simply cannot be consumed by the yeast. So those rare residual sugars are considered stubborn but flavorful.

# CHAPTER 1
## BRICK

My head is thumping like a bad Sunday morning. My side aches. Feels like a sting or graze or something that shouldn't be part of my life these days. I try to put together all the fuzziness in my brain. I got a good lump as a souvenir from some asshole who's fixin' for a face-to-face with my boot. There were two of them. One with the gun and the other piece of shit who hit me from behind. I'm not one to fall prey to that kind of bullshit and that's got me sorer than the bruises. It was planned. Last thing I remember was falling onto the pavement. It was daylight and now we're deep into midnight.

My brain is buzzing like a hive, and I slowly groan and feel around. It's sticky all around me. It's warm and not right. My side is burning but it's not bad. My fingers touch a hot scrape and the crust of dried blood. Shit. How long have I been out? And who the fuck tried to shoot me?

I slowly wedge my eyes open and I'm in my truck. I know it from the notch on the wheel where I dig my nail into it when I'm stressed. But this 4x4 should be in the shop, not here. I was driving my BMW; this is something I know. I grab the steering wheel, sitting up to look around. In my groggy state of mind, I check for my billfold. It's there. As is my gun, still hidden under my seat. What the fuck? As the curtains of my brain slowly open, I hear strained breathing.

Adrenaline pops everything dislocated back into place, and I see her. I don't know her, but she's bleeding. It's her blood on my hands, my shirt, my blazer, and all over my truck cab. With great effort I wrench myself up to my side and sit all the way up. I push back her lanky blonde hair and I don't know this soul. I see her lungs struggling to hang on. Everything has gone sideways, and I have to right it. I might think of a million ways this could go, but there's only one thing to be done. The thing my Mimi Tinker would have me do first.

I reach over and feel her pulse. She groans and squirms creating a new path for the blood. She's holding her stomach. I triage the situation the way I was trained, and I assess she was nicked in a place nowhere around the neighborhood of a major organ or artery. She was cut to bleed not to die. I know my way around a knife and so did whoever did this to her.

I reckon I should take pictures but without even looking, I know my phone is gone. Pretty sure that's gonna come back and bite me in the ass. I'll lock it remotely as soon as possible. I need to get my shit straightened out first. One thing at a time is the only plan I got right now. That's all I can focus on. The girl. The one bleeding out in my passenger seat.

I grab a towel from my gym bag and put pressure on her wound. She groans again but she's gone to the clouds for the moment. The rain is taking away the clear vision of a straightforward path. I can see the lit beer signs of a bar.

And I see some approaching red and blues. No sirens but I know where they're headed. I keep my lights off and ease my truck around the back of the establishment. It's coming on 01:00 a.m.

My training kicks in again as I pull out of the roadhouse parking lot and into a neighborhood, one I've never laid an eye on. One hand on the wheel and one on the poor filly who most likely did nothing wrong but be in the wrong place.

First questions. What are my steps for success? Where can I regroup? Where the fuck am I? And who the hell set me up? Who can I trust? I drive a little further and I'm about four towns over from where I started the day. I finally find the Napa Vallejo Hwy, which is a good thing.

I pull up to the Napa State Hospital Emergency Room doors and run inside. I see a big fella in scrubs and grab him.

"I need your help. There's a woman in my truck who needs your help immediately. I don't know what happened to her. I found her like this. I put pressure on her abdomen, but it appears she's been cut by a smooth blade. I'm ex-military and I recognize the wound. She's bleedin' pretty good and I don't know when it happened." My Mississippi accent is thicker as I speak quickly, and he looks confused.

"Don't panic, sir. Are you ok?"

I shake off the fella. Whatever attending I need will be done elsewhere. "I'm fine. This here is her blood, not mine. Now, grab that wheelchair." The man does and follows me out. He's calling colleagues.

"We need to book an OR and tell them we need all hands on deck. We have a bleeder. Get the attending, NOW."

She's slumped over now. I carefully open the door and the resident assesses the poor soul.

"Her pulse is thready. But it's there. Ma'am. Ma'am, can you hear me?" He waits to move her, but her head keeps lolling backward as he tries to stabilize her. He gets a collar on her as a gurney, a trauma team, and two orderlies come crashing out the doors and move me out of the way. They all evaluate her as they move her onto the gurney and quickly disappear. The big fella yells after me, "We need her information. Check in with the front desk and once we get her settled, we'll update you."

I search my truck for any ID or purse. I know it's futile, but I look anyway. I grab a blanket from the back and wipe my hands. Then I put it on the seat to help soak up some of the blood. The smell is acrid and tinny. I hate the smell of blood. I hate that I know it so well. I put on a pair of weightlifting gloves to hide my bloody knuckles. I have no fucking clue how that happened, but they're ripped to shreds. Nothing's making sense but I need to do what's right and that's the only thought I can put together. One step at a time. Finish this task and move on to the next. Protect yourself and move along.

I hustle on back inside. I pull out my billfold and place down a stack of hundreds in front of a stunned woman who looks to be administrative.

"She has no ID. I don't know who she is, but this is for her, you hear? She's not a lady of the evening and I'm no client. I found this poor soul and thought you'd be the ones to see after her. I don't know a thing about her except she's hurting." She nods. "If there's extra money after her care, please give it to some sort of hospital charity that helps with the bills of those who can't pay. Do I have your word there, ma'am?"

She's staring at me. I'm sure I look menacing as fuck. I'm a bloody 6'5" man who doesn't miss a day at the gym.

"Ma'am? Can I count on you to take real good care of her?" She nods but her face is all quizzical.

I'm going to take advantage of her stunned behavior and save myself some headaches. "Thank you kindly. Now if I could plug this into your computer right quick like, I'll be out of here." She nods again, still stunned. She hasn't even called for assistance or asked me a question.

I pull a pouch out of my navy-blue jacket pocket and unzip it. I find the pen drive and insert, count to thirty and return it to its pouch. Then I bolt out of there, pushing my way through the electric doors that won't work again for another twenty minutes along with the camera system.

I jump back in my truck and take off. I set off towards a place I don't come often but think about way too much. Well, fuck. I might as well go all-in on this thought. I don't really have anywhere else to turn. I take a corner and a couple of police cars go careening into the hospital. I need to get my truck off the road and get myself cleaned up. My head is still whomping.

I point my truck down the road to the only place I can think of that's completely off anyone's radar. A safe house if you will. It's become a safe house in my head too, but now I have to make it a reality. Whoever wants me to take a fall won't know where I'm headed. I've kept her hidden from every part of my life except in my mind. I'm out of moves and I don't abide by the rules of checkmate.

I take a sharp right and head towards one of the only things I've ever wanted and never got.

I've spent a good coupla years thinking about the day we spent together. The company I worked for was doing an inspection of assets we thought we owned, and she was our escort that day. But then that smart, talented woman bested us and proved we didn't own shit. In those last moments,

5

before my colleagues left with their tails between their legs, we shared a look, and we connected in that dusty old board-room. I felt seen for the second time in my life. Nobody except my Mimi Tinker could make me as secure and okay in my skin the way this one does. I don't know her, but I've craved her from that first day. Pining ain't the right word, we'd need to be more acquainted for me to pine. Every piece of me is drawn to this woman. She's the most stunning creature I've ever encountered, and I can only chalk that up to the idea of a heart song.

My grandmother, Mimi Tinker, always used to say my grandfather was her heart song. I don't know about my mama and stepdaddy. They didn't care much for each other, and my real daddy left long before anyone got to know him. Not sure if my parents were myth or mist, they took off for a life they thought they deserved, and it didn't bother me none. I had Mimi and Granddaddy Tinker. They took care of me the way a child should be. I knew the rules and if I broke them, I accepted the punishments. And my favorite cobbler for dessert let me know there were no hard feelings between us all. I got to grow up knowing I was always surrounded by love and care. I've been told that wouldn't have been the case if Mama had stuck around.

But when Granddaddy died, I wasn't sure Mimi would survive. She said she was hollow, except for me. And even though I was twelve, I knew I wasn't enough to fill up her soul. Her time, sure, her patience, always, but her soul left this earth a spell before her body did. It went with him.

Now, I know the idea of a soulmate is a fool's errand that has you chasing shadows. I've been down that road a time or two, thinking I was getting what I deserved. I ached when it all ended, and I thought I knew what heartbreak was. But now I know, I've never even been close to cherishing someone and feeling that in return. I know now that this woman, whether she's ready or not, is my destiny. She's the one that floats all my boats. I only hope I'm what she deserves. Perhaps I have been pining. This isn't quite the sweeping her off the feet moment I had hoped for.

I'm dripping wet and I remove my, worse for wear, sport coat. My shirt is stained with blood. Most people should be alarmed at the blood, but after what I've seen and done on this mortal coil, I'm immune to it.

I didn't know that poor woman. I know it was someone else sticking their nose into my business that had no bother being there. They want this stranger to be my downfall for some reason. I delivered the woman to the hospital and hope and pray she's okay. But I know they saw my face in that emergency room. There's no way to hide the puddles of blood in my truck. I don't know who left her there, but I can suspect why. I don't have no mind to think it through. My brain is still a bit scattered, and I need to pull my wits about me. I've got nowhere to turn but to her.

I glance down, looking at the tip of the wing peeking out of my cuff. It travels up my wrist and lands on my forearm. But that colorful green and purple wingtip grazes the base of my thumb. I rub my left thumb over it. It calms me. It always regulates my heartbeat and has since I got that tattoo. It reminds me that I deserve good things. It reminds me to stay on the right path. Taking her to the hospital is exactly what they knew I'd do. That I'd expose myself to save another. They can dispense with me without getting blood on their hands, only mine. But they don't know what, or who in this case, I have up my sleeve.

I hate to bring her into this. I hate it beyond words. I wanted to come to her clean when I claimed her, cleaning up my backyard before I let her know we were a forgone conclusion. I wanted to foster the flow of whatever tie that binds us together and reveal myself slowly. But plans are a funny thing, you can never count on them when you need them. I've adapted and pivoted my whole life. It's just time to speed up the inevitable.

She's not going to know what hit her little life, but it's time to expand hers to include me. I would have pined for her for forever if it kept her safe. But now that this strong goddess is about to be in front of me, I know I'll never walk away from her. She's my heart song.

I pound on the door.

# CHAPTER 2

## BECCA

can't sleep. It's almost two in the morning and I'm restless. That's all it is because I don't buy into insomnia. I'm not overthinking things because I don't do that anymore. I fixed that. I put it on a list and crossed it off.

I breathe in and out with the 7-4-8 trick. And now I feel like I'm going to hyperventilate. It's Saturday and I keep checking my phone to see if my online date from last week messaged back. I gave him the grace period of the holiday to send me a reply. I texted that he was pleasant, and I'd like to have a meal together. But I've heard nothing from him. What the hell is wrong with pleasantness?

Later today I have to deliver a whole round of paperwork for my dad to sign. I sit up and stare at a picture of my family across the room. I talk directly to my insane father, "Seriously, Gelbert Family Winery is downsizing our vineyard holdings but somehow you believe you're going to increase distribution. Sometimes I think you create challenges for yourself to create paperwork for me."

I smack the pillows behind me and rearrange them, turning away from my family. Tomorrow's agenda also has me babysitting my two-year-old niece, Sadie, because I lost a fucking bet with my brother, David. Asshole. I love my brother, most of the time. I like him more now that he's found Natalie and accidentally became a father. Not necessarily in that order.

I'm currently reading how to entertain a tiny person. It says wooden toys and peek-a-boo are a better idea than the two of us settling in to catch up on the Housewives.

As that kid grows up in our odd extended family, I want her to know I'm a safe haven. I set up my life and practice in Napa. I'm twenty minutes and a world away from the five winery families, in Sonoma, that make up my large extended found family. They say it takes a village to raise a child, well, I'd like Sadie to know that she can hide from our village here, the way I do.

A banging on my front door startles me and my book goes flying. No one comes to the front. My close-knit neighborhood all have keys and everyone uses the back door. I appreciate whoever this is didn't just walk in, but the banging is excessive.

The knock comes again. I grab a sports bra. It's probably my stupid brother, who's once again lost his key. I think he had a holiday dinner in town and probably doesn't want to drive back to Sonoma. The knock is now a loud thumping. He's probably dripping on my front porch pissed off. Whatever, use your key, asshole.

I whip open the door and lose my breath. It's filled with a menacing man whose steel-gray eyes penetrate my soul in an instant. He's so broad and his chiseled face is slightly pained. The raindrops are collecting slightly in his stubble that covers his sculpted chin. I react and try to close my door. He puts his large hand out and catches it before it can close.

"Do you remember me?" His voice is deep and laced with desperation.

My skin seizes up and adrenaline floods my system. I'm panting as I try to think of words. I know exactly who this dripping Adonis is, and I've fantasized about him often over the past two years and thirty-seven days. But how does he remember me? We only had two encounters and I'm pretty forgettable.

His deep, rich voice rumbles through my foyer and my panties. "Miss Rebecca Gelbert. I need your help awful bad, Miss." His Southern accent drips with a slow burn of embers.

I stumble backward at the sound of my name on his full lips. He steps into the light, water dripping from his granite carved features. His mahogany hair is shorter than before. He must be 6'4" and his shining mercurial gray eyes are piercing all the air and light around me. I don't usually think things like this but he's untamed and dripping on my front porch. My body is numb, but there's a deep burning low in my stomach. It's pulsing from inside of me and moving up and down my body.

His shirt is pulling and stuck to his taut torso and pronounced biceps and pecs. The top two buttons of his white dress shirt are undone exposing his chest ink. He looks menacing and delicious. Then I see it. There's blood on his shirt. It's diluted from the rain but it's there. I grab his arm.

"Let me inside, Rebecca. I won't hurt you. I need you. This isn't my blood, and I didn't cause anyone to bleed."

I don't move.

"Ms. Rebecca, I don't work for that company any longer. Left the moment after we had our exchange."

I sputter out the word, "Asher."

"I swear to you, I don't know anything about that. Last I heard there were powers weightier than me keeping him alive in prison, so more harm would come to him."

He worked with the monster who assaulted my friend, Elle. Asher served several months in prison but never made it to final sentencing. I was robbed of closure. I wanted to be the one to put him in jail to rot forever. Other than a thumb and a bag full of teeth, no other part of him was recovered. And I have it on pretty high authority an inmate was paid to keep him alive so he could be sentenced and punished by his peers. But someone else got to him.

"This is a lot to take in, but I'm a little in the weeds here and could sure use your help."

I nod slightly. It's like this is happening to someone else and the real Becca will wake up with Netflix asking me if I'm still watching.

"Rebecca, can you please open your garage? I need to pull my truck in there if it's not too much trouble." There's tautness in his baritone voice and shoulders. His broad and impossibly beautiful shoulders are so big. It's possible I'm doing something illegal, but I obey him, nonetheless. My body and soul are overriding my mind. I should be rejecting him and everything in this situation but there's something telling me I'm doing the right thing.

"Yes. Sorry. Oh, my God. Yes."

There's a heat and connection between us similar to the spark from that damn handshake when we last met back in a banal conference room. Everything else was drab but I felt colorful by the way he looked at me. No one on the planet would describe me as colorful, but I felt as if I'd landed in Oz. It was a fleeting moment when our eyes locked, and our hands held fast.

I leave the door open, reach into my purse on the hall

table and push the opener. He nods and disappears back into the rain. I stare at the spot he occupied. The weather is crisper as it turns almost to January and the rain lends a chill to the air. But it's nothing compared to the chill down my spine. It's warring with the heat between my legs and swirling in my belly.

I don't know how to reconcile all of this. I roll through all the information I know about this man, who I'd convinced myself couldn't possibly be real. I pace around the living room listing off the things I know. He was the head of the Vino Groupies collective that turned out to be a shell company for land developers. They wanted space within Sonoma City limits to build things my town doesn't allow, like Targets and McMansions. One of the men behind almost destroying my childhood home and winery. He was there the day we took back the wineries. He watched closely as I dismantled Asher's decades-long revenge plot. And he apologized; he had no idea it was a swindle, and he was a pawn. I believed him.

I don't realize he's back until he takes the opener from me and closes the garage door.

"Thank you."

"Brick Dunne." I speak his name and a flash of hope flickers across his magnetic grays. A crinkle at the corners as his lips curl upward. And it's like quicksilver is in the air and in his gaze.

"Come." I put myself together enough, but I've invited a virtual, and very large, and possibly dangerous stranger into my home. He crosses the threshold and stands in my foyer dripping.

"Thank you, kindly. Thank you so much, Ms. Rebecca."

"Becca."

"Becca." A shiver of excitement runs down my neck. It's as if he whispers my name like a prayer.

"Are you hurt?" I ask.

"A little but most of this isn't mine. I didn't know where else to turn and I'm gonna hate on myself a while for bringing this to you, but on a night like this you're the only one I wanted to see."

I don't know what to do with any of that. I pull my bathrobe tighter, untying and retying my robe several times. I'll put that away for later, there are things to be done, a checklist to be made and hormones to ignore.

My lawyer brain wrestles control from my pussy brain and is firmly back in command. "Stay here." I bolt to the linen closet, while grabbing supplies and responsible things. My arms are full of towels, peroxide, band aids, and a box of extra-large Ziploc freezer bags for the evidence.

I careen around the corner and the giant; bloody man is squatting down petting my calico. The finicky cat is rubbing up on the wet stranger much like I want to.

She's an outdoor cat that occasionally visits when there's bad weather or the mousing has turned up empty. It was a winery barn cat at Gelbert's and my mother brought it over so I could love something. My mom's cute that way. The cat is fine, but we have a very hands-off relationship. There's not a lot of snuggling. The cat does what she wants and so do I. But if you've never seen a former military, Southern hottie stroking a cat behind its ears and your toes don't curl, then you might be dead. Fuck me, that's sexy. I exhale again to curb both my blind lust and the panic of a giant virtual stranger who showed up at my house in the middle of the night, and I just let him in.

I shake my head and pull my hair up into a bun. "Is your hand hurt?"

He looks up at me and his long eyelashes dust just under his eyes as he blinks away the remnants of rain. "No Counselor, it's fine. Just the knuckles seem to be a bit raw. But I do need your help with more than band aids. I reckon I'm in a bit of trouble."

"Stop talking. You need to give me a dollar." My instincts kick in and I want to help him, I believe him without even knowing the story. He may not have seen Asher's motives but the moment I laid eyes on that man, my gut churned. I read people for a living, and I'm really fucking good at what I do.

"Who carries cash?"

He smirks at me, and I can feel my lawyer brain slipping because of that sexy little smile. Becca, get back in control. There's a bloody stranger in your house, this is not a meet cute. It's a meet cut. He's cut and bleeding and so very hot.

Shit. Bring it back girl. He's watching me wrestle against myself and I ignore his curious expression. Rational Becca is back at the helm.

"Give me your watch. Surely that's worth a dollar. I'll return it to you after the case is closed. Consider it a retainer and collateral. And here's a towel, but first you need to remove your shirt, pants, socks, shoes, and um—"

"Not wearing any, darling." Oh shit. I breathe out again.

My voice is shaky, but I think I can pull this off. "Please place each individual item into a separate Ziploc."

I plant my feet to steady myself. Ok, back to work.

"I have a jacket in the truck."

My old public defender, criminal lawyer instincts kick in. It's been a minute since I tried a criminal case, but that muscle doesn't go away.

"That's fine. Let them process it as part of the crime

scene. Is someone dead?" He looks a little taken back by my bluntness, but we don't have time to fuck around.

"Not that I know of. I did all I could to make sure she stayed breathing, then dropped her off at the hospital."

"There was a bleeding girl?" I'm scanning his features to see any flicker or tell that he's lying.

"Yes, a stranger. She was in my truck when I woke up and I immediately took her to get help."

"Napa?" I ask rapidly.

"Yes, ma'am."

What happened to 'darling?' I guess when I switched back to professional Rebecca the term of endearment switched too. Fine. I'll be ma'am. It's not like the man thinks of me as anything but a professional. He did come here for help and that's what I do. Also, there's a hurt girl who's our focus.

"Here." I hand him a giant hotel robe I stole from MacArthur Place ages ago and a beach towel. He's a big dude, I figure he needs a big towel. He nods and I turn away.

"There's a bathroom around the corner if you want..." I turn back and he's pulling his wet shirt from his body. I'm instantly aflame with lust. He's a masterpiece of a sculptured man. His body is decorated with intricate patterns and colors. Each highlights the rippling muscles underneath. My eyes are drawn to his waistband and how his pants hang low slung as if they want to slip off. My mouth waters at the sight of his chest and then he sees me staring. I want to touch his ink. I want to examine it and lick every line and know each story. The hard planes of his pecs dance in the light and reflect the vibrant hues. I've never seen anything like this man. It's as if Brick and my ex, Larry, are different species. I didn't know a body could look like this without airbrushing on a book jacket.

His complexion complements the ink in a way that's all together delicious. I finally meet his gaze and his expression mirrors my thoughts. But he's looking like he wants to devour me. How is that possible?

I'm in a tank top and a shortie robe. My pale, thick, long legs stick out of my sleep shorts making me well aware of how out of my league I am. He continues to glare hungrily, and I'm confused. And he's bleeding on the left side of his body, and it looks as if something made a six-inch-long concentrated scrape. If my addiction to *Dateline* means anything, it appears to be a bullet graze.

He begins to remove his pants, and lord knows I can't watch that. I drop all the Ziplocs at his feet and run towards my bathroom. I glance back. Anyone would for a small glimpse of a perfectly lush ass. I grab a pair of gray basketball shorts my brother left and when I toss them, I hit him in the face.

"Message received." He laughs and I duck into the bathroom. I shake off the sight of him. I grab a wet washcloth. I return to him and lift his arm.

"What scraped you?"

And he confirms my suspicions, "Well, ma'am, a bullet. And before you clean it you might want to swab it for residue if the rain hasn't ruined everything."

"Hold on. Let me google how to do it." I've read how to do this, but I want to be sure. A big crack of laughter erupts out of him.

"Darling..." My nerves jump to attention now that I'm 'darling' again. "Just go get another one of those bags and some Q-tips. If you have the sealed kind, that would be best."

"Can't say this will be admissible, but it will be something. I don't think we can wait. I have Q-tips I stole from a hotel."

"You, the legal eagle, stole? How about this robe?"

I wave my hand at him and say, "Gift."

"Liar." He is correct.

"You don't know me well enough to say that, yet."

He smiles and a laugh he's trying to stifle creeps from his lips. "Rebecca Gelbert, you said a mouthful. That 'yet' holds as much promise as I need to see my way through the night."

He's so cute when he talks. This hulking man speaks like a Southern riddle. I don't want to be a liar or a thief to him and he must see it in my expression.

"Quit your panicking, now. I'm funnin' with you. Go get them hot, stolen contraband Q-tips."

"You're bleeding. How are you teasing me?"

"Call it a defense mechanism. Just changing my thinking."

I turn to run upstairs for the supplies, and it slips out. "I always masturbate to change my thinking." I slap a hand over my mouth, and I want to die. I want to be swallowed up by my hall carpet.

He licks his lips and says, "Duly noted." I stare at him as my entire body flushes with that annoying Irish blood red color. He grins and says, "Q-tips."

I dash away and return with everything I think we might need for this probably highly illegal operation. My cat is circling him.

"What's this one's name?"

"Calico."

He raises an eyebrow. "You sure do love her a lot with a name like that."

18

"She's only here part-time. We're not on an intimate level so why bother naming a stray cat? I'm sure she has another name, why waste my time naming her?"

He grins at me. His Southern drawl amps up,

*"The naming of cats is a difficult matter, it isn't just one of your holiday games;*
*You may think at first I'm as mad as a hatter. When I tell you, a cat must have three different names."*

I stare at him blankly. I know this, it's not something he made up. I'm searching my brain and he provides the answer.

"Mr. T.S. Eliot. Poetry pops in my brain at the oddest of times." He just quoted poetry to me while bleeding in my house and petting my cat. None of these things make any sense to me.

"Becks, I'm yanking your leg again. You need to lighten up." And now there's a nickname?

"I've been told. But perhaps we put away levity until I scrape your bloody wound for gunpowder residue, call the lab to get your truck processed, and call the sheriff to take your statement." He leers at me. "You don't have a choice. You want me to be your lawyer, I call the shots."

He crowds into my space and my body floods with warmth. How can a bloody man smell this good? Do I have a gore fetish? Hell of a time to find out. He says in a deep and raspy voice, "That's about the only place I'm going to let you call the shots." He winks at me and now I know I'm in an alternative reality. I exhale and he chortles a bit, making me squirm.

He winces as I dab at the cut. It's not deep but then I notice scratches on his shoulder. Deep grooves. Like I imagine someone might do during violent sex or as they try to escape. He winces as I touch those.

"Christ," he hisses.

"Did you not know those are there?" I survey them further.

"I was more focused on the lump on my head and the burn on my rib here. I promise you; I don't know a thing about those claw marks, ma'am. I swear."

I take multiple pictures of the marks and the bullet graze. I document them by sending the photos to my cloud and tagging them with date and time stamps. I also email them embargoed to Melissa Grady, my only employee.

"Do you want to go to the hospital so they can flush this out and get the GSR flakes to find the gun?"

He shakes his head.

"Do you want to go and have the nail marks on your back swabbed for DNA evidence?"

He shakes his head again.

"I can't defend you if you won't let me."

He speaks softly and roughly, "Well, the gun's in my truck. I'd bet Calico's ass on it. And the nails are probably the woman who just about died tonight. I don't know her. But I'm right sure I'm getting framed for her murder, should she die. This is mostly her blood. I was trying to help her."

"Don't move. And don't talk." I grab duct tape and place it over the wound. "This is going to hurt like hell, but it might work." I yank it off and he grits his teeth. I place a piece of packing tape over the sticky part and deposit it into a Ziploc. I dated a forensics guy for a while and picked up a few things. I repeat the process with the claw marks. He winces.

"Jesus H Christ, that smarts a bit." I write with a

Sharpie on all the bags, put them on the hall table, then turn to the man still dripping in my foyer.

"I woke up in a place I've never been with a girl I don't know a thing about."

The intense energy between us and the gory reality in plastic bags behind me war with my head and heart.

He outstretches his hand with his watch. Instead of taking it, I run my fingers along the outside of a bright hummingbird tattoo encircled in brambles and what look like grape vines. I trace his forearm; I can't stop myself and he doesn't pull back. It's sexy and delicate and completely out of character for me. He places his other hand on my hip and pulls me towards him.

Brick slips the watch into my robe pocket, then slides his hand into my hair, pulling it out of its messy bun. My long reddish locks fall just below my shoulders. Our eyes lock while he arranges my hair. It's like it's all happening in slow motion. No, it's like I'm watching a movie in slow motion. I gently run the pads of my fingers over the wound. He sucks in a breath through his teeth. He smirks again at me, then bends down and lifts my chin towards his face. His lips are so close to mine as I sigh. I hold on to his strong chest muscles that yield slightly to my touch. I've never wanted anything more in my life than for this to happen.

Brick is staring at me, caressing and holding my cheek and chin. His lips brush over mine and it's an inferno inside of me. Something breaks loose, a part I didn't know existed snaps off and lets out a flood of emotions and desires. These are deep and dark feelings I didn't know I was capable of. I open my mouth to him. And he takes my offering, greedily exploring me with his tongue. I'm captured by him and his strong grip on my hip and head. He's holding me to him as if I'd want to leave this moment. I want to move into this moment, live here. His sensual lips connect with mine in a kiss that's scorching and yet commonplace. Like this is the way we kiss all the time, nothing about it is awkward.

Then he whispers with his lips brushing across mine, "I didn't come here for this. I need your legal help."

"But," I whisper back and brush across his lips. It's more forward than I've ever been.

"I can't help myself. You're so fucking gorgeous in this light. Your eyes tell me you've thought about me too."

"I have." I'm breathy in my admission.

"The reality of you is so much better than the fantasies I've dreamed up in the last two years."

My breath catches as I smile at him. And then just as his lips feather across mine and I move my arms around him and the tension is great, the release and reward seconds away, there's a sudden crash at my kitchen door.

Brick pulls me behind him and takes a gun from the back of his waistband. Something I didn't know he had and was covered by the robe.

He whispers, "Stay here."

I whisper back, "You lied. Said it was in the truck. Is that the gun? It's evidence. You can't shoot someone else with it."

He whispers, "I didn't shoot anyone with it, yet." He glares at me and puts his finger over his lips. I toss my hands up and realize he's actually freaked out. He slinks towards my kitchen. There's another loud noise and then some feet shuffling. The screen door crashes on its frame and suddenly I've never been more on edge. Brick jumps into my kitchen flicking on the lights and a man aggressively yells, "Who the fuck are you?"

Brick answers in a deep menacing tone, "The fucker that will end you if you take another step."

I grin knowing my moron drunk brother probably just wet his pants. It's kind of satisfying.

I round the corner before anyone gets shot.

"Bec, who the hell is this in the fucking stolen robe? Shit, are those my shorts?"

Brick lowers his gun and turns to me, now in full light I see his face clearly. It's as gorgeous as I've dreamed of. The face that I've touched myself thinking about.

Brick looks crestfallen, and I quickly explain, "This is my brother, David." Brick lets a small, satisfied smile slip out as he holsters his weapon and flips the safety.

"This is Brick Dunne... A client." I stumble over my words. They shake hands as I turn on the Nespresso machine.

"A bleeding client wrapped in a stolen MacPlace robe" David's suit is disheveled, and he rubs his hands through his russet hair. He looks like he's been on a bender instead of hosting a high-end winemaker dinner.

"I didn't steal the robe." I sneer at him and pull-out coffee pods.

"Yes, you did." He leans back on my counter, and I wince at his muddy shoes on my clean kitchen floor.

I snap at him, "Whatever. My house, you never know what you'll find. Perhaps you return to your own house."

"A shirtless client in my shorts?" David crosses his arms over his chest and flicks his eyes back and forth between the two of us.

A shirtless client who's willing to protect me, and he doesn't even know me. I'm pulled to him, and I want my brother not to be here. It's not just the kiss I want, it's him. I want to know why he's here and what he wants from me aside from legal counsel. I want to protect him and defend him. Mostly I want to be touching and tracing his ink again.

But that spell was broken by my douche nozzle brother. And it's probably for the best. He's a client and we can't be together. Fate stopped us before we did anything illegal.

"His shirt is evidence. I can't discuss anything further. Go to bed, David."

"Nope. There's a gun."

# CHAPTER 3
## BRICK

shake her brother's hand and he lifts his chin at me. "Brick Dunne. Pleasure to make your acquaintance again. I apologize for the fright."

"Fright. That's exactly what I'd call it. I'm drunk. Tell me you're a hallucination brought on by too much Cabernet. I'm David Gelbert." He runs his hand over his shorn red hair. The rain has brought some bangs down in the front that I imagine had product in it before the monsoon.

I laugh a bit. "No, sir. I'm real, and we met briefly when I used to do some disreputable work for the Vino Groupies."

"Holy shit. That fucking giant gorilla man. Becca, really?"

I answer for her. "David, I'm here to talk about some things of a sensitive nature and tonight I'm a bit jumpy. But I assure you I left that job the moment I understood what was happening."

David points to the door. "You're not here for our wineries?"

I don't blame him for being paranoid. "Scout's honor." I

put my hand out once again. My handshake means something, and I hope his does too.

He shakes firmly and nods. "Then I should go. Because I'm no longer remotely buzzed after the gun play." Becca says, "Keep your mouth shut. It's a legal matter. Seriously, no one. And you can stay."

I say, "Or I can call him a car." I don't want her brother here. She's different with him here and I want that soft, caring, intriguing woman back. She touched me and I've never felt such electricity. Becca wasn't afraid of me but wanted me. She disappears with a start and it's awkwardly adorable. She runs back and tosses me a ruby t-shirt from her family's winery that says, "It's Wine O'clock Somewhere. Gelbert Family Winery." The two of them laugh, it's a little bit of a shirt, seeming better suited to fit Calico than me.

David pulls out his phone. "I'll head home. Sorry to interrupt your client meeting. Hope it's going to be a deep, long, probing deposition for you, Bec. You could really use some prolonged release time."

"Fuck you, David. Go to bed. Don't drive. Take the guest house. I have to work tonight, things you can't see or hear. And I'm calling Robert."

He kisses her on the cheek and shakes my hand again. "Well, tell Sheriff Bobby I said hi and I didn't do anything wrong this time." He pulls her into the corner and whispers in her ear with a death grip on her arm.

She nods and says, "I'm fine. I really am working. I'm ok."

"I'll be out back. Don't murder my sister." He points at me.

He's a good man and I honor him with a salute. "I'll do my best."

We both laugh and Becca takes off down a hallway, I presume to call this Robert fella, but stops when she realizes David hasn't left yet. He stares just behind me.

"Hey, Bec, you know that bet you lost?" He turns towards the back door. "Maybe we call that off until you get the bloody rags out of the house."

She smiles. "Good call. Go to bed." They have an unspoken thing you only have with folks you know real well. I used to have that with my chosen brothers growing up.

"Um. Bye." He leaves as Becca flits around pulling things and putting others away. She's a blur of energy as she even pulls out paper towels and wipes up the mud David left behind. She eventually makes a cup of coffee. I'm watching every flick of her wrist and bat of her eye. Our unspoken tension is building real good, as she tries to avoid it.

"Here." She hands me coffee I didn't ask for. Like she didn't know what to do with herself. Again, fucking adorable.

"Perhaps you come over here and sweeten this up a bit."

"Sugar. You need sugar." Her face is getting a touch rosy as she tries to hold down the fluster. She opens cabinets in a rush, missing my meaning. I want to taste her again, but the moment seems to have fallen into porch swinging. The kinda thing where y'all keep going moving back and forth and no one talks about the sexual elephant in the room.

There's no kinda way I should have my ass in a house like this. I may look the part these days, but I feel a smidge out of step. Her massive kitchen is organized, bright, and clean. Very specific, like she has a blueprint where everything goes. She's all hard angles like her house, but I see softness in her like a caged tiger waiting to get out. I want the woman inside of the lawyer, the one caring for me right now.

I'm hoping the business of the hour will calm her down a bit.

"I got shot a spell before the second man whomped my head and the world went to sleep." She stares at me for a moment caught in a thought. Then she gets an ice pack and wraps a tea towel around it. I place it on my lumpy head.

It's not just the house making me jittery, whoever felt the need to set me up, is waiting on their plan to come together. They're out there but even though I'm standing here, like a soaking wet duckling with a bit of stranger's blood on my hands, there's a rush of calm coming over me. Like a breeze breaking up a humid day. This woman turns up all my dials. She heats up even that itty-bitty back left burner no one ever uses.

I hadn't felt it anywhere in the world but in the brief moments I've spent in her company. That day we toured the five wineries, and I met her whole extended family. I met every winemaker, vintner, cousin, sibling, family, and every close friend she has, but my eyes never left her.

She spoke to me in a way that validated my soul. I made her laugh, and all those around us reacted like it wasn't something she did often. Her laugh is light and feminine, and I think she hides it away from people. But she couldn't hide it from me.

And, just like the first time I saw her, I feel as if I can exhale. I don't have to hold on to nothing if I don't want to, but when I look in her bright exotic green eyes it's like I'm holding everything. They're as soft as a freshly cut lawn in June. The kind you lie down on and stay a stretch watching the clouds roll by along with your troubles.

She's left me in her kitchen fighting off my thoughts. I'm

going to leave her to her life eventually, but I'll savor all these moments together. There's no place for me in her world. Hell, there's barely a place in her kitchen for me. I don't have a neat shelf she can stick me on.

I coulda gone and spent a pile of money on a stranger but something brought me to her doorstep. I regret the mess I dumped here but I don't regret seeing her or kissing her. I'm a big man who has spent his life making sure attachments were a thing of my past. It's why the military lapped me up for a life not many have the stomach for. But I'm completely undone by this woman. I can't explain it and I don't want to start pulling at the threads and watch it all unravel, but somehow, I'm supposed to be at her side, even for a little while.

I hear her in the hall on her phone and she's squawking about getting processed and something about the sheriff's office. I'm keeping my ears perked, but I gotta believe she's working in my best interest.

They had to know me real well in order to pull this off. That's what's pissing me off the most. Somebody got the fucking jump on me for maybe the second time in my life. But they sure as shit made this one count.

They knew I'd help that poor filly. They knew where my truck was and where I kept my gun. And I'd bet fate, her knife wounds match the type of blade I used to carry, and I know the bullet came from my Glock. And furthermore, I'll bet a needle to a haystack, that poor girl has GSR on her hands as if she shot me out of self-defense. It's how I would have set myself up.

Time to find the fucker that thinks like I do. But that's not the story I'll tell tonight, no one needs to be wrapped up in my revenge but me. I'll tell the facts as I know them.

She flits into the kitchen with a handful of supplies and

the sway of those perfect hips has me hypnotized. She removes my tight shirt and sees all the color blazing before her. Her curious fingers trace my tattoos before I can stop them, and I close my eyes to memorize her light touch. When I gasp a tad, it pulls her out of the moment.

Her voice is low. "Sorry. They're so beautiful." She's blushing again.

I wink at her and say, "My pecs, abs, or the ink?"

She rolls her eyes and straightens her shoulders. "Never mind, that was inappropriate. You have things to attend to as soon as I clean this out."

I let her dab peroxide on the wound, and it stings. I'll start antibiotics when I get home. I keep all kinds of supplies around. Staving off infection was the most invaluable thing I learned when tromping through backlands of God knows where.

She tries to dress it, but I shake her off and put the t-shirt back on. I'll fix it up myself, but it strikes me I can't go anywhere I'd usually haunt.

"Tonight, we get out in front of this and report the crime first. It will go a long way with the jury if you're the one who offered it up. A lab's on their way to process the truck tonight, right here under the sheriff's supervision. I'm hoping your watch is worth a bit."

I wink at her. "Money's not an issue. You do what you need." Her head just about swivels off her body as she turns it around. Then her beautiful eyes land back on me.

"Sleep in my guest room, I don't want anyone to know where you are right now. Did you fight anyone off? Possibly get a few scrapes or scratches in? What's with your knuckles and how is your head? Will there be any more evidence on you? You should strip again so we can see if there are any more cuts. We should scrape under your nails, or you could cut them."

I grin as I move towards her. Her breath catches and her pupils dilate, she's flustered again, and it might be my new favorite hobby—getting Rebecca Gelbert all ruffled up.

"Let me get this straight, HB, you want me to take off all my clothes, stay in your house, shower and go to bed here without a stitch to wear and trim my nails?"

"Yes. That's what I said. But you can wear the shorts and I can get you a better t-shirt." She folds her arms over her chest missing my point.

"And you want me to do all this while you watch me? I'm going to have to ask for a touch of reciprocity there, counselor."

She looks at my shoulders as she creates a list. "I don't need to bag anything except the rug in my front hall, my garage door opener and possibly my bathrobe—oh, I get it. Stop."

I put a hand on her hip. The heat in her stare could fry an egg on a sidewalk in December. She licks her lips and I grin at her.

"I'm going to kiss you again, HB." She closes her eyes on me as if trying to scrub me from her sight, but her soft and sexy body yields to my touch.

"Doesn't matter how much I want you to, you can't," she says breathily. Now, I want her more than I thought was naturally possible for a man.

"Says who?" I whisper, drawing her closer. She sucks in a sharp breath.

"The state of California Bar Association. I'm your attorney."

"And I can't kiss my attorney?" I laugh until she steps out of my grip and backs up against her kitchen wall.

There's a knock on the door and my hand goes to the back of my waistband.

"Settle down. It's my independent DNA lab tech. Robert will watch them collect evidence then we'll turn it over to the state and local authorities when he files your arrest report."

"Arrest?"

"You have to be charged. You're the only material witness and suspect in a homicide. I'll get the charges dropped but it's easier to put it out there than be under scrutiny."

"Ballsy strategy that could put my ass in jail."

"Trust me. I'm that good."

"I do trust you, that's why I am here." I move toward her again. "Ok, that's all well and fine but can we circle back to the kissing part."

"I'll get disbarred, and you'll be charged with a massive fine or misdemeanor jail time on top of whatever they'll try to pin on you for this evening. So no, you can't kiss me again."

There's another knock. I hold my hand on the door so she can't open it yet.

I point to her up against that wall. "But you want to, don't you?" I'm close enough to see the pattern of her light freckles.

"Doesn't matter what I want. It's the law." She stares at my lips then I see the steel slide down right over that sweetness.

She answers the door and I'm like a deflated balloon who has to go and strip for a lab tech instead of Ms. Gelbert tonight.

# CHAPTER 4
# BECCA

The lab processed him and took their time in my garage working on the truck. They sealed my garage, and the police will pick it up when Brick surrenders himself. But the samples and scrapings from tonight will prove we're telling the truth when they match all the same evidence the police will find.

The Sonoma County Sheriff and head of the police department in the city happens to be my senior prom date. The only favor I asked was for him to delay the report. Robert and one of his deputies officially watched the lab bag and tag all the evidence. He took Brick's statement and believes the evidence, the story and me.

I explain to Brick the specifics, I've held back. "You surrender yourself once the charges of aggravated assault with a deadly weapon are filed. With the official police report on file in Sonoma at the sheriff's office, it buys us a little time for the lab to work. Robert officially submits the report on January 1$^{st}$, so that it's on a national holiday and I get an emergency hearing for January 2nd, due to the violent nature of the—" I put air quotes around the next word, "—'crime.' Then I claim there's zero evidence to hold you. But you spend New Year's Day, which really is the most useless of holidays, in jail and we spring you the next morning."

He grumbles a little under his breath and sits back on my leather couch. We're barely holding it together as we sit on opposite couches in my living room stealing glances.

"I'll write up the brief in the morning." I'm not sure why I'm sharing this much strategy with the client, but even I can admit he's different.

"I trust you, which is saying a hell of a lot coming from me. But, Becca Gelbert, besides having the prettiest face, it's also an honest one."

"You can't say things like that." I look away from him.

"State of California frowns on compliments?"

"Yes." I throw a butter yellow pillow at him, and he catches it and snuggles it close to his chest. Wouldn't it be nice to be that pillow?

"They won't have enough to hold you. They'll have everything we have but none of it actually points to you except it was your truck. If there's GSR on her hands, we won't know unless they swabbed her at the hospital and even that would be inconclusive at this point. And there really would be no call to swab her since she's a knife victim and there's no trace of gunplay that we know of." Brick shifts and leans forward. I continue so I don't pass out from exhaustion.

"We'll get the statement from the mechanic and the garage receptionist that you didn't pick up your truck, so there's at least some minor exculpatory evidence."

"That's some lawyer talk right there. I'm just gonna say good job. You tell me where to go and what to say, and I'm your puppet, Ms. Gelbert. But right now, I'd really like to get this poor woman's blood off of my hands." He stands up and pulls the robe around him. "Goodnight, HB." He winks at me again and it should be cheesy but it's charming in a very alarming way.

"What's HB?" Please don't mean head bitch. Or hard ballbuster. Or heavy breakfast. I don't know what that means, I'm tired, but I don't want it to be those things.

"All in due time. But consider it a term of endearment."

As tired as I should be, I'm not sleeping. My head's spinning. There's a naked man in my guest bedroom. I can feel his lips on mine every time I try to fall asleep. I believe there's a me that exists only for him. But I have to bury that and discourage him. I don't get to have anything like that anyway, there's no time and it's illegal.

But can you die from eternal unrequited lust? I google it and it comes up with a list of books I should read. I don't have time for research.

I shift in my bed and stare at the dusty pillow in the corner. The one I should have thrown away a year and half ago. Fucking Larry and his special pillow. He took everywhere except with him when he left with my law partner. I'm guessing she bought him a new pillow with the stolen half of the money in our corporate account she felt she deserved. I'd stupidly filled our coffers with my personal money to keep the firm going. Legally, it's hers as stated in our partner agreement because of our joint account. Apparently, it wasn't enough because she took Larry too. It wasn't like I desperately loved Larry the way lots of my friends love their partners. I erroneously thought he was safe and reliable. And he ticked off that domestic life box on my to-do list, I thought he was good enough.

I stand up my lip balm on my nightstand. I don't like it when it's horizontal because of the rolling potential. I pick it up and swipe my lips just once. I put it back in its place and adjust the remote perpendicular to the bed.

I'm trying to make sense of the night, putting things in their place. I like the pocket of a pop, country, or rock song. I understand the boundaries and limits of an established beat or rhyme scheme. I don't get jazz. Even though I grew up in and around a winery, the unpredictability of the harvest, the wine, and the industry never appealed to me. Made me feel out of sorts and I didn't know what to do with that feeling. I like order and the law is finite.

They broke my legal firm, my spirit, and a piece of my soul. All that remains is his pillow. I think about the hot-as-hell man who kissed me tonight. He made me feel like the Becca I'd like to be. I jump up and toss the pillow out the window. I may not get to have Brick, but I sure as hell don't have to have a Larry anymore. Everything feels different.

I DRIFT FOR A SECOND AND NOW I'M STARING AT THE spot where the pillow lived. Calico is sitting in it. If I believed in signs, I'd say that means I'm supposed to marry Calico.

My gut and heart tell me he's telling the complete truth. If I let doubt or my feelings for him see the light of day, I won't be even half the lawyer or person I believe myself to be. I've worked too hard in this life to prove myself to be above reproach. The word ice queen may have been bandied about in the past from my brother or my ex-fiancé but that is a persona I embrace at work. Nothing fucking rattles me.

Well, nothing except Brick Dunne.

I'm never going to get to sleep.

I FORGO SLEEP AND ATTEMPT TO GET MEL TO COME IN early. It's at least daylight, sun doesn't come up quite as early as I'd like. But that's what happens in winter. I hate it until the winter solstice, I always feel as if I'm on the backslide to darkness. And then once we hit that darkest day of the year, I know it's just a smidge lighter each day and I feel better about the world.

> REBECCA: Melissa. I need you at work as soon as possible. We have a new case that's going to take a lot of focus and some of your unique skill set.

> MEL: Yo. It's like the middle of the fucking night. And call me Mel.

> REBECCA: Melissa, I try to maintain some professionalism. And it's 7:30 a.m. Look, it's a criminal case. You'll like it. And I am going to need you to run a background check on Brick Dunne.

MEL: Hold your panties. Let me crawl off my beautiful wife and roll my ass into the office at this ungodly fucking hour.

Mel: Wait. Brick Dunne, like Vino Groupies Brick Dunne?

REBECCA: Yes. He no longer works for them and he's our new client. Well, my client. He has a problem. A case. He's in need of my help.

MEL: 2 things. I have a file on him from the whole winery sales thing a couple of years ago. And 2, girl, you flustered. Did he get himself some? He's got mad military skills and he's HAWT.

REBECCA: NO! That's highly unethical and illegal.

MEL: You could stand to be unethical for a minute. Be there in 20. Gonna grab some tacos. Want some?

REBECCA: No, thank you. And you should eat better.

MEL: Tell that to Tommi. She thinks I eat her out just fine. Also, it's not like you're Ms. Green Salad. Send me deets.

REBECCA: Oh God. Stop it.

MEL: Which is something my wife never says.

REBECCA: Melissa—Get into the office now.

She drives me crazy but her white hat hacker skills are

unmatched. She can find anything, get anywhere, and not be traced. She used to work for Josh Whittier's–one of the kids I grew up with–fiancée. Elle had a marketing firm in New York and Mel is loyal to her and to us now. She was called upon to help the five wineries out of the Vino Groupie debacle and stop the winery sales a couple of years ago. The five winery families are all linked for life. Our parents are all best friends and raised all of us together, basically. And when Melissa married Tommi Schroeder, she got the rest of us in the bargain. All the kids of the five families in one giant cluster.

She's loyal to all of us but her heart and first priority will always be to Elle. She exhaustively searched for Asher Bernard's other victims and aided the FBI in untangling Josh's mess with the mob. She's also the best fucking employee in the world for me.

She and Tommi have a child and a life. Even though I'm the oldest of my generation in the five families, I don't. Melissa moves through life without worries. No real concern for her health, appearance, what comes out of her mouth, or the perpetual stains on her clothing. And she's immensely happy. I should be more like Melissa, without food stains.

After her dazzling work on the Asher/Wineries case, I put her on retainer. She's not cheap but I haven't lost a case since she came on board. She's my only staff since the practice crumbled. I have a part-time paralegal but mostly it's the two of us.

There's a news report with Brick's description to investigate an attempted murder. So, that's what they'll charge him with. Or gross negligence manslaughter if she dies. But that's a big swing and will be easier to get the charges dropped.

As long as the report is filed late today, we avoid obstruction of justice. There will be a record of him being questioned and processed legally on this date.

The woman is still in the ICU and is a single woman from American Canyon who has no real ties to anyone. The spark in my stomach tells me it all feels wrong, like she was targeted. She was close to bleeding out when she arrived at the hospital. Her liver was nicked but no major damage. Her statement, if there is one, hasn't been released. How did they get Brick in the press mix so quickly? Or how the hell was she identified? Someone fed this story and put pressure on the hospital. The turnaround's too quick. There's no APB or warrant, simply looking for him, so we're still within the law.

Now to deal with the other issue, I hold my stomach for a moment and let it all wash over me so I can get rid of it. He's here and I've dreamed of him for years. He's in my house. There's a sensation swirling I've been able to turn down to a low simmer but it's the feeling I've carried since we met. But now it's like an—on crack, dialed up to eleven, hurtling towards the pavement after a swan dive off the Golden Gate bridge—out of control sensation. I feel as if I'm trying to run on ice.

Just as his door was closing last night, I peeked. He saw me but didn't see my reaction to the elegant magnolia on his shoulder. It's beautiful but almost looks nostalgic as if he's mourning the tree or the flower. I know he's from Mississippi, but I wonder the last time he was back there.

Mel needs to work fast. Robert made sure everything was completely handled and documented thoroughly. I owe him. The last thing I need is something inadmissible. I've covered my ass and the lab will make sure I have the exact information the police have.

David must have left this morning. My brother tends to get up early so he can exercise or sculpt. Sometimes he walks the vines before daybreak to get his head in order. I do Wordle.

I pull open my pod drawer and it's empty. Shit, no coffee, and I think that's going to be the key to me being human today. My cabinets have been rifled through. I think Brick is still upstairs in the bedroom, so it has to be my asshole brother. I put everything back where it belongs and clean his dishes.

**B-**

**Always the charming hostess - bloody stranger and all.**

**-D**

**P.S. Call Mom**

**P.P.S. You're out of eggs, cream, and coffee now.**

I blow out a puff of air and try to calm myself. Fucker. He blabbed to Mommy last night because my family texts are out of control.

MOM: Call me.

I ignore it.

POPPY: Come to the café. I'll make your favorite. I have things we need to discuss.

My cousin already knows. What the hell? She's so freaking nosey. No, my darling cousin, there aren't things to discuss because somehow you found out about Brick. Ignore.

41

> NATALIE: David has concerns. I trust you, of course, but he wants me to get the full story.

David's wife is now involved. Ignore.

> POPPY: Answer me or I'll shut my restaurant down and come over there.

Ignore.

> POPPY: Not kidding. And I'll tell all my starving customers it's your fault.

My rule-following, ever cheerful and ever influenced cousin, Poppy, hates not being in the know. She gets it from my aunt Tina.

> SAM: Heads up. David told me.

SHIT. Sam Langerford. He's a notoriously terrible secret keeper. I'm trying to keep a man from going to prison and they're gossiping.

> ELLE: Don't forget brunch tomorrow. Be warned it's a massive family affair. And Happy New Year. And we might all know that there's a half-naked man in your house.

Fuck me.

I like Elle a lot, completely straight shooter. She gets me and I care for her well-being. I don't know anyone who doesn't adore her. Josh Whittier was lucky she fell for him.

The two are perfectly suited, she doesn't let him get away with anything. She's probably the strongest of all of us but you'd never know since she hides all her strength behind the perfect lipstick and designer outfits. Even pregnant she looks perfect.

I grew up surrounded by four other winery families. Gelbert Family Winery is still run by my dad. Although he's relinquished some control to our vineyard manager and winemaker in the last couple of years, he still lords over the property and the vines. Occasionally growing up I felt left out because I had to watch out for the rest of them. Ingrid Schroeder is the youngest. We call each other Alpha and Omega. Why can't she text me? I like her.

I'll stop by the brunch briefly after taking Brick to jail. They're all a bit much. I blurt out, "Shit. Puzzle club." I have to call and cancel our New Year's Eve plans. "Oh, my God, that's the most depressing thing I ever said."

I look around to make sure Brick didn't hear me utter the words 'puzzle club.' It's only sometimes when I hear myself, I realize how far I've retreated. I love puzzles but a New Year's Eve invite shouldn't say BYOCT (Bring Your Own Card Table). We weren't going to work on a joint puzzle, just individually near each other.

*POPPY: I'm on my way unless you text me back.*

There's a knock on my back door and my relentless cousin didn't even give me a chance to fucking answer her. I pull my robe around me ready to unleash on Poppy and notice a spot of blood near the pocket. And for a brief moment I remember the feel of his hands on me.

I whip the door open and my breath catches.

"Well, darling, it appears I owe you some dry cleaning." His voice wraps around the room and then slides down my body with his words. He reaches out and takes my silk robe between his thumb and forefinger and all I can do is try to regulate my breathing while I watch his masculine grip on the light fabric, and I feel feminine.

I don't say anything as I stare at the tray with two coffees and a bakery bag.

"I sure am sorry about last night. I figured the least I owed you was breakfast for your hospitality. I also filled up your car with gas since I had to commandeer it."

I don't move because then I'd have to look away from his giant corded and brightly colored biceps peeking out from his dark gray t-shirt. I wonder if he knows all shirts are too small to contain him.

He's so vivid as the morning sun streams through the kitchen highlighting his intense decoration. I should be more professional at this moment, but the world is spotlighting his beauty. His tattoos are a picture book to this otherworldly, stunning man. He's like a movie star or something and he's talking to me as if he actually wants to talk to me. I need to pull back to professional mode. I don't get why he's here. There's lots of other lawyers in the world. Why my doorstep? And does he want to kiss me again? No, Becca. Bad Becca, do not think of the manslaughter assailant that way. He's your client and you took an oath.

"Step aside, now. I've got things to say, and you and your sexy Irish bedhead are distracting me."

My stomach gets all warm and gooey as he calls my insane hair sexy. I move slightly as he passes. Then suddenly he kisses my cheek. All the parts of me explode and are put back together by reason and purpose.

I close the back door and follow him. How can his ass be as good as his chiseled face? That's not fair to the rest of the faces or asses in the world.

For a giant man he moves so gracefully and exact.

There's a slight bulge in the back of his waistband. Holy shit, it's still in my house.

"Is that a gun?" My voice is high and sharp.

"There's that sweet voice I want to hear for a spell. Yes, ma'am, it's a gun. We don't know what these people will do if I'm not arrested soon. And I sure as hell don't want to be caught without it again. I surrendered the other one so, I promise you it's a new gun."

"You got up and went home for a tiny t-shirt, muffins, and another gun?"

"I didn't sleep. After you left me for your room, I headed to Richmond to grab some things before everyone got into my business."

He's been in Richmond. That's forty-five minutes away. He was that close to me this entire time?

I watch as he removes a gun from the back of his pants, and it looks like a toy. Then he puts it on my kitchen island and it squinches like metal, not plastic. There's nothing juvenile about this piece of hardware sitting in direct opposition to my well-manicured and safe kitchen. It's so out of place in my life, as is he.

I can't glance away from it and speak again while staring, "Why are you here?"

"You're my lawyer. And your brother drank all the coffee, so I thought you might like a cup to get all lawyerly. And I like looking at you."

He steps into my space, and I have no rational thoughts. He reaches into my pocket and pulls out his watch. His lips are so close to mine. Last night's kiss was the most thrilling thing that's ever happened to me. Especially in comparison to what I did an hour ago, quitting the puzzle club.

He stares and the heat between us is a tangible thing. As if someone could pluck the sexual tension from between us and hold it. It's a living and breathing entity that scares the shit out of me. Then he steps back. This has to be in my imagination, he came to his senses and so should I. I'm not a silly woman, and those feelings are for fools.

"There are several things that need to be said here, HB."

"What is this HB business?"

"Tell you later, don't we have more pressing issues? Like what are we doing for New Year's Eve and when do I have to go to jail?"

I smirk at him, toss my hair up into a top knot and metaphorically roll up my sleeves. I have no intention of lying or losing. He stares at me as if I'm a riddle and I can tell he's seen the shift in me. I'm not fucking around anymore, and his gorgeous face will not distract me—much.

"Right now, tell me anything pertinent to the case. And HB is not something you'll call me. I'm Ms. Gelbert or I'll allow Becca, but do not be mistaken, I am your attorney in what seems to be a rather serious matter. This weapon is of no use to me, and I'd like it removed from my house. And as for your comings and goings, I'll need you to document all the places you frequented within the last twenty-four hours. Before and up to the incident." I reach into a drawer and grab a pad and pen and place it next to the gun. "We fight with facts not bullets."

"First, I'm going to go change and take a quick run and I'll be back in a bit. Is that enough facts for ya?" He winks.

"I'm serious."

He clears his throat and rushes his hands to his shorn rich brown hair. He pushes the Olive Tree bakery bag towards me.

"Eat up, now, you're gonna turn into nothing but a whisper." He bites into a muffin and whispers, "But I'm more partial to the way you look right now." Then he places a piece of muffin in my dropped jaw. My eyes almost bug out of my head that he's not taking this seriously.

"Brick?" I say with a mouth full of Olive's ridic amazing muffin.

"I sure do like the way you say my name." He's in my space suddenly and I'm off my axis again.

I have to pull up all the reserves I have to move past this and put us squarely into a working, professional relationship. His hands are on me, and I have to ignore every single fucking tingle that's spreading.

"You can't kiss me again."

He feathers a finger over my jaw, and I shiver at his touch. He grins slyly knowing the effect he has on me.

He whispers, "Who says?"

I clear my throat and answer as sternly as I can, "We've been over this, the California Bar Association."

"Thought maybe that law changed in the last coupla hours. Did you check?"

He steps away and takes all the warmth in the world and in my body with him. He walks toward the hallway and my heat ebbs across the kitchen.

I put a period at the end of our sentence. "And me. My job is important to me, and you've given me your retainer. I can't be seen as unscrupulous or amoral. But if you can behave, then we can share some takeout and a bottle of wine, and you can stay until midnight tonight. But there can be nothing between us."

He sips his coffee and I see his grin over the top of the cup as he leans against my kitchen wall. His eyes are mischievous and dangerous.

"Darling, there already is."

# CHAPTER 5
## BECCA

nother hour and half passes before Melissa graces me with her presence. My family doesn't know I only see clients in public spaces or in the library of my house. I don't want to hear my father's judgment or take my mother's handout because I can't afford office space any longer. We don't talk about those kinds of things. David does, he talks about everything. If I were going to tell someone about all this, it would be him, but given today's blabbermouth performance telling Sam "The Mouth" Langerford about Brick, I'll pass. No one needs to know my business imploded along with my personal life.

Touching him last night was as if a famous painting came alive or waking up and Monica's making Joey breakfast in your kitchen. The two dimensions of it all shattered the moment he spoke my name. Even when I opened the door last night, he was still a story I tell myself. And then he said things. Like way too many heavy things. And then there was blood and heat and rainwater dripping on my floor and a gun.

I flop down on my desk chair and turn to Mel coming out of the bathroom.

"Do not eat tacos from that one truck on the far side of Agua Caliente. The one with the blue and gold stripes. That's a whole morning I'm going to lose to the porcelain throne."

"You have something on your sleeve." It appears to be a piece of lettuce and she picks it off her shirt and deposits it into her mouth. I cringe.

I'm wearing a mint green button-down and jeans. A little casual for a client meeting but he's in gym clothes and currently eating yogurt and granola from my fridge. It's like the awkward morning after without all the benefits of orgasms. Not that I remember what that feels like with another person in the room.

The air in my house is charged. It's all swirly and magnetic since he arrived. My house is big, but I can't help but feel suffocated. He's like a weighted blanket on my life, settling me into a false sense of security and acceptance. The moment he walks out of my house and the blanket gets ripped off, I'll be back to neurotic and obsessive Rebecca again. He called me Becks. How cute is that? Shit. I don't say things like cute. I refocus on Melissa who is tapping away already.

"We knew this dude was a bad mutha at that meeting. He's a highly decorated mercenary and graduated *magna cum laude* from Emory in Atlanta. He was a Navy SEAL. He occasionally gets called out on missions still." I react by standing ramrod straight and spilling my coffee. No. I don't want him in harm's way. Also, holy shit how did Mel find that?

"Stop prying into government records. Legal things."

"I did that check before I had to go all legal." He fills the doorway like a TikTok thirst trap. White ribbed tank top and low-slung slate sweats. Even Mel takes notice. He leans on one side of the doorframe, and I sigh like I'm a cartoon swoony girl. They both look at me and he smiles.

He nods to Mel. "Well, I guess in this situation, I've got nothing to hide. So, darling, pry away. See what you can find and ask anything you need. I'm Brick Fernando Dunne and I'm awful appreciative of you making me a priority."

I put my finger up. "Fernando? Really?"

"Apparently my folks, who I don't know at all, saddled me with their favorite ABBA song. Never been a fan but it sure is a conversation starter."

Mel gets animated as she says, "Jesus fucking Christ on a cracker. You're fucking good looking. Look at those goddamn guns holding that tiny container of yogurt. Yes, sir, you are a snack."

"Hold on now. You're going to make me blush."

I don't speak, I'm afraid my tongue will ruin the view. I need to get my professional head around this before I put my mouth on all his body parts, specifically one.

Enough penis thoughts. I glance over again and it's seriously taunting me. That thick outline. I'm trying to look anywhere but his dick, but it's got its own gravitational pull. I'll bet he needs a third flip flop at the beach. He's a freaking tripod. How can he look like that? Talk like that. And apparently have the Grand Canyon of dicks. The Washington Monument of mounting. The ultimate rod of destiny. The divining rod to my reservoir. I've never been so wet in all my life. I need to go to the bathroom. I'm sure my skin is—

"Becks, you alright? Your face is a bit flushed there, darling, like you're taking in all the heat and not letting go."

Mel turns to me. "She's fine. She's just turned on by

your insanely large cock bulge. I'm a clam eater myself but I applaud that whole thing you got going. Good for you. I'm hoping you know what to do with it."

He leans down to Mel. "You're going to be mighty blunt now, aren't you?"

"Yes, sir."

"Let's see if we can rustle up some manners while Ms. Rebecca's around. You and I can talk like that when she's not here. But I do thank you kindly for the compliment. Now. How am I not a murderer?"

I turn away from him, which is a bit like turning away from the sun. It's cooler as I face my wall, but my back is warm as hell. I breathe in and collect myself. I hear Mel mumble behind me.

"Damn tacos. I'll be in the can. Start without me. I'll catch up." I hear the door shut and the air is charged again. He's behind me in a flash and so close to my ear, I gasp.

"If I were the blushing type, I'd be red too. I don't know what to do with all that I'm feeling but looking at you, smelling you, being around you in just this space makes me insane. Turn around." I don't move because I'm paralyzed. He has turned me on so much it now overrides all neural systems as well as my musculature and my fucking free will.

There are goosebumps erupting all over my skin but I'm having a hard time believing this man feels like this about me. He leans forward and places his coffee cup on my desk. Then he puts his strong fingers on my hip and turns me around into his sexy arm cage.

He moves a piece of hair back into my makeshift bun. "There's not a strong enough word for how beautiful you are. Especially when you're flustered." He takes one of his undamaged knuckles and gently sweeps it over my cheek. "Darling, I've waited my entire life to feel like this and I'm going to need you to follow me down this rabbit hole as it leads us to Wonderland. I'm helpless against you."

"That's both the most absurd thing I've ever heard and the sexiest. But you know we can't. You're my client," I manage to whisper.

His smile curls up. "Then we better get my charges dismissed soon. I've waited long enough for you."

And cue my damn heart flutter.

# CHAPTER 6
## BRICK

Tomorrow, I go to jail, and my mind is picking at old memories of Gulfport and the only other time I've been in a cell. We may have switched the north and south highway signs. Fleabag, Cy, and I took the brunt of it but that ole slickster, Chase, talked his way out of jail by seemingly throwing us all under the bus. Then he switched them all back without anyone catching him. They couldn't hold us because there was no crime anymore. Mimi Tinker walloped me pretty good. She made sure I knew what I'd done was wrong and didn't let me forget for a month.

I add my diced onions into the pot with the hock. The greens are stewing, and the cornbread is cooling. Becca ran to her parents' house to grab something. I throw some butter in the pot and let it melt into the onions. Then I check the temp on the rib roast I got going for tonight.

The onions, hocks, greens, and beans are for tomorrow. I know she's headed to a brunch while I take up residence in the Sonoma jail but that doesn't mean we throw out tradition. I'm making a big ole double batch of Hoppin' John for her to take with her. That whole family collective needs a bit of luck, as do I. Greens and black-eyed peas might just be what sets all our worlds right this year.

I also want to make up for what I've done, bringing all this chaos into her life. I wanted to be worthy when I saw her again, not a blood-soaked idiot with a murder problem. I'm not one to trouble others with my issues, I like to solve things on my own, but this time, it was too big. It's selfish of me to come here. Look at me in this perfect fucking kitchen cooking up a feast for someone whose life might have been a bit better off if I'd stayed away.

Mimi Tinker used to call these the 'not good enoughs' and would scold me for letting them into my thinking. I'm pretty good about beating them back but I'm smack dab in the middle of an ethical and metaphysical crisis. Is she going to be better off in the long run if I slip back into the night and get another lawyer? Or do I double down on the simmering between us and believe she's the one. I only hope I've not put her or anyone she cares about in danger.

Ms. Mel stumbles into the room, the woman is a wonder of confusion and contradiction. So skilled behind that keyboard, so cocksure of who she is, yet there's no filter or care for personal appearance or propriety. I'm fascinated by her and look forward to meeting the woman who stole her heart and their son.

"What the hell are you doing?"

I laugh and continue to sauté the onions with a sprinkle of fresh thyme. The ham hocks have set to boiling and the beans are soaking.

"I'm cooking."

"I'm not sure the stove's ever been turned on. She's more of a button pushing cook. Smells damn good." I shuffle over to stir a few things and put the potatoes in the oven to bake in their foil jackets.

"This here is Mimi Tinker's Hoppin' John for tomorrow. Tastes better if you make it the day before. I'll send it along with Becks to that family thing."

"You bringing some to Robert too?" She leans back against the counter and pops a piece of onion in her mouth. I thought her stomach was wrecked but I guess she's a raw onion eating kinda gal.

"It's the neighborly thing to do. We could all use a little luck this year." I wink at her.

"And the beefy thing I smell?"

"That's a standing rib roast for dinner tonight and I made a King Cake, complete with plastic baby for tomorrow."

"You know she'll never cave. Sorry, about your lonely cock, but that one will never bend."

"Thank you kindly for the advice. I made you a banana bread to take home to your boy." I push it across the kitchen island and her eyes light up.

She picks it up and takes a bite right out of it whole, like it's an apple and not a loaf cake. "Fuck him. I love banana bread."

"Then by all means, take two. Becks had a whole heap of rotten bananas. I cook and bake when I need something to do."

"Instead of raging against everyone and everything for what's about to go down?" She sprays quick bread bits onto the floor as she speaks.

I turn my attention back to my onions, which are starting to stick, and I deglaze the pan a bit with some broth. "Something like that. Did you come in here for something? I thought you left for the day."

Her face hardens and I can tell she's trying to get down to business.

"Ask what ya need, Ms. Mel."

She puts down the cake and leans over the island towards me. "I need pieces filled in. How did you get into the truck?" All jokes are gone from her demeanor.

"Dragged." I flash her the knuckles that are all ripped up.

"And why were you at that roadhouse?"

"I wasn't. I was at the Safeway, down in Richmond. Not so safe now, was it?" I waggle my eyebrows to try and crack her.

There's no reaction to my cheeky joke. "In a sport coat?"

"I'd had a meeting earlier." And that meeting is none of Ms. Mel's business right now, but I'm sure she'll go digging. There's nothing to find.

She's all rapid fire now, "Did anyone see you there?"

"Sure, but the timeline wouldn't work out. My suspicion is the girl didn't get hurt until after I was in place, knocked out."

"What about your phone? Where's that?"

"Lab found it deep under the bloody seat in my truck. I remote wiped it first thing after dropping her at the hospital. They told me it was smashed up. Maybe from the dragging or maybe it was done on purpose. Doesn't matter, they won't find a thing."

"Can I double check the wipe?" She scurries out of the kitchen and is back in a flash with her beat-up and over-stickered laptop. It seriously looks like a schoolgirl's math class binder.

"Have at it, but I'm pretty fucking good at this too, you

won't find a thing on there." Her keyboard hums, then she nods to me.

She says, "Later, fucker. Headed home to plow through dinner, toss the kid in bed and get down to a really Happy New Year's Eve. Keep your hands off her."

"Pretty sure Ms. Rebecca can take care of herself."

"Farts out!"

I roll my eyes as she takes off though the front door.

# CHAPTER 7
## BECCA

'm driving up and over the Carneros Valley, between Sonoma and Napa. It's a little desolate except for the Christmas lights still adorning the houses set back from the road. Domaine Carneros' entrance is festive and melancholy set on either side by sleeping, naked vines.

I like having someone at my house. Using my things and making himself at home. Shit. "Becca Gelbert. He is not at home. He's a guest."

Ok, new plan. No dreaming of him fitting into your life or house. That's fucking ridiculous. Tonight, we'll eat take out, I'll put on ugly comfy clothes and firmly put him in the friend zone. Client, attorney—that's our defined relationship. "Good," I say and flip on the radio.

I drive on and realize I talk a good game, but I can't stop my mind from envisioning my hand running up his torso and licking his biceps. Shit. I'm getting a little heated thinking about his pecs and the way he smiles at me. I breathe in and out, counting to four each time. They're now all I can think clearly about, and the outline of his dick in those damn sweats. Hopeless.

Fine. Let's do this. I drive and let my mind float to my tongue on his chest circling his peaked nipples as I reach down and take his cock in my hand. I grin at the conjured moan that follows me kissing his dick hello.

I hold on to the image for another couple of seconds imagining his musky salty goodness hitting my tongue. And now my face is beet red, and I'm going to have to run past him and take a shower to get myself off before I can even face him. I roll down all the windows and hope that helps. "You're a mess, Becca."

"GIRL, WHAT'S GOT YOUR SKIN SO WORKED UP?" I ignore him as I come through the back door.

"What are you doing?" I'm completely confused by the mess in my kitchen.

He laughs pretty loudly. He takes my bags and deposits my purse and bottles on the counter. Then he squares my body to the island in front of a cutting board littered with the leafy carcasses of celery and carrot tops. He stands behind me and I might spontaneously combust. He slides a knife into my hand and positions his fingers on top. We chop slowly and I focus on the sound of the knife hitting the board through a sliver of carrot.

I feel his breath on my neck, and I know it's as red as the rest of me. Fuck Irish skin. Fuck my heritage. And Jesus fucking Christ I want to fuck this man. I use all my reserve and passion for the law to say no to him.

My voice, despite my best efforts, comes out hoarse and low. "I know how to chop."

He's in my ear. "Do you, now? Haven't seen it yet. Your pots still had a plastic wrapper around them, and that pan hasn't been seasoned. Ms. Becca, are you saying you can cook?"

I put the knife down and steady myself on the island. He pens me in his arms. I can't answer him. He presses into my back and it's a bit too much. Apparently chopping excites him too.

I turn quickly in his arms. His eyes are dark and his stare predatory. I like it but I don't want to say the thing I shouldn't.

"You're annoying the shit out of me with this. Please step back."

He tosses his arms up and steps back. He laughs at me, and I can't help but smile back. "You didn't answer me."

I straighten up and tuck my hair back. "No. I don't cook. But this all smells great. Thank you. I have to go to the bathroom." I run out as I hear him chuckle. This is a dangerous game and yet I cannot stop playing it.

I JOIN HIM AGAIN AFTER SETTLING MYSELF DOWN AND he's dumping things into a pot. I reach into the bags that all say "Wine FTW – Gelbert's Got You Covered For The Holidays."

"Cheese. Salami. Wine. A perfect New Year's Eve feast. What the hell are you cooking?" I survey the kitchen, which is worse for the wear.

"A proper dinner, worthy of the evening and the best damn lawyer." He stirs something and I wish he were wearing an apron over a hunter green t-shirt. He's put on a pair of smokey gray knit pants that might be wool. And he's barefoot. He's his version of casual dress up. He has product holding back his russet hair and I want to grab a hold of it.

I smirk at him. "I smell that. Are you cooking every recipe that's ever existed? This is a lot of pots and pans I didn't know I owned."

He sips a finger of bourbon. "You didn't own all of them, we needed a few more. But you do now. Go on, get to mixing up the middles of them twice-baked potatoes." I give him some side eyes. "It's easy, you dump stuff in a bowl and smoosh it together. I'll guide you through it."

"What is all this food? And why are there canned items?"

"Mason jars to hold the peas you're bringing to your brunch tomorrow. You eat them for good luck, and I insist you do." He glares at me. He's deadly serious about these peas.

"I don't like peas. Certainly not beige ones."

"They're black-eyed peas or field peas. It's a bean and you're going to love them. Mel confirmed Ms. Elle has a pot big enough, so I don't need to send mine along."

"What is even happening?" I sniff the air. There are loaves and colorful cakes and these drab beans, but things are still in the oven.

"Tonight, we eat a rib roast so I can sustain myself in prison tomorrow. A last supper if you will."

"It's hardly a prison, the cell is carpeted." He laughs and I can't help but be in a good mood. "Um, we're just friends tonight, right?"

"As far as you know." I point at him, and he continues. "I'll do my best to abide by the rules of the house. Just good food and conversation, then we can watch Andy and

Anderson make snide tipsy comments about how cold Manhattan is tonight. I promise."

"Can I trust you?"

"With your life."

The mood shifts but I know he means that.

I collect pots and start to suds up the discarded bowls and utensils.

I toss over my shoulder, "Not my life I'm nervous about." I can't fucking stop myself from flirting with him.

"Your virtue?" He covers his heart pretending he's shocked at my statement.

Laughter bursts out of me. "Sure. Let's say virtue."

"Promise. Dinner and a peck on your cheek at midnight." He crosses his heart.

"I can live with that." I wink at him like he's always doing to me.

# CHAPTER 8
# BRICK

watch her cute butt scamper out of the room instead of facing the thing between us. I promised her I'd be good. She took all the light with her.

I'd give up peanut butter if I could taste her. Lick her up and down while she's still all hot and bothered. I'd make a meal of her clit and make sure no part of her isn't kissed and sucked properly. I take the roast out to rest, adjust my ever-present hard-on, and wash up. When she burst through the back door with multiple packages, I got a warm easy feeling all over. It wasn't only sexual and that's a frightening road I'm running down. I'll have to face it won't go my way eventually, but for now I can pretend this is what we do on New Year's Eve. I cook and she tries not to tell me about her emotions.

She appears with folded swan napkins and picks serving pieces out of the cabinets. She's in soft tan knit pants that highlight that pert and luscious butt of hers. Her fuzzy cream sweater is more inviting than she probably intended. She doesn't pay me no mind as she slides back up next to me and that light white flower smell, could be lily of the valley, could be a gardenia, something white and pretty, is overpoweringly feminine on my ginger gal. She's simply lovely.

SHE SAYS LOUDLY AFTER WE'VE BOTH FILLED OUR bellies, "I need to know before it's midnight. Are you safe? Are the people who failed to pin this on you coming for you still?"

I'm a bit thunderstruck. I speak as I close the back door, headed outside, "You're safe. While I'm around. While I'm not around, I don't think they're desperate enough to try something with all these people around me. I was easy pickings when I was by myself in the parking lot."

She points across the lawn. "You sit ALL the way over there. In fact, stay where you are." I'm about ten feet from her fire pit surrounded by Adirondack chairs overlooking her pool. She's got big fluffy white blankets out here and she pulled out stuff to make s'mores, forgoing my butter cake. Imma let her have this one. She's stumbling a bit and fuck me if even that isn't sexy. Dinner was divine but a real practice in manners and patience. What I wanted to do was throw the food off the table and fuck her into tomorrow. What I did was eat too many potatoes. She's dragging a chair towards the pool and is now returning to the fire pit.

She pops a hip and looks at me straight. "That's your seat, Mr. Fucking Eyes."

"What does that even mean?"

She's trying to light the starter log and points at me with

the long stick lighter. "You know exactly what I mean, which is why you're sitting over there. I left you a blanket."

She sure did. I make my way over there next to the guest house. The one she's never asked me to move into. She put me in the room next to hers, which is where I intend to stay until I'm in her bed. I flop down on the chair and glance around at her huge backyard.

"What do you do with all of this?"

She shrugs as the logs catch. "Look at it."

"Do you have pool parties?" I almost can't even get the question out. I'm laughing so hard.

"What am I Annette fucking Funicello?"

"My Mimi Tinker used to love them old surfer movies."

"So did my dad's mom. That's when I saw them. But no. I don't throw parties."

"Then what's all this for? The giant kitchen you don't cook in. The guest house no one but your drunk brother uses and a pool that sits there waiting for a purpose."

She falls back into the chair and wraps herself up. I hear her mutter something.

"Either speak up or let me rejoin the circle."

"I DON'T KNOW!" She stares off.

"I'm sorry if I hit a sore spot. That wasn't my intention." I scoot my chair closer when she's not looking. I do it again before she catches wise.

She gestures to the air. "This is my favorite spot."

I ask, "The fire pit?" She nods "Why?"

She pulls the blanket around her and tucks her feet up into the chair. "I don't know, it calms me down when I'm alone."

"Then why are there nine other chairs if you're the only one enjoying it?" I push. I shouldn't have. I'm sure I've ruined my evening.

I scoot the chair a little closer but she's not speaking to me.

Her face is open and vulnerable. "I'm not alone, I have you. At least for tonight."

"That you do, darling, that you do. Now I'm going to have to come a little closer, we're coming on about five minutes until I get my cheek kiss."

"I'll give you a two-minute warning." She sighs and rolls her emerald eyes at me.

I get my chair to the circle before she notices and then she just shrugs. I keep scooting it until it's directly in front of hers.

"There. Now that's a better view."

We hear hooting and hollering and I ditch my blanket and lean forward as she presents her cheek. I linger a bit too long then brush my lips over her ear as she shivers. I say, "Happy New Year, HB."

She turns her head and says, "Happy New Year, AH."

I cock my head to the side.

She laughs and says, "Asshole."

My belly laugh echoes through the yard and I'm pretty much sunk, all those "not good enoughs" can go to hell. She makes me want to be good enough.

# CHAPTER 9
## BRICK

One wall away from paradise about drove me nuts last night. I went after myself like a teenage boy who discovered porn is readily available on the World Wide Web. Every time I thought I couldn't get hard again, the sucker jumped right into my hand at the thought of her. Surrounded by her smell perfuming the world and only a whisper away from me caused a chapped hand situation this morning. I need to have a sit down with him so that we can proceed in the world. I won't be anyone's bitch, certainly not my dick's.

I wish I had a suit to wear, but I can't go home, I don't know who's there. And the one I did have is sitting in a lab. Those reports won't help at the hearing because they're not done yet. She said not to worry, and I choose to believe her.

That funny gal, Mel, hacked into the hospital's mainframe. The woman's name is Hope Beardsley. She lost a lot of blood, but they stitched her up and the police went to see her, but she's still sedated. She's a single gal. The charge is officially attempted murder with an aggravated assault charge thrown in for good measure. Because she's currently recovering from a knife injury, unable to identify me or say what happened, they can make up any damn thing they want.

Becca called the DA and Robert filed the report at six am this morning. I don't know who the fuck did this to me. I've kept my rage tamped down a bit but the moment I'm on the other side of these charges, it's game fucking on.

Just in case I called my bank and have them on standby for a large amount of money in a cashier's check. I don't know what my bail would be set at, but I don't want that burden to fall to anyone. I can cover whatever it is. I've lived humbly, invested wisely, and done things Mimi Tinker would be ashamed of me for, but I was well paid, and I don't intend to squander it.

She knocks lightly.

"It's open."

I've showered and am all set to go to jail. Just one little piece of business first, I walk past her, inhaling those flowers as I go. She follows me to the kitchen, and I load up her cooler with the Hoppin' John. I put in a couple of bottles of Texas Red Hot sauce. I don't know if they like that around here, but I find it essential with the greens. I load up a batch for Robert and myself as well. She stands there leaning against the doorframe with her arms crossed.

"Pretty quiet." I take in her face and it's a bit pained.

"I'm sorry I couldn't stop all this."

I rush to her and take her face in my hands. Fuck boundaries. "No. This isn't your fault and I feel a bit of a shit-heel bringing all this trouble to ya."

In a shocking turn of events, her eyes glass over just a hint. "Thank you," is all she says, and I pull her to me before that bottom lip starts to go. I can't think of what she'd thank me for, but I'll hold her close until she's able to get herself right.

"Now, let's go lock me up."

ROBERT'S A GOOD FELLA. WE SHARED SOME PEAS AND now I'm reading a book about the history of beer. Kind of interesting and also kind of not. The door to the cell room flies open and in bursts a small blonde and a hurricane I recognize.

"Brick Dunne?" The itty-bitty blonde woman breaks my concentration but it's the brassy ebony-haired one that breaks everyone's peace.

"You know it's him. Robert fucking told you so. And is there anyone else in the room? Did you think Sonoma had a run on criminals and this place would be swamped?"

The blonde rolls her eyes and turns back to me. "Mr. Dunne. I'm Natalie Gelbert and I brought you a better pillow and some melatonin for your jail night."

She places a shopping bag on the ground while her fierce companion almost hisses at me. "It's not a fucking sleepover. He might have killed someone." She turns quickly to me. "Did you?"

"No, ma'am, not recently. And thank you, I wasn't sure how I was going to sleep."

"She's efficient like that." Now she's growling at me.

I grin and greet this loud hurricane of a woman. "It's nice to see you under better circumstances, Ms. Aganos, or is it officially Mrs. Schroeder?" She was a bit outspoken when we met a couple of years ago. She's a hard one to forget.

"Wait, jail is better circumstances?" Natalie inquires.

I smile and say, "For Tabitha, they're better. Also, congratulations on all the recent motherhood." I take a walk around my cell and turn towards the nice one. "You're David's wife?"

She nods but Tabi points through the bars. "Look, motherfucker, the last time you were breezing through here was on Asher's coattails with the idea of turning my family's winery, Stafýlia Cellars into a TJ Maxx."

"You're nothing if not loyal. I admire how fiercely you defend your loved ones. And I'm sorry about all that, I'm sure Ms. Becca filled you in on my parting with that company. I live a life of honor and I stepped away from them as soon as I found out."

She gets right to the bars. "How the fuck—" and the sheriff comes in holding a screeching little ball of beautiful brown skin. That lil' cutie seems to be fussing a bit much.

She rolls her eyes and the fire in them tamps down a bit. Seems as if Tabi the hurricane is having a bit of trouble adjusting to being a new mama. Becca told me the tall tale of how Tabi and her husband, Bax, became parents on Christmas.

Robert passes the baby to Tabi with an exasperated expression. "Really? Come on, Tab. I don't know what to do with this?" She takes him and pleads with the babe. She's cooing at this little one.

"Nick, shh. Come on, baby. It's ok. I got you." She puts him on her shoulder and starts to bounce. She kisses his head but he's still squawking.

Robert says, "Is he hungry?"

"How the hell should I know? I did all the things I know and yet the crying persists. I suck at this."

I put my hands out through the bars. "Ms. Tabi, let me give him a snuggle." They look at me as if I've offered up a dead possum.

"The man who tried to destroy us?"

Ms. Natalie adds, "And made Becca laugh." Tabi nods to Robert as if that's some kind of secret signal.

He pops open the cell and points to me. "He can't do any worse and that sound has to stop."

Tabi says, "You think I don't know that."

She surrenders the tiny cutie. He don't have mind to know who's helping him out, only that there might be comfort. I start the Mimi Tinker shushing and he calms down.

Tabi's mouth drops open. "Will you marry me?"

The little one goes right to sleep, but I don't stop moving.

"What are you doing with your hips? It's like they're hypnotizing me. Is this how you got Becca to agree to be your lawyer, you did this hip thing?"

I laugh. "It's a figure eight. My grandmother used to make me mind the nursery in church. The figure eight always worked on a colicky baby."

"He's colicky? Oh my God. There was something actually wrong with him and I didn't fucking figure it out," Tabi says as she stares at her son calm as a bug in my arms.

The blonde squeezes Tabi's hand.

"And you're both here to what? Set the baby right?"

Her tone is softer, but her words are still trying to intimidate me. "We're here to make sure you know, don't fuck with Becca." Tabi takes some kind of power stance. "My people know curses. I was raised in a curse culture. The Greeks do not fuck around with fate or assholes."

Natalie chastises her, "Tabi, stop saying things."

"Nat, that ship has sailed. I don't know how to not say things. Look. She laughed today. Like full-on lilting feminine laugh at something that wasn't even funny. Rebecca Gelbert doesn't do that. So, you either fucked her or she likes you."

My body pings and lights up internally. "I promise you and the California Bar Association I've done nothing disreputable."

Natalie goes up on her toes and squeals. "Then she likes you. Oh, frizzle. Don't tell her I told you that." Tabi mirrors my movements while I keep the baby sweet.

"Frizzle?" I ask.

Tabi reaches for her child, and I surrender the little darling. "She doesn't swear. You'll get used to it."

Robert enters. "Can we wrap this up? Holy shit, did he stop that kid from crying?"

Tabi nods and whispers, "He's a goddamn genius."

"I see you're not worried about the swearing thing."

"Got that fucking right. But I will need a lesson in that baby spellbinding thing when you get out of the clink."

Robert hands me Natalie's supply bag.

She says, "You've made quite an impression. Everyone has noticed. And you swear you didn't hurt that woman?" It's a sweet and lovely thing for a person to maintain such openness these days and I can see in Ms. Nat's eyes that she's a good person.

"I swear, Ms. Natalie, I didn't hurt that woman."

Tabi adds, "And you're not here to take our wineries in some strange long con?"

I hold my hands out. "I swear on sweet sleeping little

Nick. I know I shouldn't have brought y'all into this by way of Becks. But in a pretty damn dark and desperate hour, she was the only light I could think of."

Natalie gasps and pretends to let her knees buckle. "That's really swoony!"

Tabi says, "Meh. Do better. Do better by Becca. She's dealt with a lot of our shit but has had enough of her own too. She's prickly, but worth it. Prove yourself worthy."

"Yes, ma'am."

She smacks Robert. "See. That I like. You should call me ma'am."

"Never gonna happen." He flicks his head to indicate it's time for the ladies to leave.

The women are almost gone when Natalie pops back in. "We're not the last visitors."

"You mean like I'm going to be visited by three ghosts?"

"More like the rest of the 5."

"Bring it on, not like I have anywhere to be."

I WAKE TO THE SOUND OF A SOLO CUP BEING DRAGGED along the bars. There are four men standing there and I know exactly who they are. The other four owners of Prohibition Winery and the children of the five vintners of the wineries my old company tried to steal out from under them.

"Howdy there, fellas, is this a reckoning or you coming to call on me?"

David says, "Did you actually just say howdy?"

"Should I greet you as, I believe your sister referred to you as, douchenozzle?"

The gregarious redhead high-fives me through the bars. "Respect."

"If I'd known company was coming, I'd have set the kettle on. Wait, I'm in jail."

Josh Whittier, who took over for his father at LaChappelle/Whittier Winery, speaks first. "There's some questionable people in my past, but you, fine sir, will never crawl out of the fucking hole I dig for you if this is a scam or you're a murderer. I have no time for bullshit or anyone fucking with my family. Speak, asshole."

He's got every right to be this aggressive. I would be if the tables were turned but I'm not what he thinks. "Coming out of the gate hot."

"What do you expect?" He's in my face and I don't back down.

I pull out my military tone to match his aggression. "What do you fucking want from me?" I stand to my full height, and we stare each other down for a second and no one does a thing but stand there stupid. Message fucking received. They're here to bully the truth that sweet Nat didn't get for them. Fuck them.

"I want to know your plans for my family," he finally hisses at me.

"I have none." I grit out. "Take your shit and your posse and go. And don't send another fucking person in here to ask me the same fucking questions I've already answered. My actions should speak louder than the words you people are demanding of me today. Roll up your alpha bullshit and shove it up each other's asses, because I won't tolerate it and don't fucking need it. Do you want to fucking tape this so you can play it for the rest of your cast of fucking players and I can get some damned rest?"

"Ok, muthafucker, answer the fucking question one more time." He shakes the bars as if he can't control himself. And that's where we differ. I may be able to get to a place of rage, but I know exactly what to do with it. And it's time to shut this down.

"First off, bitch, I don't have to answer shit. I have my entire life folding in on top me and your fucking pissant worries about nothing are clouding my world. Listen up, all y'all cunts, I have no ill intentions towards any of your families. And I'd appreciate if you get the hell out my face."

There's a tense moment where I might crawl out of this cell and pummel him if he keeps at it. It takes me a while to get riled up but when I do, watch the fuck out.

Sam Langerford clears his throat. I almost don't recognize the fucker, he's totally cut, probably dropped a hundred pounds and his friendly beard is missing.

"Did you just call us cunts?" There's a long pause and we all break up, including Josh.

David's leaning along the back wall sipping something from a small keg. He pipes in with, "I don't think we're as intimidating as we think we are. But, dude, do you really like my sister?"

"Don't you?" I spit back at David. It's gonna take me a moment to come out of the red zone. I step back and breathe in and out slowly.

Sam says "Look, we're only being tough guys because you, Mr. Fucking Muscles, are locked up. None of us are that brave. Josh likes to think he is but he's not. Wanna beer?"

"I'm incarcerated," I answer cautiously.

The silent blond man says, "Potato/Pahtato I'm the mayor, I sanction it."

"Then hell yes, thank you, Baxter Schroeder." He's the most even keel of this group. The five friends grew up together, and he married the most unstable.

"On one condition." He puts his finger up just as David stops pouring my cup,

"Let me hear it," I respond. I'm not rolling over for this guy.

"My wife told me you're a bit of a miracle worker. Tabi needs you to teach me how to get Nick to sleep?" He steps closer and I see the blueish smears under his eyes.

Josh jerks his chin to me. "Work on girls too?" Becca told me he has three little girls and another one almost here.

I smile and say, "Yes. It's a figure eight with your hips and a shush shush shhh."

I demonstrate and Baxter, Josh and David mimic me. Sam slams his beer and pours another. He doesn't have children.

"Like this?" He's jutting his pelvis out but not in any kind of pattern.

"No, Josh. Open your hips more."

"I'm not fucking flexible like that," he grumbles.

Baxter has a huge grin on his face. "It's easy, let go, like you're dancing. I can totally do this."

Sam pipes up, "You look like a bunch of hula dancers."

David smiles. "Yea, and I'm fucking great at this. It's why I'm good at fucking." They all groan and Sam hands me a beer.

"Thank you kindly." They all stop and find chairs or walls to lean on.

Josh says, "She laughed."

I raise my glass to these men. "So I hear." Inside my

little heart is doing the happy dance but I won't let them see.

David sits on the floor and finishes his drink. "She doesn't do that. Not like that. And we had to lock the aunties away from coming here."

"The aunties?"

"Our mothers. Jana was all hot to see who you were, she didn't go to that meeting two years ago," Josh explains.

"That's right. But I look forward to meeting her."

David grumbles at me, "Watch yourself. Are you looking for a blessing or a cut bait situation?"

I'm a little ruffled at their presumption either way. I'm not looking for a damn thing from these gentlemen.

"Josh, what are your intentions towards Elle? I mean you've knocked up that girl several times without making an honest woman of her. And, David, you didn't even know you'd fathered a child and then you expected Natalie to simply jump on board. Now, Mr. Sam, I know your love took off, so I don't have anything for you." He throws his hands in the air like he's victorious. "And, Mr. Mayor, well, you've saddled yourself with enough trouble, you don't need pointing out that she's, well—"

They all step forward, but Bax speaks distinctly, and it carries a hell of a lot a of weight, "I get your meaning, but if you say one more fucking word that even alludes to Tabi's character, we'll all kick your fucking ass. And I don't care what kind of training you have, we're—"

David interrupts him and I see that I've crossed a line. "Making sure you're not using my sister. That you're not in this for her to get you out of jail or somehow swindle property or vines from anyone. But mostly, don't fuck her over for your own cause. Because she fucking—"

Josh finishes his sentence, "laughed."

I back up and put my beer down. "What y'all are telling me, is that Becca doesn't laugh much. And I am sorry for disrespecting Ms. Aganos, was not my intention. She's a fiery, loyal, and highly intelligent human."

Bax is quick to correct me, "Mrs. Schroeder."

Sam replies, "I wouldn't push it, asshole." Seems harsh from him but I've found their limit and I get it.

"You don't fuck with family, and I wouldn't never do that to yours. My loyalty to my own got me in this situation. Once I realized my own agenda was affecting y'alls so badly, I removed myself from the situation. And before you ask, I would have, but I didn't kill Asher Bernard."

Josh's nostrils flair and his face hardens. I'm sure if he was given the opportunity he would have as well. Asher roughed up his fiancée quite a bit and she escaped before it all went tragic.

"Good." Josh nods sharply.

"Don't break her." David puts his hand between the bars, and I shake it.

"I would have warned him how she could probably snap his psyche but if you want to play it that way, you go ahead." Sam shrugs.

We all laugh, they refill my cup and pull up some folding chairs. I think it's going to be a long, good night.

# CHAPTER 10
## BRICK

I hear a series of metal-on-metal noises and wake from my shitty sleep. I'm a bit hungover. There's a knocked-up blonde woman holding a suit bag. I recognize her as the real victim in that Vino Groupies scam. The one that piece of slime tried to claim. I don't forget names or dates.

This woman's green eyes sparkle differently than my Becca's but they're stunning.

"Ma'am, are you wearing a wedding dress?"

"Yes. I won't get married while I'm pregnant and I'm always pregnant so I'm wearing all the fucking dresses I've ever purchased over the last several years until this one pops out." She wipes a purple stain from her lips. It's like she's been sucking on a lollipop or something. She resets and smiles at me. "I'm not a good pregnant person, sorry."

"Noelle Parker," I say, and she nods.

"Yes. But it's Elle to my friends. Noelle's a bit formal."

I'm a touch confused she'd be this open with me. "You barely know me."

She doesn't hesitate. "She trusts you. Here. Mel said you needed a suit. This is Josh's."

"That man can hold his beer." I take the suit and hang it on the bars and step back a bit.

She flings her arms around. "Yes. I'm so proud. It was fun waking up with three little girls singing Moana and me puking from this one"—she rubs her white satin clad belly—"while Daddy slept it off in the guest room."

I crack up but she breaks the laugh in half by taking on a more serious tone.

"The least trusting of this brood has embraced you. The rest of us are catching up, but we'll follow her down this path without question."

"Tabi." I roll my eyes a bit.

Elle smiles. "No. That girl gives everyone a chance. Don't get me wrong, she'll judge you instantly, but she'll give you a chance to defend yourself. Apparently, you passed her test. But Becca holds too much for all of us. We've relied on her when we probably should have let her find her own life. But you somehow take some of that weight she carries. I know you have a lot of shit to deal with but somehow, she seems lightened and it's only a couple of days. Imagine what would happen if you stuck around?"

My mind races and my body feels like that first spring day, the one full of possibilities of a long warm summer. But I can't let on because I can't have her, so I deflect a bit.

"Congrats on the blessing, the ring, and the promise. You gettin' hitched soon so that little one—"

"Isn't a bastard?" She cocks her eyebrow and I laugh as she mocks my old-fashioned mindset.

"I didn't mean to offend."

"No offense taken. This one will join the other bastards. What's a group of bastards called? A burp of bastards? A barbarian of bastards. How about a bellyful of bastards. That's what we have. And Josh and the universe can't stop knocking me up. This was with a condom after a vasectomy. It's like we're in control of nothing in the universe. It's chaos. I have three small children and another one on the way and all I want is for my ankles to look human and not part rhino. Is that too much to ask?"

I cross my arms. "That's a whole hive of bees you got in your bonnet and a bit of an overshare, but I appreciate you."

"Sorry. You'd think I'd get better at being pregnant by now. Instead, I'm slipping into madness." I smile at this very beautiful and exact woman. "If there's anything else I can do, just reach out. I'm not sure I have clout enough to pull you from the press. Mel might be able to curb some of it, she's very good at pixel and code manipulation. And she saved my ass a bunch of times and helped with the whole Asher..." She looks down. Her voice drifts off and her vibrant eyes glaze for a second, then she snaps out of it.

I clear the lump in my own throat to speak. "Thank you for this. And I need to say this—I'm so sorry, Ms. Elle." I don't know what to do in this situation but I'm sorry seems like a good idea.

She takes my hand through the bars. "It wasn't your fault. No one saw him coming. Even those of us with impeccable taste or the most distrustful of us, none of us could predict he was a monster. But thank you."

I nod. "I appreciate you saying it."

She shakes it all off and says, "Robert's taking you to court, and she'll meet you there. You'll have to stay cuffed going into the courthouse." I figured as much. She hands me a phone. "It's a burner. The 5 basically have stock in them. It's ridiculous. But she has the number and it's the only one programmed in there. And be warned, Mel can monitor anything."

I'm flustered as this woman forgives me for working

with the lunatic who tried to hurt her. There are some things that are harder to forgive yourself than others. Mimi Tinker's death will forever be etched on my soul, but this cut pretty deeply too.

"Thank you for coming back for her and for having the integrity to walk away from what I can only imagine was a lucrative job."

No one knows why I took that job in the first place. That's no one's business for now.

"Wait, coming back for who?" I'm confused. She waggles her eyebrows. I continue, "Ma'am, you have me mistaken with someone who would try to make a pass at their lawyer." I grin.

"Look, I'm aware of the parade of people who busted through here yesterday, but we did it because she laughed." I imagine her having a good time. Elle continues, "Often and loudly. The only thing different in her life is you. We held the moms and dads back from coming. I didn't know Josh and his boy band came by until after he came home drunk. But your next audience will be with Josh and Bax's fathers. They're the heart and soul of the five and if they deem you worthy, everyone falls in line."

"Which is the heart, and which is the soul?"

"Stick around and see for yourself."

"Ms. Parker, I do thank you kindly for the suit and the conversation, but I believe I have a hearing to attend."

"Are you nervous?" She leans in and I whisper her a truth.

"As a cheater in church."

She laughs then yells, "Robert. I'm done."

Robert looks at her. "Is Yia Yia on her way in?" She laughs. I have no idea who that is.

"Nah, I think we're done."

I shoo the woman away from me. "Now, if you'll excuse me, I have to go tell the judge I most certainly didn't hurt that woman."

"Do you think they'll believe you?" she asks, holding her belly full of hope.

"Wishes and Tinkerbell."

"What?"

"People believe in all kinds of things; I only hope I'm one of them."

She smiles. "I'll clap as loud as I can."

"I appreciate that, Tink." I wink at her. Now to face the truth of things and hope it's enough.

# CHAPTER 11
## BECCA

There're way too many people at the courthouse. I'm waiting for him to show up. My gamble paid off and the judge cleared his docket to take this high-profile case. He's up for reelection and has something to prove. I hoped he'd jump at the bait. But the DA did put us off until almost the end of day so they could review the case and what evidence we have. I sent everything over the moment Brick headed to Sonoma to spend the night on New Year's Day. They've had a minute, not a lot but neither have I. I'm going to lean heavily on character and facts. But it's not my job to prove his innocence today, it's their job to prove there's suspicion of guilt.

He glides into the court escorted by Robert but in hand-cuffs. It's upsetting but I tuck it away. Then he takes his place at the table next to me and even restrained I'm awed by the way he moves around me as if we're constantly danc-ing. I demanded he not be in cuffs and the compromise is that they'll be removed once court is called into session.

There's no reason because we've cooperated since the first night, but it's a fucking power move on the DA's part.

Like subliminally, if the judge sees him in handcuffs, he'll automatically agree the charges should stick. We brought the crime to them but I'm here to officially state there's no case. He shouldn't be remanded into custody if we keep it simple. And the DA doesn't appear to be out for blood, but the truth. My brief is compelling and precise, as always. The arrest should go away.

There's not enough evidence to hold him and no one can find the hospital nurse he paid to fix her or the orderly who helped get the woman onto a gurney and out of his truck. And the CCTV footage from that night was damaged, which doesn't look great on our part, but is helpful. They'll argue *prima facie*, that the case is the first impression, and the charges should stick. I'll counter argue that they haven't made their proof. He has an alibi for the bulk of the evening thanks to Safeway and Mel. The truck wasn't picked up from the garage by Brick and he took the victim to the hospital.

Brick takes his place by my side and the heat coming off this man is palpable. I missed him last night and that's not natural. He's been in my house, suspected of murder, for three days and I missed his presence last night. He broke me. I'm not acting normal and I'm not sure how I'll put the pieces of my life back together after he leaves. It all has to go back to exactly as it was before, so I'll know how to deal with things.

He's in Josh's custom navy-blue suit and it's disturbing how my focus is interrupted by the thought of him out of this suit. My knees buckle a bit when he brushes his hand with mine.

The bailiff calls the hearing to order, and we stand as the judge enters. He nods for us to take our seats. I don't take mine until the bailiff removes the cuffs. Brick thanks the man, who seems a bit taken aback by that. He leans over, and his breath tickles my ear.

"Why is there no jury?"

And I snap back to attorney mode—a terrible attorney that didn't explain what was going to happen today. I didn't prepare him because somehow, I felt he knew everything. Or I didn't want to be lawyer Becca with him. But if I don't want this man to go to jail, I need to get my shit together.

"It's a preliminary hearing to determine whether the charges against you are even valid. A full-blown trial has a jury. This judge is simply going to tell us whether you'll need to be remanded to jail to await trial and then we'll get bail set. Or if I can get you the hell out of here, we can figure out what happened for real."

The District Attorney blathers on about the sanctity of life. The woman is still alive so that's a good thing. But if something changes, they can arrest him again. The prosecutors are scribbling notes and conferring.

I scribble on the pad in front of me, then Brick takes a pen and writes "Hi" and I try not to laugh.

I smirk at him and turn my attention to the questions being asked.

"No, your honor, we don't believe there's a preponderance of evidence on the prosecutor's case. And we further ask that all charges be dropped immediately."

"Ms. Gelbert, I've read the brief, but put this into terms both the DA and I can understand."

"My client, Brick Dunne," I gesture to him, "has zero prior criminal activity, is a highly decorated veteran and most importantly, didn't hurt that woman. He only attempted to aid her by driving her to the hospital and covering her medical expenses. He was in shock from his own injuries and refused treatment in a state of emergency."

The DA asks, "If he's such a seasoned member of our military, why did he leave the hospital?"

"As I stated, he was in shock. But more importantly, having no idea how or why this woman ended up in his truck, he was exercising extreme caution and keeping himself safe. Was it wise to leave with a gunshot wound and a possible head injury? No. Was it illegal? Also no. Other than my client's testimony as to the care of Hope Beardsley, there's zero proof he was even with her at the time of her injuries. He simply delivered a wounded woman to the emergency room. And currently no one but my client was a material or physical witness to this even happening. The prosecution has stated they're unable to find the three people Mr. Dunne interacted with to save Ms. Beardsley's life."

I walk towards the bench and turn back to the DA. It's a move I enjoy as if the pivot puts extra emphasis on what I'm about to say. I never think of myself as a showy person but if you put me in a courtroom, a piece of me sparks to life. I glance at Brick and his eyes are dancing and his expression is almost reverent.

The Assistant District Attorney takes the wheel for a second and I can't wait to squash him because I know what's coming.

"Ms. Gelbert, Mr. Dunne was arrested and accused of a homicide." He stands there indignant, not even doing his job.

"Accused. I could accuse you too, Mr. Kaplan, but the point of this hearing isn't accusations, it's you and the state of California proving there's merit to this arrest. An arrest, mind you, that Mr. Dunne basically volunteered for. He reported the crime. He brought you all the evidence and his testimony the very night all of this happened. If it weren't for Mr. Dunne and his cooperation you wouldn't have even had enough to get a search warrant pushed. He's the reason you think you have a case and the exact reason why you don't."

I pivot back to the bench.

"Your honor, the prosecution has failed to make their burden and I ask again for an immediate dismissal of all charges."

Kaplan tries again, "Your honor, the blade is consistent with a blade Mr. Dunne used to own."

The judge speaks, "As do I, sir. It's a common hunting knife and unless you have something that uniquely ties those wounds with a knife Mr. Dunne was actually holding, I will ignore that line of thinking. There are no fingerprints, no weapons, and no witnesses. And according to this preliminary report the angle of the wounds are consistent with someone standing and inflicted by someone shorter than Mr. Dunne. Mr. Kaplan, I'm inclined to side with the defense on this and all issues."

"Thank you, your honor," I say smugly.

The assistant DA protests, "Rebecca, you can't be serious?"

"I don't joke, especially in a situation like this."

Brick sits back in his seat and his bird tattoo pops out of his sleeve. I like that one. I need to stop thinking about his tattoos and get back into this game.

"Your honor, I request an immediate ruling, so we're not wasting this man's time any longer."

"Objection," the District Attorney says loudly.

"Ms. Gelbert, I hear you and I agree." The judge scoffs

at him, "This is a hearing, Mr. Kaplan, you can simply speak your mind, no need to object."

Kaplan tries again, "He has zero ties to the community."

"That's not what the arresting sheriff's report said. In fact, he set a record for visitors last night in Sonoma. But that's neither here nor there. You have only proven there was a crime, but I've heard zero evidence this man committed it. In fact, you can't even place him at the scene. You don't have a crime scene. It's not been discovered."

Brick raises his hand and I shake my head.

He ignores me. "Roadhouse out on 29 just south of American Canyon. That's where I woke up. Must be the scene or at least part of it. And the Safeway was where I was shot and walloped on the head pretty good."

I glare at him.

"Mr. Dunne, I must caution you, anything you say can and will be used against you in this very room. You are about to walk out of here a free man, do you want to jeopardize that?" The judge admonishes him.

He says, "The crime location was in the arresting report, I'm not telling tales out of school."

"Is this true, Mr. Kaplan? It's in the arrest record and you didn't think to bring it up?"

He responds, "There's nothing there and it's simply his word."

"Then I defer to the law. There is nothing tying this man to this crime. Other than the victim's blood on the accused's clothing, which was surrendered without question and before arrest, there's not a single piece of evidence pointing in this man's direction. And why aren't we looking into his injuries and who assaulted this man? Suspicion and supposition have no place in the law or my court. Mr. Dunne, I'm releasing you to Ms. Gelbert's care, but there's still the matter of the victim and your role in her injuries is nebulous at best, therefore you're a person of interest. This court will ask that you remain close by and in the custody of Ms. Gelbert until further determination can be made of your involvement with this crime."

I exhale and hope that's the last of this.

"The state has failed to prove their burden and this case is dismissed and all charges against Brick Dunne are dropped. And will remain that way until further concrete evidence is provided to bring about new charges pertinent to this case."

He turns to a stunned prosecution, not sure why they thought this was a slam dunk but it's far from it. "And, Mr. Kaplan, keep looking, that woman deserves justice."

I blurt out, "So does my client."

The judge glares at me. "Don't push it, Ms. Gelbert."

"My apologies, your honor."

I return to my seat with a slight grin but the steely expression on Brick's face isn't helping things. He looks like a hardened criminal and I'm pretty sure he's not. Or he is and I'm a fool and my career is going up in flames just like my underwear when he looks at me. This all might be the worst idea I've ever had. I should have told him to leave and called the police immediately. I should have referred him to a true criminal lawyer. But I'm buzzing all over for the first time since I can remember. He might be what I need to get me out of the rut I didn't even see that I was in.

We exit and Brick doesn't say a word. The DA rushes after me and touches my shoulder and Brick cuts him a death gaze.

"Mr. Dunne, would you mind waiting over there for me? I need to confer with a colleague."

"I mind very much. It seems like this man here doesn't

have my or your best intentions at heart. Mind your manners, sir."

He sneers, "I have only the law to think about and justice will be carried out to the fullest. Your intentions are none of my concern and Ms. Gelbert, trust me, she can handle anything. That's why they call her Elsa."

I wince a tiny bit but hopefully no one saw it. I hate that fucking nickname privately but publicly, fuck 'em, let them think I relish it. I look over at a confused Brick. "Ice queen from Frozen."

"Can he talk to you like that?" Everything in me wants to throw myself at him and thank him for being offended for me. But instead, I give him a nod and he reluctantly walks away.

"I don't know what the fuck is going on between you and, let's face it, a murderer, but get out of this case. I'm prepping a plea bargain for after sentencing. The evidence doesn't look too favorable. They're going to charge him again, first hint of a connection."

I respond as coolly as possible, "Look, there's nothing to find. But I'm going to find the truth and that's what you should focus on as well."

"Fucking Elsa."

"Jim, I thought you were a good attorney, but instead you're an opportunist who has a hard-on for this case. There are accolades in your eyes, and I won't have it. Law to the fullest extent my ass. You're a fucking social climbing piece of shit and I could shred you any day of the week with less than I have already discovered about Mr. Dunne's innocence. That's why you want me to step away from this case. Make your career somewhere else, there's only smoke and mirrors here."

"You really are a grumpy bitch who needs to get laid."

"Not by a needle dick with his head so far up the mayor's ass he can barely keep the brown off his nose."

I put my hand out to shake his and smirk at him. I hate being a bitch, but he started it by evoking Elsa in front of my client. He doesn't know the nature of my relationship with Brick. Not even I understand what the hell is going on, but he was simply trying to undermine my client's confidence in me.

He's the guy who tries to make up for his lack of legal talent by marginalizing women around him. He wants to make me feel less than, but it won't work. I grew up at the hand of the master of that little kind of jab, I learned to dodge them and turn them back around at a young age. My dad can be an asshole, but he made sure I was never going to be anybody's fool. Kaplan walks away and I turn and run directly into Brick.

We walk out of the building and Brick turns to me. "I'm free?"

"Yes, but on thin ice basically. They want you for this. We need answers first. You can return to your house but you're in my custody."

"Nope. They clearly know where I live and there's a good vibe at your house."

I blush a bit. "Only while we work the case. This will all depend on evidence discovery and now we're both in a race to prove you did or didn't do it. If she dies, this will get a whole lot stickier. Let's go home." A sense of calm tickles my nerves and I exhale at the idea of him coming home with me.

"Hot damn, we're having a slumber party!" I laugh and move away but he's in my ear. "And I heard every word you said to that weasel. It's the sexiest fucking thing I've ever seen in my entire life. A woman who not only knows how to handle herself but can dress down a foe with a look." Then he growls and all decorum is lost for a brief second.

"I can't be sexy to you. We need clear boundaries."

He laughs and walks past me towards the parking lot. "Whatever you say, counselor, whatever you say."

# CHAPTER 12
# BRICK

Been about a week we been at it and I'm starting to have a set running route. Her large reimagined modern farmhouse comes into view. It's no doubt an impressive thing to show your childhood bullies and competitive types but it's not her. It doesn't suit. It's all so calculated and ordered. She should move and create something of her own, not feed into an antiquated version of herself. She's more than this house can hold.

I sneak in the back door and sure enough, Calico, who I've been calling Lil' Bit, because creatures need names not categories, is sitting in the sink. She only dares do this when Becks isn't home.

Lil' Bit is licking the faucet. I turn on a drip for her and she dives in, the only cat I've ever met who wants a touch of water on her fur. She purrs loudly while I grab some yogurt and granola.

"Shit and shinola. That's what we don't know the difference to."

Mel's presence, although jarring, is not surprising. Her voice fills up the house whether we want it to or not. Becks ran off to the courthouse so we're alone. Mel's always intrusive but somehow loveable. Her dark-brown hair is in all directions with a smear of what I hope is chocolate on her cheek.

I look at her and tap my finger on the spot on my face where there's something on hers.

She shrugs, wipes her cheek with the back of her hand, then proceeds to chug milk directly from the carton. Becca would never stop scrubbing out her mouth if she knew.

She blusters, "Where the fuck you been?"

I'm dripping in sweat, wearing workout gear with a red face.

"Library."

She laughs and slaps me on the back. "We got work to do."

"Ain't you up a little early for you?"

"Not up. Never down. I'm onto something and you have to help fill in the gaps because I don't know—"

"Shit from shinola, I get it. Don't try to talk like me and I won't try to dress as dazzling as you."

A large guffaw fills the room. I walk over and turn off the faucet and the cat curls up in the damp sink.

I scratch between her ears. "Ok, Lil' Bit, you chill here but if you hear your mama, skedaddle. And, you, let's hustle up and ride."

She pumps a fist in the air, and I follow her down the hallway to Becca's study. There's a giant whiteboard taking over the room and a corkboard with string to match on the other side.

"I thought you were more of a digital kind of gal?"

"When digital fails me, I go analog. I need to understand your connection to these people and theirs to you and to each other. It's a fucking mess in my head."

I stare at what she's put together and some of it's wrong but some of it eerily right. I don't know how much to invest or trust. If I go ahead and expand this research and we work together, there's no going back. My history becomes public. Imma need a think on it.

"Ms. Mel, this is mighty impressive, and I will definitely weigh in on it but first, I need a shower."

"And what the fuck am I supposed to do?" She slurps one of the open cans of Red Bull littering the desk. I heard her come in around two a.m. and snuck down to see what the hell was going on, hoping it was a drunk David again, but it was Mel. I relocked the back door and got some more zzzs.

"You need to stop drinking that shit. I'll make you something when I'm decent and we'll talk it through. Then we'll come back to this nonsense and make it right. But for now, you go have a lay down in the guest house and find yourself a moment of peace. I need you sharp, not manic."

Her voice is unmodulated, "There's no moment of peace if I can't figure something out. Won't rest until the problem is solved." She makes a grand gesture, then flops down in a comfy chair. She's there a millisecond before her eyes flutter. I drape a light blue cashmere blanket over her. I figure I have a couple of hours to figure out what the hell I'm going to tell her, cover my tracks or possibly admit a few uncomfortable things about my past.

As I leave the room a damp Lil' Bit jumps on her lap and the two of them purr loudly.

MEL STIRS AND I POINT TO A GREEN SMOOTHIE ON THE table. "What the fuck's this wet spot. Did I have a wet dream?" She feels her lap.

I laugh. "Never mind that, you're a right impressive person." I'm sitting behind her desk staring at the two boards and I've filled them in. No sense hiding the inevitable so might as well see if all of this can help my situation.

She looks at them and gasps. "I knew it. I fucking knew it!"

"Now, we got to prove it." I shoot her a finger gun.

"But that one spot, the big one, is empty."

"That's on account of I don't know who pulled the trigger or in this case, wielded the blade. I can suppose who paid for it and who might be cleaning all this up, but the faithful, deadly foot soldier is a mystery to me. And this stays between the two of us. If we need to reveal all these things to Becca, we do it in a timely manner, and it comes from me. But for now, ask away, I know you're itching."

She sits up and leans forward. I add, "But you have to drink the smoothie."

"Fucking healthy shit. Fuck you." She takes a sip and then turns and addresses the glass, "Fuck off, you suck." I laugh and she turns to me. "How many men have you killed?"

"I believe that's on my classified service record, which seems to be pulled up on your laptop."

"But is that a complete number?"

"No. But it was all in the line of duty. Never killed a man in anger. But that doesn't mean I won't or can't."

"Shit." She lets that one slip out.

I tuck my white button-down into my jeans, buying me a little time before I launch into this. Mel continues to sip on her drink. I'm pretty sure it's the first real vegetable outside of shredded iceberg lettuce, salsa and guac she's had in ages.

"You're a scary badass?"

"Nah." I grin at her.

"You are."

"I do what needs to be done."

"Badass."

"Can we get back to it?"

She pulls her legs into a crisscross sort of configuration and balances on the edge of the chair.

"Let me tell you a story. Like you know, the Vino Groupies were a shell for Rex Construction." I point to the five different names that are all Rex employees. I take a red marker and cross out two of them as well as Asher.

"Dead?"

I don't know what happened to the other two, but one was from a European division, and I know for sure he's no more. A man I've worked some extraction jobs with informed me of his passing. More as a warning. And the other was a woman who only came around if something looked wrong in our department.

"Asher and I were the only ones on record for the Vino Groupies and I was only in an advisory capacity to make sure the deal went through. When shit got out of control, I was to rein in Asher, but I didn't see his fucked-up mind because I was too busy looking above me, not below."

"Forgive yourself. Not even the Capo saw him coming." I bristle a bit at her reference to Sal Pietro. The mafia don of Los Angeles who used to work with Josh and somehow is involved with all these people. He's making moves to legit-imize his business. I admire that, but his reputation does give me pause. There's even rumors he's involved with Becca's cousin, Poppy.

Mel must have seen me wince. "Stop. He's a fucking pussy cat. You'll see. You can't be around here without running into that wall of Italian menace."

"I appreciate you." I point at her and tuck away the info that she works for him too.

"Continue. What am I missing?" She scratches under her bra, and I turn away, but she doesn't pay me no mind.

I explain, "No offense, but quite a bit. But in your defense, the scope's a touch wider than you were looking at. Took me the last six or so years to unravel this shit and it's not what you think."

I go to the whiteboard and make seven boxes and off of one, a larger one. Rex Construction, Juris Shipping, twelve senators and minority whip, Appropriations Committee, Incan Trust, Hayslip Pharmaceuticals, and the Diana Group.

"What the hell?" She grabs her laptop, and her fingers fly over the keys. "They're not connected."

"But they are"—I pause for dramatic effect for my own amusement—"by this man." I tap the name she has randomly on the board as one of the Vino Groupies. I write Phillip Cady into the top box. Fucking man sets my teeth on edge.

"He's the one pulling all the strings and the one I suspect is gunning for me. He may think I'm a loose end, but I'm not sure if he knows I'm a threat."

"Get the fuck out of here." Mel leaps up and then plops down in her chair. "That's the dude Mark has a hard-on for."

"Mark?"

"Shit. Never mind. I'll tell you later." That might be the

name of the FBI agent who was attached to Sal Pietro for a time. Josh Whittier's former college roommate. She's not the only one doing background checks and making boards and lists.

I take a seat directly across from Mel. I need to be heard and seen when I say this. I have to tell Becca this part and I'm not sure if I'm proud or ashamed of it. I know I'll always blame myself for Mimi Tinker's death but the rest of it, well, it's time it all comes tumbling out. I haven't confided in anyone in quite a while, and this seems as good a time as any.

"Are we about to break up? I feel like there's a 'it's not you, it's me' moment coming."

I take her laptop and place it on the desk. "I need you to focus on me with that big brain of yours. There's a lot of information coming I don't readily share. And I ain't gonna repeat myself."

"Is that why they want you in jail and not dead?" She's too smart for her own good. Sure am glad she landed on my side of things.

"Yes, ma'am. First off, I knew Asher/Darren was ex-military by the way he maneuvered around the truth and the room. But he's the kind of military man that hangs his morals at the door instead of being a part of something greater than himself."

She doesn't blink or hesitate. "Did you kill him?'

"I would have, but that wasn't me. I suspect he found himself labeled a loose end as well. Vino Groupies were a front for Rex Construction, which is just a larger lie for the Diana Group. They own everything. You won't find it on record, but you will find it in the smaller holding companies and the employees that cross the boards and payrolls if you look hard enough. I have some skills too." I wink at her.

I stand and cross to the decanter of brown liquor on the shelves of the library. I don't know if it's decor or if Ms. Becca sips, but I know I need it. I stand with my back to the door staring at both boards. I move her pins around to the correct spots. Matching the people to their companies. I talk and she listens.

"Phillip Cady is the man who destroyed my home and my Mimi Tinker—"

"The woman who raised you. Oh, hey, do you want to know where and who your parents are?"

I turn around quickly. "Just because you can find something doesn't mean you should. It's in the not knowing where I take my peace. You can tuck your research right into that recycle bin in the upper left-hand corner of your screen." I don't want or need to know a thing about them.

I take a sip and she pushes her green juice away from her. "When my mama left, she took the mystery of my father with her. And by leaving, she gave me a rich and full life, one I don't plan to pull apart wishing things were different. You follow?"

"I think I want to be you when I grow up."

I laugh. "You don't, trust me." I lean back against the wall and cross my chest with one arm while propping up the other. She lifts her arms over her head, lacing her fingers and stretching. She's a sweaty gal but Imma let it pass.

"You went to Rex in order to get the goods on him?'

"Yes. In a way it's all been motivated by revenge. He stole her land three days after she died. I was overseas, called away for some classified business. Now, mind you, it had been over four years since I set out on a mission. I felt this was important enough for me to put my civilian life on hold, so I went. While I was gone, she was killed, and eminent domain was immediately enacted, and the government built a road within a month right through my bedroom. And because she'd passed, they didn't have to pay out for the land."

"Holy shit. They're not tied to anything like that."

"No. But Incan Trust and their development project won the government bid to build the road and was able to sell the land for US Interior contracts for a hefty price."

"The Senators."

"The Appropriations Committee, all financed, backed, and elected through, see if you can guess…"

She leaps up and moves one of the red strings. "Juris Shipping. Fingers in multiple states so therefore can contribute quite a lot to different candidates without looking like carpetbaggers." I nod at her. This is like playing tennis with a better player. She's quick and I appreciate it more than I'll be able to tell her. If we get out of this, I might buy her a taco truck.

I push her further. "What about the other major donors to approximately twenty-two strategic house seats and a dozen or so senators? Don't forget the multiple plants in different states owned and operated by—"

"Hayslip Pharmaceuticals!" I slap her on the back. She writes down three more slips of paper and pins them to the board.

I sit in the closest chair, but she doesn't move, staring at the board as if this chaotic string theory of hers makes sense.

"I left the company right after that winery mess, so no one could dig into what I'd been really doing for the company. I moved closer to my target to keep an eye on him under the guise of corporate competition. I took what I knew and set forth a trap."

Mel turns and picks up a piece of chocolate from the desk and licks her fingers.

I shake off the image and tell her the newest piece of this saga. "I became property manager of a large parcel of land I knew Cady had an eye on for development of a high-speed rail proposed in California as well as cross country. It's a dusty nothing of tumbleweed beige land outside of Bakersfield on the other side of the fault line. I know it's his crown jewel. He's been slowly buying up parcels of it for close to a decade. The man likes power, and this would give him power enough to charge the US government rent on the land. Power enough to hand the governor of his choosing a win. Power enough to gerrymander districts that would vote the way he chose in national and state elections. The man craves control and lusts for domination. He's well protected and well funded. He's also smart as fucking hell and from what I can tell, ruthless."

"So, there's a Big Bad?" Mel says and slaps the desk.

"I don't follow." I'm totally confused and then a voice from the doorframe startles me.

Her eyes are a little glassy as if she's overwhelmed. I stand and nod at her. Then I curl my toes into her soft carpet and try to shake off this feeling of anxiety. I wasn't ready for her to know all of this.

Becca smiles at Mel and turns to me. "Like *Buffy the Vampire Slayer.*"

She puts her bag down and points to the row of papers that have the fewest red strings. "These are low-level vampires."

"Y'all are talking crazy," I say, hoping it becomes clearer.

Mel waggles her finger. "As soon as we make sure you don't go to jail, we don't die, you get revenge, and we figure all this shit out, clear your schedule for some binging, Mister. You do know of Buffy, right?"

Becca grins at me and I nod yes. Then she explains, "Every season she'd fight the good fight against paranormal evils but there was always one big underlying bad thing pulling the strings or creating all the chaos from the beginning of the season. It was quite clever. Sure, there were one-off episodes that had nothing to do with it, but you get the idea, right?"

Mel is super animated. "Don't even get me started on Dark Willow! Then there's—" I hold up my hand.

"Ok, settle yourself. Save it for our Buffyfest. I get it. And yes, Phil Cady just might be the Biggest Bad. He's not even in this country. The SEC was onto him for a while, and he violated a bunch of things. He got suspected in one of those Madoff type things, so he disappeared himself from the country. Even though they couldn't find a thing about him. But little bursts of chaos are what feed his machine. If the law is focused in one place, they don't glance in his direction. So, if you see another blip in the economy or a bank scandal, he probably tugged that string."

"And he wants you gone?"

"He wants me useless."

Becca takes the glass from me as if it's completely natural and normal for us to share a sip of something. My dick twitches when her fingers scrape over mine. She turns to me and says, "I'm sorry."

I don't deserve her sweetness.

"What else?"

She offers the glass back and touches the wing of the bird on my hand, then stares at it for a millisecond too long. I catch her and the left side of my lip curls up.

Mel snarks at us, "Back to the story!"

Becca leans back onto her desk, but her eyes never leave

mine. "I can take it. And I was in the hallway the whole time."

I pace like a tiger that's had too much time to think. Back and forth until finally I can't contain the story or who I am completely any longer.

My voice is colder than I intended. "Fine. You want this fucking story. I'll give it to you. This is the trust and the long of it. No holding back, you want to defend me then fine. I didn't kill that girl. I didn't carve her up into a bloody mess, but it doesn't mean I'm not capable of it. This fucking man has fingers into everything and who knows what his ulti-mate plan is, and to be frank with you, I don't rightly give a shit. I don't fucking care if he buys up the whole fucking world. My motivation is personal. He killed her. I know he did. And I'm going to kill him."

I turn swiftly to leave the room and get a couple of steps down the hallway, but she's faster and steps in front of me. My face is hardened. I'm the machine I keep tucked away.

Becca turns to me, unaffected by my words. I didn't intend to let her see the real beast inside of me. The one that wars between what is right and what is just. She holds my face and I simultaneously want to turn away and lean into it. She's not afraid of any part of me.

I stare at the ground and say in a quiet breath, "I don't remember how to rely on people."

She gets into my field of vision. "That's good, because I'm not very reliable." My small laugh erupts, and she liter-ally pulls my fucking chin up.

"I'm not afraid of you or your past."

Well, now I know how my life will shake out. There will never be a day that isn't about her in some way.

I walk back into the room and Mel nods at me but doesn't judge or say a word. Becca picks up my glass again and refills it. After taking a sip, she hands it over to me and takes a seat, tucking her feet up onto the couch.

I stare down at the drink and try to stall even more, but it's time, I guess. Face it all. "Alright. See, what I did was set about slowly buying up the land I knew he wanted. I did it over the course of six years and created an untraceable company to be its front. If he can pretend to be a businessman instead of a beast, then I can pretend to be a property manager."

I take a long draw of my whiskey. I don't know what it is, but it's delicious. I'd feature this as a couple finger pour and make sure no one mucked it up with a cocktail recipe if I was offering it to people. My mind is wandering to a life beyond all this shit. Back to the problem at hand and opening up a vein to these fine folks.

"He's made several attempts in the last six months to purchase the land. Each offer is higher and higher. I don't know if he figured out who I am or I'm just someone in his way. I don't believe he recognizes I'm the same person who worked for the Vino Groupies or if he knows about my grandmother. But we should assume he does."

Mel sucks back a sip of her smoothie and makes a terrible noise and Becca laughs. She then says, "But how is that possible and why not kill you? Not that I want you dead." She utters the back half of that sentence with a lovely urgency.

"He thinks I'm a whole different problem or maybe I'm the same. Who the hell knows? But I do know if I'm dead, that land is in an iron-clad trust to a non-profit preservation society. If I'm in jail, a case can be made for his old classic, eminent domain or better yet, he could swindle some kind of sheriff sale on it. He owns the California regulatory board."

Becca whispers, almost in awe, "Motive."

Mel points to her screen and it's a picture of the repair shop where I took my truck.

"I've been in sort of hiding but when I took it in, the plate must have drawn some attention."

Becca says, "Opportunity."

I nod, finish the whiskey, and put my hand out again. I'm aware we're only a touch after breakfast, but I'm terrified of the conversations we're still going to have today.

I squish my toes into the comforting rug again. I'd normally walk in the grass barefoot when I'm turning a thought over, but this soft cozy golden rug will have to do for now.

# CHAPTER 13
## BRICK

t's six days after my confession and nobody seems to care. I'm not the beast I think I can be or at least she's real good at pretending I'm not. We've been working non-stop, and my eyes are bugging out of my head as I search for this asshole among the rubble of his destructive path. Becca's hand hasn't stopped moving and she's been through almost a whole yellow pad. She said she writes better by hand. The analog of it all is adorable. We've moved from the study to the living room and I'm getting hangry, but she won't stop working.

Her red hair keeps falling over her left eye and it's been the joy of my life to tuck it behind her ear four separate times today. But this machine of a woman needs to slow the hell down and find a moment to be her. I've set up a thing with her cousin, Poppy. She's a chef, and I've learned, she's the reason they all trust Salvatore Pietro.

There's a secret spot that will do just fine for what I have planned. I need to get this girl into my car. With the truck being a crime scene and all, I thought it was best to buy a new shiny Volvo. I like the way it hugs the curves of the road. But we're going a block or two. I don't think she'll walk with me so I'm going to have to trick her.

I stand and tuck in the back of my favorite gray t-shirt into my jeans and I worry for a quick second I might not be dressed appropriately for the level of this dinner thing.

But then again, she's in a long pink-and-green-striped rugby shirt and leggings. It makes her look like a carefree girl scribbling in a journal instead of the badass lawyer writing my case. I hear her pen scratching on that yellow pad of hers like a broken needle on a record and it's oddly comforting.

This room has those real small white lights tucked into ribbon and garland all around. She has a little tree in the corner, nothing big or flashy. The only ornament is a piece of construction paper cut in the shape of a Christmas tree. It has some scattered glued macaroni and a lot of glitter in one place.

"Did you make that when you were young?"

She doesn't even peep at me. "I've always been old." I laugh at her, and she smiles. "My niece."

Well, that's a cute little move on Becca's part. Loving that little girl.

"Have you ever thought about having a bunch of macaroni decorators of your own?" Her spine goes pretty straight, and she stares at me as if I pissed in her pudding. "Sorry, understand. Boundaries."

"No. It's not that. No one has ever asked what I want."

I turn to her on the couch and put my arm along the back of it. She faces me and tucks her feet up under her. "Becks, explain."

She bites her bottom lip. "I've been told I was going to have kids by my ex or friends. And my mother talks and makes plans as if it's a foregone conclusion. David and the rest of the 5 assume I'm not interested, but no one has ever asked what I want. I just helped and witnessed two of the best people I know create a family overnight." She told me that Christmas story, it's a good one. "And I cried when those boys were adopted and held Tabi's belly and felt her relief and sheer terror that she actually got pregnant, but I don't know if it's all for me. I'm pretty settled."

"Are you now?"

"I am."

I raise an eyebrow at her and fight not to touch her. "I'd say your world is a tad small and it's my job to stretch it out a bit."

"You don't say. I mean you do have a way with entrances." I chuckle at her, and she laughs as well. Every time she laughs, I hope she releases a touch of the weight of the world that she leaves sitting comfortably on her shoulders.

"That was a mighty nice thing you helped those folks do, but it's not your job to carry all of them and their problems. Seems as if you're always there for them. Who's there for you?"

Her face contorts for a half a second, then she pulls her mask back on. Now, I don't reckon to know one damn thing about being a father or even having a hoard of people surrounding me the way she does, but I do know lonely. And like recognizes like.

I put my hand on her knee and she winces for a millisecond. She then straightens up and shakes out her hair while standing.

She gets to the archway leading to the foyer. She turns slightly. "If I don't, who will? And I'm here for myself."

"Not anymore, darling. I'll volunteer for that duty, take

a load off, I'll carry it awhile." She tsks, even though we both know I'm serious.

"Come on," I say and put out my hand. She looks up at me skeptically, which seems to be her default setting sometimes. "You know I won't bite." She cocks her head to the other side, and I laugh. "Unless the bar association says it's ok."

I'm going to push that little limit as far as I can. Surely there must be a loophole for a man, who did not commit the crime, to be able to lick every inch of their lawyer.

"We don't have time for games. They're looking for a reason to arrest you and the lab reports are coming very soon. And they will put you back in jail. No more Robert jail and my idiot brother tailgating your incarceration. Real prison where I can't protect you."

My heart bursts open, she wants to protect me when that's all I want to do for her. I exhale. "I can take care of myself. And you don't think that I know it's a race?"

She holds her hips and says, "Then where do you want me to come?"

I can't help but grin. And then I stare at her and twist my lips in my thumb and forefinger. It takes her a moment to realize what she said.

She gets frazzled and tries to correct it, "I mean come with you. Oh shit. I mean where do you want me? How do you want me?" I howl and she throws her hands up. "Christ." She pulls her giant collared sweatshirt thing down. "Fine. Where?" Even her lips blush when she gets embarrassed. They're a deeper pink, instead of the normal light pink. I wonder if they get darker during sex.

I pick up her boots and point towards a chair in her foyer. She sits immediately. My dick jumps at the idea of her listening to all kinds of demands. I kneel and take her leg and slide one of her boots on slowly. She's staring at my hands and I'm trying not to look up at her in this position. It's one I'd very much like to see without clothes. She offers her other foot and I slide that boot on as well. It's more sensual than I'd like and a hell of a lot more sexual than I want. Not sure I can handle being around her when she's this pliant.

I stand up and she pushes past me.

"You don't even know where you're going," I point out.

"No, but I assume there's a reason for all of this, so I'll trust you have a rational thought in your brain. My eyes are starting to cross from all the research and writing so this is a decent distraction." Hell, even I know I'm more than a decent distraction. I smirk at this enchanting and infuriating woman and wink. She rolls her eyes at me.

"Let's get on with this."

WHEN I PARK, SHE STARTS LAUGHING. I'M BEHIND A wine cave at this Napa place she must recognize.

"That's my cousin's car. Is there lasagna in there?"

I shrug. "Perhaps."

"You know we don't have time for this. Let's pick up McDonalds." She's fucking serious.

"That shit is garbage of the highest degree."

I hurry to open her door. She scoffs at me as she passes by, "Delicious garbage. But I'll indulge you."

"Well, let's say I made sure you had all four food groups represented instead of the naughty fifth."

She pulls open the large, weathered handle on the entrance to the winery. "Fifth?"

"Fried."

She laughs as we enter the small room, and it fills the whole damn place.

"Don't forget I'm from the south, fried is a religion as well as a food group."

"Maybe I should live in the south, it's my favorite." She walks on, leading the way to the surprise I planned as if she owns the place. Mel told me her dad helped launch this place in the '70s.

Her cousin did well, there's a candle, and it's more intimate than Becca would like and perfect for me. Poppy must have scurried out of here because there's no trace of her. Even though Becks doesn't like to admit she's close to people, I know she texts her cousin goodnight and good morning every day. Despite whatever's going on there's at least one person checking in on Becca, and I like that.

I pull out her chair and the food is already plated. I asked for lots of veggies and protein for me and whatever's her favorite, as long as it has some nutritional value.

She shuffles her feet and takes her chair. I scoot her in and sit across from her. She has her elbows on the table and her fingers tented in front of her.

"We can't do this."

"Eat? Enjoy a conversation? I'll give you the bill and we can call it a working business dinner." I'm trying to find that lighthearted woman underneath all that skepticism.

"It will never work."

"You're so damn sure of yourself, aren't ya. You're never wrong."

"No."

"Must be exhausting." I reach over and brush my fingers over this intriguing creature. Her lips tilt up slightly.

"Yes, it is," she says.

"I told you, tell me your troubles and I'll hold 'em for a while."

She leans back in her chair and crosses her arms. Then she looks to the left and to the right. She rolls her eyes, and I can't help but smile at her.

"Fine. My day both sucked and was oddly fucking interesting."

I roll my hands towards me. "Hit me. I'm not kidding. I'll hold your concerns while you put some nutrition into that damn fine body."

"Watch it." She picks up her fork and gestures and points at me.

I say, "Just an objective observation, not an overture. Boundaries, Ms. Gelbert."

She cracks up as she shoves a giant piece of melon and prosciutto into her pretty piehole.

I sit back and sip the ruby red liquor in front of me. I'm sure she could name the vintage, patch of land, and damned name of the man who picked it, but here's what I know—it's fucking delicious. I told her brother to give me the best Gelbert he had.

She's all business again. "I didn't sleep well."

I lean forward, squinting at her. "Me neither. But it's only on account of—"

She quickly interrupts me. "Don't. You want to hear my worries or not?"

I twist my lips like I'm locking them up.

She smiles. "Good. You could stand to zip it a little."

I gesture to her to continue.

"Everything is crumbling beneath me."

I start to speak, and she puts her finger up.

"No sympathy and don't try to fix anything. Just listen. You want me to unburden, let me do it without judgment. I can't handle the clients I have. I'm afraid to hire anyone and build the firm back up because it collapsed in on me. And I'm the one who has had a financial plan and business model since high school. But I'm the one failing. How the hell does that happen?"

I squeeze her hand right quick.

I want to hold her so fucking badly. I want to kiss away those lines on her forehead and tell her she'll be ok. But instead, I listen.

"When my law partner ran off with my fiancée..." She's never said it aloud, but I knew it happened. "...I had only ever known myself as one way. It all made sense and this person, who I am now, is confusing and scary to me."

"She's also fucking amazing. As you rebirth into the person you're supposed to be, know it's exquisite to watch." She's quiet as she pushes food around on her plate.

We're in a clearing inside their cellar area. There's old brick all around, like the kind that holds stories better left alone. The smell is slightly cold and musty. I don't know a whole lot about cold but here in this cave of sorts I swear it's all around me until I look at her eyes. They're molten fucking fire.

She whispers to her pasta, "Thank you."

# CHAPTER 14
## BECCA

O h, sweet muthafucking Jesus. What the hell is wrong with me? I told him things. I felt better after I did it but now, I want to hate this man. That's bullshit, there's no way anyone could hate this man, he's charming, sweet, kind, thoughtful, all that crap people dream of. Conversely, I gravitate to losers who will either bend to my will or break my heart when I attempt to be what they want.

This one is in dogged pursuit of me just as I am. I know I have little patience and I hate most people outside the families. I don't have a reason to spend time pretending to be interested in their dogs or what the fuck they ordered for brunch. It's why I loathe social media, mostly because I have to be social and that's not a thing I want to do.

But Brick's gray eyes are sparkling like dimes in the rain as the candle flickers off them and not only is it sexy as hell, but he's also never once clouded over his enthusiasm for talking to me. Most people tune me out or write me off. But this gorgeous, funny man begs for attention that I'm not used to doling out. I don't have an exit plan for the first time in my life.

I know that decorum, law, and my own moral character need to keep him at bay. That's not to say every single part of me didn't light the fuck up when he touched my hand earlier. I mean my dusty vagina sparked to a fancy, ready pussy in a second when he said he had a surprise for me. She's been waiting for the green light since he walked in the door. But I have to push that shit down. No time and I think we're becoming friends, not that I'm any good at that either.

He says, "I see the wheels spinning. This isn't a date. It's nutrition." Then he takes a giant bite of salad. He's already wolfed down two chicken breasts and I have picked all the cheese off the top of the lasagna.

I come back at him. "What makes you so cocksure this isn't a date? You planned it. It's empirically romantic. I assume you did research and crab cakes are on the menu as well. You even procured my favorite wine from my family's winery. Which means that either my asshole brother swiped it, or you braved a conversation with my rigid and condescending father."

He puts his finger up to stop me from talking and I continue, "I say condescending because he's a bit backward and your size and tattoos would intimidate him, so he will try to cut you down to make himself more comfortable. Which wouldn't work because I'm not sure I've ever met anyone as confident in themselves as you."

"You wanna take a breath or you have more bullshit to espouse?"

I bust out laughing.

I pick up the wine, which is literally mother's milk to me. It hits my tongue like a familiar wave of nostalgia. It's tart and rich with a touch of chocolate on the end of the finish. I swallow down the Cabernet that put my family winery on the map and grin at my dinner companion.

"Permission to speak freely, counselor?"

I nod. "Always. I don't like secrets or bullshit."

"Direct is hot."

"I'm not hot." I reflexively suck my gut in a little

"That's not for you to decide." He leans forward and I can barely concentrate on anything except the way his lips curl when he's trying not to kiss me. "You, smelling, sipping and savoring that wine was watching flirting, foreplay, and fornicating all in a couple of moments."

I blush. I'll pretend it's the wine.

He looks at me and the air around us seems to still. It's like if I could look away from his intense eyes, I'd be able to see particles and atoms frozen in time and space. I don't know how long the air holds us but there's a scrape of metal in the next room that pulls us back into normal gravitational orbit.

I lean back. "Why me?"

He leans back and sips his wine. His eyes light up when it hits his tongue. "Good stuff."

I ask again because I need to know why he's in my life. I'm not good without facts and details and he seems to have all of them, and I have none.

"Why me?" I repeat.

He puts his glass down. Brick stretches his arms out wide and has a massive wingspan, then they move above his head, and he locks his wrists together and groans.

"I've watched my back my whole life and my guard slipped right down that day in front of your family's vineyard before our corporate tour. You said to y'alls' colleagues, 'Today won't be a total wash if I can grab a good glass of Pinot.' I laughed and we locked eyes."

I breathe in and I don't say it, but I remember that exact moment. My vision went into iPhone portrait mode and the only thing in focus was Brick.

He continues and I can't fucking breathe, and I have no idea how to stop him from pushing us closer to that line I'm terrified to cross.

"For the first time in my life since Mimi Tinker's arms, I didn't worry about a thing. For a split fucking second, I was at ease. You ask why you? Well, I've been asking that question since the very second, I met you. And the only thing I can come up with is why me? Why do I get to feel this intensely about a stranger? Why me? Why is it that I'm driving close to madness imagining time with you or the feel of you? Why can't I shake ya off and move onto a sensible life with a perfectly lovely woman? Why am I so captivated by a complicated, stunning creature, that it turns out, I legally can't have? Why me, you ask?" He pauses and I'm breathless. "I counter with, why you?"

I'm breathless and he's relentless. "Near as I can tell the only answer that makes any kind of sense to our questioning is, you're mine. Meant for me. And I'm hook, line, and sinker, yours."

I toss my hands into my hair. What the fuck is he even saying to me? He's got me jumbled and confused. What the hell? My body is all tingles and surges. I can't stop this feeling from spreading to all my extremities.

I don't say anything for a moment as he speaks my truth out of his mouth. There's no air in this wine cave and his words are bouncing off the bricks and stones all around us. He leans forward again, and I feel myself drawn to him, and my Mel phone rings.

It breaks our spell and I'm grateful for it. I'm not ready to crack all the way open. I'm still clawing at yesterdays and trying to understand who I'm supposed to be in all the tomorrows.

"You can't hide behind work forever. Eventually, I'll be free and clear because of you and that's when we'll see all about getting into some trouble together."

I answer the phone and ignore him. "What?"

Mel says, "You know that's why I like you. You don't even pretend to be polite. It might be my favorite thing about you."

I just need data, not her brand of approval. "Mel, you needed something?"

"It's not public and I don't know if it's something, but I saw a strange item in the lab reports."

I say, "The lab reports are back? Does the DA have them?" Brick takes my phone and smashes the speaker button.

Brick clears his throat. "How ya doin' tonight, Ms. Mel?"

"If it isn't the hottest piece of ass from under the Mason Dixon line."

"Don't do me like that, ma'am. I know you're spoken for, and it only blurs the line between us. You break my heart when you speak such things."

She guffaws through the phone, and I grin a little at their exchange. His eyes don't leave mine. His jawline shadowed by the candlelight covered with a light stubble is distracting me.

Mel's voice snaps me back. "Fine. Listen up. The lab reports aren't official and haven't been double-blind verified yet. And what I did isn't technically illegal, I promise. See, reports like this, if not completely sealed by a judge or the police, aren't exactly open to the public but they're not off the radar either."

She's under strict orders to never break the law so I know this is close. "This better be legal. I do not want to get down the road and have inadmissible evidence."

"It won't be. You need to jump on it now. And I'm not sure anyone will find this significant, but I think it is. I think I found something everyone else will ignore. You need to get an investigator on this."

Brick traces a circle on the back of my hand. He might as well be circling my clit because I'm pretty sure just the heat and spark of his touch can do that anywhere on my body. I try and pull my hand away and he traps it while still holding it rubs his thumb back and forth. It's sensual and hypnotic and I don't pull away again.

He nods, then whispers, "Stop being so jumpy. We're inevitable."

And my breath is gone and replaced with the warmest of coziest of feelings. I might suffocate in his words.

Then in a louder voice he stops Mel from droning on. "Ms. Mel, I'm going to need the point, darling. And until this gets bigger, I can handle the investigating part."

"There's mud on your truck's running board and in the passenger seat. And on the floor mats on both sides."

"Hell, Ms. Mel, there's mud everywhere on my truck."

"Yes, but this was clay."

"You know as well as I do, there's clay in California." He puts my hand down and stands up circling the small space. His giant frame fills the room with an anxious energy.

Mel says, "But not Yazoo clay."

Brick's eyes go wide. I don't know what that means but I grasp his wrist as he passes me. He looks sideways at the phone.

"Are you shitting me, Mel? There was Yaz in my

truck?"

"I'd never shit you and yes, 100 percent confirmed, Yazoo clay. They even listed the likely origin town and county. Do you want the location?"

Brick is quick to answer. "No need. It's Harrison County and if I were more of a betting man, I'd clean up because I'm going to say it also contains a bit of oyster shell from down Gulfport way."

Mel exclaims quickly, "I tried to pinpoint your origins, but you're hidden. I got you now, you little scamp. I'd like to buy whoever hid your shit a whoopie pie."

Brick doesn't smile at her teasing.

"Thanks, Mel. We'll talk later. Good work." He hangs up on her. I turn my attention to Brick whose gaze is a million miles away.

"That's where you're from, isn't it? You know this Yazoo clay?"

"Mimi Tinker used to eat it. Said it made her young. It's more prevalent deeper into Mississippi, Alabama, and bit into Louisiana but the coastal region where I'm from has its share. It's nowhere else on the planet."

I reach my hand across the table, and he stares at it for a second. But he doesn't take it. I don't know what he needs because I'm shitty at this part of life. The affectionate, caring part. Fuck it. I remove my hand and pull my chair back. He clearly needs the night to be over.

I stand and he puts his hand on my lower back. My body floods with warmth as he whispers in my ear, "Let's get home, so you can pack a bag."

"Where are we going?" It comes out breathy and wanton.

"Home."

And now I'm totally confused.

# CHAPTER 15
# BECCA

wake as we land. I twist to see him a row back. I'm in his thrall like idiots who fall for vampires in B movies. Edward, I get, I'm not made of stone, but the ones who hypnotize with a strange look. That's what's happened to me.

He wasn't remanded to California, he's simply a person of interest; it's a gray area. That's my new life, living in the gray area. Wanting a man I can't have and watching the ever-moving line of my morals disintegrate. I didn't know what to wear for our traveling out of jurisdiction, trip to the homeland, investigating mud mission. But jeans go with everything.

I can feel the humidity before the plane even stops pumping recycled air. I went to South Carolina once and it was a kind of heat I've avoided since. We may have fires and earthquakes and insane temperatures, but we don't have thick air you can swallow with a spoon. He wanted to fly commercial, but he didn't use his name. He had another set of identification like he's a spy or something. I didn't ask because if I don't know, it's for the best. Everything is getting hazier by the minute, then his hand eases down my back and now it's murkier.

I FOLLOW HIM TO A PARKING LOT. "WHOSE CAR IS this?"

He opens the door, grabs a towel, and eases me into the car. I'm sweaty and it's mid-January. My joints feel looser, like the blurred air is a lubricant. He wipes a thick layer of dust off the two-seater Mercedes.

"Is this yours?"

"Yes." He doesn't elaborate. He paid my retainer within twenty minutes, but I didn't know he was 'abandoning cars at the airport' wealthy. Land baron wealthy.

"How many different airports have cars?"

"A few. It's easier to remain hidden."

"Do you have the ticket to get out of the parking lot?"

He laughs as he opens his door. "Nah, darling, I guess I'll have to pay the full twenty-four-hour fee. Shoot." He winks at me, and my insides feel like warm caramel. Everything about this godforsaken state is sultry.

He revs the engine and glances over at me. "Now, there's no need to do anything drastic like pull away from me. Can't have none of that."

It's out of my mouth before I can stop it, "Just trying to stay out of the forbidden areas of our lives. Touching is bad."

He growls a bit along with the engine. "Is it now? What if I promised to be very good at touching?" He exhales loudly, then turns his attention to the road.

"Promise." I bite my lip and slam my eyes closed because I just said that.

"It's a goddamned vow."

"Noted. Verbal or do you need something in writing?" I tease back as my sense slips from me.

He pulls out of the space and turns towards the exit. "I think we're friendly enough for a handshake deal, don't you, darling?"

I mutter a yes because I need to get off this subject.

"What was that?" His hand is on mine as he pays the attendant. Never looking at them. I see the wings of that vibrant blue and green hummingbird and can't help but touch it.

We don't move as he watches me tracing the bird. Then he covers my hand with his and puts the car into gear.

"Handshake good," I mutter.

For someone who prides themselves on their intelligence, coming to Mississippi might just be my undoing. The final piece of my unraveling into madness. I'll become a babbling idiot worshiping at his altar and he'll discover I'm kind of boring.

I'm going to try being present and not worry about all that could happen. I'm a mess, but I'm a mess with a sexy-as-hell man sitting beside me who keeps telling me I'm his destiny.

Calico will never believe this story.

# CHAPTER 16
## BRICK

I only have one destination, but she doesn't know I'm making a flash of myself around town. I spot the one person I was hoping to wrangle, Reverend Paulson. He's a real good man with fast fingers and a gossip-ready mouth. I slow down a bit and give him a polite nod. I'm barely out of range when I see him pull his phone out of his pocket and get to work. He's got that church lady gossip phone tree to service and I'm prime news. I haven't been here in seven years. Since the day I was able to finally get home from my mission and bury an empty box that should have been Mimi Tinker.

Becca's skittish about this whole manner of being here, but I can't help but let my soul ease when the magnolia buds and Spanish moss hit my senses. It's like my body chemistry jumps to attention. The south is a living breathing thing that people take part in but are never really part of unless you're from here. You can enjoy sucking down oysters, BBQ, and crawfish. You can hand over your hard-earned money at our beaches, but you're a tourist in the truest sense of the word. Passing through, trying to take a little piece of charm back with you. Y'all are lighter, more hospitable after being in our company, but we don't know any other way of being. I've been all over, but the south owns me.

Her face is resting on her hand. She has long delicate fingers and I'm fascinated with them as I am with all parts of her. I know the rules, but I've never been one to follow the letter of the law. I have to convince her it's more fun on this side of the fence. I feel her yielding. Life would be a whole lot simpler if she'd get on board with forever so I can worry about something else. These past weeks have been perfect, despite the homicide charges, of course. But every day she moves further into my soul.

She takes my hand as she gets out of the car. That damn sizzle runs up my arm again. I let it drop like it's as hot as she makes me. I roll up my sleeves a bit as that jangly old piano, that changes pitch and tone as the humidity swells and contracts through the year, spills out into the gravel parking lot.

"Where the hell are we?" I laugh as she stares at all the cats roaming around. There's a giant live oak that's seen it all before, reaching its branches over the cars, sprawling and claiming the land around it. As if the cottonwood in the corner might challenge its grandeur and make a claim on its roots. But it's owned this spot for a century or so.

There's life in the honky-tonk music, in the laughter of the people inside, and in the smell of the crawfish boil that I think is about ready. I guide her to the back door and her head is about to plum swivel off her body. "We shouldn't let our guard down. You never know who's watching us."

"Hush your mind." I think I know exactly who's watching. I invited them to come and find me by gallivanting around town. They know where I'll be.

A voice, big and bright as the day, barrels out the back door. "Ain't nothing you can do about that. Except lay down your worries and maybe dance a bit. Brick Fernando Dunne, you lying piece of shit. Who said you could come round here?"

Becca looks alarmed as I take the weary and wise woman into my arms. Her hair is whiter than I remember but her eyes are still sharp as a razor. That steel in her veins and honey in her voice reminds me a titch of the squirmy, gorgeous redhead standing to my left.

"Ms. Lucille, I know I told you I'd be by sooner than this. But you gotta cut me some slack."

"You ain't been home since they laid your sweet Mimi Tinker."

"And I ain't had a decent meal since." She jabs me in my ribs and whistles when she comes in contact with my abs.

"Boy, you all meat, no fat, that's no way to live. Maybe we start with cobbler."

"That I can get behind," I say.

She turns to Becca. "This one here is right perfect but she needs some cornbread. Come, them heads ain't gonna suck themselves there, stranger."

I laugh easily as Becca's eyes get wide and her lips straighten out. I lean over and brush my cheek along her jaw as I slowly make my way up to her ear. I leave a path of gooseflesh as I get closer to her. I know for sure her body wants me, just need to work on her brain.

I whisper softly and let my tongue flick a hint onto the shell of her ear. "Come on. You're gonna love it. Float on this air with me." She nods.

Lucille's voice rises above all the frogs and toads in the local bog. It's a natural hot spring so they croak to the tune of that piano all year. "Oh, child, you are very much in trouble." She fans herself. "I ain't seen that kind of heat coming off a pair since I put the pots to boil for the first time."

I let my lips brush her jaw on my retreat and she lets a small but sexy little sound slip from her full, damp lips. I bite mine so she knows for sure the only head I truly want sucked is my own.

I turn to Lucille. "Lu, this here is the charming Rebecca Gelbert, attorney at law."

"It's a pleasure to meet you, Ms. Lucille. You may call me Becca."

Lucille gets sarcastic, "Well, get a load of those manners. 'A pleasure to meet you, Ms. Lucille.' Woo, child, do you know he's the devil with a crocodile smile?"

She laughs. "I do." I pinch her lush backside and she laughs louder.

"It's a pleasure to meet you too, Ms. Rebecca." Lu does a little curtsy, then straightens up while all three of us laugh.

"Becca." Lu finishes with a flourish. "I got stories to tell and people to feed. Get your caboose inside and I'll get you something fine to drink."

I follow Becca, putting my hand on her lower back. I can't help myself, but she stiffens up like a jackrabbit sensing a predator.

That's right, Hummingbird, I am that predator. Something about the heat and the smells have unleashed me a bit. I hope it's got her insides hopping as well. It will literally be the death of me if I can't tease this woman's skin soon. She's coiled tight and I'm desperate to unwind this little spring and see how high she jumps or how twisted she can get.

Lu escorts us to the corner of the bar and Becca sits her

ass down gingerly. I laugh and slide in next to her. "The chair's clean enough."

"How did you know that's what I was thinking?"

"How many times do I have to tell you? You're mine, darling. Of course, I know what you're thinking."

She blushes and picks up the piece of paper with hand-written specials on it.

Lucille whips the paper away from her and sets down a beer and a glass of her special sweet tea in front of each of us.

Becks sips her beer while Lucille talks. "Ok, are you two hungry, peckish, or just plain snacking?"

Becca says, "I could eat."

"She's peckish and I think you know what to set on my plate."

"Can I look at a menu?"

The bartender cackles and Lucille answers her by walking away and yelling back over her shoulder, "Nah. You can look at it later. Promise no chitlins. Drink a spell. I'll be back."

I swallow down the best iced tea in the world, then quickly turn to the pretty redhead to my left. Her hair is getting curlier and wilder with each moment in this swamp. I love it. She keeps patting it down.

"Leave it be and let it find its own path on top of your precious head."

She laughs and asks, "Why are we here? And don't say it's for the food, atmosphere, or dirty bar glasses."

"Family. And the food." I raise my eyebrows at her. I turn towards the rest of the bar as a tall, painfully skinny but muscular man approaches us with conviction. Becca holds onto the bar like she's bracing herself. I leap up and wrestle him into a hug.

"Becca Gelbert, this here is Chase Carlyle. Not a thing gets done in this part of the world without Chase knowing about it." I'm flattering him because I need him to rat out the bastards who paid him a penny for his services or silences. I'm appealing to the part of him that should still exist deep down, the root of the root and the bud of the bud, to quote Mr. E.E. Cummings. We go back to diapers and I'm hoping the man won't forget that when he starts looking down the long hallway of loyalty.

"Ma'am." He stares a bit too long. I shove him a bit, and he squeals with laughter.

She puts out her hand as formally as this girl can be. "You can call me Becca."

"Well, Ms. Becca, care to come on over to our table and learn yourself how to eat like a southerner?"

I didn't tell her I wanted her to charm this man. I think it would make her nervous and she'd tighten up even further into her lawyer/cross-examination mode. She gulps down the tea. I don't tell her it's twisted up with some whiskey.

"Damn, you move fast there, Chase. We'll join you and y'all's crew, but keep your hands to yourself."

"And my thoughts?" He raises an eyebrow.

"Well, those are all yours. Unless you're in a sharing mood, then let me get Cy over there to pluck out some Kumbaya."

The two of us laugh loudly and we move towards the table. Cy, short for Cyclops, on account of losing an eye to taunting a rottweiler, is sitting there with a shit-eating grin taking up most of the table. He's a big man whose hobby seems to be to get bigger.

I know he helped bulldoze Mimi's house. He tried to call me and tell me what was what. But I let it go because there were bigger pieces to make fit into this convoluted puzzle than ole sweet Cy. He was earning not scheming.

I would like to know if he's aware who signed that order. He only did his job, but that doesn't mean I'm not sore at him for calling me after the place was flattened. By the time I got stateside, the house and her body were gone. Chase couldn't have done the deed, but he's the sort might know who did.

I slap him on his back. We all played under the Friday Night Lights together. I happily caught every pass he flung at me. And he caught all my castoffs from under the bleachers. Cy was on the defense holding down the downs.

"Wow, are all men from Mississippi this tall? It's nice to meet you all."

I say, "The word is y'all, darling." I smile at her, and she laughs. She should do that more often, let her light spill out for all to see. It sets me on fire both spiritually and crotcherly. I adjust myself in my jeans before he jumps out and takes possession of her the way I'm dying to.

The boys are a bit jumpy, not anything a regular person would notice but I'm sure Lu has paid mind to it. They all keep slyly looking at the door.

Lucille saunters over and puts down a dozen oysters and Becca picks up a glove and knife.

Chase crosses his arms and I know he's going to tangle with my girl. And I know she's going to bury him deeper than his accent.

"Fine filly. You know how to handle that knife?"

She picks up an oyster and stares at him. "This little knife? I'm used to handling things much bigger, but I think I'll manage." His mouth falls open into a fly catcher. She jabs in and twists, popping it open like a pro. She slides it onto a cracker, tosses some hot sauce on it, and slurps it back. Those lips curl into a smile, and I want to chase that oyster with my tongue. I glance around the table, and everyone is staring at her with the same lust I'm trying to keep crammed down.

No one else is eating as she picks up another. "Surely, strong burly men like yourselves don't need me to shuck these for you. I can teach you."

Cy's deep rumble shakes the table a bit. "Little lady, whereabout you from to shuck like a pro?"

I laugh. "I know you're working with a handicap, but you really think oysters only come from one coast? Becca's from California." She nods and smiles at me.

They all dig in. "Becca, darling, can you shuck for me?" She laughs and picks up another oyster. "Find a luscious, wet one for me to suck on, can you do that?" The boys all hoot and holler, and she bumps me with her shoulder.

I want them to stay fascinated with her while I assess who they're waiting on. About this time of night Cy is usually knee deep in a jam session over at the Pole Cat. You can set a watch to him showing up for his standing gig with the boys. But he's here giving Becca shit for knowing how to shuck an oyster. Chase is usually balls deep in some stripper or whore about now.

"Fleabag, how's your mama?" He smiles wide with the teeth he has left. He loves his mama, good to know nothing has changed much around here. He's my real person of interest. He's made a career out of looking harmless, but he's ended every fight he's ever been in. He'll also do anything for a dollar. He once tried to bribe Chase and me into throwing a football game for a betting scheme he had cooked up with the neighboring town. He was sixteen years old trying to pull that shit off.

"She good. You should come by and let her talk at you a

bit." Fleabag is exactly that, he may love his mama, but my gut tells me it's his lack of backbone that helped displace my sweet grandmother and get her killed.

"Might so," I say, trying to hide my suspicion under a heap of brotherly hospitality.

# CHAPTER 17
## BECCA

I slurp down my third sweet tea and finally I'm drinking my beer. I refused a drink earlier, trying to keep my wits about me even though I'm a bit lightheaded. I'm chalking it up to travel and lack of sleep. I suspect as always; this man is so much deeper than anyone sees. Everyone's laughing and joking, and I can see his mind spinning. I don't know the role I'm supposed to play here, but I suspect that's the way he wants it. He has to know I'm savvier than he's letting on.

Brick's friends, although a bit leering, are funny and I'm having a good time. And I'm stuffed from fried things and a gumbo that in the words of Cyclops, "Would do your taxes and get you a refund every time." Not sure if the metaphor lands but I got the point.

I'm trying not to be too lawyery or stiff. Brick is always easy and open, but he seems a touch on edge, except when talking to Lucille. There's an ancient jukebox blaring and when Lucille left for the night, she left a pile of quarters on top of the bar. There's constant music from the box or a piano that people keep taking turns playing.

Brick stands up and motions to Cy. "I need you, man."

"You got me."

Chase looks at me. "You're in for a treat."

Cy settles into a chair on the corner of the dance floor. He plucks a guitar and Brick plunks the piano while people flood the dance floor. My mouth drops open and I stand to get a better look. Then Cy sings about this being "Every Little Honky Tonk Bar." A woman comes from the kitchen and picks up a random violin adding to the song. People are doing that two-step dance and now Brick is doing a harmony underneath Cy. There's clapping and laughing. What can't this man do?

I have a smile on my face that seems like it's going to be permanent and I'm clapping along. Chase is standing and clapping too. Fleabag is hooting and most of the bar is screaming, "That's what happens in Every Little Honkey Tonk Bar." Then they bring it down for a moment and Cy sings the last line and cheers erupt.

Brick searches the crowd for me and I'm screaming and whistling for him. He nods and turns back to the piano, and they spark up a song I recognize. It's Luke Bryan's "Rain is a Good Thing." A group of us sang it to the vines a couple of times in a bit of a drought. Tabi looked up every song about rain and we learned them all when we were home for the summer between college one year. I sing along and people stare at me.

"What? I can't like country music?"

Chase puts his hand out and I shake my head. "I don't dance, but thanks." He pulls someone else from the table next to me and runs out to the dance floor.

After that there's one more tune, a bit slower and sweeter, but it's just Cy playing. Brick's in my face in a heartbeat, sweeping me onto the dance floor before I can say no. He pulls me to him, and I get lost in the idea that I'm someone else. He sings only to me, "...your hand in my hand, and I could die a happy man." I don't know the song but it's my new favorite.

There's probably forty people here and half of them are dancing all kinds of dances. There're some more formal gentlemen, spinning their partners around the floor in a perfect two-step and others are just rocking and holding close. Cy stands and carries the guitar by the neck. He slaps Chase on the back, then shakes Brick's hand, and I nod to him. He pulls me into a hug that starts with me being stiff and then I toss my arms around this gentle giant. He leaves and Chase flies around the dance floor with a brightly dressed woman in clothes strategically placed so as to not get arrested, but barely. I ditch my blouse and pull my black t-shirt down.

I'm staring at the dancers and when I glance sideways Brick's watching me with an intensity I'm beginning to rely on. His gray eyes gleam like chrome in this light, making me suspect that's my color. The rest of the world gets his dusty gray, but the bright, shined-up quicksilver is for me. My heart races and I wipe my palms on my hips. He curls his finger and gestures for me to come closer to him.

He's like a fucking magnet and with every second around him my strict code of conduct slips a little further.

I lean over and he's in my ear, "You good, darling?" His breath ruffles all the tiny hairs on my body but there's a real concentration of them reaching from the back of my neck. How can one man be this attractive?

"I think I know what you're up to, but I don't see it working. We're no closer to answers. And it's so late."

"Just another couple of minutes. Do you trust me?" I have no reservations at this moment. I feel the heat and humidity crammed all around us and between us pushing us together and holding us a smidge apart. He pulls me with him. He puts his hand on my back, guides me to the bar, and grabs a quarter. I plant my feet and he slams into my back. I don't hate that hard, sexy, wall of a man at my back, but it's not happening.

He's on my ear again, so close but no contact, then his fingers graze across my wrist and it turns me into the hottest most wanton woman. My back is rigid as my mind wanders towards a more domestic thought, but his voice pulls me out of confusion.

"I thought you trusted me." His voice is dripping with molasses and sin, and I attempt to give up a piece of who I think I should be.

His hand snakes around my waist and splays out low on my stomach as he pulls me to him. I lean back, and it's heaven resting against his shoulder. I tilt my head up so I can talk directly into his ear.

"I don't dance."

He grabs my left forearm and spins me to face him. "You do now." And then I'm in his arms. I hear and see nothing but this man who feels more like home than anything I could fabricate or want. And as he twirls me, I fall deeper into a pit I'm not sure I can climb out of. But right now, I'm not sure I want to.

# CHAPTER 18
## BRICK

pull her back to me and breathe her in. It's not smart what I'm doing but it is right. I see Chase out of the corner of my eye madly texting someone. I don't like the looks of that, he's hiding but he's not. Like a raccoon sitting on the edge of a garbage can staring 'atcha, daring you to deny him his work. Chase is slicker than he should be with me, and I feel it. He looks weathered since the last time I saw him and that chip that hovers above his shoulder is firmly in place. He's one of those 'but I deserve everything' guys without working for it. Always needs to be just a smidge more successful or resourceful than everyone else.

Fleabag's talking to some known shady characters and my focus is on him. And Cy leaving. I know full fucking well they don't need him down at the Pole Cat, they're all set to survive a couple of sets without him. I think Chase sent him away and is about to set Fleabag out of here as well. They all know or suspect something I can't crystallize in my brain yet. I don't think the boys know who did all those wrongs in my life, but they know Chase knows.

I spin this goddess in my arms and cuddle her close.

Chase nods at me and realizes I'm watching him. I nuzzle my nose into her neck, and she becomes more mine with each second. I lightly brush my lips along her jaw and then those bright-green eyes are staring at me, dark and liquid. She's lush and ripe for picking. We're dancing and the world drops away and it's just us holding on to the impossible.

Her hips mirror mine as we sway, and you couldn't get a slip of paper between us. Not that someone would try, seeing our connection, sensing our heat, there ain't a person alive who doesn't know this thing between us. But there's only one who won't admit it.

Fuck it. I move closer and the song switches. I throw my head back and laugh at our timing and she moves back out of my arms breaking the spell.

"Not so fast."

I grab her wrist and twist her around and she lands right in front of me. I put a hand on her hip and lace my fingers with hers. Then I rock her back and forth and we dance a little this way and that. She's a terrible dancer but she's laughing in a way I haven't seen before. There's a wild look that says she's tamed herself for way too long.

"I suck at this!" She throws her arms in the air and shimmies a little and I laugh.

"That you do. But I suspect you're having fun." She twirls on her own and trips a bit. Then tosses her out-of-control red curls all around. The humidity suits her. She dances back towards me, out of rhythm and out of breath. I take her in my arms again and scoot our butts around the floor.

"What was in that tea?" She smiles like a winter sunset, bright and bold.

I grin at the sweet tea magic. "Whiskey, probably more towards moonshine than whiskey. It's homemade."

"That explains why I'm enjoying any of this."

I pull her to me and guide her in a rudimentary two-step. "And here I thought it was the company."

She fists my t-shirt and looks at me and says, "You undo all my sensibilities and rules." Then she lets go and rests her head on my chest. I can't help but drift down to the top of her ass and she not only doesn't react, but she leans into it.

I lift her chin to face me and put my forehead to hers.

"Counselor, can we pretend we're strangers? Just for one second."

She whispers, "We can't." I haven't undone all of her yet and I respect the hell out of her for that. Her hands float up and down my arms, tracing the tattoo on my wrist again. I have to tell her all about it. I may not get to have her but at least she'll understand how I've kept her with me since we met.

Fleabag slips out the back door and Chase nods at him. We can go. There's nothing else for me to figure out tonight. I nod to the bartender and make a locking motion and he tosses a rag on his shoulder and salutes me. I put my key on the bar. I'll pick it up tomorrow. I've had a key to this place since I was ten and picking up deliveries for Ms. Lucille.

I whisper to her, "We should go." I inhale her heady scent and put distance between us for a hot second. I need to cool off the situation, so she doesn't regret it. She's in control, I won't push her, but maybe nudge a little.

"You can't sleep in a chair." She's all settled in bed. She's got a silly smile on her face and it's enchanting. She washed away the day and tried to contain her hair in an elastic band that's on the losing end of working. The curls are wispy and framing her lightly freckled face. I've got my arms crossed over my broad chest and I'm barely able to keep my dick in place. Thank God for the small, embroidered pillow on my lap. Hope she doesn't realize it's raised about an inch or so.

I tease her, "You sleep here then."

She tosses a pillow at me. "Sleep here. It's fine. It's a big bed." She gestures to the spot I've been dreaming of inhabiting. Sleeping every night next to her room in that house, working my hand thinking about her, is wearing thin.

"I'm a big man."

"Yes, you are." Her eyes go wide as she realizes what she's said. It's cute to watch that heat crawl up her chest. "It's fine. I'll sleep way over here on the edge of the bed."

"Ok, but I need to ask you something as my legal counsel."

She sits up and lord help me, her nipples are hard, even through her bra. Now that data tells me she's either cold, but the air isn't blowing too chilly, or she feels the same heat I do.

She says, "Go ahead. Ask me anything." I stand at the end of the bed and toe off my shoes. My jeans are pretty comfortable, but I might want to slip into some athletic shorts. The problem with that will be the thin layer of fabric between my cock and the ultimate object of its desire. I keep telling him there's no way this can happen, but he doesn't listen well.

She takes my breath away on the regular, but this is

next-level beauty. Dancing with her close was not enough, I need a whole bucket more of touching her.

"Now, is it against the law to cuddle with your counselor? Legally speaking, of course. We need to get our parameters straight. And I know you love boundaries." I smirk at her.

She smiles and rolls her eyes at me, and I cross my arms.

"Look, that watch and cash I gave you was a hefty retainer, I expect prompt answers, Counselor."

She clears her throat and clutches the sheets next to her. "Legally speaking, if we're cuddling close for say, survival purposes, then it can be overlooked. If it's an advance or attachment, I'm going to have to say we're in a gray area. Intimate touching is a no go. And if it's an overture to relations, then it would be on its way to illegal."

I leap onto the bed without warning and grab her around the waist before she bounces off the bed. I pull her to me and bury my nose deep into her hair. Heaven. She moves herself into a better position to hold me closer and I can't want her more. In my life, in my bed, and most definitely on my cock.

She says in a voice that's a little too authoritative with my arms around her middle. "This is only because I'm very chilly in this air conditioning. And..."

Dammit, I thought her nipples were reaching for me.

"And you're warm and cozy. But all I can give you is this cuddle."

"That sounds about perfect then, I get to hold you all night while we try not to break all the rules and shimmy down to our bare selves and let instinct and nature take over." She smacks my chest and I curl my fingers around her hand.

Every new way I get to touch her is an explosion in my

brain of neural pathways opening up and digging a memory into my brain. Wires crossing and sparking to life a piece of myself I never knew existed. It was lying dormant until this hummingbird of a woman flitted into my life and flitted right back out. But somehow, right here, in this beachside motel in Gulfport, Mississippi, a couple miles from where I was born, I caught me a hummingbird in my arms and it's shaping up to be a pretty damn terrific night.

My phone vibrates in my pocket and it's the last thing I want. But I squeeze her and stand up.

"I'll take this in the hall. You find yourself a place to settle into a dream, you hear? I'll probably be a minute." She breathes and moans a bit in agreement. I step into the hallway and answer a call I probably don't want any part of. It's Cy and I'm guessing he's got a heap of things to get off his chest. I saw it weighing on him before he bolted out of Lucille's for his so-called gig.

"Cy. What do you need to tell me? I got a woman to tend to and sleep calling my name."

There's a silence.

"You alright, buddy?"

I try again, "You can tell me what you need, and I won't pay no mind if it's nothing and I won't bring trouble to your door."

His voice is croaking. "Don't matter. You know I live in a state of trouble and tunes."

"That I do."

"Your Mimi Tinker was a right special woman. She was always good to me. And your ginger girl is special."

Now my back is up. Not sure why he's speaking so.

He continues, "You gotta go, Brick. Go live a life far from here. Live one for me too."

"Cy, I can handle myself fine and you know I got a good

sense about me. Thank you for your kind words about those women. We're not in immediate danger so I'm going to let Becca sleep a spell, we'll say our goodbyes to the Spanish moss and tumble towards our next step. But I need you to do something for me."

"Just about anything, Brick. You're like blood."

"Not sure that means a whole lot around here anymore, given what I've been hearing about some of our friends."

"You got good hearing, Brick, you always did." I get his warning and the confirmation that one of my friends is someone to be warned about. He was always too much of a punk for his own good, but I worry for sweet Cy.

"Cy. You got somewhere to go? If I stir up some shit, I want you out of the storm. You follow?"

"Loud and clear. I'm on my way to New Orleans as we speak. Gonna lay low and play. Maybe find a honey pot or two."

I laugh. "Go get that pussy, boy. Care 'atcha."

"Care 'atcha too." It's what we say to each other as Southern men are taught not to show our true emotions.

I stand in the hallway another second mentally shifting gears to return to Becca. Now my nipples are cold.

I open the door as quietly as possible and slink to the foot of the bed, the lights are off. But when I get there, she startles. Her nighty is hitched up around her hips and she removes her hand from the one place I want to be. My dick goes from curious to painfully hard in a millisecond when I see what she's doing.

"Well, darling, tonight just got a whole hell of a lot more interesting. Don't you dare fucking stop."

# CHAPTER 19
## BECCA

Oh, God. I should be embarrassed but I'm not because I'm a mess of need with too much home-made whiskey in my system. I'm filled with want for this man. I've been pent up since the second he kissed me. His voice, the dancing, the musky smell of that man. And now he's caught me, and I don't want to stop.

His voice takes over my rational thought. I only hope he can uphold the law because I'm not sure if I'm capable. I was on the brink and now it's like I'm edging myself. I move my hips, desperate for relief. I have to go into the bathroom and finish, or I might die of blue pussy if I can't come soon.

My voice is raspy and needy, "I'll be in the bathroom."

He's direct and his voice is deep and gruff. Fuck, it's sexy. "You'll do nothing of the kind. This is a fucking Pandora's box of treats and there's no way you're going to sleep without coming hard."

"Brick," I whisper.

"Stay there." He walks over to the curtains, cracks them a little, and lets the moonlight spill over the bed. "There. Now I can see your gorgeous face and get a peek at that perfect pussy. Christ, you're fucking beautiful. It scares the breath and fear out of me."

I draw a breath in quickly. I should pull my nightgown down, but I don't. I'm even wetter at the way he's speaking to me. It's hot. I've been doing it with men who would never use the word pussy. Just thinking that word gets me hotter. And then there's this deep, rumbling, Southern dripping voice commanding me in a way I never imagined possible.

Under the cover of absolute night maybe I can be this person, but I'm wired differently. I have lived by so many self-imposed rules.

"You're not buzzed or impaired, right?"

"No." If I'm honest, I'm not impaired, I'm ready.

His voice wraps around my good sense and pushes me to the other side. "Then put your hands back on yourself while I get a hold of me."

I slide my fingers down my body and he groans.

He stands at the edge of the bed and removes his jeans. His dick pops out long and hard. Jesus, it's like one of those cottonwood branches we saw today. Thick and ropey and so hard. He strokes it and it's like I can feel the power between us. It's gorgeous and I want it so badly.

"That's right, darling. I need you to see what you do to me. This dick belongs to you whether that's legal or not. I'm harder than I've ever been watching you touch yourself and screaming my name. Fuck. I like the wild in your eyes."

He steps out of his jeans. "Pull your nightgown up and let me see all of you. I'd be much obliged if you remove it all together, but if you need it for modesty's sake, that's fine too."

Modesty? I'm about to spread my legs so a man can see how wet I am for him. There's no modesty. But I do hesitate, that last piece of the Becca I was raised to be holding on tightly to my so-called morals. He senses my shift and before I know it, he's on top of me.

He's planking on top of me. He's not touching a part of my body, but our faces are close.

"Brick." I gasp.

"Stop it. Right now. I'm not a man of shady convictions. I made you a promise I wouldn't fuck you the way you deserve to be fucked until I'm in the clear. But lord knows we both want it. I'm not alone here. Thinking about it isn't illegal, Ms. Gelbert. Giving yourself pleasure is not abnormal or illegal. It's a fucking turn-on and it's your right. Give yourself pleasure, and I'll take mine freely."

His breath is hot on my cheeks and the power of this man hovering over me is too much to take. His Branch brushes against me slightly and he pulls his hips back into a perfect plank. I'm trapped under this man like we're playing that force field game and whoever touches the other first loses.

My voice explodes out of me as he traces my jaw with nothing but air. "Ok. Fine. It's all I think about." He grins and his lips are impossibly close to mine. "But we can't."

"I'm not about to do anything to put your soul or job in jeopardy. Do you trust me?"

"Yes."

"Then here's what's going to happen. You're going to fuck yourself in my stead and I'm going to watch. You do what I tell you and I'll get you off."

I whisper yes as he leans down and blows on my nipples. Then he lifts himself off me with his abs doing a dance that few men can pull off. He doesn't touch a single part of me as he stands back up. I want to rip my nails down his perfect torso, then explore that perfect muscular V framing that thick branch. He's more stunning than I could imagine. He strokes himself hard while his perfect abs contract and his neck muscles cord in tension. My mouth waters and I lean forward, drawn in by his dick. It's like I'm hypnotized by his penis. I'm dickstruck.

He opens his eyes on a moan and smiles. "Get yourself situated and toss that nightgown." I lift it off and throw it on the floor next to his jeans. He licks his lips and groans.

"Hell on a stick, those are perfect tits. I knew they would be. Stick your finger in your mouth, sweet girl, and give that right nipple a swirl. And I'm going to need you to pinch the left one to the brink of pain for me." Then he leans down and blows on my wet peaked nipple and growls, "Pinch harder."

I do as I'm told. I put my whole finger in my mouth and his eyes are dark but unwavering. I'm not sure I've ever been anyone's fantasy, but I'm going to embrace it. I arch my back on contact and never stop staring at him. He's fixated on what I'm doing. And when I knead and pinch the left nipple he groans.

"Christ. Pinch it harder. There's nothing in this world I want more than to watch you fall apart. I need you to come hard, darling."

"I want to come."

"And somehow, I'm harder when you talk like that. Slide that right hand down to your clit but just rest it there. Maybe give it a tap."

Like a forbidden game of Twister, he commands where my hands should go. "In my bag." I breathe out, desperate to touch myself. The heat of my own hand resting on that bundle of wanton nerves is fucking beyond. He's in such control of this situation and himself that I can let go a little. I rub in a circle.

"NO! Do not touch yourself yet. I'm not missing a second of that show. What's in your bag?"

"Something for you. Lube."

He stops stroking. "Did I hear that right? My girl has a dirty side to her that thought she'd need lube on an overnight trip with her client?"

I sit up a little. His eyes flare. "Sit up more and pull your knees up. Spread them apart so I can get a good look at your cunt."

I do it and groan. "It wasn't intended for you. I keep it in my cosmetic case. Will you use it?"

He's at the foot of the bed staring at me, and I open wider for him. He licks his lips again.

"Taste yourself." We are down quite the rabbit hole now. I reach down into my glistening mess and drag my finger through it. I take it to my mouth and lick it clean. I've never tasted myself before.

"Fuck. How perfect do you taste? When this legal obligation is over, I hope you don't have plans because I'm going to feast on you for days." I laugh a bit and he grins. Then his face goes deadly serious. "Fuck yourself with that finger. Put it into that wet, hot chamber and pull it out. Just once. I want to see how dripping you are. My cock is weeping for you."

"That's why I thought you could use the lube."

"In a minute, first show me how you fuck yourself. I need to learn what you think is good. And you leave that needy clit alone for a spell."

I slide my hand back down and lightly graze by what he told me to leave alone. And the forbidden zing of this all has me almost coming at that non-contact. I'm on the edge, my body is coiled up tight, ready to explode. I slide my finger inside of me and toss my head back.

"Now out. Now slam it back in and see how deep you can get it."

"I'm so close."

He disappears and I stop doing what I was doing. It's like a douse of cold water. He yells from the bathroom. "In and out. Do not stop fucking yourself. Imagine it's my cock teasing that entrance and pushing through. So deep." I do as I'm told, moaning as loudly as possible. I've never been this out of control in my life. I've never felt so free, safe, and wanted.

As he returns, he views me with a cocked head. One hand on his dick and the other holding things. Oh shit. Oh shit. I know what he's holding, and I never imagined that was with me. But now I remember the last time I traveled was to the most boring conference in Portland and I packed a couple of extra things. I sit up.

"Let me explain." I put my hands up.

"Babe, you get to explain nothing. I'm happy to know my girl—"

I'm so desperate to be his girl but didn't imagine it was possible, but when I think of every move he's made and everything he says, he's proven himself to be mine. I choke up a little until he flips a switch, and my eyes go wide.

"—is just as switched on as I am. You filthy, fucking gorgeous and perfect creature. You rev me in a way I thought I'd never know. Tell me you want this."

He waves it in front of me with his dick reaching for me. I want that but I can't have it. He can't touch me but steps closer to the bed.

He amps it up. "Prop yourself up, legs wide, knees out of my fucking way. Hands on your tits. Keep them there doing the lord's work." I do all of this. His tone is rushed and authoritative, handing out commands and orders like I imagine he did in the military. These just have a deliciously dirty slant.

He stands at the side of the bed and drizzles lube over my tits, and I rub it in with a groan. So slippery. "Those are mine. Do to them what you think I want to do." I squeeze and moan.

"Tell me." He commands.

"Tell you what?"

"What do you think I want to do to my tits?"

Oh shit, this got turned up. Hottest. Thing. Ever.

"Tease my nipples?"

He stands up straight and puts his hands on hips. "You fucking kidding me if you think that's a question. Try again."

"Pull on my tits until I scream. And then with all this lube, pull them together and slide between them."

"Fuck yes! I've been focused on this view down here, but that's an excellent suggestion. Imagine my dick between those perfect tits, then sliding between those big pouty fucking lips of yours."

"I want that so much. I want to feel you hit the back of my throat so I can swallow you down." Words tumble out without thought or reason.

"That's a fucking promise I intend to cash in on. But now I need to be wordless in seconds. But I have to come soon, just from watching you. I'll keep my oath of not touching you. But you've got to do your part. Keep your hands away from me or I'll break. I'm going to fuck you now, the only way I can. Then I'm going to come hard, and I'd much appreciate it if you'd watch me spill all that cum just for you." His hand is jacking himself harder now as he positions himself closer to my pussy.

And then he turns on the power. OH MY GOD.

# CHAPTER 20
## BRICK

'm out of my fucking head for this woman. This won't be enough, but it will be enough for now. I'm imagining all the things I want to do to her and I'm not sure I can stop my dick from punching through my hand to get to her. I drizzle lube over her soaking wet pussy. I want to make sure this feels good, and I can't gauge if she's as open and wet as I need her. I start at the lowest speed and keep my hand at the end of her large hot-pink vibrator.

"I need to be the one to make you come, even if I can't touch you."

I take it up the inside of her leg slowly, carefully making sure I don't touch her. Look, if she wants to play a technical game, I'm in. I'm very good at games. She's so beautiful when she's turned on. Her eyes are dark and hooded like deep emeralds in this moonlight. Her perfect alabaster skin is dotted with slight freckles, and I imagine this soft place between her legs is warm and rich. I trace her clit with the lowest setting of vibration and see her clench and ratchet higher. Nothing else in the history of time is as important as making her perfect mouth form a perfect O and softly gasp.

She's so close. I travel the toy south and circle the very core of this goddess. I've never felt more honored than in this moment. She's open and mine and yet not. But she's handing over her whole self to someone like me. If she'll have me, I'll never let her go. I don't even know what she feels or tastes like but as I enter her with my proxy cock, this will be the moment I let all the walls down and climb behind hers.

"FUCK. YES! Oh, Brick. Brick. This is so good." She reaches out and I jerk my head back.

"No touching. I don't want to break any penal codes." I grin and refocus my attention to where the vibrator is disappearing in and out of her. That hot-pink flashing as I pull it all the way out and slam it back into her. Her hips move in rhythm with my hands and my dick is on fire. I turn the switch up once more and move it around inside of her searching for the spot where she'll scream, then it will take me two pumps and I'll join her in that moment.

"There. Holy shit. Hit that spot. Hit. Fuck me. Brick, fuck me harder. I wish this was you. I want this to be you. Can you fuck me harder?" I don't want to hurt her, but I do pick up the pace.

"Work your needy clit. Give it a pinch right fucking now. Christ, you're so goddamn beautiful and sexy." She snakes her hand down and finds her apex and pinches hard as I coordinate that moment with entering her swiftly. And she fucking explodes. Her body bows and she sits up, and I barely get out of the way as her knees slam together and her body shakes. Her head is back and when she snaps it up, I'm finishing myself off in a fury. I lube my hand to get it done and I'm madly pumping away as she watches me. I stroke faster and my balls draw up. There's lightning on a dry night zapping my lower back and shooting out through my cock. I roar as I come all over the towel I positioned before all this.

"Becca. Fuck. Fuck. I can't stop coming. So much, all for you. Fuck. Fuck me. Becks."

She's trying to catch her breath and I bend over doing the same. I grab her foot and feel the energy she's radiating. I hope that foot touch doesn't get her disbarred or send her psyche reeling into nasty territory.

I look at her with her hair insane all around. She stares at me as I clean up a bit. I look back at her with the biggest hangdog grin I've ever sported.

I take her foot back into my hand. I don't know the rules. Is aftercare covered by a legal precedent? She pulls her foot away and goes up onto her knees, then slams her hands down on the rumpled sheets. "What the hell just happened?"

I chuckle wide and deep, and I'm filled with a light I don't ever want to dim. She's a tad confused. Hot damn.

"One of the best things that's ever happened in my whole damn life. Imagine if I could touch you?" I smirk and she giggles, sweet and girlish. It's like a gear dropping into place, my whole being hums with all the parts of myself. I love her. And I'm not afraid of it anymore. She will be, but I'll walk her through the specifics.

"Seriously, imagine." She sighs and there's the weight of the world creeping back in. Her shoulders slump a half tick and I can't have that. I run to get her a warm washcloth to wipe down the lube and the toy. She yells after me, "Have I told you how spectacular your ass is?"

"My, my, so forward." My life's purpose becomes bright and shiny in front of me. I want to spend a lifetime making her happy. I disappear into the bathroom, so I don't run and scoop her into my arms and kiss the hell out of her.

She calls after me, "And I can't wait to climb that thick cottonwood branch." She rattles my brain and soul. I return to the room with her nightgown and travel kit so she can put my hot-pink proxy away.

"Did you just call my cock a cottonwood?"

"I did, but I may shorten it to branch. You'll know what I'm talking about." She laughs at herself, and in the moonlight with her red curls all around, she's the embodiment of all I dream of.

"As long as you don't shorten it in general, my dick's always happy to be in the conversation."

She cleans up and I grab some shorts and sit on the edge of the other side of the bed. She's gentle and relaxed. I touch her cheek because I can't fucking stand it. She relaxes into it.

"I want to answer my own question," she whispers. Her eyes fill and I'm filled in the places where hope and joy hide.

"You can say anything you want, Hummingbird."

She grins and says, "Whatever it was, I don't want it to stop. I don't know how to let people in to take care of me."

"You're doing a bang-up job of it tonight, darling."

She sighs and rubs my thumb across her cheek. She closes her eyes, and a tear drops down onto my hand. "This can't be real."

"Don't you go back to hiding from me, because that genie is out of the bottle and my branch can't go back to dreaming."

She sits up and shakes her head. "I can't talk about this anymore tonight. You're a giant ball of scary words and feelings. So, I'm going to sleep."

"And dream of me?"

"Maybe. Or maybe I'll dream of Lucille's greens."

I lay myself onto the bed. She turns away and gets under the covers. I let her think she can get away, but she already gave me the green light to cuddle.

"Still life-threateningly cold?" She's quiet for a long stretch and I turn to face her back. I'm about to tuck my hands under the pillow and try to find some rest.

"I might have frostbite." The words are barely out of her mouth when I haul her to me and snuggle her into my arms. I fall asleep instantly with my face buried in that beautiful bramble hair of hers.

# CHAPTER 21
## BRICK

wake up alone. Her gentle purr missing from my life and suddenly I can't sleep without it. She's my soundtrack. I know we got close last night, and we got the information we needed and that should be wildly satisfying, but I don't like her so jumpy. I'll lean on Fleabag a bit before we leave, and he'll tell me the next name on the chain that takes me to Cady.

I want her safe and protected. Like for the rest of my days, safe and protected. I hope to fucking God I get to do that by her side, but if I have to step away to keep her safe, then that's the hole I've dug myself. I'm too far down this path and I won't live with myself if the only other person I have loved in this godforsaken life is taken from this earth because of me and my actions. I won't do it.

MEL: Yo. Man meat!

BRICK: Was thinking of you—I have too much shit on my plate. Find Fleabag, his name is Ronnie Donato. And he don't got a whole lot of sense but he does like money. Bank accounts and plane tickets to the West Coast in our timeframe ought to help us a bit. Left in a hurry from my sight last night. Who has his leash?

MEL: I'm on it. But contacting you because I've discovered some disturbing crossover in your world. And I alerted interested parties. Someone close to Becca's cousin requests a meet.

BRICK: What kind of crossover? The hell you say?

MEL: It's best if the interested party explains. This isn't a meeting request, it's a command performance.

The only reason I'm going to do this is to make sure this individual knows not to summon me again. If there's work to be done together, I'm open to it, but I'm not someone's boy to be ordered around no matter who you are.

BRICK: Set it up.

MEL: Copy that.

It's not a meeting I can say no to. Her bag is missing, and I quickly pull on a pair of jeans and head out to find her. I don't think she'd leave, but she might be reevaluating. I search the lobby and there's nothing to see but a couple of people peddling lukewarm coffee mixed with some sad nondairy fake hazelnut shit. Just buy cream, it ain't that hard and everyone will be happier except that one person who can't live without her pretend, froofy shit. I wander out to the Mercedes and she's not there, but her bag is in the car. My heart leaps to my throat and I try to settle myself before I tell her all my inner thoughts.

I mosey around the back and stare out at the Gulf. The smell of brine and sea oats mix in the air to make a powerful perfume of memory. There's a part of me that always settles a bit with salt in the air. Being by or on this water in particular, speaks louder than any drug or activity to calm my ass down.

I see a flash of red moving near the shoreline. She's picking up shells or stones on my water's edge. She's capturing even more of my heart without even knowing it. I walk towards her but give her some distance. I want her to notice me first, so I give her the proper space to adjust to who she wants to be this morning. I'll let her hide if she needs.

She stares at the water and lifts her face to the sun that's popping out of the clouds not too high in the sky. It's early and we have a lot to do, but the south's gotta hold of her. When I'm here I'm reminded everything comes in its own time. Mimi Tinker used to remind me often, "Your lack of patience will be the death of me." I'm afraid it was, but sometimes I can't stop my impulsive need. Some call it a gut instinct and others, well, they call it brash. There's nothing to be done about it now, she lived a good life, if not a long enough one.

She opens her eyes and sees me down the beach. Even God could see the size of her smile when she spies me. Last night was blisteringly hot and I'd gladly repeat it all, letting me know her heart, her mind, and holding her will always out do coming hard in my mind. And I really like to come, but I thought I knew how I felt about her, had it wrapped up with a bow in my mind, and I wasn't even fucking close. I'm going to need a much bigger bow to tie her up with.

She runs to me. My hummingbird moves quickly and with purpose towards me and I'm luckier than a butcher's dog. And because I want to push that luck, I open my arms and she falls right in them.

"It's so gorgeous."

I pull her closer and whisper in her ear, "Yes, gorgeous is the word I'd use myself."

She squeezes around my middle, and we watch the sun rise a bit higher in the sky. She lets go suddenly but links her hand in mine, and I'm shocked at the intimacy. The Gulf still has a bit of magic in it. Or maybe the humidity she's not used to has opened her up in a different way. Either way, I'm not complaining.

"Thank you," she says quietly, and I kick an old crab shell in front of me.

"For what, darling?"

"For bringing me here."

"I'm a touch confused. It was against legal counsel to leave the state of California during an ongoing investigation and yet, you, Ms. Rebecca Rule Follower Gelbert, are thanking the likes of me?"

Her laugh is louder than the surf as it rushes through my heart.

She pulls away.

"It's different here."

"I'm different?" I ask.

There's a long pause, then a sly smile. "No. I am."

I grab her hand and haul her to me. I can't take another minute of this. Goddamn if I don't feel complete looking into those green eyes that never cease to confuse, amaze, and surprise me. She's still smiling up at me and that's it.

My self-control snaps. I'm a problem solver, it's what I do, and this is the toughest thing I've ever had to figure out.

I groan, "How can you be so stunning and ethereal and so fucking sexy at the same time? Tell me you want to be with me as bad as I want to be with you." I glide up and down her arms and stare into her way too earnest face.

She's open to me like a camellia in the spring, all her layers on display for me. I glide my thumb across her soft jaw. She's changed but the same. I adore both pieces of this hard-as-hell woman along with the soft, vulnerable girl in my arms. I want to protect her, and I'm turned on and proud she can protect herself. I'm not sure anyone has ever gotten to see the Becca that's in front of me. I'll never take it for granted.

She traces my tattoo again. Then she looks at me. "I don't know how or why I know this, but I have to ask."

I pull her hair behind her ear and say, "You can ask me anything."

"And you'll answer?"

"I'll answer, might not be the truth, but I'll answer," I tell her.

"Wait, you'd lie to me?"

"Never. I will never lie. But there are things you shouldn't know and don't need to know. But if it comes down to important, you'll have my straight and narrow truth."

"Then my question can wait until you tell me everything."

I kiss the top of her head, I'm not sure I'll ever be ready for that.

# CHAPTER 22
## BECCA

never thought I'd be ok with not knowing all the facts. I trust him completely because every piece of me is telling me this is right. He pulls me tighter.

"Oh, my darling girl. We're helpless and hopeless."

"I think I might be. You don't think less of me?"

He nuzzles into my neck and I'm ready. Brick grazes my neck with his tongue and teeth, and I get goosebumps everywhere. My resolve dissolves along with my morals and rules. They're silly platitudes in the face of this man's power over me.

"You have to stop," I whisper.

"Why? This isn't sex with a client. This is trying to grab a taste of the woman I dream of owning, of commanding, of having in every fucking way possible. I will spend my life protecting and possessing you the way you've possessed me."

"Brick, it's so fast."

He grins. "And yet, not fast enough. We were written long ago. We've been lying in wait to be awoken."

He shifts his arms to settle around me again, then says,

"Deep in the man sits fast his fate. To mould his fortunes, mean or great.'"

"Is that Emerson?"

"You identified it, see *Fate*."

I grin at his pun and at everything good there is in the world. It's the first time I've ever let this reckless joy into my soul. Him holding me is the only thing besides the law that's ever made sense to me.

Rules are rules. I can't argue his way to innocence and be respected if I can't follow the law myself. Everything is on the line, but the lines are so damn muddy when he holds me like this. If we can hold on until after this mess, we can see what this is. But currently he's actively not holding back.

I gasp, "Brick."

"Becca. I'm done pretending I don't need you in all things. You're what's right."

"You don't know me." My weak excuse sounds pretty damn silly but it's all I have.

"Yes, I do. From the second we touched, and I handed you my card in that conference room. I've known you and owned you from that moment on. As you have owned and known me. Catch up, Becks." He touches the tip of my nose.

My watch dings in the middle of this moment that defines and defies everything. I've never wanted something more in my life. Actually, that's wrong, what I want more than anything is to find the fucker that did this to him so we can be done with the lawyer-client contract and can move on to our life. I'm starting to believe him. But my moral and professional character was literally saved by the bell.

I glance down and he kisses my head and steps away.

Shit. The moment might have been broken and I'm about to irrevocably fracture it.

"She died."

"Ms. Beardsley?" He scrubs his hand over his head and yells to the ocean a loud guttural scream. I want to comfort him, but I don't know what he needs. I step closer.

He says, "That's bad for us but just about bust a gut worst thing that can happen to that family."

"She didn't have one."

"Bullshit. Somewhere there's a mama or a sister or a friend of hers weeping up a storm because of this shit. Is that it? Because you look like a fire that still got an ember smoking."

I don't know how to be anything but blunt. "There's a warrant out for your arrest and they're headed to my house to find you. We have to go back so you can surrender yourself to the authorities."

He picks up a stone from the shoreline and almost knocks a bird out of the sky.

"I'm sorry."

He turns to me and holds my shoulders. "It's not time for sorry. It's time to fucking fight. You with me, Darling?"

"You know I am."

He hauls me to him and my heart beats so rapidly. I have to keep it under control. I know people find me prickly. Hell, my family can't stand me at times, but I always thought that's who I was and that's all there is. But he makes me discover so much more. And for the first time in my life, I'm exactly where I'm supposed to be and comfortable in my skin.

I slide closer to hold him a little longer before I put my Becca game face back on and lawyer the hell out of some things. I'll wrap up this sunrise, the feel of his arms, and the way he looks at me and carry it with me for the rest of my life.

I break our perfect instant with the surf as our soundtrack and the pine smell of this man.

"We'll find the witnesses from the hospital and get this shit dropped. I'll put some investigators on it."

He slides his hand down my arm and interlaces our fingers as he says, "Do you trust me?"

"Beyond reason." His smile hangs on his face like he can't help but stay smiling.

"Then we have a plane to catch."

"Tell me it's back to California, so you're not a fugitive. I can't get disbarred, that's too much paperwork." He laughs, but I'm serious. I don't have time to get disbarred. Walking back to the hotel, he's quiet but never lets go of me.

I remind him, "We have to do the right thing. Safeguard ourselves." We hustle up to marble stairs, the ocean becoming a faint sound as the doors close behind us. He turns to me, the glow of the sunrise highlighting his beauty, and words pop out. "I'm powerless against you."

"It's me who's powerless," he replies.

His lips are on mine before I can answer him or overthink anything. It's a firm kiss that's demanding everything of myself and I give it freely. He licks and nips my lips and I open for him. He finds my tongue waiting for him. They dance and swirl in a kiss that stops time and reason. I can't get close enough to him as he holds onto me like I'll run. He breaks away from me and takes two steps back.

We're both breathing heavily and he's wary. We've shoved that line a little further back, but I still haven't legally crossed it. I grin at him.

He runs his hands through his hair and points at me. His lips raise into a giant smile that takes over his face.

"Fuck. You're the best thing that's ever happened to me. Do you know that?"

"I didn't do anything."

"Fate did it for us."

"Did what?"

"Chose us."

FOR THE SECOND TIME IN MY LIFE, I'M KNOWINGLY doing something illegal as I board a private jet that's not registered with the FAA to take an accused felon across a couple more state lines. Who am I? Myself pre-Brick at my front door would be appalled, but this Becca wants to make sure he's cleared. My moral center is warring with itself over what is legal and what is right.

This man, despite how he makes my stomach jittery and my nerves jangle not to mention what he does to my heart, head, and vag, is a good man and he's innocent. I know he's innocent.

He hits the top of his phone and punches the overhead.

I ask, "You ok?"

"I'm fine. We're going to be fine."

He sits across from me not next to me and I feel the loss of his warmth and gaze. The detached military machine is back. He's not the same Brick who danced with me last night or held me on the beach an hour ago. I guess in the light of day and gearing up for battle, we're both closed off again.

He pulls a cashmere blanket from the overhead bin. He

covers me up and leans into my face. A flicker in his eyes warms and the icy demeanor gets pushed back.

"What are you doing?" I inquire.

"Wrapping you up tight like a bug. You didn't sleep. I have a little work to do, so you go ahead and rest. I'll wake you when it's time to do some side-kicking or lawyering." I laugh. I'm exhausted. I haven't wanted to miss a second of this adventure with him since he knocked on the door.

Girls like me don't get much in the way of adventure. Even the boldest, ballsiest thing I've ever done, sending Asher to jail, was done from the comfort of my home and office in Napa. I didn't realize how closed off my world was until he dripped on my rug. He turns away from me and reaches for a warm cup of something from the flight attendant. He adds a touch of sweetener.

"Tea. It's the sleepy time kind and I added a little Splenda so it's the way I know you like it." I reach out and he waits a moment, then nods at me.

"Thank you."

He puts down the tray beside my chair and places the cup down. After a kiss on my forehead, he holds my face. "No, dear girl, thank you. For all of this and for so far not hating me. Hold on to that, would ya?"

I laugh. "The not hating you part?" I sip my tea and it's exactly what I need. It's delicious.

"That's the one, darling. I'm gonna need for you to remember that for the near future."

"I'll write it down, so I don't forget."

He quickly pulls a pad from his bag and scribbles a note stating, "I won't hate Brick Dunne in the future." Then he signs it. I take another sip, put down my cup, take the pen from him, and sign it while laughing.

"There. Now, it's legally binding."

"Is the flight attendant a notary?" I ask.

"He can be whatever I say he is, so yes." He strokes my cheek again and my whole body is a warm puddle of cashmere and puppies and crackling comfortable fires.

"Sip, sleep, and dream. That's what I need for you to do now."

"And what are you doing? You're tired, this blanket is big enough for both of us." I have no shame.

He groans and throws his head back. "You're something else, my Becca. I have to work a spell. Maybe I'll crawl in next to you while you snooze away and steal your thoughts for my own. Then I'll plant only good things in your brain, involving me and my rocking body."

My face flames. I yawn as I finish my tea. As I drift off these words slip from my head directly out of my mouth.

"You don't have to steal anything; you can have all my thoughts and time."

And then I don't remember a thing as I'm pulled under the weight of exhaustion.

# CHAPTER 23
## BECCA

'm still in that state of intense cozy sleepiness when he scoops me up still in my blanket and carries me. I flop my head against his chest. I want my bed so badly and I'll tell him if he doesn't hold me, I might freeze to death so he has to join me.

"Shh. Sleep now. I got you." I glance around at the private airport, and he carries me through the small lobby. I giggle and snuggle into him, shielding my face from anyone who might be watching.

He places me in the backseat of a car and joins me, pulling me into his chest. It's the most comfortable place in the world. I'm still drowsy and thinking about going back to sleep. It's only after we're on the road about ten minutes and my mind flashes. It fixates on palm trees surrounding the entrance of the airport and lack of hills. I sit up and he puts his hands up as his eyebrows reach for his hairline.

He holds up the piece of paper I signed before the flight. My head swivels around looking at our surroundings.

"Where the fuck are we?" I shake my head out of my

sleepy state. It's the middle of the night but not far in the distance is some glittering pieces of shit that can only be the Strip.

"You're savvier than that."

I move as far from him as I can. My lips pursed, my brain buzzing, and my blood boiling.

"Fucking Vegas. You kidnapped me and that's a felony offense."

He says aloud to the driver, "She don't mean that, sir. Tell them, HB. You do not mean what you just said. The last thing we need is the law involved." Holy shit, we most certainly do not.

I think fast. "Sir, I am kidding. I'm not good with surprises."

"No, baby, you're not. And I wanted this to be special, so I didn't tell you all the details but there will be a spa visit for you." I don't know what the hell he's playing at, but the driver seems less alarmed.

I lean over and begrudgingly kiss him on the cheek. "Always thinking of me." I dig my nails into his thigh, and he holds back a wince.

I want to cock punch him hard. He fucking didn't take me home so he could respond to the warrant. I'm in a place I hate with a man I can't trust. He said he'd never lie. What the hell is this?

I take our contract from him. "Is this our itinerary?" He nods, thinking I'm playing his dumbass game. I rip it in half, and he cocks his head to the side. "Let's just wing it, darling." I glare at him, and he bites the inside of his cheek. I don't know if he's trying not to laugh or it's a reflex from me putting the death grip on his hard thigh. Fucker. Mutha fucker.

He answers me, "Winging it sounds just fine. No malice or malcontent here, just straight up doing what's best for us."

The driver is starting to pay attention again and I try to cover it up with another quick kiss to his cheek. Then I whisper in his ear as if I'm saying something sexual.

"I'm so fucking angry. I'm going to throttle you. I'm going to literally squeeze you until you beg for mercy. This is beyond the pale."

He looks at me and says, "Sounds like a perfect evening."

I growl at him because I can't say anything. And then I paste on a strained smile and move to my side of the car.

"Baby, that's too far from me." He yanks me onto his lap. I squirm to get away.

He's in my ear. I don't want it to be sexy but unfortunately everything about this confounding man is sexy.

"Now, you sit right still, and I'll explain everything once we're in the room. I need you to mind me. You're making it difficult for us to get out of here safely. I don't know this man. I assume he's just a driver for UBER, but Cady has fingers everywhere. So sit your ass still, look alert, and pretend to like me."

My body freezes. Not only have I been taken against my will, I now have to pretend to like him so we don't die. We are certainly in a different place than sucking crawfish and admiring a sunset.

I turn to him. "Fine."

He kisses me lightly and I scoot away. But not too far away.

WE'RE BARELY IN THE DOOR WHEN I ROUND ON HIM. He stands there, legs apart, arms crossed, and says nothing.

I yell, "TELL me the truth. Do not lie to me."

His voice is sugary sweet. "I didn't lie. You never asked where we were going. You assumed it was California, which it never was." He holds up the ripped piece of paper. "Don't forget about our binding contract."

"Duress. I signed that under duress, that's what I'll tell people." I turn to him, and his shirt is off. Fuck me. How do I stay furious with that chest mocking my conviction? So cut and hard and so many abs to count. His tattoos only high-light the taut muscles. I step back and adjust my shirt. Then put my arms up to keep him at a distance.

"Tell me everything, right fucking now. And why are you shirtless?"

He rubs his hands down his torso. "I need a shower." He walks away towards the bathroom, and I follow.

"You can't shower now," I sputter.

"I'm dirty. Join me, you can yell at me while I'll soap you down."

He turns on that damn twinkle in his eyes over his shoulder. They sparkle and I'm losing my resolve. But that's his hope. I dig deep and find trial attorney Becca. The one who never reacts to anything. I cross my arms over my chest and give him the look. The one that brings opposing counsel to their knees, makes judges wary, and scares the crap out of jurors.

He mirrors my stance and bites his lip. "Now, darling, I know you're trying to be intimidating. I'm sure the rest of the world finds you formidable but to me you look delicious when you give me that look."

I growl a bit.

"Adorafuckingble. Now, Imma let you yell at me a spell after I tell you about my well-researched actions." He smirks. "And while you scream at me, I'm gonna watch those perfectly succulent lips of yours."

I grit my teeth and say, "Tell me what happened."

"Short answer is I was never going to Napa." He rolls his wrists to encourage me to keep going. "Let me have your best, Elsa." He widens his legs into a more secure stance and smirks at me.

My voice is low and powerful, "Let's set aside the kidnapping charge, I'm now on the hook for aiding and abetting an alleged felon."

"Let's simmer down. Isn't that the very definition of a criminal lawyer?"

Not fucking funny. "Not the abetting part." My voice cracks with anger as the next words slip out, "You're a fugitive now, do you know that? And my career is fucking done. But then you have the audacity to tell me that you had a good reason. That all of this makes sense to you, deceiving and lying to your attorney, and well, um..."

"And what there, HB? Finish your thoughts, I'm all ears."

"AGGH." I scream in frustration. "How are you this nonplussed about breaking so many laws and dragging me down with you. I'm not going to do well in prison. My brother—who I thought at one point, given the dumbass stuff he used to do, would be tossed into jail—he'd make friends with everyone, and they'd all end up working for him. But me, no one likes me. I'm difficult to get along with and I have no idea how to have a polite conversation. I will be an utter failure at prison yard chit chat. I'd bond with a lunch lady or something and get beaten every day because she feels bad for me and gives me extra tater tots. And so, my inordinate unlikability will result in being claimed by the cellblock boss for legal advice, and who knows what else I'd do for protection from the tater tot beatings. Why doom me to a life of being a prison outcast? Answer me and give me all the details. Why would you do this to me?"

He doesn't hesitate. "Because I'm in love with you." He doesn't move while my entire world flips upside down.

I blurt out, "You like me." I can't feel my tongue.

He shifts his weight, and his lips curl up. "I more than like you and would move heaven and earth to protect you. Especially from prison bosses using you for advice. But mostly, I can't keep you safe unless you're with me."

He found a way to make me smile in a situation that's impossible.

There's a knock at the door and I jump about a foot. He puts his fingers to his lips, then pulls a gun from his bag.

I whisper, "Now you have a gun with you?!"

He's on my ear in an instant, "I've always had a gun. I know who this is, but I want you far from this. Go to the bedroom and stay there no matter what." He pats my bottom and I run and hide in the closet. I don't know what this is all about, but my nerves are a little frayed from being kidnapped and now shushed. And as if that's not enough, the man thinks he's in love with me. I have to bury that under the pile of felonies he's racking up. Can your elbows sweat? I feel like my elbows are sweating.

I listen intently as if I'm going to be quizzed on this mysterious meeting. My powers of concentration and memory are unmatched by anyone I've ever met. And there's a second and third voice, and holy shit this can't be happening. I charge out of the bedroom calmer.

# CHAPTER 24
## BRICK

"It's a pleasure to meet you, sir."

"Not sure any of this is a fucking pleasure, but nice to meetcha all the same." We shake. I'm meeting him eye to eye. He's about as big as they come, and he says we have things to discuss. This is not a man who makes a habit of meeting with strangers and certainly not alone. Tonight, he brought along his federal tail.

I gesture to the couch but before they can sit that damn woman comes swinging around the corner. I didn't want anyone to know she was here.

He stares at her while my heart and body flood with ice. He said come alone and tell no one. I know the repercussions will be swift, but I'll protect her with everything that I am. I know the rumors, but I don't want to tempt fate until I understand all the players and where I fit.

I command her, not that the infernal hummingbird will listen to me, but I try, nonetheless, "Please leave us to our business." I turn to the men and they're smiling too big. Then the giant gestures to her with his enormous hand and his coat lifts and I see he's packing.

The other man, who's been standing back, raises a hand to wave to her. This is a disaster.

"I see you brought some legal counsel." His thundering voice says with amusement.

Steam is building in my brain.

I play it off, "Darling, scoot along now."

She pops her hip and gets a salty look. I'm going to kill her if she gets us both killed.

"What are you doing here?" she accuses and points to both of them.

He points to her. "You. Trust me, that's a question you should be answering. I know why this guy's here but I'm a little sketchy on why you're here, Red. I was told you were laying low. Did Mellie Mel lie to me?"

"Yes." She walks over to us, and my jaw drops as Sal Pietro, crime boss, opens his arms to Becca and she walks in them. Well, I'm going to say the rumors about her cousin are true. The mafioso is hugging my woman. Then she rushes to the other man. He's about an inch shorter than me and although I consider myself muscled, this man is a tight coil. He's wearing cargo shorts and a faded Stanford t-shirt. His hazel eyes are sharp, as well as the rest of his features. His casual attire is in opposition with his shorn efficient hair. And then a smile spreads across his face as wide as the room.

"Becca Gelbert, always a pleasure." And she hugs yet another man in my presence. She hugs the Fed.

"Mark! This is a surprise. And you should know this alleged felon gave me the gift of plausible deniability when he kidnapped me and brought me to Vegas."

I roll my damn eyes. This woman is maddening and playing a game I don't know the rules of.

She finishes the hug and stares at me and says, "And now you're associating with known criminals?"

Sal chides her, "Watch yourself there, Missy, who's known?" She laughs. Well, my brain's flipping like an internet browser with too many tabs open. I can't keep up.

She steps back over to him followed by the G-Man. He puts his giant hand on her back, and I want to cut it from his body.

"Sir, I'd like it a whole lot better if you remove your hand from Ms. Gelbert." He smirks but does so, holding it up so I can see it.

Sal says, "I appreciate the dance, Becca, but it's fine. It appears someone's a bit possessive. I recognize the instinct. Poppy Gelbert is a known associate of mine, Mr. Dunne."

Neither Mel nor Becca ever confirmed that fact. That five families' loyalty is impressive. Sal sits pats a cushion for her to sit.

I speak again, "Now, I didn't want her to be any part of this. I need you to run along while I hear Mr. Pietro out."

"Bullshit. She's the best thing you got on your side, wise counsel, a cool head, and nobody can zing a fucking idiot like Red can."

She laughs, then her face drops when she glances at me. "I only use my power for good unless you piss me off, which is where that shirtless, painted man is falling right now."

Sal's laugh booms through the room. He turns to me and straightens out his face. "We're family." She pats his arm. "You ok? Lou's outside the door and can walk you right the fuck outta here if you need."

The Fed puts himself into an at-ease stance, but says, "I'll take her." As allegiances reveal themselves, I see she's a lot safer in the world than I thought.

For the first time, I realize she might leave me. I've marginalized her. These powerful men lined up behind her, and I pushed her into a bedroom because I wanted to protect her.

That's no way to talk or treat a woman. She has the opportunity to be done with this mess because she has power on her side. I jerk my head in a stiff nod, so they know I'd let her go if that's the route she chooses. I don't deserve her. I got twisted up in the idea that I could lose someone else I love to this fucking mess.

There's a thudding silence filling all the space around me, and my heart is out of my chest, beating like hummingbird wings as I wait for her verdict. All I care about is this woman, who apparently can tangle with the mafia and remain unscathed.

Her glance goes from the door to me, then back to the dark-haired, dark green-eyed lethal panther in the room. Her voice cracks the room.

"My place is with him," she says these words as a matter of fact. My blood jumps like a jackrabbit.

Sal squeezes her hand and walks to me. I don't flinch or move because I'm bolstered now by that woman choosing me.

"Before we get to business, this is your one and only warning. You hurt her, get her hurt, fail the Gelberts or the five in any way, and I'll not only make you answer to me but, Arthur. Now put a fucking shirt on, we get it, you're goddamned cut." Becca laughs as he mentions her dad. He slaps me on the back, then pulls me into a giant hug.

"Any man who tangles with Becca and comes out the other side hung up on this dame, and it's reciprocated, well —that's a man of true character and grit."

She states for the record, while I toss on a t-shirt, "He's innocent. What do you know? And why are you here?"

"Who's Lou?" I ask.

They all laugh but don't fill me in and I exhale for what seems like the first time in my life. She had her out and she stayed. Not because she was legally bound, because lord knows I've broken a few laws today, but because of me. She moves a bit on the couch to make room for me. Sal sits across from us.

"Sir, if you don't mind getting down to the brass tacks and answering a few questions, that I believe only you can."

"That's why I'm here. And because the fucking Gingersnap told me I had to help unravel some messes creeping into all our lives. Our paths are no longer separate, and someone has us in their crosshairs."

"Gingersnap?" I ask.

Becca turns to me and smiles. "Poppy."

Sal sits back and pulls out a cigar, looking as typical as I'd expect a man like that to look. He doesn't light it but holds it. "Your friend is gone. But you should know he wasn't a good guy."

Becca panics. "Who?"

"Ronnie Donato," he says, and my heart drops.

"Fleabag."

She gasps. I guess I'm not surprised but it is a shame.

Sal says, "Don't worry. He had that coming to him. Not by me but by those he's betrayed. He was a slave to the buck and smack. He did a lot of dirty in his life in the name of those two pursuits. The friend you knew was long gone. But we followed him here, which is why we're meeting at the devil's playground."

She's switched on and he sees it. She leans forward and asks, "What's the connection to Brick's grandmother's death, Hope Beardsley, and the Vino Groupies?"

"Ah, that dumbass shell corporation that tried to swindle all the wineries. Your boy was Asher's cellmate."

"Fleabag killed Asher?" I suspected as much. But now Becca demands, "You need to tell me all the rest of it. It's under privilege."

Sal puts a finger up, points to me, and adds, "Not so fast. There are things I'd never tell you, even though you're technically one of my lawyers. Because if shit's harmful or blatantly illegal you'll rat me out. So, dance lightly there, cowboy. Only true privilege is spousal."

Becca's back straightens like someone struck her with a hot poker.

I am going to be honest with this man, I have no other alternative. "I went hunting the man who took my grandmother's land and who I believe in my gut killed not only her, but that woman, and tried to frame me."

Mark clears his throat. "That's a hell of a story. You're not going to find him. He's a ghost and a good one. I know a thing or two about hiding and he's the best."

Sal adds, "And if you find him, I'd like to be by your side to fucking tear him apart tiny fucking piece by fucking piece."

Becca says in strained voice, "Are you saying you all have a connection to this man?"

He gestures his cigar at her. "So do you. He's the one who put Asher in your life. And your buddy was unhinged but our ghost weaponized him. It's what he does, he gets the pieces of shit of the world to do his grubby work."

Becca asks, "And does this ghost have a name?"

Sal sits back and laughs.

Mark answers, "He has many, but you'll know him as Phillip Cady."

"Holy shit. That guy again," Becca says.

Sal says, "He owns all the companies and all the people. Except mine. He sure as fuck was the puppet master behind my nephew's attempted coup. And my nephew's number one cut man is your fucking piece of shit."

I look to Mark. "That's why you're still with Sal? You know he's not dirty but the two of you are hunting him?"

Mark nods and there goes my stomach right down to the floor.

Sal stands up and says, "Now the three of us are."

Becca stands. "Four."

Shit.

# CHAPTER 25
## BECCA

can't process all of it, so I go procedural in my brain. Talk to Mark, hug Sal, avoid jail, keep Brick. His possessive, protective thing is more of a turn-on than I could ever imagine. I'm terrified, oddly not for my life, but his. But between the Don, the mercenary, and the FBI guy, I think I'm safe in this room. Oh, and Lou, the bodyguard in the hall.

My father, although a prickly asshole, made me feel safe as a kid, and certainly growing up in a small town where literally every single person knows your name made me feel safe, or so I thought. But this morning getting tucked in on the plane by that inked bicep was the first time I truly felt it.

Procedure. I walk back into the living room area, and the men are talking, and breakfast is on the big table. Brick is putting on a more formal shirt. He's buttoning up and slowly hiding his broad shoulders and the giant snaking vines on his arms. His chest remains a blank canvas, but his back and his arms are stunning works of perfect art. His muscles highlight the ink and pictures. My mind wanders from all the laws I'm breaking, and I stop to admire his ass.

His tight, shapely ass makes me giggle, thinking about flat-ass Larry.

"I'm just calling to say that the cannoli is rotten and I'd like to return the whole lot." A warning to Poppy and Mel, be alert.

Sal tosses the phone to Brick, who breaks it in half. We always use burner phones to contact Sal and when Mel tells us to. It's her system. Poppy has a whole list of burners written down by her bed, she moves on to the next number when told. She's the only one who can find Sal at all times. I breathe in and out before I join the conversation. I want to be the only one to find Brick because I'm pretty sure he's the only one who can find me.

Mark says, "The room is clear. I double checked."

Brick nods to the two of them. "Just cuz I talk slow, doesn't make me dumb."

"Far from it, Mr. Dunne." He clears his throat and puts his hand on Brick's shoulder. "Chase is the one who did you dirty. He's also the trigger you're looking for. I'm sorry."

I scream, "WAIT. Not Fleabag? CHASE from the other night? Chase? Is he dead too?"

Sal smirks. "Not yet." He chuckles a little under his breath.

Brick circles the room. "I had him and got blinded by a running around together childhood bond. I'm better than that, I let him fucking get me. Shit."

"Brick, we don't know each other well, but if Becca wants me to take care of this, I'm bound by family."

Mark says, "Nope. You're not doing shit. Sal. You're not in that business. Nope. And that piece of garbage is one of our only living ties to Phil Cady. He and Sal's nephew were the ones who set up Mr. Dunne. All trails have dried up, from his she-devil to your nephew. All gone without a trace."

I say, "I'm so fucking confused. Just lay it out for me and what I need to do to get my client off."

Sal snickers, "Get your client off, huh?"

Brick clears his throat. "Mind your manners. I don't care how fucking close you are, you don't speak to her that way."

Sal puts his hands up. "Was just kidding. Bygones."

"Becca, it's a losing case. They want Brick neutralized and caught up in litigation or jail time. They're pushing for a bench warrant. You'll never find the nurse, orderly, and doctor. Their families pulled up stakes. Cady doesn't do loose ends. It's why Asher was doomed. It's why none of you have ever heard from Shawna again." Mark shoves some bacon in his mouth.

My blood is cold. How can this be connected? "SHAWNA? Bax's ex-fiancée, nightmare, political pariah, Shawna? Holy shit. All her hidden political sex videos. She set up—"

Mark finishes my sentence, "Senators, house reps, governors, mayors, advisors, that girl had a lot of political power in her pocket so to speak. She'd been setting up the pieces for years."

"Was she a plant the whole time?" Sal's face goes ashen, and Brick looks confused. "She did her best to ruin Bax and Tabi when he ran for the US Senate a couple of years ago."

"Shawna Moran?" Brick says, and I realize he's been keeping tabs on us.

"Not initially, but Bax became a long-term strategy to grab control of California. When Bax didn't do as he was told, they tried to ruin him, so he'd step away from politics. She's Cady's niece and her parents are gone. So, he's all she has and knows. All those sex tapes and blackmail files. And super PACs she had were all under—"

Brick finishes his sentence, "The Diana Group. All groundwork for the high-speed rail. I didn't see that connection even though I was monitoring the situation." I knew he was looking after us. "Where's the troublemaker now?"

Mark points at him and says, "She skipped out of our federal offices and other than a facial recognition hit, eight months ago in Sweden, not even Mel can find her. It's killing her not to tell Bax. But it's not safe, and it's classified."

What's even happening? I'm in a room listening to conspiracies to take down my extended family.

Mark's up at the door with Sal, and I ask, "What do we do?"

Mark shrugs. "Nothing. Not a fucking thing, do you hear me? You can't say a word to anyone outside this room. We operate with extreme caution."

Bricks exhales and half laughs.

"For now, we keep the rope loose on Enzo and Chase so we can trace them."

I ask, "Was Fleabag cut like the girl?"

Mark nods. "Worse. He was carved."

I bristle with the thought.

Mark addresses both Sal and Brick. "I'm not fucking around alpha males. Do nothing. Be seen in everyday life. Brick, go back to Napa and surrender. Becca file motions so you're seen in court. Discuss this with no one."

I'm pacing and land next to Brick. He puts his hand on my back and Mark chides,

"You two need to look like client and attorney. I don't know what's going on, but I do know Chase sent this picture to a contact."

I peer over his shoulder. It's us dancing at Lucille's. Shit.

"And to be honest, Becca, I need you to step back. Get off this case if you can."

"A judge will deny my motion."

Mark implores, "Anything you know is a danger going forward, especially if asked to testify against your client if the evidence is overwhelmingly against him, which it's looking like. They're introducing an iron-clad eyewitness."

"WHAT? Who?"

"Father Carmichael was helping out at the hospital when Brick took the woman there. He can place him, and his deposition states Brick made threats to the staff if they talked."

"That's a fucking lie."

Mark puts his arms out. "Misdirection, lies, and money. That's how the man has amassed power and fortune. You have something he wants. I don't know what that is, but this is larger than your grandmother."

Brick doesn't play his hand, so neither do I. And I'm impressed Mel didn't tell them about the land. But I guess she figured we would.

Sal pulls me to him. "You be careful. Gingersnap will never let me live it down if something should happen to you. I'm going to check in on you but for now, I have to scurry back to Los Angeles. I have a fucking weasel to hunt."

Mark admonishes him, "Stay out of it. This was fact-finding and courtesy. Do not confuse me with a friend. I will fucking put you down if you shit all over this mission. Leave your nephew alone unless he pulls a fucking gun on you. Welcome him home. Let him in."

Sal gruffs. "Understood, but you can only keep me away from him for so fucking long. Tick tock."

Sal kisses the top of my head. "He's a good man, I can tell. Trust him like you trust me."

Mark hugs me, then addresses Brick, "I'll be in touch if I need to be. But do not make a move on Chase. When the moment is right, I'll let you know. I'll toss you in jail myself if you fuck with this."

"Understood, sir."

"Mark."

Brick nods, and they both exit the room. I fall into the chair behind me unable to process anything. Brick puts his gun away, turning to me with his face showing the pain in his heart and I wish I could take it away. He's so close to getting the closure. But I pull out some pressing issues we need to discuss.

"You love me?" I move across the room, hoping the physical distance from his scent helps me get to the truth and stop addling my brain.

I'm rooted in my spot, but he rushes to me. My body is alight with a million tiny fires and all of them need to be put out. There's so much going on, but in my procedural brain, this is first on the list.

"That's what you're taking from the last hour or so?"

"I'm taking it all in order. And this was the second mindfuck of the day, we'll circle back to the kidnapping." He laughs. I turn in his arms to try and walk away, and he pulls me back to his front. His lips so close to my neck and ear. He's trailing his words.

"But I do."

"You can't. It's impossible." I gasp.

"Fine, then I like you a real, real lot." With each word there's a whisper of a kiss on my neck and now all rational

Becca thoughts are gone. I'm one sensitive quivering mess in his arms. Instinct has me lean my head back, stretching so he has better access.

I hold onto the thin thread of morality and reality that's zinging the back of my brain. I stare at the large windows overlooking the strip with its garish lights, and it looks a little magical.

"This is all lust and will go away."

He continues to feather his lips over my jawline, and I involuntarily moan. Fucking body betraying me. Doesn't it know this is career suicide? I glance down and his tattooed hand is on my collarbone and the brightly colored hummingbird is catching my eye.

"I don't think it's going to go away for a while, but if you think you can do something about all these feelings swirling around us, Hummingbird, you do that."

I gasp at the nickname and pull his arm away from me. "Tell me." I point to the bird that's so colorful and bright, the wings wrapping his thumb.

He bends over me and takes my lips without warning. I lean into this incendiary passionate kiss and moan a little. It takes all my resolve to pull away. I don't want to because in his arms and in his kiss, nothing else matters. In this space somewhere tucked into a pocket of time, there's no murder investigation, no mafia bosses, or FBI warnings. There's no law saying I can't be with this man and there's no moral code I've lived my life by in the secret moments with Brick.

This is a war with myself not to jump on him and dive deep into the abyss where I can't hear the pressures of our life and only the pleasures of us together. I'm exhausted from denying how I feel about him. But I give it my all to stay legal.

"Hey! You kidnapped me."

"I did and I am sorry." He'd do jail time for me. Balls-to-the-wall love has always been reserved for my brother and his friends. They live loud, bold lives and demand happiness from the world. I've been content to be content in mine. But in the last six weeks I've been more excited to see him or tell him something or share a meal or little things about my day with him than anything else that's ever happened to me.

There's a small crack in my contented shell, allowing in the light of his eyes. I don't know if that's love or hope, but it's definitely something new and unexpected. I'd like a couple of years to analyze it and make sure it's not going to hurt me, but I don't think I have that kind of time.

He approaches me with a determined look, and I snap back.

"No. That's not right. I'm not sorry. There are no limits or places I won't go if it keeps you safe."

My jaw drops at his words. Seems a pretty good definition of love, no limit to what you would do. I sit on the floor right where I'm standing. He lets me process. I pull my knees up. Perhaps it's the utter chaos and time flux, but I get it. I've echoed his behavior, there are no limits to what I would do for him. I have that instinct to protect what's yours. He told me he's mine and I'm starting to believe him. And if I let myself drift to a totally insane and lucid dream space, I can admit, I'm his.

I collect myself, stand up, and pull up my hair. Mostly because I have zero idea what to do in this situation. Do I tell him? Or let it play out? I'm going to fix my hair instead of saying anything.

He says, "Nope, I like it brushing your shoulders and reminding you you're feminine. Such a beautiful woman that drives me crazy."

"Brick."

"Damn, if I don't love my name on your lips."

I smile and try to tuck that feeling away again.

"Brick. Next steps. All that remains is footage of you arriving with a bloody woman, who's now dead. And the word of a priest to condemn you. We have to get back to work and do what Mark suggested. We go home and not be seen together." My stomach cramps and twists as I say this.

His face is unreadable. My heart feels like someone's sitting on my chest. I let the rest of it stumble out of my lips without conviction.

"I'll find you a temporary residence. Only appear together in official capacities."

I don't want to cry but the idea of ripping him out of my life is painful. He stares at me and I'm not going to be able to keep standing. My knees are locked, my back straight, but I'm breaking apart inside. Silence builds and it's pushing in on us. I squeeze my sides tighter hoping it helps. I wait for a response. Wait. And wait.

He laughs and says, "Nah. We ain't doing that." He sucks in a breath, and I clutch the edge of the couch, so I don't launch on him.

My voice is weak but flooded with relief. "How?"

# CHAPTER 26
## BRICK

'm standing in front of this magnificent woman while she pretends she's anything but special. She's worn out. I see it. The tension of not being together completely is gnawing at both our souls. And of course, the state of California would still like me to get drawn up on some bullshit murder or manslaughter charges.

We'll find that nurse and that fella who helped me and heard the doctor say she's gonna be right as rain. The bloody rocks on a rainy night. The closed bar. The lump on my head. Our loopholes that keep getting sewn shut. But we have the mud.

All those worries fade when she lets me hold her. She's flumped down on the couch, and I pull her feet into my lap rubbing them.

"I promise not to do anything, but you look like you need to be held. Let me do that for you, darling." She flips around on the couch, and I'm shocked but grateful she heeded my request.

She places her head on my chest and my arms reach around my goddess. I kiss the top of her auburn head and she sighs. She's tracing my arms. I know she's a woman of boundaries and principles beyond reproach. I also know she's using them as a shield to deny her heart. I scare her as much as she frightens me with this powerful emotion I got no business knowing.

I may not have done this bad thing but that doesn't mean I haven't done my fair share of things that will get me judged in the afterlife. I've atoned for what I've done for personal reasons and for country. But there's always the part of me that won't forgive myself and kept me from pursuing her before. I lived in the agony of the "what if." And now I live in the agony of what I could lose.

She's turned and now her body is molding to mine, her back to me, but her fingertips still tracing my tattoos. She brushes over the bright-green and gold hummingbird, the color of her eyes.

My voice comes out pushed, "This is you. I know you know that." She slaps my wrist and I hold her tighter. "Hush now, darling. You're going to take account of what I say. Take it, sweet girl."

"I'm not sweet." She huffs. Always the one to make sure you don't know there's a vulnerable heart underneath. I never wore my heart on my sleeve until fate stepped in and let Rebecca cross my path. Now I wear it on my wrist, with those delicate wings peeking out of my sleeve to remind me she's always with me.

"You're so beautiful and strong. You're the vibrant one, not me. I'm more of a fade into the background, can you file this paperwork for me kind of gal. My signature colors are beige and cream."

"Someone's been seeing themselves all wrong. That final day back in the conference room. When I took your hand just before I left, knowing our business was through.

You hummed at a higher frequency, one only I can hear. I'd never felt that type of vibration or sound."

She folds her graceful legs under her and looks up at me. I touch her face for a second and she thinks about biting off my finger, but I move it too quickly.

"You were only with me for a moment. Your fingers lightly hovering over mine. A delicate wave of energy that flitted back out of my life as unexpectedly as you flitted in. I didn't know what to make of it or the look in your gorgeous green eyes as they locked on mine." I shift her closer and collect myself a minute.

"Surely you noticed the magic as I did. Mimi Tinker used to call it the mojo. And said she never knew it except with my grandfather. But she understood it existed and long after he passed, she bathed in that memory every night. Said the moon made her feel it all over again. I was content to know it did exist. And I never wanted to be without that magic, but I had no intention of chasing you. Wasn't sure I deserved it or could handle it right then. It's a big thing to tackle, meeting your other half. I was resolved that it be just that. I'm not something for everyone and certainly not my delicate, gorgeous hummingbird."

"No one would call me delicate." She scoffs and I won't have it.

"I would and I just did."

A soft tear hits my arm and I know neither of us is walking away from this moment the same as when we sat down. I need her to know that it's her and the mojo I need most. This chaste path we've been walking will end soon. It fucking has to. But I do love her and will continue to do so if she'll have me. She's going to deny it's real again or rationalize it away like the tide going out. But I'll wait because I'm not going anywhere. I run my hands up and down her arms as she clutches me. Her fingers never leave the hummingbird tattoo.

"Say more things. I can't speak right now."

"Get your thoughts together and get back to me then. Maybe draw up a brief you'd like to submit to that bastard judge who won't let me fuck you properly." She laughs as I pull the tension back a bit.

I turn her around in one swift motion and she gasps. I'm looking straight into her eyes that will forever be both my damnation and salvation. I need her to see when I speak my heart.

"Becca, mind me now. I'm gonna get serious and cosmic on ya. Can you handle that?"

"Probably not. You'll have to pardon me if I roll my eyes, it's instinct."

I kiss her without warning. I know I'm not supposed to, but I can't help but indulge for those magnolia pink lips of hers. She softens in an instant and sighs into my kiss.

I pull her hair behind her ear and linger on her delicate cheekbones. As I speak, I trace her face and her jaw.

"Listen up now, Missy. When we met, I know it wasn't that long, but I saw all the things I'd never have in this life. All the beauty that would always slip through my fingers. I never thought I could have something so precious like you in my arms for real. When I left that last meeting of ours, where you bested those assholes and saved everyone's wineries, I immediately went to get this tattoo. I described what I wanted based on how I felt."

I flip my wrist so she can see it up close. She examines it. "See the coloring, the green and gold of your eyes and wings tinged with auburn for your hair. This was the only way I could think of to make my dreams come true. To have you in my arms forever."

Her face is like stone, and I don't know what my girl is thinking. I almost never do. Hell, I've been hers for coming on two and half years. I'm not the type to pine, but I'll be a horse's ass if that's not who I ended up being. A little pining pup mooning over a juicy steak, all for her.

She puts my arm down and she's filled to the brim with tears, and that's the soft perfect woman I know instead of what she lets the world think. Those ever turning and whirling little gears in her head working overtime.

"HB or Hummingbird, always in a hurry, delicate but strong. I can hear the smoke coming from those ungreased wheels turning in your brain, darling. You don't have to think through anything. You don't have to say anything. I'll wait until you get on board with the mojo and fate."

She closes her eyes and one of those tears escapes, and she wipes it quickly, but her eyes never leave mine. Becca simply nods a lot. I know whatever she's about to say she's never said to anyone else and it's hard for her.

I put my forehead to hers and say, "Let the mojo fill you and say what's deep down in that perfect soul of yours. Becks, my love, let go. I'll catch you."

"You sound like someone who owns one of those stinky candle mystic shops."

"Try again," I say quietly, letting her get her awkward humor out.

It comes out in a whisper and changes the course of our lives.

"Forever. I want to live in your arms forever." She traces her bird once more, hiding deep in my chest. The tears fall as she lets her resolve go and embraces the color instead of black and white. I pull her closer.

"Good. Now, marry me."

# CHAPTER 27
## BECCA

I leap up.

"You just want to have sex with me."

"That is a considerable part of moving up our inescapable timeline, but it's not like you're opposed. I am of sound mind and want to be of your body."

How the fuck can he say something like that to me? Okay, yeah I just said all the mushy stuff but my walls slid back up pretty fast.

He laughs at me, and I want to crawl away. "Let me interrupt to say, I know what your face looks like when you orgasm, that's far from being strangers. It's downright neighborly if you ask me. And even though you'll be Mrs. Dunne, you won't stop being my lawyer. Also, I know exactly how to fold your towels and that the blue ones belong in the guest bath and the gray flowery ones go in yours. Your cat, who I call Lil' Bit, likes to sip from a dripping kitchen sink. And you keep a jar of that cookie butter hidden behind the serving platters in that buffet in the dining room. Here's the point. I know your heart and your preferred yogurt flavor. I fucking know you. I'm not a stranger and we're getting married now." His tongue darts out and swipes at his top lip, and lord help me, my stomach flutters.

I hold up a finger to stop him from talking and he tries to grab it. I pull it away quickly. He folds his arms over his massive chest. The hummingbird glaring at me. The most romantic fucking thing I've ever heard of is staring at me. Mocking my stance. Fuck you, perfect hummingbird tattoo, I said, fuck you.

"You're sexy when you're fretting and thinking you can stop this from happening. That's fucking funny. Now come over here and kiss your fiancé. Your skin's got that summer-time blush to it. It's almost as stunning as when you're coming."

"This is not fretting." I do not want to get disbarred. I repeat it like a mantra.

He sways back and forth in his stance.

"As an attorney, in the great state of California, I'm bound by privilege, decorum, and the law that says you and I cannot be involved in any way that isn't appropriate attorney–client related. I don't know what I was thinking. There's absolutely no way I can be back in your arms, let alone show up in court as your fiancée. We cannot have sex."

I step back from him because I've put all of this to rest. But he pulls me quickly towards him and I realize he was only ever toying with letting me walk away from him. His arms wrap around me, and I'm transfixed.

The sizzle of want and mojo, for lack of a better term, crackles all around us. It's our own personal biodome of lust. I have to escape, or I'll lose everything.

"Well, Ms. Gelbert. If it pleases the court, I'd like to enter this into evidence: According to the California Bar Association's Rules of Professional Conduct—"

I'm about to speak and he snaps his head back and covers my lips with his finger. He puts his forehead to mine and sways. I'm hyper-aware of that cottonwood branch on my hip. The vision of it burning into my brain. I'm going to short circuit or orgasm thinking about it. Shit.

"Hush. I have the floor and all your objections have been overruled." He steals a quick kiss, and it sends a Zeus-sized lightning bolt to my clit.

He clears his throat in an overexaggerated way and continues, "According to your precious laws and conduct code, I am citing precedence and, I'd like this entered into the court records as defense evidence, exhibit A. The book clearly states in rule 1.8.10 Sexual Relations with Current Client: A lawyer shall not engage in sexual relations with a current client who is not the lawyer's spouse or registered domestic partner, unless a consensual sexual relationship existed between them when the lawyer-client relationship commenced."

I know all this. I've scoured it so my vagina could find a loophole and be filled by this gorgeous man.

He continues by licking his lips, "You see."

I shake my head no.

He keeps talking, "You're mistaken. Not often. But I caught ya this time. I'm gonna set ya straight so that there's no misunderstanding me. I don't intend to be your fiancé. And don't intend to be your boyfriend. I intend to be your husband and right there in that rule book, you love so much, it says I can. Also says, I'm legally entitled to a honeymoon." He waggles his eyebrows.

He shoos me away. "And we should get going because it's happening now. Hustle up, darling. Woman. I'm not waiting one second more for you to find an objection or to overthink. The moment you say, 'I do' you won't need clothes until at least tomorrow."

My skin is hot and cold at the exact same time. I'm blistering and numb. I'm also elated and enamored.

I run to him, kiss him hard on the mouth, and say, "I do love the law. And citing things gets me hot. You might want to brush up on some other statutes."

# CHAPTER 28
# BRICK

This is a dress I haven't seen, and it knocks me over. We don't say things we're thinking, that's for a different time. I know her mom and massive family will make us do this in front of them, especially since her brother eloped. And I want to stand in front of that football stadium crowd of hers and let them know that I've got her. I'll take it from here and they don't need to worry none. Becca Gelbert might be the one to save us all, but I'll be the one to save her. I slide a ring on her finger, and she looks shocked I have one. It's the only thing I had left and now it's on the only thing I'll ever need.

For now, I see all she wants to say in her eyes and my heart hears all the words unspoken. And that sly little grin and dilated pupils speak to an entirely different part of me.

"I now pronounce you husband and wife." The words are barely spoken when we rush to each other. Our mouths collide and devour the moment and each other. We're tongues and teeth slashing at each other while our lips can barely contain us. She's open with me and I'm lapping up every second. I lift her up and there's music playing and people around us are cutting up and hooting. But the beat of her heart is all I hear. She hitches her legs around me, not paying any mind to anything anymore. She's unfettered and unraveled, and all fucking mine. Finally.

WE BOLT OUT OF THE HITCHIN' POST CHAPEL AND into the UBER I ordered and had waiting for us. I paid for his time and wanted him ready the moment we exited. Having money for dumb shit like this makes all my scrimping and saving worth it. If you can't splurge on finally getting to be inside your woman, then what can you splurge on.

In the car, she snuggles close to me. My arm is around her and I smile down. I kiss her nose lightly, then she moves her face to mine. My intention is an innocent sweet kiss and that lasts 'bout a half a second or so.

In one bold move, she straddles me. I can't help but follow her lead. Branch doesn't even come close to how hard I am. She grinds down and gasps as our tongues search for the meaning of life by swallowing the other person whole. My fucking wife is hot.

I kiss up her jawline and we act as if we're alone in here.

I nip at her ear and say, "There's just so much I'm going to do to you, I can't contain myself."

She gasps, "All of it. Do anything."

I whisper, "Anything."

I skate my hand up her thigh and under her dress. I search for the apex of all my thoughts and desires and slip my finger under her flimsy thong. She's already dripping for me. We both groan as I graze her clit. That initial touch is fucking magnetic. Like one of the superconductor mega magnets, I'll never be able to let go. Not on my own.

She bucks her pelvis and I'm pretty sure I'm going to mess myself pretty soon and come just from her dry humping me in this here—

"GET OUT." I didn't even realize we've stopped and pulled over. Her face turns scarlet as we realize just how carried away we've gotten.

"Not kidding, get out of my car, you perverts. You get zero stars and a warning." Well, that's enough to calm down my cottonwood.

Becca mutters sorry and bolts out of the car, pulling her dress into place.

"I apologize, sir."

"Get out. I'm going to pray on this for you. But you are a bad man. You are bad."

I shrug. "Not bad, just a newlywed." I exit quickly and I'll make sure to double the fare in the tip.

I pull Becca to me, ready for her to retreat into herself a bit. But as I have her huddled into my chest, her body begins convulsing and I realize she's laughing. I join her and the two of us find ourselves belly laughing until we lock eyes. I take her lips again and all our heat amps right back up. It's like it simmers just under the surface and now we've been given the green light, legally, there's no putting that genie back into the bottle. She moans and pulls my head as close to hers as we can. Our tongues thrashing and our heads wobbling out of control as we attempt to deepen a kiss that already has a hold of our souls. My hands knead that fine ample ass and I'm in another dimension. Her ass teleports me through this universe to somewhere I'd never thought I'd get to visit.

We both gasp and she pulls away while we both look around. Now, I'm pissed.

"Darling, we're about six hotels and like an hour walk to our room."

She looks behind us and hooks her thumb. "Then we stay here. It's faster. I need you to fuck me now!"

"Good girl. Seems I've unleashed a beast."

She begins running towards the entrance of the Bellagio, yelling behind her, "You have no idea."

I'M NIBBLING ON HER NECK IN THE ELEVATOR AFTER taking a suite without a second thought. She's laughing and holding onto her slip of paper.

"Do you want my winnings to help pay for the room?"

I laugh and take her piece of paper. "They're our winnings, now. Shared property." She won this $125 on a slot machine while I procured our room.

I wink at her, and she gasps. I don't think the weight has settled on her yet, but I'm all-in on this marriage whether she's prepared for it or not. Her hand drifts from my back to the top of my ass. She dips a finger and scratches a cheek, and I laugh. I can't get to her discreetly, so I whisper something only she can hear.

"This first time, ain't gonna be pretty. And it ain't gonna be long. I'm going to take you on the first surface available. The second time, I'm going to dine on you like a Sizzler buffet. The kind that you take your time with to get the most for your money."

She laughs. "Will there be ice cream involved?"

I raise my eyebrows. "Possibly. But you know what will be involved? That dripping and perfect pussy and my weeping cock. I'm going to fuck you harder and longer than anyone else, but also more than you've ever even dreamed of. Get ready to ride my cock until you come so hard the stars shuffle themselves around in the sky."

She bites her lip, and the doors open. I pull her behind me and then push her up against our door. I roughly pull her neck to mine.

"I can't be contained."

She kisses me quickly. "Then open the fucking door already."

I pick her up and she bites my neck. I growl as I carry her over the rented threshold.

I set her down and she exhales loudly. No fucking thinking right now. Only fucking.

Once we're inside, I snag her dress, pulling her back to me. I reach down and whip the entire thing off her and toss it. I don't even flip the lights on because where I'm taking her, I won't need them. The sunset is blazing over the strip and the lights are just beginning to take over the night sky.

I turn her around quickly and cover her mouth with mine. Her soft full lips going hard as they stretch to take my entire tongue. Her arms go around my neck and I lift her up and carry her to the far end of the room. I place her up on the slightly raised windowsill facing the sparkling hotels, billboards, and restaurants. I kiss her back as I release her breasts to the glass. I push her slightly forward so her nipples kiss the window.

"The glass is cold." She backs up and I pop her ass, and she sucks her breath through her teeth.

I remove her bra, grab her tits from behind, and peak her nipples. I kiss the back of her neck and once they're twice the size they were, I guide them to the cold glass again and kiss her neck.

"Holy shit." She sucks through her teeth.

"Keep them there." I unhook my pants and let my cock out. He's so fucking happy. I rub it over the crack of her sweet ass, then up her slit.

"Yes."

I pull her thong to the side and step out of my pants. I don't have time to take my shirt off. I pull her slightly backward with my arms around her middle, lining my cock up to her perfect pussy. She's wet and there's no time to lose. I turn her head to find mine and hold her face in place.

"I love you." And as I say it, I ease myself into her ready and waiting body. Her eyes spark and she moans. I take her lips and she sits back slightly to take more of me inside. I gasp and move my hands down to her succulent tits. There's nothing either of us can say as she wraps herself around my dick. She drifts one arm up and behind her to grab a hold of the back of my neck and then she's on display for me and the window in front of her.

She leans back to kiss me and it's soft and vulnerable as she acclimates, and I try not to come just from the feeling of this soft, velvet perfection. I spread my hand out on her lower belly and reach around to her breasts, kneading. Her hands are grasping at anything she can get a hold of.

"You're so deep. So big. Deep. I need more."

"So sexy. Don't worry yourself, deeper is coming and so are you."

I lick my fingers, reach down to her clit, and spread her wide. I look over her shoulder so I can see. I rub her and pinch and she convulses a little.

I move my hand up to her chin and whisper in her ear as she moans, "Good girl."

She takes me deeper as she relaxes. I reclaim her clit and her gorgeous red curls frame my fingers in perfection. She's leaning back on me, and I move her forward so she can take a bit of her own weight. I support her and push up against the glass again, so the chill from the glass can send a shiver through her sensitive nipples. I tear her thong off, and I rut up into her.

"Yes. Fuck. Brick." Her heels and the height of the windowsill are perfect. I adjust her a little, then grasp her breasts from behind and she slides back on my cock.

"Fucking tight and perfect. You're fucking perfect. I knew you would be. I knew your pussy was meant for my cock."

"Yes. It's all yours. You feel so good. You're so, oh God. That. That feels amazing. Do that." And I slam back into her while squeezing her tits. I pinch the nipples until she cries out with a beat of pure lust. Then I take my hands and slide them down to her hips and step back a little, pulling her onto my cock.

"Hold on, darling. We need to come."

Her hands go to the glass and the thrills of fucking while on display for the strip has me even more overheated than I should be. Even though I know no one can see us, I can live in the fantasy that my girl is everyone's fucking fantasy, and she's all mine.

"Oh. God. That." I reach my hand around and put my fingers in her mouth. She sucks on them with a preview of how she'll suck my dick later. I take my wet hand and move it down to her clit while hammering away at her from behind. I'm watching my cock slide in and out of her glistening perfect pussy and it's the third best thing in my life, behind her face and her heart and soul.

I groan loudly "Baby, I have to come." She screams my

name and slams on the glass when I hook my fingers and scrape by her clit. She loses control, but I don't stop moving, I'm too close. I stare at her reflection as she comes and her gorgeous mouth and body release at once. The sounds driving me to fuck her faster until my balls are tight and ready. She leans forward and her ass is fucking perfection in front of me. I pull on her hips and then drive into her like a damn beast fucking up into her. Then I freeze and groan as I come inside my bride. And come. And come. Until I don't think I've ever been this spent. My knees buckle as she collapses back into me, and I groan.

I lift her off my cock and place her on a chair. I bend over and try and catch my breath.

## CHAPTER 29
## BECCA

"That was worth getting married."

He laughs, but I'm not completely joking. That was epic.

"You're worth marrying." He's on the ground and crawls over to me in the chair I can't move out of. "So fucking hot. You're quite good at that, Hummingbird."

"I am?"

"Not fooling. You take that compliment and own it. And I'm here if you need to prove it to yourself."

I nod and my body is a blaze with something brand new. Whatever we were or will be, this was the moment our life will pivot between the past and our future.

He rests his head on my knee and holds onto my calf. He looks around, then jumps up, finds a towel, and takes care of me.

Then he's walking around and looking at the suite we took in a frenzy to have sex. His sleepy dick is bobbing around. The buttons of his shirt are mostly undone and one of them is missing. No idea if I did that or he did. I know my undies are toast, but at least my bra survived.

"I'd like to brush my teeth."

He rushes to me, pecks me on the cheek, and hands me a bottle of water. "You just say any foolish thought that runs through that beautiful brain, don't you?"

"What would you say?"

"I'd say, 'Brick, my virile and perfect husband, you're the best fuck of my life and I can't wait to ride your cock every day of my damn life. And have I told you how handsome you are, and can I go get you a steak?' That's what I'd say if I were you. Not this toothbrushing story you're starting."

I can't stop laughing at him.

"But if you want to go with the dental hygiene angle, have at it, wife."

I stand up and gather a cashmere throw around myself and walk up to him. I kiss his full lips and he smiles into our kiss.

Then he pulls back and says, "I like our other suite better."

"See, that's a foolish thing to say. You want to leave this place?"

"I want to take moment of regrouping and head back to our things." He's jumpy.

"What's back there? In the suite at Mandalay."

"So much, I don't want to get into it right now. But I do think we should get back there unless you're not satisfied."

I peek into the bedroom and it's gorgeous, very old-school Vegas. There's '60s era chartreuse velvet chairs and a cream tufted headboard. I turn back to him and stare at his gorgeous face. I put my hand on his cheek.

"Let's say I wasn't satisfied, is there something you might be able to do about that?"

He instantly scoops me up and walks a couple feet to

the edge of the bed. I'm not someone people pick up or hold or carry often. As a kid, sure, but Brick doesn't think twice about carrying me around. And until this moment, I hadn't thought about it either, somehow my bullshit slid away. He's already made me think differently about myself and I didn't even notice. Maybe I am just different and that's how life works. You change the way you think, carve a new brain-wave, create new habits, and don't notice until they're done. Then you get to look back on how far you've come and marvel at how much better you feel and how useless all your worrying was in the face of being happy.

He places me down and pulls me into an embrace. He asks, "Is that pussy ready for what I'm about to do to it?" I smile at this insane man that's now my husband.

"I don't see how she could be."

"Scramble up there and let me get a good look." I'm not sure when I became the girl who does things without question. Perhaps it was that day we met or maybe it was the slow and steady process of taking over my heart. It could be a chemical thing in which his scent activates a certain part of my brain and creates these false feelings of trust and comfort. But I would appreciate if that brain part doesn't shut off, ever.

He stands there in just his half-buttoned oxford shirt, his chest peeking out and his dick not quite hard, but impressive none the less. I open my legs to him, and he licks his lips. I feel sexy and good in my skin. I'm not trying to get away from myself but embrace all I am.

"You know that night I caught you red handed was one of the best nights of my life."

I grin. "Because of what we did?"

"No, because of who I got to see. All of you. And I knew that you wanted me and not just sexually. You trusted me and something snapped into place. Suddenly I knew exactly where I was going in life."

I sit up on my elbows. "Because I was masturbating?"

He snorts a small laugh. "I didn't know I was aimless until I realized my path was with you."

My eyes fill and I'm finding it odd because I'm spread-eagled on the bed, naked.

He says, "That's enough sweet talk for right now. I have a pussy to devour, and my fingers are itching to make you come. You ready for some good coming?"

I nod and before I can say anything his hands are bracing me in place and his tongue swipes up my slit completely.

"Defuckinglicious." His tongue begins to concentrate on my clit, and I buck into his face. "Slow it down, darling. I'm just going to keep feasting"—he slips a finger inside of me and I gasp—"and fingering until I'm done. You just keep coming, as often as you like, but I've got some work to do here until I say I've had enough."

He sucks my clit into his mouth, and it scrapes on his teeth. I moan, "Yes."

He looks up at me with a glistening, grinning face and says, "Gonna be a long night, settle into it." With that, he thrusts another finger into me, and I grind down on it. It's all happening so fast and yet not fast enough. He was right, I'm his.

# CHAPTER 30
# BRICK

After some tasty pussy time, my hummingbird passed out to the world. I swear at one point she had come so hard she was speaking in tongues and telling folks in Neverland how to find nirvana. And it turns out my wife can suck a cock better than my imagination. I didn't think anything could top a solid dick sucking fantasy, but she did. I roused her about an hour ago so we could go back to our other suite. We have to leave earlier than I'd like in the morning, so this way we can try and get some sleep. And there will be more fucking, but we need to shuffle back to Mandalay.

I PLACE HER IN THE BED AND SHE'S A RAGDOLL. WE both need to shower and set ourselves up for some sack time, but it seems she's going to drift off as is. I pull her to me, and my mind goes blank as my wife snuggles into me and validates every part of me. I kiss her on the top of her head.

"I love you."

Her eyes are closed, and her breathing is rhythmic already. It's a solid minute of listening to this beauty purr. Then she reaches her hand up my chest, lifts her face to mine, and says, "So I've heard."

I can't help but smile at her. She kisses me softly and drifts back off to sleep. The world falls away for me as well. All of it except the feel of her on my chest

# CHAPTER 31
## BECCA

'vе never been the girl to swoon, but I look over at this man who married me in order to make me come more times that I can count. My body is spent and floating like six feet above the earth. It's early, like seven, and we're flying home in a couple of hours. His back is to me, blazing bright and beautiful like the sunrise I'm lucky enough to catch on a perfect morning. I'm probably going to have to process this forever, but when I evaluate all that's happened in the last three days, this moment will be the one I draw upon to try and conjure what happy can look like.

My mother's going to flip out, she didn't get to decorate and throw an elaborate party. David fucked me over good in that department when he and Natalie eloped. He showed up to brunch one morning after a trip to Ireland, married.

My mom loves a good shindig and now I'm the one that's going to have to give her that. Hope my husband doesn't mind. AHH. He's my husband. I'm a wife, his wife. I look over at him and it's wrong and right in the same basket of confusion and acceptance. But I guess that's how you could describe me.

I slide out of bed and toss on his t-shirt, a hoodie, and a pair of sweats so I can run downstairs and grab coffee.

I don't want to wake him, so I'll pop down to the casino floor. It will give me a moment to process things without the smell of him reminding me I can have sex whenever I want it. And turns out I'm amazing at sex with him. If it were appropriate, I'd like to video us having sex and send it to Larry so he's aware of how not frigid I am. And if you actually take care of your partner, everyone gets to come.

I toss a note on the bedside table, and he's still snoring and looking perfect. I bend down and kiss him lightly on the temple and he moans in a satisfied way. I sneak out of the room before he threatens to make me come again. I need a minute, a muffin, and some freaking caffeine.

I'm going to need a real ring at some point. This one is sparkly and pretty, but I assume it's from the check-in desk at the chapel. The elevator is an endless parade of people coming in from the night, sneaking back to their own rooms, or proudly flaunting their conquests, either carnal or financial.

I don't know if Grammie Tinker's Mojo Magic is real or a line he fed me to marry me and get me into bed, but I got swept up in it. I married him because of the tattoo story. How does a girl, even those of us skeptical black-hearted types, possibly resist that story?

I swerve around people and make my way towards the casino area to pass through to Starbucks. The noises and manufactured music all blending together in their own odd symphony of false hope.

When I was four, I announced to my mother, who worships Christmas, that Santa Claus was them. Aside from the absurdity of a man traveling around the world in one night and knowing exactly what I wanted, I found David's presents unwrapped in their closet when I was playing office. When he got them on Christmas morning I had irrefutable proof, and my law career began.

Every year they'd try to make me believe in something that wasn't there, like the Easter Bunny, the tooth fairy or bipartisanism, and I found a flaw with each. The only existence of magic I've ever found, is my parents. They're still madly in love but shouldn't be.

My mother's the believer, the artist, the dreamer, and the first one to pull out seasonal decorations with gilded glee each year. Michaels, Target, and Hobby Lobby alert her when the seasonal aisles change over. When she finished decorating for Christmas this year, there were thirty-four trees ablaze, including a creepy Victorian doll tree, on our winery property. She created an attraction from her obsession with spreading joy. She then turned to my brother's winery and after that she still had enough lights to create an actual helipad on a Pro/Ho's basketball court.

Then there's my dad, a cranky, belligerent asshole. He's a stark realist and skeptical of everyone. He doesn't suffer fools, he's aggressive and rigid, but yields to my mother every time. He'd do anything for her and she for him. There must be some kind of magic in the world if they're still completely in love.

Brick might be the first thing I believe in wholeheartedly, because for the first time I might be tapped into my whole heart.

"Miss? Can I help you?" I shake my brain back to reality and order a bunch of egg sandwiches, muffins, and coffee. I grab sugar packets. Other than lapping me up, copious amounts of sugar in his coffee is the only vice I can come up with for this guy. I do have a court appearance late this afternoon and will need all the caffeine. I scoop up all my stuff, bumping right into a man.

"Fancy meeting you here, counselor." Shit. "You look like you're seeing a ghost. What, no sugar for me? I thought we were friends."

I sputter out, "We are." He's oily and I should have seen it. I felt it from the start, but Brick didn't seem concerned. I put him out of my mind, but my instincts are never wrong. Brick was blinded by nostalgia and loyalty. I was blinded by Brick and too much *sweet tea*.

"What brings you to Vegas, Chase?"

He crowds me a little and the drink tray is the only thing between us. I could dump hot coffee on him and run, but I don't know what he wants. Or how he knew we were here.

"You neglected to tell me you was such a fancy lawyer with a big ole farm of sorts at your back, when we was swapping stories. I know all about your winemaking daddy and brother." I don't like him referring to my family.

"I didn't see the relevance in it, it's public record, and it's all over Google. It's not my f—" I pause as his hyena smile overtakes his face. He pushes closer to me, and I see the sheath beneath his jacket. He's not a gun guy and that knife terrifies me. Poor Fleabag.

"As you were saying." His sick tone snakes around his words, making a simple sentence sound menacing. I won't be underestimated. My lawyer's brain crackles, and I know how he found us. It's the only way, it's how he'd know where we were, right down to me being alone at Starbucks. It feels strange to go there in my mind, but I did sit with the FBI yesterday, listening to warnings and security measures. And Mark did tell us who pays Chase's bills.

"It's not my fault when you borrowed my phone to snap

a picture that you didn't google me. But you were busy planting a tracker instead. Pity it wasn't a bug, you could have heard an earful from the two of us."

"Watch yourself."

Thousands of people are walking by the restaurants off the casino floor passing with multicolored lanyards to some corporate thing and not one of them is observant enough to see I'm being threatened.

"You and your husband?" His eyes drift to my makeshift ring. He crowds me until I trip backward down a stair, and he pushes me into a backstage corridor.

I say, "If you'd shown up earlier you could have been the best man, seeing how the two of you have such history. *Almost like kin* was the phrase you used."

His voice gets low, and his face is in mine. The drink tray shakes as I attempt to hold on. Acid is burning my stomach and crawling up my throat. I push the fear down so I can get out of this. I'm going to survive because I have to bury this fucker and protect Brick.

He yanks the tray and tosses it down the hallway. And now, aside from being terrified, I'm also pissed. I need that caffeine.

He presses in closer, now I'm unarmed, so to speak, and I'm still shaking.

"I don't like lawyers. I don't like people asking questions. Your job is to fail. Do you fucking understand? You send your husband to jail for the murder of that woman."

I nod my head.

"Good. Let him do the time and your life continues on. You'll have conjugal visits to keep the home fires burning."

"Chase? Why not kill him instead of her?" I need confirmation. I'm an idiot for pushing this further but I need information to protect Brick.

"You accusing, chere?" Where Brick's accent is honeyed and sweet, his is acrid and rough.

"Why not just kill Brick if you want him out of the picture? We all know you killed his grandmother who you loved dearly? Why the circus of a trial where he could get off?"

I've been a badass most of my life in the courtroom but then his strong hand wraps around my upper arm in a death grip. I realize, we're not fighting with words. The sharp and insistent point pokes my stomach.

"That's not my call." He's Cady's bitch.

"You cut her up." I gasp.

"I'll carve you too when time's right. Like I did precious fucking Mimi Tinker. May hap, nick a coupla your loved ones along the way. Stop asking fucking questions. You holler at that judge what we tell ya. Or next time we gonna have less of a civilized conversation."

I'm numb. His best friend killed her cruelly. She knew pain before she died, and I can't tell him. Brick will never bounce back knowing she died in such a horrible way. I want to yell, "cut me and not them." Not any of the 5 or Brick. I do nothing but stare at him and wonder how this will end. His knife tip feels like acid as it sits there. His nostrils are flaring and I'm speechless.

Chase jogs away into the bowels of the hotel. I slide down the wall and pull my knees up. I can't stop shaking. I don't know if I was incredibly stupid or brave. Perhaps they're the same thing, but I don't want to be here. I want Brick.

I SIT ON THE EDGE OF THE BED A VIBRATING, HEART palpitating mess. I concentrated on the carpet in front of me one step at a time. I don't know how long it took me to get here. Brick reaches out and hauls me to him. I can almost pretend nothing happened as he spoons me. His hand moves under my hoodie then Brick flips me over. He whips my clothes off dusting his fingers over my skin. He runs to the bathroom and grabs a damp washcloth, placing it over my stomach. His eyes are hardened into steel, and I don't know what I've done wrong.

"Baby. Why are you bleeding?"

"I didn't know I was. I'm sorry."

I look away from him and everything in me evacuates my system as he grabs the ice bucket and catches it. He wipes my face with my t-shirt.

"Rebecca, listen to only my voice. You're so cold. You're in shock, baby. I'm going to lay you down and put your feet up, but you need to breathe with me, darling. In and out slowly for me. I've got you."

"But who's got you?"

# CHAPTER 32
## BRICK

'm pushing the panic and cocksure notion that I know exactly who did this down. It's not a deep wound but enough to bleed up a washcloth or two. I reckon, I'm gonna have to return the favor. It's a real eye for an eye situation we got going. No one touches her, ever. I will end him.

I flip into military mode and find the burner Mark left for emergencies. I plunk out a series of letters and pray he's able to figure out the cipher. Then break the phone in half and drown the SIM card in her puke and place it out in the hallway.

I rush back to her. Her heart rate is back, and that sweet rose blush is creeping onto those high cheekbones of hers. Her eyes are shut, and her chest is rising and falling in a rhythm I want to dance to for the rest of my days. No one will fucking hurt her or take her from me.

I grab a new t-shirt and place it next to her. I lift the towel and the blood has slowed. I slip into my duffle and unzip that secret compartment I had created in all my bags. I bypass the passports and extra money and find my version of a first aid kit.

I cut some fresh gauze and soap up a non-fiber cloth with Betadine. She moves but I hold her in place. Her lithe and beautiful body has been sapped of all adrenaline, and her crash will be epic. I'm not sure what to do about her court appearance today, but I don't give a shit about anyone but her. Once she's disinfected and washed, I apply a bit of Dermabond to seal it over. It's possible she needs a stitch or two, but this miracle glue has healed me from worse.

"Honey, this is gonna pinch." I flip the cap and hold her in place as I jab her with an antibiotic shot. She says nothing but moans.

As I hold her still so the Dermabond can set, I have few moments to ponder what the hell is happening. I only hope she played delicate flower instead of the steel magnolia I know she can be. It's a skilled knife cut meant to alarm not harm. Saints above, I need her to be ok. The hotel phone rings.

I pick it up, it can only be Mark. "Yes."

"He's gone. You should be too." And he hangs up.

My worst fears are confirmed. I stomp out of the room and try to calm down. I'm a raging mess of junkyard dogs and redneck justice. I want him in slow pain for treating her like a pin cushion. The world can do without me, but she's a different story. Her brand of magic deserves to be here.

I toss all our stuff in my bag and place her simple wedding dress carefully over her head. The bandage is holding well but I don't want to risk it none by getting a waistband involved. I know she'd be horrified at being in the same clothes, but she looks stunning. I hold her to me and she's waking up a touch.

"Becca, honey. We have to go."

"Brick," she whispers.

"Baby, you're ok. Your body's exhausted."

"Brick, I want you."

"Music to my ears as that is, I'm afraid for the only time in our marriage, I'm going to have to deny that request." She's limp and spent and I have to get us the fuck out of here.

"No. I need you. I don't know. The muffins are gone." Her brain is shattered for a moment.

I whisper to her, "Stop trying to make sense of scribbles."

Her voice gets panicky. "Scribbles is fine. Don't touch Scribbles. She's fine, right?"

"Hummingbird, I was speaking in a metaphorical manner, but you seem to think it's a person. Everyone is right as rain, except you. But if you need me to look after this Scribbles character, I will."

"She's the only one who likes me." Her brain is fried. I have to get her back to her bed.

I get her to stand and hoist our bag on my shoulder. "Just come with me and try not to look too drunk."

She can barely walk, she's wobbly as hell. As we get to the floor her knees buckle. I pick her up and rest her head on my shoulder and carry her out to the portico. It's Vegas, no one's looking at us. I'm scanning the horizon for anyone I recognize. I'd have to fucking kill them, and I don't want to do that today.

I hitch her up as we hit the outside and walk toward a cab.

"She ok?"

"The wife had a real good time in Vegas. Take us to Henderson Executive airport, and if you don't care about tickets, I'd appreciate it."

"Yes, sir."

I sit back and pull her to me. She rouses and stares at me. I smile.

"For the record, Hummingbird, this Scribbles character isn't the only one who likes you."

"She loves me," she says dreamily

"She ain't alone."

WE'RE PULLING INTO HER DRIVEWAY WHEN SHE finally gets her faculties about her.

"Morning."

"Chase." Her voice is dry and rough. She shakes her head as if clearing all the cobwebs of shock and newly-wedded bliss.

"Chase what, darling?"

"Chase. He killed your Mimi Tinker. He did it himself. He cut that girl, Mimi Tinker, and Fleabag. He did it all. And he followed us to Vegas and it's my fault."

I put the truck in park and bounce out so I don't crush the steering wheel. I scream and punch the side of my truck. My hand is doing more damage to the metal than vice versa. Fuck me. I didn't want it to be true. I know all signs point to him, but when did he go corrupt? When did he cross the county line into unscrupulous and dangerous? He's going to die for what he did, fuck Mark and Sal. I'm not waiting for shit. I'll lure his deplorable ass here and fucking kill him. Not just for my Mimi Tinker or the poor woman he carved up and left in my truck, but for daring to touch Becca, he dies slowly.

Flashes of my training and background pop out of their

hidey hole deep in my brain. Things I don't talk about or feel guilty for because they were the right thing to do, but I am prepared to be judged for those acts if and when I meet my maker.

But what I do to Chase Carlyle will be calculated, cruel, and vengeful. I didn't think anything could take down my mood or rattle my cage anymore, but I am an unleashed beast. Her scent surrounds me, then her delicate hand wraps around my middle and her head is on my back. And instantly I'm calm. I'll never deserve her, but I will take comfort, pleasure, and grace in her arms for as long as she'll have me. My wife.

"Are you ok?"

"I don't think that's a question you want to ask," I say.

"Fine. Are you going to punch metal again?"

"Not planning on it." I twirl around so I can hold her to me. "But the day is young, you never know."

"There's a tracker in my phone somehow."

"Christ, he was fiddling with it the other night and counted on me being stupid on nostalgia. I gave the fox the key to the hen house."

She pushes me away for a moment. "We controlled the last arrest, they're in control now. They'll file right before five on Friday and you'll spend the weekend in an actual prison. I won't have access to the arrest report, the charges, or their evidence until you're already locked up."

"That's pretty damn shady."

"It's what I would have done. I need to file a motion in court for this banking thing, then I'm going to refer the case out. You have to surrender."

"You'll do no such thing. Get it moved." I react as a caveman, and I realize it, but there's nothing I can do to stop it from happening.

She bristles and raises an eyebrow. "It will take half an hour, and I'm perfectly capable of working. I've already fucked up enough for one lifetime, it's time I set it right. Then I have to stop by my parents' house in Sonoma. Wanna meet the folks before your arrest?"

"I guess I'm going to have to, considering you don't leave my side until I can get some safety measures put into place."

She pulls me closer to her and says, "By my side as I go to the courthouse and you're a wanted man?"

"I'll wear a mustache."

"So, I'm an abettor now."

I laugh at her and smile. "You're just a wifey." She hits me gently and then winces. "Stay here." I reach across to the passenger seat for her phone.

I place it under the wheel of my truck and reverse over it. I know he knows where she lives but I want him to know I got his message.

I grab our bag from the truck and head to her door, punching in the code and turning back towards her.

"How do you know that?"

"Mel. But more importantly, your security is shit. Things are changing around here now." She chuckles a little but has no idea this is calm before the shitstorm. I can fucking feel it like a phantom pain, something's off. Something ain't where it's supposed to be, and it's gonna scratch at me until I figure it out.

# CHAPTER 33
## BECCA

He's on my heels and ass and will be until Mark finds Chase or Brick's in jail. I got the bench warrant dismissed after I filed a motion with a lower court stating he's dealing with emergency family issues. He wasn't on bail, not a flight risk-ish, and it was ego stroking, dick sucking by the DA's office. I bolstered Brick's upcoming case with a couple of public record motions I'll pull last minute for the hearing. But they have yet to present new evidence other than she died. They have it, but they can't remand him to jail without showing their hand. It was all scare tactics, and I'm only afraid of that knife and telling my family I got married in Vegas to a virtual stranger.

I didn't tell Brick about Cady's demand or Chase's threat. I filed this paperwork to let them know I'm not fucking taking a dive and sending Brick to jail. I can barely stand when he's in another room, so being locked away from me is not a fucking option. Jesus, that flipped fast. It's the black and white of things. I guess I may be resistant to change, immoveable on some points, and kind of obtuse to human emotions, but once I'm in—I'm all the fuck in.

"Mom, are you here?" I smell mac and cheese which means my favorite person is here.

"Bec! Bec! Ebeebody come quick. Daddy. Bec is at Nana's house! My aunt Bec!!!"

Sadie barrels around the corner, then stops because there's a giant tattooed man at my back. She twirls, then yells, "DADDY! There's a man with drawings like you."

I squat down and open my arms. "Come here, Scribbles."

Bricks says at my back, "This is Scribbles?"

"It's a long story, but this is my niece, Sadie. Sadie, this is, well, um." I don't know what to say here, so he fills in the blanks as he squats. I'm hugging her and he puts out his hand.

"I'm Uncle Brick, mighty proud to meet you. I don't have much family to speak of, but I'd be honored to be your friend."

"You're still around?" My brother comes around the corner holding a pink stuffed squirrel.

Brick stands. "You do know she's my attorney, right? It's kind of all over the news."

"I don't read much." David shakes his hand.

"No shit." I stand and lift Sadie.

"Sssssit!" Sadie repeats.

"You know, Nat's going to blame me for her knowing a new word," David scolds me, and I love it.

"Sadie, surely you've heard that word before. That's a Daddy word."

She giggles. I turn into the living room and run into my dad. My mom enters from the kitchen.

I kiss my father's cheek and he tickles Sadie, who reaches for him. Brick leans in and I whisper in his ear.

"That little girl's been doted on since the moment she showed up in our lives abandoned on our family winery's bar. All the note said was David was her dad. Took us all a moment not to hate her mom. She did it shitty, but she did what she needed to do. Scribbles is Sadie."

He smiles at her. "Ms. Sadie, it's an honor to meet someone who loves her auntie so much."

"She's a aunt. Not a auntie, dat's different."

I laugh. "Yes, that's a very different thing. Good job, Sadie. It's hard to remember it all." I let Brick in on a little more of our five families lore. "The Aunties are what we call all our mothers as a collective. They're a fierce bunch, good luck."

Brick whispers, "I remember. I'm still a little afraid of Tabitha's mom."

"Goldie's a sweetie, but good with curses." I laugh and his eyes get wide.

My father interrupts, "Becca. It's been ages."

I quip right back, "I saw you a week ago. Remember, I'm the responsible adult redhead you sired."

His eyes are fixated on Brick. I ignore it and move towards my mother.

Aunt Tina enters the room, and her eyes bug out of her head. I've got a love-hate thing with her. She's cranky and gossipy, which I love, but also vindictive and petty. Her daughter, Poppy, at her worst, emulates her mother sometimes. At her best, she's evocative of her name, bright, light, and cheery.

I hand my father the papers to put David's part of the

winery in trust for Sadie and his upcoming spawn. The rest is divided equally between Poppy and myself. I leave Brick in the foyer with David while Sadie traces his arms. She does it to her dad all the time. Brick's showing her the magnolia on his shoulder.

My father moves swiftly towards Brick, but David puts his hands up, telling me he's got this.

"Weren't you the villain?" My dad, ever the asshole.

Brick straightens up and Sadie scampers away. "Sir, I'm mighty sorry about all that. Once I understood what was happening, I made sure I tucked tail and headed home. You bested the best. You should be proud." He's brilliantly buttering up my father.

My brother comes up behind me and whispers in my ear, "Your crack and your face appear more relaxed."

I hiss back to him while my mother officially meets Brick, and we all stand to the side while Aunt Tina scrutinizes all of it.

David whispers in my ear, "You got fucked. You fucked that giant magnolia tree in our foyer."

"It's more of a cottonwood branch if you must know." I flip him off with my left hand and as I do it, I realize what a mistake I've made. I didn't take it off. Wasn't going to tell them yet. I never get away with anything.

"Becca, darling sister of mine. You *married* him? Congratulations!" He's loud and then sticks out his tongue so only I can see.

"Sadie, time to celebrate!" She begins a rudimentary squealing beat box and David dances a bit with her.

All conversation stops and everyone stares at me with slack jaws except Brick. He's got a shit-eating grin on his face. He's enjoying this way too much. David picks up his daughter and they bring a hush to the crowd.

I shrug. "Oh, yeah, he's my husband." Everyone in the room, including Sadie, speaks at once. I head towards the kitchen to grab a snack.

"Get back here, Rebecca," my father bellows, but I don't even break stride. David's faster than me and in front of me.

"This is fucking awesome. They're going to be so pissed at you they'll finally forgive me for knocking up a stranger and eloping."

"They LOVE Sadie. And like Nat more than you."

"Everyone does, but it's me they keep giving the irresponsible digs to. Shockingly, I'm a freaking great father. But this time, Mom's gonna kill you and Aunt T looks like she's about to swallow her tongue."

"She did go a bit pale." We both burst out laughing.

"I think she wants to fuck your husband," David spits out.

"Who wouldn't?" I laugh as I say it.

"True story. He's hot as fuck." David tears up he's laughing so hard.

"It's the reason I married him."

David bends over laughing. "You're so goddamned practical. You married a guy so you could legally fuck him, didn't you?"

"Kind of."

"You're so fucking uptight."

I look at him and I can barely get out my words, "Not anymore."

We roar with hysterics as my family enters the room. The two of us can't stop. I'm doubled over trying to catch my breath.

Our mother lifts my finger to the light as Poppy enters the back door.

"WHY IS THERE A RING? And why is David laughing?" And the two of us guffaw again trying to contain it.

Pop's mother offers up, "Because she married the thug who tried to take our wineries." Poppy skips over to me and inspects.

"Brick?" I nod. Poppy continues, "Very good taste in diamonds. This piece is bigger than that rock of Gibraltar Josh gave Elle. Clarity is fab and the setting is so classic. Very you. Nice job, sir."

I turn to the door of the kitchen and filling the doorway is my "I can't believe I married him" husband. I sigh and David bumps my hip.

Poppy looks to Brick. "This is what, three karats?"

"3.4 karats." There's a gasp. I know it's a piece of glass crap he picked up at the wedding chapel. But it's square cut and kind of old-school with tiny little crystals in the inlay on the side. It's something I would have picked for myself. I let them believe it's real, who cares?

He grins and crosses his arms over his chest, his hummingbird on full display. The amusement is gone from his eyes, he's just staring at me and my family with a sense of wonder.

Then my father breaks the spell. "I don't care for this shit one bit. This isn't like you, Rebecca. I thought you were smarter than to marry a thug in a flashy suit." He's currently wearing black jeans and a blue t-shirt. "I raised you to be more than this and I'm ashamed and furious I'm going to have to undo this mess."

"Can we all stop calling my husband a thug?" Everyone starts up again, and I look over as David sits down in a kitchen chair, puts his hands behind his head, and leans the chair back smiling. This is the first time he's ever been the gray sheep instead of the black one.

I spin around and my mom's crying. "Mom. I'm so sorry."

She hugs me and sobs on my shoulder. "I'm so happy you have love in your life."

There's a pause in the chatter. Brick's voice cuts through the din. "Ma'am, she does. And I'll do my best to honor, protect, and love her the best way I know how." My heart flutters and my breath gets ragged as I breathe out.

"I'm so happy for you. I'm so sorry you thought you had to hide it." My mother hugs me and Poppy squeals and claps like an overtrained seal.

My mother scolds my father, "Artie, you get on board with this right now. Your daughter is glowing."

His entire face softens as he says, "Yes, my love."

Magic.

My mom is forever the optimist. "This is so romantic. I want to hear all of this!"

Oh shit. Well, I guess we'll see if the story we concocted last night will hold water. My mom moves to Brick and opens her arms.

"You're wonderful. Simply wonderful, Brick. So charming and you love our Rebecca. That's a thing I didn't see coming." Then she sobs again. My mother does love surprises and celebrations. I don't ever have to give her another gift in life.

"Are you fucking kidding me? That's it. You're apologizing to her for denying you the opportunity to throw a lavish party and be the center of attention." David stamps his foot. This is my favorite part. "You're sorry because she hid a relationship that was this important to her. This is bullshit." Sadie is weaving between our legs and twirls in a circle.

She says, "Bullsssit," as she scrambles up on David's lap.

Poppy crosses her arms and rolls her eyes. "Father of the year."

DAVID AND BRICK DISAPPEAR, AND THE WOMEN FOLK attack me. I hate every second of discussing dresses and dates. I don't adore the spotlight, except in the courtroom and that's only because of my pathological need to be right.

"Enough. Plan whatever you want. Leave me out of it."

Poppy says, "You are getting a celebration, even if we drag you there to be the center of it. Some of us will never get this moment, so you get to have a giant party to remind us the world is a good place and you have found your missing piece. Shut the hell up and show up where and when we tell you to."

I growl at my cousin. I know it's a veiled comment. She can never have a big wedding with Sal. Not until he's free from his life. They won't even admit they're dating. I escape and as I reach the kitchen door, I say, "Fine." I point to my mother. "This is for you. And only the 5. No other guests. Just our circus of family and friend network. That's IT. And I'd like an Olive Street Bakery cake please."

Poppy thrusts her hips forward and pumps her fists. "Yes!"

# CHAPTER 34

# BRICK

"Y'all really know how to welcome kin."

David slaps my back. I grin as David says, "You shoot hoops?"

"Been known to toss the rock a time or two. You itching for a beat down?" David laughs, as do I. I know all about his all-star college career and his almost NBA life. I'll have my backside handed to me, but maybe, he'll have an off day.

"Cool. Meet us out at Pro/Ho on Thursday night. We play a pickup game with whoever shows up. This week should be a bunch of locals and possibly an internationally famous popstar. Who I thought would be an asshole but turns out Ian Reilly can hang. Little Ingrid Schroeder hooked us up with someone we can stand. And there's beer and Mary's pizza shack pesto breadsticks."

"I don't think I've had the pleasure."

"Then allow me to change your life, and your carb intake." He pats my stomach and I wince a little, not used to intimate gestures from men. But it's something I could get behind. However, the last friend I thought was a ride or die threatened Becks and killed my grandmother, but I'm guessing David might not have that level of evil in him.

I squeeze his shoulder. "Thanks, man."

"Least I can do since I finally have a fucking brother in this family."

"What about Poppy, isn't she with—"

"Shh. Nope, we never say the S word in reference to my cousin. Worst kept secret, but we all play along."

I nod. "I don't want to step out on a bad foot with any of y'all. I've always lived by a code of right and wrong, but I can't say I've painted in the lines all that time."

David follows me out to the truck and doesn't say anything for a moment. "Are you proud of the man you are?"

"Yes," I respond honestly.

"Were those things done in service to others?"

"Yes, sir. I'm not wired any other way." I cross my arms.

"Love my pain in the ass sister?"

I laugh hard. "Very much, sir."

"Seriously?" He laughs and says, "Then we have no issue." He yells back from the front door, "See you Thursday."

I'm waiting out front for my wife when the newest burner rings. I know I've got some damage repair to do. I pick it up.

I speak without a greeting. "Now, I know what you're getting at, but we have a plan."

Mark roars, "Low profile. Be seen. Keep it respectful. You fucking married her?"

I knew this would all boomerang, but I had no idea how fast this would all bite me in the ass. "Mind yourself, now. I respect you and the authority you have, but I will not be cast the fool simply because of my accent. They threatened her. I need her. And I'm in love with her. I'm not gonna be doing anything to put any of us in jeopardy, but if you think it through, simply because it's not your plan don't make it a terrible plan."

"Continue."

"If we get it all out in the open, they'll come after me, but they can't because it's in the open. They'll get sloppy and we pick up the pieces."

"Sloppy gets people killed."

"Ain't no one getting killed on our watch, but remember although we're aligned, not all of our goals and outcomes match up."

"I want Cady."

"And I do too, but I also want to protect my wife." I grin just thinking that. "I want to spend zero time in jail. And I want justice for my grandmother. Ultimately, I'd like to bring down that fucker like a house of cards, but for now let's focus on the immediate. I need Chase. You're a patient guy, you do stakeouts and shit. I'm a slow burn of a man, myself, one who can wait for it to all fall into place the way it needs to, but not this time. I won't be a pawn and I will not let my queen be taken. Ya, hear me? I'm not one for repeating."

There's silence on the other end.

"I respect that. I'll be in touch."

The phone goes dead, and I break it in half. I'll move onto the next one and toss the pieces out along the way to our next destination. Which I hope will be inside my wife. I'm itching because it's the only place that makes any kind of sense.

I text Lucille on the next burner phone.

*UNKNOWN NUMBER: Sweet mama, you need to know our jumpy friend done us dirty. He's the one.*

*LUCILLE: Boy, you talking nonsense to me. And call me proper.*

*UNKNOWN NUMBER: Can't but will soon. And I married that girl.*

*LUCILLE: Then get your puny ass back here so I can toss you some love and a boil to end all boils.*

*UNKNOWN NUMBER: In a while. Be careful now, you're one of the only things I got left. Do as people tell you. Ya hear?*

*LUCILLE: I ain't nothing but an old fool, but I do love your dumb ass.*

I pace around the truck waiting on my woman. If Chase is dirty and working contract for Cady, then Sal's nephew must be the one pulling the stateside strings? I need to go back to the roadhouse, someone very large had to drag my 6'5" frame into my truck. And I may not be as big as I used to be, but I'm fit as hell. There's a lot to take down. And someone brought the woman. And somewhere there's evidence of them returning my loaner car to the auto shop. I call Mel.

"What's up, tree trunk?"

"What in the hell does that mean?"

"Your arms are tree trunks." Trees again.

"Clever. Y'all should take up a comedy career. I need footage from traffic cameras all around the garage."

"Already done but I didn't look since it's technically illegal."

"Of course, and don't tell Becca."

"The wife?"

"Damn, you're good."

"You don't think that shit popped to an alert the moment you made it legal? Also, I imagine boning you would be good for Becca."

"It's a two-way street. Scan the footage. We need to know who the fuck picked up my truck."

# CHAPTER 35
## BECCA

As I bolt from the house with a head of steam and a vague notion of dislike for my family, I blurt out, "I'm so sorry. They can be snarky."

David yells from behind me, "You know we can fucking hear you."

"Ducking hear you, Aunt Becca!" Sadie mirrors him and we both laugh.

I'm greeted with a smile that breaks me apart every time. It's like Christmas morning in his eyes.

He takes me into his arms. "Darling, it's all a little hazy around me until you step into my field of vison. Then everything snaps into focus. How do you do that?" He's grinning at me, and I kiss him lightly.

"Mojo."

He leans down to my ear and whispers, "We've spent too much time in our clothes, Hummingbird. What do you say we take a moment to strip down and reward ourselves for a productive morning?"

I laugh at him. "Mel filed an updated witness list, including our best friend, Chase Carlyle. But I have an idea how to draw out the rest of the players." Chase is the sort of man who craves feeling powerful. That's why he was bragging and confessing to me. I'm sure Cy knows everything that piece of garbage has done. I want to rattle him into making a mistake. And want him to know that aside from this military hunk of a giant man at my back, you don't fuck with me. I may have trembled and ran from him, but that's not who I am and it's time Chase fucking figured that out.

"That wise?"

"Probably not, but I will not be bullied into submission or fear, and I can protect the people in my life too. It puts him on the DA's radar without drawing direct attention to him." I kiss him on his cheek, and he growls. "You have to drive carefully."

He laughs at me, but I'm serious. "Is that your love language there, Hummingbird?"

"No, I just think you should be careful driving." I'm confused why this has become a thing. What's to not understand?

He holds open the truck's door and I climb in, aware my entire family's watching me through the window like some sort of sitcom goodbye. I wave but only to Sadie. She blows me a kiss and it warms a part of my heart that only belongs to her. I don't function well with children, except Sadie. As for the child Natalie is currently carrying, it's a wait and see situation.

Brick slides into the driver's seat and the way his body moves is graceful and powerful, even doing something as benign as getting into a car. We pull out of the driveway and we're not even a mile down the road when he pulls under a tree on the side of Highway 12.

"Come on over here and give me some of that sweet honeysuckle lip service."

I peck his lips. But before I can draw back to my seat, he captures me with one hand behind my head, anchoring me to him. His kiss is open and aggressive.

My tongue is automatically tangling with his and dancing in and out of our mouths. I gasp and moan as we maneuver closer, and everything dissolves around me, including my sense of decorum. My pussy clenches when his strong hand clamps my thigh and claims me in one small motion. Fuck. His thumb rubs the crease in my inner thigh.

I gasp and his hand moves inward, tucking a finger under my thong and searching for my clit.

"Take me home. We're on the side of the road."

"Well, if you weren't such a rabid temptress, we wouldn't be in this situation."

I laugh. "What situation is that?"

He kisses me so deep, it's like he's trying to remind me of how deep I can suck his cock.

He draws back and stares at my chest as it reddens up. "Quit getting me hard all the goddamned time."

"How fast can you make it to Napa?" I put my hand on his upper thigh and he moans. I need him inside of me as fast as possible.

"Not fast enough, darling. I'm cocksure of that." I burst into laughter. Then he says, "Is Mel at the house?" Shit.

He glances over as he pulls into traffic, and I groan loudly. "Imma take that as a yes, so I'm going to tuck back my wonder cock and think about cilantro." I belly laugh. "I fucking hate cilantro. Gets me angry how much of it people use or how in love with that weed they are. It don't have use for it, excepting making everything good taste like soap."

I can't stop laughing as he crests up over the Carneros Valley, headed over to Napa from Sonoma.

"I NEED TO FILE A CONTINUANCE ON THE BOWERS dispute."

"I got you. I'm wrapping things up at your house, then I gots to get me a meatball sub and go find my wife. It's been a couple of hours since I felt her up."

"You know I don't need all that information."

"Both are a real handful and mouthful." I roll my eyes at Mel's confession and toss it out of my memory. She's insanely inappropriate and socially awkward. Then I scoff at my own thought, we all are in our own way.

"Fine. Enjoy your—lunch." I hang up and turn to Brick. He's humming some simple song that probably has its roots in country and western music.

"Those wheels are turning awfully loud, now. Give me your questions, Hummingbird, because there's no talking when we get home. Unless it's, 'Brick, you're the best. Fuck me harder, Brick. I've been an idiot sitting around waiting for you when I could have been out hunting you down, Brick.'"

I giggle. "I'm so exhausted my thoughts are going to come out blunt and unfeeling."

"Not sure you're aware of your everyday demeanor sometimes. I see you underneath that pile of wood you've chopped for yourself. Built it up tall and sturdy with plenty of hiding space behind it. I know the soft center of you. So, despite what you think, you almost always come off as blunt. I like it."

"You like my obnoxious traits?"

"When I said I loved you, I didn't just mean part of you. I married all of you and not just for that golden pussy of yours."

I stare at him and grin and shake my head. I don't know what to do with him, where to place him in my life and brain. Everything had a neat little order and place like a well-thought-out garden and now he's running amok through my flower beds and pulling up the carrots.

I sit back and say, "How are you this kind when the world has been so cruel to you?"

"I had a good teacher who reminded me every day of the power of gratitude and grit." His grandmother comes to mind, and I'm overwhelmed with gratitude she cared for this man the way she did. I need those fuckers to rot in hell.

As Brick turns into my driveway and we wait for the garage door to open, things slow down and speed up at the same time. I open the door to the truck, Brick shouts, and the door slams back as glass showers around us. My brain can't understand any of it. I feel the intense heat and I'm on the floor of the truck and Brick is cut. There's blood. There was a loud sound and now muted, muffled noises through the constant ringing. I don't move because I'm not sure I can. My system is flooded with adrenaline and nausea again.

I can't sense him. An acrid singe of smoke is covering me, and I can't shake it. I can't get on the other side of the sound and smell. Then I see nothing.

# CHAPTER 36
## BRICK

'm instinct and sinew. I am gut and purpose. I shift into the machine that assesses and calculates odds and situations in a flash of an easy trigger pull. I push the desperate down and work to save everyone.

I rip her out of the car in a matter of moments and place her on the lawn across the street, knowing that shock is all my Hummingbird's gonna suffer. My triage of the situation states my attention should be on the empty VW bug parked on the side of Becca's street. It shouldn't be here. She's supposed to be gone. I quickly assess the best course of action. The office has to be the ignition point. I pray there's no bad news today for Ms. Mel.

The front door isn't hot yet, but the keypad won't work. I kick it open and step back, letting the black smoke spill into the calm around us. The neighbors are out, and on their phones, not sure if they're taping me or calling the fire department, but I have no mind for them.

I remove my t-shirt, wrap it around my face and rush forward, scanning the perimeter of her dining room and living room. Flames are lapping at the curtains and

247

engulfing the couches. The back of the den has been blown out. I rush to the kitchen. I open the back door to get rid of the pressure building to avoid a nasty backdraft. The ceiling is going to give way on the other side of the house, but the kitchen is still relatively fine. I scream down the back hall-way, while there's oxygen. It's smoke filled but no flames. Something darts behind me and out the back door and I know Lil' Bit is taking care of herself.

"MEL! MS. MEL, IF YOU CAN HEAR ME, BREAK SOMETHING. DON'T YELL. MAKE SOME MUTHAFUCKING NOISE. I KNOW YOU CAN. MEL, BREAK SOMETHING, PLEASE. FUCKING BREAK SOMETHING." I dart to the back hallway hoping to get to the office, but it's a precarious path. Sirens are wailing, but they'll be too late to save her, and they'll make me leave. I don't leave a man behind.

"MEL, it's now. Now is your moment to save yourself and me. NOW! MEL. TELL ME WHERE YOU ARE. MAKE SOME MUTHAFUCKING NOISE. BREAK SOMETHING RIGHT THE FUCK NOW."

I get low to avoid a waft of smoke. It's chemical, I can smell it and I'm sure there are accelerants all over the house to make sure it all goes down. We have moments until those flames find their next path to destruction and I have no hope.

Fucking hot. I squint my eyes shut trying to clear them. I have to get her and get the fuck out of here. In about a minute, I have to get the fuck out of here. It's too much. Shit. And then there's a crash halfway down the hallway coming from the little bathroom. Her office and that wall are all but gone, but the bathroom remains. I crawl down the increasingly dark hallway and I'm grateful the doorknob is cooler than a summer day but not quite cold.

I open the door and Mel's on the ground barely conscious, the bathroom mirror broken all around her as well as the plunger she must have hurled at the mirror. Cuts dot her face. She must have been blown back by the explosion but protected by this room. I scramble to her and there's a deep gash in her leg, lord knows how, but again, you want me by your side for this shit. I was built for this. I rip a towel in half and tie it above the wound as tight as I can to try and stop the flow of blood. And now the smoke is getting to me, a wall of pain hitting my face and lungs. Each breath is harder. The noise, no one talks about how fucking loud a fire is. My nerves ping all at once and I'm a fucking rocket. Hurling her up onto my shoulder and running as fast as I fucking can down the hall, around the fiery staircase, and out through the back of the kitchen to clearer air. But I don't stop running until I've hit the other side of the street, because I heard the hiss.

I heard the snake of the fire winding its way up that staircase and it's a matter of seconds before my sweet Rebecca's bedroom explodes and bursts into impossible flames and the roof is blown out.

First responders rush to Mel. I don't know when she passed out, but I'm so relieved they have her. I pop up on the balls of my feet, discarding my blackened makeshift mask. I gulp in as much good air as I can and cough out the bad.

"Sir, follow me. I need to check you." I frantically scan the crowd. The firemen are moving my truck out of the driveway, and I see the remains of her car in the garage. "Sir. You've been through something. You need oxygen. This is vitally important."

I walk away, there's too much chatter and anger coming from behind me but there's nothing I need more than her. I panic that the explosion is a diversion. I weighed those odds, and I took the risk to go and grab Melissa. But did they take her? Christ. I'm running through the crowd and on the far side of the scene, she's surrounded by first responders and police. I push people out of the way to get to her. They put a hand on her to stop her from getting to me, but she shakes them off and runs at full speed to me. I open my arms and catch her and pull her as close as possible. She's shaking and I hold her closer. She's sobbing and I'm kissing her cheeks.

"You're ok. We're ok. I found Mel in time. You're ok, darling. I got you and I'm not going to let anything happen to you. Nothing's going to happen to you. It's all things." She sobs harder and her trembling gets worse. I panic until I realize, I'm the one shivering. I can't contain it and gasp out a tearless sob at what could have happened.

She's in my ear and saying, "You're ok. We're ok. I got you. I'm not going anywhere. You're all I have left. You're all I need. But the evidence is gone. The case is gone. I'm sorry."

I pull her back and stare at her.

"You pay that no mind, hear me? Right here is what we need, not some papers. Mel was bleeding pretty bad, and I gotta get checked out. Come with me."

"I have to tell them things." She points to the sheriff, police, and assorted others waiting on her.

"The story will be there. I need you more." Christ, do I need this woman by my side. I can't stop shaking and it's only in the cloud of being near her that I might find peace.

They've taken Mel to the hospital. And I sit on the edge of one of the rigs.

They shove some oxygen up my nose and I understand we have to make sure there's not some sneaky smoke problems gonna pop up later.

"Ms.?" Rebecca's cuddled in close to me.

"Mrs.," she responds and it's all the air I need.

The paramedic asks, "How are you not in shock?"

"I'm too fucking angry to be in shock."

"Fair enough. You don't appear to have any injuries except cuts and scrapes. You're lucky."

I put my arm around her. "The luckiest."

The firefighters are running around with hoses in full swing. The battalion chief comes close like he has things to say to us but is interrupted by a call.

"Fuck me. This is too much. We're already stretched. See if you can get Santa Rosa and Tiburon to send back up. We're going to be here a while. Christ, that café is too close to historic buildings. Get it the fuck under control."

I'm on the edge of my seat and Becca tightens up.

She gasps, "Poppy."

# CHAPTER 37
## BECCA

I slept in the hospital bed on top of that man. I didn't move an inch as we both passed out from the safety of our situation. Poppy and Sal were in the room next to ours and there were large, muscled men outside of both of our doors. Men, who with the crook of an eyebrow, wouldn't hesitate to hurt someone. That's so different from the world I live in it's hard to process, but I've never been so tired in my life. Sal bought out the floor from the hospital like it was the top floor of the Bellagio, had non-emergency patients moved, and fed the entire staff steak. I'm grateful to be in his sphere for the privacy and the care.

Mel lost an insane amount of blood and cut her Achilles tendon when the mirror shattered. I was informed in a loud manner by her wife, Tommi Schroeder, that Mel's retired. I get it. Good thing I only have one client, no office, and nowhere to live. Seems about right to lose my only employee. I'm so fucking grateful it wasn't worse.

Mel has to stay but the rest of us checked out this morning. I'm headed to Poppy's with insurance forms for the café. Brick has another breathing treatment and reassessment, so I'm doing this to keep my mind off things. I left him a note and he was finally sleeping when I left. Well, escorted to my car by Lou. He's a very large man who we all know as Sal's number two guy. He doesn't go anywhere without him unless Lou is protecting someone else for Sal. I'm grateful he's following me to Poppy's, but it's not necessary.

As I knock, I hear a loud and welcoming cackle of a newly pregnant, Tabitha Aganos.

I've known her since she was born, and she's always had this cackle. Whenever people call me blunt, I refer them to her. Well, she might not be blunt as much as she has zero filter and rather enjoys making everyone around her participate in her brand of chaos. I simply tell people how I see things; she forces them to see things her way.

Poppy is hustling around her mom's house, and it smells like she's cooking everything all at once.

"Pop."

Tabi mocks me. "Well, if it isn't married up, reckless, slutty Rebecca?" I laugh at her as she tosses her short black hair up into a scrunchie.

"That's the best you got? Nice haircut."

"This baby is sapping my cleverness. Seriously, congratulations and I'm terribly sorry about your house. Hey, we're both homeless."

Tabi's dilapidated farmhouse recently collapsed in on itself after an unfortunate overly amorous session with her husband and the bed fell through the floor.

"Losing your house was more fun," I say.

This is exactly what I need. I don't want to worry about all the millions of details pushing at the edges of my mind. The police have talked to me no less than five times about arson. And they're having a hard time believing that Mel didn't smell anything. I believe it, the girl is a wizard and observant in only two areas. Her family and food. She probably thought it was a new cleaner I was using.

I want to sit here and do nothing for a minute.

Poppy runs out and shoves a bowl of something at me.

"The walk-in freezers and the fridges didn't burn up, but they don't work. I sold as much of my inventory as I could but as for the rest. Mangia, per favore, mangia tutto."

She's given me a steaming bowl of pasta and I sit and eat it greedily. I'm not sure the last time I ate.

"You speak Italian now?" I raise an eyebrow.

Tabi says, "Pretty sure she swallows Italian too."

Poppy gasps, "Tabitha." Tab shrugs and I laugh at my cousin getting offended.

I ask the ladies, "Hey, did Elle and Josh name the new kid yet?"

"No. Josh keeps calling her Four."

Tabi fills in some gaps. "I think that's as good a name as any, there are too many people in that house."

I quip, "Says the woman with three boys and another baby on the way."

"Yeah, well, two of mine can wipe their own butts and do laundry. I think I win." Tabi shoots me a finger gun. I smile as she refers to her adopted boys, who I adore.

Tabi rubs her belly. "Poppy hasn't stopped moving."

She was opening the café when the explosion went off. It was more controlled than the one set at my house. Mine was set to destroy, hers to warn. Sal's going to create some kind of war room place, according to Brick. Poppy wasn't injured except for some scrapes and cuts. Sal forced her to stay overnight in the hospital. Brick's banged up and inhaled some smoke, but he's thankfully, fine.

"That fucking shit brickhouse of a man of yours, he's

like mercenary military seal hero. That's not a brand of man we have in high stock around here."

I shove more pasta in my mouth and let her talk. I'm sure eventually she'll have a point under all her snark, but I don't have to listen to the lead up.

She waves her fingers around and points. "Poppy, sit down. You're making me dizzy."

She appears in the doorframe. "I can't anymore. Not since he forced me to sit and spend the night in a hospital. I'm a mess." Just then, something attaches itself to my back. I shriek, stand up, and toss pasta into the air. It lands open bowl down and the two of them roar with laughter.

"Get this off. What the fuck is this? Ouch. It's sharp. Oh God. Is it like a raccoon? I fucking hate raccoons, they're shifty and so damn cavalier. Get off me, you smug bastard. So fucking smug with your masks. AHH. Get it off." Poppy's laughing so hard she can't concentrate on getting the animal off me. I twirl around but the thing hangs onto my back.

Tabi yells, "Relax." Poppy pulls it off and I flip around to see Calico in her arms.

"She found her way here, not sure how." This can't be the same fucking cat. We're at the back end of the vineyard where this Calico came from, but that cat ran out of my Napa house. That's a fucking trek. I take her from Poppy, and she purrs instantly. Holy shit. I whisper to the cat, "Lil' Bit?" and it purrs louder.

Tabi smirks. "And we didn't think you had the mothering instinct."

I shoot back at her, "Look who's fucking talking."

She pats her belly. "True."

Poppy stirs something else. "There's a war room and people are going to bed and there's so much going on I'm not allowed to know and now they all know, and no one will get to live a lovely life because I messed it all up."

She cries after her breakneck pace of word vomit. I swear to God she got all the Gelbert family emotions. David and I are pretty good at holding it all in, but Poppy lets everything out.

Tabi gestures to me and I wave her off. We're not the ones you want in the room when you fall apart. Breakdowns are usually handled by the Aunties, Elle, Ingrid, or Natalie. They're good at this shit. Tabi and I silently play rock, paper, scissors, and I lose.

I pat Poppy and she instantly stiffens.

"What are you doing?"

"Consoling you."

"Did you get hit in the head by debris? That's not something you're good at. You either." She points at Tabi, then shrugs. "Look, I needed to fall apart a bit. I'm better now."

Tabi puts her feet on the couch. "What's for dessert?" I glare at her. "What? You can't tell me you don't fucking smell that oil? There is some kind of fried pastry and I'm here for it. Fire it up, Pop."

It's strange but Tabi being herself pulls Poppy back to us. "Raspberry Zeppole. And I'll bring them right out. Does anyone want pot roast?"

"Seriously? You made a pot roast too?"

Tabi doesn't miss a beat. "Send it to the war room. I'm sure the generals are hungry."

Poppy says on her way out of the room, "They have two already, this is my backup."

Tabi quips, "Send it to Pro/Ho. We'll give away a slice with every bottle of 'What the F Happened? Red.'"

Their wines have the dumbest names. I'm sure that one was my brother's brilliant idea.

I say, "Solid marketing, but I'd run it past Elle and Evan before you throw in cash for that idea. How's Mel?" I ask.

Tabi answers, "Stable. She's still sedated so they can make sure the smoke stuff is cleared out and give her wounds a minute to calm down. They'll do surgery on the tendon in a day or two. Tommi's kind of a mess." That's her sister-in-law, of course she has the most up-to-date information. Their son is with Tommi's dad while she stays with Mel.

Poppy covers her heart and scurries out of the room.

I ask, "What's a war room and why are people going to bed?"

"Sal can't tell me things. But they're about to huddle in a secure space with a bunch of his men, and no one's allowed to leave or come in until Mark says we're all safe."

"You mean go to the mattresses, not go to bed. Do they think this is related to Sal's former businesses?" Even though he's working with the FBI, he can't outrun all of his past.

"His nephew is coming for him and somehow we got sloppy and now he knows the best way to take down Sal is to hurt me." Her voice is low and sad. Shit.

"This isn't your fault. Everyone is ok, Pop."

We all knew they were together, but they'd kept it quiet. Poppy blames herself, but I'm the one who taunted Cady with my witness list and dared him to pop out. It's my fault.

Tabi yells for her doughnuts. Poppy picks them up. "Stay here."

I glance into the living room and Tabi sits up, rubbing her hands together. "It's about damn time. The service at this restaurant sucks."

"Shut up, Tabitha," Poppy says with a smile.

"Thanks, Poppy. Hey, now that you and Sal are 'out' can I ask a question that's been killing me?"

I give her a look. "It's about his penis, isn't it?"

Tabi doesn't hesitate, "Of course it is. More long like an Italian sausage or a big fat cannoli? My money's on cannoli."

Poppy turns scarlet and turns back to the kitchen.

Tabi yells after her with a mouthful of Zeppole, "Definitely cannoli."

In the kitchen, I run my hands over the tawny stained oak of our grandmother's table. I remember rolling out cookies with Poppy under her guidance. Her nails were always done in a bright color, usually a hot pink, which matched the crystal sugar she'd give us to decorate. Her sugar cookies were always wafer thin and they'd snap when you ate them. Or sometimes we'd make her family recipe shortbread. We'd help her box them up with real silk ribbons for holiday presents.

I don't remember the last time I baked. It used to be something I loved because it was measured and controlled. Poppy's a good baker and great chef. In the kitchen she can improvise and be outrageous without drawing too much attention, just praise.

Poppy squeezes my shoulder. "I miss her too." Our grandmother was a spitfire and we're both blessed with her hair and spirit, we just use it in different ways.

"Why am I here? You're not ready to file your insurance claim."

Poppy exhales. "I'm so sorry. We're the distraction."

"What are you talking about?" I panic.

"Brick was discharged an hour ago." Poppy says sheepishly.

I leap from my chair. She pushes me back down. "Sal

took him to the mattress place in protective custody with Mark. It's to keep us safe."

"He's going to be furious. He needs to be with me."

Poppy smiles. "Sal said he'll make sure Brick knows you had nothing to do with this plan. You can lawyer, cross-examine thingy to me all you want, but I won't crack because I'm in the dark as well."

I unravel in an instant. I don't know how to function without him, he's a part of my everyday. Woah. That's the truth and it's crushing me. It's so odd when random moments line up and you realize they've become history. All those times I chose to be around him or do things for him or pick up food he might like, have been woven into our story over the past seven weeks.

He's never left me before and I didn't realize I'd gotten used to him. That I settled into a place where not only do I want him around, but I need him. I shake my head from the sappy thoughts and push them to the edges. I'll solve this.

"Poppy, this doesn't work for me. Let me talk to Sal. We'll be fine in a secret VRBOO. The fire set so much back, but the case still lives on the cloud. I pushed all my other cases to friends and colleagues because of the fire. Ironically, the judge said I don't have to be Brick's lawyer anymore, but I want to be. He won't go to jail anymore; he was a victim in the arson. But we need to prove it was Chase so we can be free of this. I know you have a way to contact him. Do it. I need to talk to Brick. I need to see him and know that he's ok. I can't do this." My cousin's eyes get wide. My voice has reached a fevered pitch and there are tears popping out of my eyes defying my will.

Poppy tries to talk me down. "Becca, it's going to be ok. I've never seen you like this."

"I've never been like this. Who will take out the garbage and empty the dishwasher?"

Tabi yells from the other room, "Wait, he looks like that, and he fucking empties the dishwasher. Marry him. Oh, shit. Never mind. I'm not helping."

I go to the archway and stare her down. "No, you're not."

Poppy takes my hand. "I know what you mean."

I throw my arms in the air and I'm unhinged. I'm crying. I don't fucking cry, and I know Poppy is probably disturbed by all of this, but this has been a week like no other and now he's hidden. I didn't tell him. I forgot. That's a lie, I didn't forget, I cowered away from it. My voice is crumbling, from fear and frustration. But mostly it's weak because I'm weak. I thought I knew how the world worked and I didn't. I have jack shit figured out about myself or the way things should be until he kissed me, dripping in my hallway. The Rebecca I always thought I could be was found in that moment.

I look at Poppy and say with a withering girly voice, which is a sound I didn't know I could make. "I thought I'd have time to tell him. I was indulgent and thought there'd be a perfect moment, but the moment didn't come because everything is the moment. Life is happening right now, not in a minute or a perfect second. It's now and everything we do is building it and I didn't tell him. And we have this together and I don't want to be apart from him. I don't want to be in a place of not knowing. I didn't tell him. I didn't know this was happening."

Poppy asks, "Tell him what?"

Tabi yells from the living room with a mouthful of pastry, "That the Tin Man got a heart. But seriously? Pop, she's literally the smartest of all of us. Remember when she felt the need to prove it by showing a graph of her IQ test compared to the rest of us? And you didn't realize what was happening, Bec?"

I yell at her, "Book SMART! I never claimed to be emotionally smart. And you're not a genius at that either. You're the mother of three screaming the word fuck throughout the house because you love them all so much."

She nods and I crumple on the floor between the kitchen and living room. Poppy envelopes me in a hug and it's nice. Poppy and I smile slowly at each other and laugh as Tabi keeps talking. "Elsa's heart is unfrozen. Mr. Darcy just snapped and can't keep his hands off Elizabeth."

We're laughing very hard now.

I nod and as my surefooted voice returns, I say, "I didn't tell him I love him."

Poppy throws her arms around me, and Tabi replies, "Fuck yeah, you do. And good lord that man is a smoke show."

Poppy speaks while I slowly stop leaking water. "It will be fine. If Sal contacts me, I'll let him know you need to talk to Brick. That's the best I can do, Cuz. In the meantime, get to know Murray."

I pull out of her arms, completely confused. "What the fuck? Who's Murray?"

Tabi yells from the other room, "I'm assuming he's the pit bull-looking muthafucker eating all my doughnuts."

"Zeppole," he says gruffly.

I look in the room. "Was he here the whole time?"

The women nod affirmative.

"What if I don't want a Murray?" I ask and gesture to the beefy man in the corner.

He shrugs. "Not your decision, toots."

Tabi looks at him. "Did you call her toots? Cliché

much? Dude, are you mob? Or like an actor hired to play a mobster. You're very convincing."

"I work at the pleasure of Mr. Salvatore Pietro, business owner."

Tabi smiles and says, "Business of what?"

"Business of business, there, nosy. Now, where do you need to go? Because I'd like to get the hell out of this hen house."

"Take me home, I guess."

Tabi says, "You know it's still smoldering."

"I know. Take me to Gelbert Family Winery."

Tabi laughs. "Ugh. An audience with Arthur." I nod as she mocks my father. He's an asshole but I love him. And I have nowhere else to go. I don't know where Brick's house is, and I don't want to stay with any of my friends or brother. I want to be in the comfort of my melon-colored room with the Spice Girls on the wall. I always said I loved Sporty because she was the practical one. Secretly, I wanted to be Scary Spice. And if people keep fucking with my family, I may just get my wish.

"Let's go, Murray. Time to meet the family." Poppy hands me seven Tupperware containers and Murray gets another four and a bag.

"Just a few things I made."

"Is that a ham?" Tabi asks, and Poppy waves her off.

"What, no lasagna?" I inquire.

Poppy says, "I'm so sorry, I was just—"

I interrupt her by kissing her on her cheek. "I'm teasing."

Tabi remarks, "It's a new fucking world when you're the one making the good jokes."

"It certainly is."

# CHAPTER 38
## BRICK

'm jumping around like oil in a hot pan, pacing this fucking warehouse. I've lapped it going on sixty times.

Lou and I shot some hoops out back and all it did was make me miss Becca more. I don't get the philosophy of running and hiding. That's never been my thing, but I do understand the idea of the regroup so I'll allow Sal to call the shots for a moment. I trust him with her life, and that's saying a hell of a lot. But he's on a short fucking leash. All I want to do is saddle up and choke the life out of Chase. Fucker. Muthadirtyfucker.

Lucille's been sent on the vacation of her dreams for the first time in her life. I collected her "card playing" friend and the two are under a watchful eye in Punta Cana. At my expense, of course. I'm sure she'll be running the kitchens at the resort inside a week, but I need her safe. Chase has been running his fucked-up business out of her restaurant. I want him on the run, no safe harbor for that fucker.

I smelled it the moment I stepped out of my truck, then the series of smaller explosions throughout her second floor confirmed he left cans of turpentine through the house to make sure nothing, and no one, could be saved. After the initial blast it was a matter of time before the cans would heat up, burst, and spread the fire faster. They were able to put Poppy's fire out faster because the cans didn't burst, but the café is ruined. I'm out for fucking blood. Poppy's café was a distraction for Sal, but Becca's house and almost Mel's life were an act of goddamn war. They wanted her dead, but thought I wasn't with her for some reason, because if I died, the land goes away.

I sit on a ratty plaid couch and Sal hands me a phone as Mark walks over to us.

"Pull the SIM card and you can keep the phone."

"Why in the hell would I want to keep a burner phone?"

Mark smiles. "Sorry, but, um, we read what's on that phone and thought you might want to keep it close."

"It's like a letter you're never gonna wanna lose." Sal's deep voice is dripping with sentiment. He puts his paw on my shoulder and I nod at him the way men do when faced with emotion.

"Come see us, we have fucking worlds to conquer and men to slay."

> BECCA: I don't know if you can get this to Brick, but if you could, I'd appreciate it. I'm trying to be patient, but I'm not enjoying it. And if it speeds up your revenge bullshit, Poppy is not enjoying my company at all. I'd be much better company if you'd return my fucking husband to me.

My face cracks open wider than the Mississippi; my fierce little hummingbird called me her husband.

BECCA: I'm not cut out to be the wife sitting at home knitting or some bullshit waiting for the men folk to take care of things. We're a team and I want him back as soon as possible. Now, if you could tell him something for me, and I'm embarrassed you'll read this, when he should hear it from my lips first, but here we are. Tell him I love him. That I love him more than the law and that's quite a lot. I love him more than my soul can contain. Tell him I actually cried when I realized what a fool I've been not telling him sooner. And tell him that the part of me that rationalized his words away when he told me he loved me is completely obliterated. I believe him because I believe in myself now. I love Brick Dunne. I love my husband. Please tell him how much I love him and don't do anything stupid. Mojo and Magic are real, and they live inside him. And I need him back in one piece.

BECCA: Oh, and tell him that Calico/Lil' Bit is here and ok. And I'll call her any name he wants. I want to name things now.

There's not a spec of me that ain't glowing. I rub my thumb over my hummingbird tattoo sending up a secret thought I hope the universe will deliver for me. I whisper it to my tattoo like that's our magical connection. "I love you, beautiful. And I'm hurrying back to you."

I tuck the phone into my front pocket and turn to face the men who will help me stop this fucking bullshit.

"GENTLEMEN, I BELIEVE IT'S TIME WE PUT SOME things to rest."

"Agreed." Mark turns his laptop towards us. "Mel's laptop was destroyed in the fire, but I have her cloud password. Well, part of it. She has multiple systems in place, but this is our shared directory since Sal was the bad guy four years ago."

Sal laughs and it booms throughout the room. "Yeah, some bullshit that was."

I'm not amused. I want fucking action. "Where is this fucker? And do we need to cut off the head of this hydra in order to take down the pissant asshole who keeps fucking with my life?"

Sal corrects me, "Our lives."

"Enzo's in LA, and we've sent for him. They'll grab him when they can," Mark says.

Sal grins and puffs on a cigar. "It's time we had a little family reunion."

"And we can't get to Cady through this Chase fella. He's work for hire with no loyalty, as you well know. He's a cruel marionette, but an effective one. His strings are debt. He's in fucking deep in Vegas and Biloxi." Idiot. "He killed your grandmother so the land could be annexed while you were dark." Sal scratches his stubble and I put the last piece in place.

"Cady pulled on my puppet strings: duty, honor, and justice. He put me on that mission."

Mark nods, and Sal says, "Fuck, I thought I had power."

"It's a stupid patch of road. I'm not seeing something."

Mark continues, "Worth several billion and someday will top that trillion mark in trafficking drugs. Also pulling in cash from government contracts for that one swatch of road which traverses the state instead of going down through the bayou or by the ocean. There are multiple ports and a road that now leads in all directions."

Mark stretches his neck and cracks it side to side. "Next to 95 through Miami, it's the biggest inflection point in the last forty years for key distribution of not just drugs, but guns, weapons, illegal pets, and Squishmallows."

"The plush stuffed animal toy?" Sadie has like twenty of them.

"They're a hot commodity, and after that trend fades, they'll be hauling the next one. Toys and drugs always trend. Heroin turns to meth turns to oxy turns to fentanyl, which will in turn become a different horror that some lab junkie is thinking up at this moment. Can't stop the demand, but we can sure as hell try to stop the supply. The road straight through is completely controlled by Cady."

"How the hell is he getting all these things into the country and onto that fucking road?" I'm stunned that I missed the full scope. I thought I had a master's degree in Cady, but Mark has several PhDs on the man.

Sal stands and his presence fills the space around all of us. I would not want to meet him under other circumstances. His coal-black eyes and dark hair, pulled back just so, match the way he carries himself. His custom suits tell the story of a man trying to prove himself and succeeding.

"That's where I come into this little fucking play you assholes got going."

Mark jerks his chin to Sal and says, "The ports." I get it now. But I need to take care of my backyard first before I plunge into international chaos.

I turn to the special agent. "Sir, I won't admit to plans, but is Chase Carlyle of any importance in any ongoing investigations."

Mark pushes the laptop towards me. "There's nothing

more we need from him currently unless Cady reaches out to him. But you might need him to clear yourself once and for all. And I'm sorry to inform you but last evening a known associate of his was found dead in a bar in New Orleans."

My blood is boiling, he doesn't need to say it. I hold up my hand.

"Cy. He silenced my friend." I look up and blow out a breath. Cy wasn't a bright fella, but he was a good man, even if he did bad things from time to time. Wouldn't hurt anyone. My fingers flick thinking of him, and I want to play the piano. I want to play through this hurt for him. I push it down.

Mark clears his throat. "I've known a lot of criminal minds, but his only allegiance is to money and addiction which makes him ruthless. Couple that with the randomness of his acts and he's truly dangerous. He's too dumb and his ego is too big to make him any good at being a criminal. Enzo is the calculating, industrious one, Chase is the blade and that's all."

Sal circles the chairs we're sitting in, and I realize we're swiveling to keep him in our view. He's commanding where we look. Fuck that. I stand up and face him, no man is going to tell me what to do unless my country demands it. Sal doesn't wield or collect it; he just is power. But so am I.

I'm not anything to be trifled with, so I don't turn my head, but I do catch a smirk from the corner of my eye.

Sal's voice reverberates off the walls. "Why keep that fucking liability breathing?"

"Am I the long game?" I ask. Cady knows someone owns that land with my description, but I wasn't sure if he had all the pieces worked out, since I scattered them about.

Sal looks confused but Mark does not. He holds my

history and has since the Vino Groupie days. Hell, maybe he knew before I did. I need the setup exposed and my record cleared, so I can disappear for a minute, then help take all this shit down. But Chase is first.

Mark leans forward with his hands on his knees and asks, "How long have you known?"

"A while. When I initially became involved in that snake in the grass's business it was strategic and all about my Mimi. It wasn't until I dug deeper, I found out he's a man of infinite patience and deep pockets."

Sal says, "What the fuck are you assholes jawing about? Tell me right the fuck now."

I turn toward Sal. "I apologize for leaving you in the dark. I realize y'all don't know how I'll react and that sits wrong with you. I'm more methodical and strategic than brutal. That's not to say there hasn't been violence or I can't take care of things quickly and efficiently. I'm well trained with a cool head, but I understand I'll have to prove that to you."

"You love Rebecca Gelbert, that makes us family, you don't have to prove shit. Hell, I trusted my nephew until he killed..." Mark scowls at him. Then he corrects himself, "Disappeared my right-hand man and lifted a ton of unauthorized product."

I clear my throat. Mark crosses his legs and taps his watch.

I chastise, "No, sir, this isn't for recording."

"Fair enough. I'll ask a different time."

Sal says, "Tell this piece fast because I sure as shit am confused as to why he's so hellbent on putting you in jail and not in the ground."

"There's so much fucking death swirling around and all I want is to move into the light," I say.

"Ain't that a fucking mouthful. Shit yeah, let's all get to the light," Sal says while unwrapping a cigar.

"Settle in. I worked for the man under a different name, didn't want him to tie me back to Mimi Tinker. It started with trying to find my grandmother's killer and get the land deeded back to the county in her name. I researched him and his ill doings from inside his own fucking company, I did it as Tad Stone."

Sal laughs loudly and takes a seat. "Brick, Stone. Come on, that shit's funny." Mark half laughs.

"When I met Becca, I wanted her to know me for real and dropped the Tad Stone. It was then I popped on people's radars and since I was leaving the company early, I took a few mementos when I left. I've been buying up land for the past six years under a shell corporation. He wants it badly."

"Wait, you bought his fucking acquisitions while taking a paycheck from the fucker? You bought up his land with his own goddamned money."

I tilt my head. Sal applauds and Mark salutes me.

Mark pulls out a map and points to a line across the country. "The high-speed rail path. Fuck."

"It's gonna be awkward with Congress next month. He doesn't have the land he promised them. I do."

"You fucking land swindled a land baron? Jesus, the balls on you."

Mark jumps up and down in place.

"Bakersfield." I nod. "Just California or did you cross state lines?"

"Oh, I have stretches that skirt the edges of national parks and avoid roads or play upon existing rail lines in Nevada, Utah, Colorado, clear up to Colby, Kansas. I have a piece in Virginia right near Incan Trust's headquarters, that's one of his companies, just to piss him off even more. My plots of land are all along the rail route proposed by Rex Construction. And already miraculously have EPA approval to build."

I move around the room. I need to be up on my feet. I know this is a lot for them to take in but it's been my preoccupation for a while now.

"He must have figured out the nine different land development companies who hold the deeds, are all me." I raise a finger and silence them again.

"If anything happens to me the land's in an unbreakable trust and goes to a series of nonprofits: environmental groups that can claim endangered species, Native American tribal lands protected, wetlands, expanded state and federal protected parks, and my favorite, birds."

"Birds?"

"Yes, it turns out in Utah, you can fucking leave your land to birds and not one person can touch it because, what, they're going to fight the sparrows for it?"

Sal raises a cut crystal glass with brown liquor in it and gestures to me.

"And tossing your ass in the big house instead of dead, gets him his land."

I point at him. "Bingo. I upped the ante on an eye for an eye. I stole his land, but that fire wasn't meant for me. It was meant to prove to me he can take what I love too."

Sal claps a meaty paw on my shoulder and hands me a glass of whiskey. "Fuck. Remind me not to cross you."

"Same, brother, same."

Mark rolls his eyes. "This is fucking trouble. I need to work this, and I need a copy of those deeds and your will."

"Ms. Mel can get them for you, since she's in and out of my damn server all the fucking time, whether she's invited or not. Soon as she's up, I'll bother her about it." She's like me that one. Sitting still will kill her faster than a fire.

Mark passes me his laptop and I see the new Cady profile I asked Mel to work up. I needed fresh eyes on it. I haven't seen it yet because I was getting married and running into burning buildings.

Mark lays out a plan. "First step, find Chase, nail his ass for the murder of that poor girl and the arson. That's his best bet of nailing your ass into federal prison, and the case is almost rebuilt. Charges are coming soon. Sal, neutralize Enzo. No. Keep him alive, and busy. See who Cady brings out to take their places."

I'm reading, and damn that girl is good. "Hey, y'all, Mel spotted a weakness."

Mark flips the computer back to himself quickly. "I've read this a thousand times, what did you see?"

I point to the screen. "His wife went missing seven years ago and he's never married again or issued a death notice or even filed a missing person's report. Only his inner circle and employees talked about it in emails, according to Mel. He spent a massive amount of money trying to find her. Only accounting line items and a couple of emails. But there's nothing public."

"Yeah, so what?" Mark shrugs.

Sal says, "A man like that doesn't lose things. You know where all the fucking pieces are at all times. It's the only way to play the game at the level he's playing at."

I finish the thought, "And if he did lose her, he's probably sore about it. Press that wound. Find out if she's dead or alive and hiding. Tell him you have her, and he'll pop right up like a whack-a-mole. Or better yet, put all those government resources to good fucking use and find her, see if she'll turn."

Mark sits back and sips his whiskey. Sal sees me eyeing Mark's drink and slides the bottle over to me.

Mark slams the glass down. "We've been looking so fucking hard for a flaw in his money, his real estate business, his political superPACs, the people in his employ, I forgot about the personal."

Sal says, "Don't beat yourself up, Brick here is a fucking newlywed, he's got pussy on the brain. And you see how fucking ornery he is without it, and it's only been days. Imagine how pissed off that muthafucker is." Sal raises his glass. "Chin muthafucking chin, boys."

# CHAPTER 39
## BRICK

'm jittery as we make it to the offices in Los Angeles that are more secure than all of Fort Knox. Sal never shows his emotion or anger when he's around any employees. He's the walking persona of the Sal Pietro that he wants you to see, invest in, and believe. I'm stunned by this man who is now my comrade in arms.

He pushes the doors open. "This ends today. John, you got my shit together?" A well-dressed man in an apricot three-piece suit appears and bows to us.

He puts the back of his hand up on the edge of his mouth as if he's telling a cartoon secret. "Always such the hurry with this one." Then he announces, "Yes, it's all here. Coffee all around?"

"John, this is Brick Dunne. He needs some help finding a known associate of that piece of shit nephew of mine." John looks to the left and spits on the floor, then wipes his mouth.

He shrugs and says to me, "I can't stand even thinking about him. Mr. Dunne, I am at your disposal. And, Sally, my dear, this man is simply delicious." He gives me the up down and I toss him a curious smirk.

Sal waves him away. "Josh'll be here momentarily, and I need him in here immediately."

He claps excitedly and squeals. "Been way too long since I've seen that beautiful soul." Sal glares at him and the man exits in a flourish. Lou remains standing off to the side of the room.

"Hell of an assistant. No one navigates tricky situations better than that man. Pay no mind, he ogles everyone, totally worth it for the job he does. No fucking HR and no tension. Just work being done and an occasional off comment about my ass. He's too good to worry about the shit that comes out of his mouth. I stole him from Josh when he went vintner."

"Stole what from me?" He enters the room as Sal says his name.

"Joshie!" And now I know who he's talking about. Wasn't sure why we're pulling up another chair for a stranger to this fucked-up table. But it's Josh Whittier, who owns Pro/Ho and runs LaChappelle/Whittier Winery.

I stand and put out my hand.

"Good to see you again on the other side of the bars."

Josh's grip is strong and secure. "You've been busy since jail. Holy hell, congratulations on wrestling Becca to the ground. Fuck, if you do nothing else to prove yourself to me, finding your away around that grumpy, prickly woman to wedded bliss proves your mettle of a man."

"That's not a hearty endorsement, but I'm going to forgive you on account of I've been wearing your shirts. And congrats to you."

Josh laughs and Sal stands up and embraces the man.

"Joshie, I do love when you answer my beckoned call."

John saunters in with a tray of coffee and places the platter down. He plants himself in front of Josh and pulls him into a hug, and he slaps his back.

John backs up from him and clasps his hands together over his heart. "How is my darling Elle? And all those wonderful little girls?"

"She's a bit hormonal. I'm happy to be here."

"She got a name yet?" Sal blusters.

"Elle can't decide. She's so freaking tired. It's fine. We call her baby girl or baby four."

"Blessings. So many blessings." John cocks his head at Josh. "I got you. I'll send Prada."

"That will help. It's like her chicken soup when she's sick." He sighs and rubs his hand over his stubbled face. The man looks worn out, but that's to be expected with four under four.

John tosses back as he exits, "Well, time to find her a couple of more wedding dresses."

"Jesus, no more fucking dresses. The woman's been in tulle and silk for months. I want my Elle back."

I say to him, "I don't know you well, but I think that's probably gonna take about eighteen years."

Everyone laughs again, then Josh's expression switches, and all the air leaves the room as John shuts the door.

"How bad is this? Like coming to my fucking doorstep bad or something you can keep on your own side of the fence? Mark gave me his take but now you start fucking talking, Capo." Josh is all business like a switch flipped from hospitable to hostility.

Sal doesn't take offense to the term, but there's some aggression floating around and I'm the one to blame, not Salvatore.

"Pardon me for getting in the middle of y'all's pissing contest, but I'm to blame too."

Josh sits back in his chair and says, "Fix it and keep far away from my valley. I really did mean congratulations on marrying Becca, and it might appear I don't care for her. But that's where you dead fucking wrong. Rebecca Gelbert is family, and if you get her hurt in any way, trust me, there will be retribution. Now, somebody tell me what the fuck is going on."

Sal straightens up in his chair.

I say, "Hold on there a sec or two. I have only love and the best intentions towards my wife. And if for one second you think I'm not doing everything in my power to unwind the situation then you're the one who's dead fucking wrong, sir."

Josh puts his hands up. "Got you. Can we get some shit done? And you still didn't kill that woman, right?"

I shake my head no. Sal laughs and his voice booms all around us. He paces behind his desk. He nods to Lou in the corner, and he exits.

"Why am I here? I handle your legit investments."

Sal says, "We all little pieces of this bullshit picture and it's time it came into focus."

Josh turns to me to explain shit I already know. "Mr. Pietro and I met about a decade ago and he started investing capital into large projects." I grin. He thinks I'm an idiot who doesn't do his homework.

I cut him off, "And diversified his organized crime holdings therefore shifting his business into something a mother could be proud of. He's also the one who kept all that Pro/Ho distribution a secret from my former employer and company when they tried to wrangle those wineries from y'all."

Josh says, "Exactly. But there's one slice of Sal's dark portfolio left. The holding company."

Sal points at Josh then moves to the couch stretching out his arm on the back and crosses his legs. Josh gets himself some more coffee, and I feel the tension in the air.

"Not sure I can prove shit all to y'all, but all I have in this life is my word. Josh, if you say she's family and, Sal, you said we're related now, I swear on that prickly redhead's heart I'm not here to backstab anyone. Trust me with all the information now so I'm not flying off blind. Chase is my issue and I'll thank you kindly for leaving him to me. But all the shit comes out now."

Sal leans forward and says, "The harbor."

"LA harbor? You ship shit in and out of it," I say.

"I own it."

Josh explains, "And he doesn't want to. But for now, he's the largest distributor of legal and illegal goods in the United States. He owns the people, the containers, the ships, and slips. Nothing legal or otherwise comes into Los Angeles without it touching Sal in some way. And he can't pull out of the arrangement without exposing himself and pissing off an awful lot of people."

Sal points at me with his cigar. "You'd have an all-out war between each fucking faction who hauls their illegal shit in and out of there. I'm talking like weird fucking pets, furniture, Cuban cigars as well as stolen art and, of course, the ever-fucking-popular heroin."

Sal then fills Josh in on my story and I nod along.

"Joshie, this shit is already at your doorstep. It's all fucking connected and coming at us in a weird mutha-fucking way. I can't wrap my head around some of this bull, but this web is sticky. Shawna—"

Josh's eyes get wide, and he puts his coffee down to

scrub his face again, then it hardens. "Bax's bitch of an ex-fiancée, Shawna?"

"Seems as if a lot of us were playing in a game where we didn't know all the rules," I add.

Sal continues, "Right now our only fucking weapon is he doesn't know we pieced this shit together. Now if I can get into the mindset of stupid for a second, Becca was the target. I think this dumb muthafucker honest to fuck didn't know Becca and Poppy were two different people because of the last name. Like Becca was a lawyer by day and restaurant owner by night."

I pull my hands behind my head. "Phil Cady is now acutely aware of our association."

Josh's voice comes out as a roar, "Stop fucking talking. We have to stop this shit. You have to fucking stand up, put your fucking coffee down, and go get this cocksucking cunt."

Sal doesn't react, I'm assuming he's seen a touch of devil in Josh before. In light of his rage, I'd be happy to have him at my back.

There's a tough silence in the room, settling on us like the eye of a hurricane. There's pressure and anticipation for what the back half of the storm can bring. It's never the front that destroys you, it's the dirty side that'll get you every time if you look away. It's time to be on the dirty side and saddle up our storm surge.

Josh breaks our tension, flipped to the calm methodical man I've encountered. "Well, shit." We laugh and he continues, "So we dismantle it all. The way Bax and Tabi put Shawna down. One bit at a time."

Sal puts his arms up, and I speak before he can. "Exactly. Each piece gone should open this fucker's soft belly for Mark to take him out."

Sal's voice is low, "But we do it how we decide. I love Mark like a brother, but he's the fucking tattletale brother who will always make sure Mom is watching."

Josh sips his coffee. "Agreed."

"Cady, or as Mel might call him, the Big Bad, he wants your port?"

Josh looks curious. "Like *Buffy the Vampire Slayer*?"

I point at him. "Exactly! I've got to see this show."

"It's good. Elle was on bedrest with the twins and kept calling them leeches, so she wanted to watch vampire stuff."

Sal grins. "Back to me, girls. Everyone wants my port, he's just the fucker who thinks he can get it. He's got Miami and most of the Gulf coast buttoned up, but he pays me. Pays me a shit-ton of money and he got sick of owing. Not a high profit margin out of my fucking port. He tasked my nephew with wrangling the business away from me. Shot up good among personnel and found his way back into the game with some former associates. But they couldn't get it for him."

I ask, "Where do we start?"

"Enzo."

WE'RE ON OUR WAY TO HIS NEPHEW'S BECAUSE CHASE was spotted but he hands me a phone.

"Mel needs you."

I'm tired of this relay shit and I need a fucking phone back. But I have to begrudgingly admit, I would absolutely have called her. I would have jacked off while my wife talked to me. I desperately miss the feel and smell of her.

She validates every part of me and reminds me all this shit is not my fault, despite what I've told myself my whole life.

Fuck therapy and dealing with mommy and daddy issues, all I need is her. That woman who moves and thinks faster than any creature on the planet and is so beautiful. It's awe inspiring when she stops and focuses only on you. I've seen a hummingbird perch back on my Mimi Tinker's feeder and I was blown away by how powerful something that small could be. Not that Becks is small, but she's mightier than she can ever imagine.

> MEL: Ask him his cloud password. I can crack it, but it will be easier this way.

> UNKNOWN: Girl, you think I left shit on a cloud? Mind yourself.

> MEL: Tree Trunks! Don't underestimate me. Your phone.

> UNKNOWN: What about it?

> MEL: Chase might have taken pictures and if Apple auto uploaded them to their cloud - we can see them. And basically, unless you spend some good minutes wiping it all out, it's all there somewhere. And you haven't had the time to do this properly. Just on the surface.

> UNKNOWN: Again, I'm not new. There's nothing on there. I universally delete everything.

> MEL: Not YOUR Apple account.

> UNKNOWN: Oh shit, you mean the company's server?

MEL: Exactly.

UNKNOWN: Lucielle76Rebecca-35Mimi8930.3674° N, 89.0928° WaaaeeeaaJX2345@iz!

MEL: Your women and their ages when you got your phone. Coordinates from Gulfport and your factory issued WIFI Password from your Richmond house. FUCK ME. So easy. I'm an idiot for not getting it.

MEL: I'm in and holy shit. Do your thing and I'll do mine. Farts out.

She's just broke into Apple headquarters' server. That's some straight-up balls on that woman.

# CHAPTER 40
## BECCA

He's going to end up in jail and my marriage will be pretty one sided. I've poured over every possible angle and I'm not seeing how to prove him innocent without Chase.

I unload another round of books onto my father's desk, which I've been using, and they fall off because something has made the surface uneven. I smile at the sight. I didn't know these still existed in the world. My father's advice floats through my head. The only way to get unstuck is to do something else. I used to think he told us that so that we'd do our chores or be free labor when things were lean around here. But I need this right now, so I clutch my things and bolt off to find some boots.

I'm racing through block 122 on one of our gators. I forgot how fun it is to go fast whipping through the vines. The block I'm headed to is one of the many Cab blocks on our property. Cool thing is that it's right next to this Pinot block. Usually, they both need very different terroir or soil to grow, but somehow in this little microclimate up on this hill, it works. They share cherry and other stone fruit characteristics, but the grapes couldn't be more different.

Just because I've shunned the winery, doesn't mean I don't remember everything about it. And this was one of my favorite parts, the ritual of pruning to lay the groundwork for the show to begin soon. Bud break is close, and you can see the vines starting to swell and come back to life. I don't always understand the creative things David does with flavors or blending. But tending to something to make sure it's got the best possible chance to fulfill its potential, I get that. They say there are flowers and gardeners in every relationship. I've always been pushed down and put into the gardener roll. This is the first time I think perhaps I see it differently. Perhaps in the best relationships, you take turns blooming. But right now, I know exactly how to do this, and it has nothing to do with my problems, or legal precedence.

I put on my gloves and pick up my sheers, the ones monogrammed with my initials that I got for my fourteenth birthday. I don't say a word but set to work studying the vine and seeing what it needs. I examine the spurs and canes or, as Poppy used to call them when she was little, the knotty things and the skinny sticks. I cut the canes as low as possible without damaging the buds just starting to form under the bark. The canes drop at my feet, and I don't notice as I move down the row.

My bet is David will drive the flail mower through here later, grind up all the canes, and leave them for mulch. Sadie loves the crunching sound. The vines aren't bleeding a lot yet, the water isn't pushing up. Budbreak isn't too close but close enough that I'm excited to see it. But we're not in danger of frost so pruning a touch early is kind of my dad's signature move. Cab usually breaks late for us, so we're just doing a cleanup and maintenance rather than a full-on bud prune.

After about an hour and a half when I'm lost to the vines, he speaks. I'm totally in this moment and grateful for the break from panic or longing.

"Yo. Daughter, come."

I laugh as my father, who is in the row across from me, flomps down onto the ground. He's got a giant sandwich dangling from a Ziploc bag. He's been doing online grocery shopping lately and there's an inordinate number of types of ham in our house. From prosciutto to Black Forest. He hasn't quite gotten the hang of it yet. Or he thinks we all really love ham.

I push through the vines and sit next to him. He pulls out two pink and red cloth napkins and spreads them in front of us. Then removes two bags of chips from his hip pockets. My mother has a themed napkin for every holiday, and this one has embroidered cupid's bows and hearts on the scalloped edges. I grin at the napkin and notate the passage of time.

"Happy Valentine's Day, honey. I know he can't be here, but I'm sure your instahusband is thinking of you." He places the sandwich in front of me, and I toss the Ziploc bag at him. He presents two beers from worn hunter-green barn jacket pockets.

"Thanks, Dad. I remember a time when you'd fill my room with pink and red balloons and stuffed animals claiming to love me. And more chocolate than we'd get at Christmas. But a multi-ham sandwich is nice too." I take a bite and somehow the man has made it work. There's like four different types of ham in here. It's like the Artie Gelbert version of a Cuban sandwich. I'm worried about his sodium intake, but it's a good sandwich.

"That was your mother."

"What was my mother?"

He bites and gestures to the napkins. "The holiday crap."

"And you took credit for it?"

"You'd be surprised how many of my good qualities, and your good memories of me, were always your mother."

I chomp into the sandwich. "Nah. We knew and loved your cranky ass anyway."

He's just there for me right now. There's no judgment, which is a little shocking, but I'll take it. There's a slight chill in the air and I feel it in my butt as we sit on the ground, but there's a peace surrounding us.

"You know, right now, you're oddly comforting." I smile at him.

"Love you too, honey." His voice is gruff and teasing. He gestures to me. "Find anything that might help out your fella?"

"Do you like him?" I don't mean to ask, but it slips out. The sun is warming my face today, and it's rather breath-taking seeing it play among the shadows of the unpruned wild canes. They almost look like long Halloweenesque fingers jutting out from the old vines' hands. I've always thought they looked like Tim Burton creatures or backdrops.

"Does it matter?" he asks.

"No."

I answer very quickly, and it's the first time in my life that I've thought that. Their opinion really doesn't matter.

Not that it stopped me, but I always gave it a passing thought. But now, I don't care what they think.

"Good," my father says.

"I don't know how to help him. I keep hitting a brick wall, no pun intended." My father laughs anyway, which irritates me a little. "No. I'm serious. The law is failing me." I stretch my legs out in front of me and breathe in deeply. The smell of soil and Sonoma itself reaches out and gives me a comforting hug.

"You're the only one who can do this, pumpkin. You single-handedly saved our five wineries with your contract loophole. You found it when teams and teams of lawyers and all of us missed it. You're the one with the gift of looking outside the box while remaining firmly inside. It's that big-ass stubborn heart of yours that won't let yourself fail. I'm so fucking proud of who you are."

"Can you repeat that last part please?" I'm stunned.

He laughs and finishes his sandwich half. Then he stands up and puts a hand on my shoulder. "I'm so fucking proud of you."

I have food in my mouth but say anyway, "Can you repeat that with David in the room?"

He grins. "Do I have to tell him that I'm proud of him too?"

I laugh. "I'd prefer you don't so I can bask in the glory, and he can labor under his inferiority."

He chortles again. "You do know I'm proud of him too."

"I'll pay you a million dollars to never tell him that."

"Too late."

I laugh just as there's a slam of a car door. I bolt to standing and my father straightens, pulling his shoulders back in an exaggerated way, moving his large belly a quarter of an inch higher to indicate that he's ready for anything. I love him so.

Mel screams through the vineyard, "BECCA! Where you at? This is a fucking bomb. I've got it. I fucking have it."

"We're here!"

Melissa runs up and my father stares at her; he'll never understand her but tolerates her because she's part of the extended fam.

"Hey, pops! What's shaking?"

"Please don't scream swear words all about. What if Sadie were here?"

"She's with Giuseppe over at the park. I've got a tracker on her."

"You've tracked my granddaughter?"

I didn't know that. She shrugs, opens her laptop, and shows us a map of Sonoma with a massive cluster of moving red dots all over the map. "You're all in here."

I zoom out on the map and, sure enough, there's a blue cluster of moving dots in Los Angeles. There's a couple of purple ones in Chicago.

"That's them. And the purple are Ian, Ingrid, Meg, and Tabi, well, she'll be landing in about an hour at SFO."

"Meg Hannah? Wait, what's Tabi doing in Chicago?"

"Yeah, well, it's Meg Turner, now. Ingrid and Ian are working. They'll turn red again when they get back to Sonoma. Tabi's doing her last sales call before staying close to home. And she's visiting some people she met at an airport or something."

"Ok, I don't care." I put my finger on the LA cluster and his name pops up. I grin and follow the dot with my finger as it moves down the 405. "If something happens?"

"The dot turns black if there's distress."

"How did you d—never mind. Don't tell me."

"I will tell you it's taken a while to get it all in place. I started after what happened to Elle. And then expanded it to the rest of you when Sammy went missing." Sammy was Sam's girlfriend. We've never heard from her after the day she disappeared. Sam's never been the same. Even Mel can't find her. It's her obsession and her biggest annoyance. I pull my lips together, Mel may not act it most of the time, but she's a softy.

I try to console her, "You know those things were no one's fault? Jesus, between you, Josh, and Brick. Sometimes shit things happen. Elle took care of herself and is totally fine, now."

"Shut the fuck up. We have bigger shit to do than fucking analyze me." She pulls up another tab. There are photographs of a blonde woman laughing and posing.

"Who is this? What am I looking at?"

"The victim, duh."

"You know you work for me, right?" I bristle.

"Yes, but do you know what I just did?"

"What?"

"I got you some evidence no one else has."

I pull the lap top closer to my face as bits of ham fall from my sandwich she's begun to eat.

"You cannot fuck with me, is it good evidence?"

"We'll see. If not, I can destroy it." I run my hands through my hair and give her the stern Rebecca look. "You know when you do that it's just sexy, not intimidating."

"I'm telling your wife."

"I've already told your husband and he agrees." There's a low flutter of need bouncing in my stomach as I think about pulling out that look in an intimate setting. God, I want to fuck my husband, but I need to focus on getting him off. Ah. I mean getting charges dropped.

"Do not destroy evidence. Do not do anything to it. Tell me what you found."

We wander to her car and set the computer on the hood. She clicks through and there's a bunch of pictures of people I don't recognize.

"I didn't peg him for a sunset man."

I swipe past a sunset that reminds me of Gulfport. "What is this? Whose pictures?"

"Brick's phone."

"The only thing they have is a partial print on the phone. He remote wiped it, all the information is gone."

Mel laughs. "Nothing in the digital age is ever gone. When you have an Apple account, pictures automatically upload. He deleted the pictures, pulled them off the iCloud, and emptied everything, except Apple's corporate Fort Knox of a mother server. He's super good at hiding. But I'm really fucking good at seeking."

"Grandstanding. Get to the point."

"Look, I'm just a woman with a dream, the dream of running the whole world from my laptop with one hand on my wife's pussy and the other wrapped around a barbacoa burrito. Let me have this."

"I bow down to your prowess. Now tell me how we save Brick with these photos that shouldn't exist but do."

"I found his phone contacts too. Wanna know who he spends time with?"

"No." I pause and shake my head. "Yes. A little, but let's move on. They help him how?"

I take the sandwich out of her hand so she can drive back to the house.

The blonde woman is on a date and poses for about a dozen pictures with different expressions and angles.

"If our timeline works, Brick was already drugged up

and beaten and dumped in his truck while this little dinner went down." Holy shit. It was part of the frame up, pictures on his phone of the victim.

"And we're the only ones who have these?"

Mel explains, "Yes. And legally, you don't have to turn them over to anyone until discovery, right?"

"Legally, but ethically—" I scold.

She slams her hand on the dash and I'm startled. "Do you want him to get off or do you want to send an innocent man to jail?" She cares so much it pulls me into the gray area. I want her to have this victory as much as I want Brick to be free and I want to bury Chase.

"Are these timestamped?"

Mel screams, "Hell, yeah they are."

"We don't need to prove Brick didn't do it if I can prove that someone else did."

Mel says, "And I assume Chase was sitting across from her. There has to be someone who fucking saw him." She slams the car in park, and we head to my father's office. We walk and talk the whole way while she clutches her laptop.

"Chase isn't one to fade into the background, his ego won't let it. So, we need to find that restaurant. From the billions of restaurants in Wine Country and the Bay Area. This isn't the slam dunk you think."

She nods again. "Hungry for Italian?" I smack a kiss on her cheek. She's so fucking good.

"You found it." I gasp.

"I figured out it was Italian because of the cannoli pictures, but I can't get a location on these. But don't mess with me and food."

These are the last pictures of her alive and they're on Brick's phone. I look closer at the pictures and my cousin pops into the room. "And there's no location tag on them?"

"Please, woman. I checked and no."

She rolls her eyes. I tap my cheek and try to come up with a way to figure this out.

I screech, "Poppy!" She knows every restaurant in the area and certainly Italian restaurants. Sal is always on the hunt for the perfect braciola.

"Tell me what you see."

"A blonde in need of a touch up."

"Where is this?"

"Looks like one of those white tablecloth places down in North Beach." I hug her hard.

I run out of the room, yelling, "Send those pictures to my phone! I'm headed to the city."

I'll need help and there's already one of us in the city.

BECCA: I'm picking up your wife. I might need her Italian language skills.

BAX: I've learned not to ask when it comes to rando texts. Fine. Can I have her back by dinner? There are too many fucking mouths to keep feeding by myself. Tell her to bring food.

BECCA: You're in luck. In the mood for Italian?

BAX: And you will be safe?

BECCA: We'll have Murray with us.

BAX: Good. Joaquin wants to interview you for career day.

BECCA: Really?

BAX: Yeah, he said everyone was doing wine people and he wanted a real job. {eye roll}

BECCA: Spoken like a true vineyard rat. He's catching on quickly. Tell him early next week. And I'll get your Valentine back to you ASAP.

BAX: Shit.

BECCA: Throw chocolate at your children and make sure she gets some Basque morning buns and you're good.

BAX: Nat, can you do me a favor? I need Valentine's shit for Tab and the boys.

BECCA: Still me. And come on, man, she doesn't work for you anymore. Give her a break.

BAX: I HAVE TWO CHILDREN, AN INFANT AND A CITY TO RUN.

BAX: Ingrid, hey. Do you have time to get a bunch of Valentine's shit for the boys and Tab?

BECCA: Still me. And your sister is in Chicago.

BAX: I'm so fucking tired.

"You've basically kidnapped me. I'm being held against my will and you're a fucking officer of the court." I roll my eyes. "You said I'd get lunch if I came with you. I'm fucking starving, pregnant, and ornery. And an ornery Tabi is not what you want."

"Is there a difference between ornery Tabi and regular Tabi?"

"The eye rolls are more severe."

We've been to three places and none of them match the picture, but the last place told us to try Trattoria Contadina. I drag her across the street to the corner with the green awning.

"Whether you like it or not, we're eating. Or at least let me grab some focaccia for the road. I'm weary and ragged from the journey." She pulls at my sleeve and laughs.

"It's been twenty-five minutes. And you ate In and Out on the way here that you grabbed in the airport."

"That, my friend, was a snack." She rubs her belly and grins. Seems the baby is her excuse to let loose with shit food. She normally eats healthy and Bax eats like shit.

I glare at her. "A double double with fries and two shakes, is a snack?"

She waggles her finger at me. "Don't know what to tell you, this baby is going to be a monster. The heart wants what it wants." She grins.

We're walking down Mason Street and Tabi's reveling in every pregnancy cliché she can. She's earned it, so I'm not going to say anything, but it's annoying.

She opens the door to the restaurant. "I feel a maternal pull to some fettuccine right now and baby Nick is napping so I have time to eat a full meal." She shows me her phone with a live feed of her sleeping baby. He's so cute with his butt in the air.

I should probably find out if Brick wants them. And then my heart pangs because I can't talk to him and have no idea if he's in mortal peril, and I'm here trying to identify place settings and candles.

I follow her inside and the manager greets us.

"Can you help us out with something? Do you have a seating area that looks like this?"

Tabi interjects, "More importantly, how fast can I get a meatball?" I elbow her in the ribs.

I show him the picture. "We're trying to identify the restaurant in this picture." He looks very Italian, exactly why I brought this pain in the ass friend of mine. I nod to her, and she doesn't hesitate.

"Mi dispiace disturbarla, signore. Ma la mia fastidiosa amica vuole sapere se il suo marito di merda a due tempi non va bene l'ha tradita. Ha trovato questa foto e vuole sapere se era questo ristorante. E c'è del pane?"

He then puts his hand on my forearm and disappears.

"What did you say?"

"You want to nail your cheating husband and does he recognize this woman or this table." He reappears and gives Tabi a basket of bread. "Oh, and I asked for some bread. Want some?" She shoves an entire roll in her mouth.

"No. And, I might need this man as a witness, I can't lie to him."

She gulps down the roll and says, "You didn't. I did." She tears off another giant bite and moans.

"You're the worst."

The man walks several feet deeper into the restaurant. We follow him and stand behind him. Nothing is on the tables yet, they're not quite open. He holds up my phone and the picture matches the corner booth. Oh my God. We found it.

"Sir, wow."

In a thick accent, he says, "Yes. This is our restaurant. Is there anything else I can do for you..." He looks to Tabi. "Besides the meatball?" He grins at Tabi. How the fuck does that happen? She's obnoxious and the world loves her, and I get labeled fucking prickly.

She nods. "Good, just don't want that order to get lost."

"May we sit? I'm sorry if my friend misled you. But I have a sensitive question to ask, and I'll need to record our conversation. I'm an attorney investigating a case and this restaurant might be the key to letting an innocent man go free."

He gestures to his heart and breathes quickly. "Oh my. Let's get the owner involved if that's alright with you."

"Please, that's fine with me."

I squeeze Tabi's hand and she grins at me. Then yells at the nice man, "Yo. About that meatball. Can it be on top of some spaghetti? With a side of fettuccine Alfredo?"

"Salad with house dressing okay?"

She continues to call after the man, "If I must." She turns to me. "Happy?"

"Around you? Almost never."

She laughs big and bright, and it fills the room. She fills almost every room she's in. I grin at her and realize I should take up a little more space in life. She should probably contract a touch, but it's time for me to expand.

# CHAPTER 41
## BECCA

"My client is still under medical observation for literally running into a burning building to save someone's life." It's this phrase that got the bench warrant squashed. He's under medical supervision in Los Angeles or at least that's what they told me and gave me paperwork to back it up.

An emergency closed preliminary hearing was called by the prosecutor who has taken issue with threat of the Great Writ. If they even try to put him in jail, I'll bring Habeas Corpus on their asses so fucking fast. He's not spending one more second behind bars.

But we need more time. I've had unsolicited calls from old friends, law professors, and colleagues this week all asking to co-chair or take this burden off my plate. All of it is bullshit. They need me to hand off this case to someone else who will lose. Then it's all neat and tidy when Brick gets life imprisonment. That's why they burnt down my house and now this new prosecutor, who came down on high from the state's attorney's office, is pushing for arrest without bail. All tactics to stop me from winning.

We all rise and I'm aware of my solo status at this table. I should've brought a friend to pretend and sit next to me. There's seven people swirling around the prosecutor's table.

"Your honor, the litany of offenses, including not appearing today in court, should be all I need to prove that Brick Dunne should be remanded, arrested, and incarcerated immediately for the first-degree murder of Hope Beardsley and the possible arson of two separate buildings."

I leap up. "Is there a reason I wasn't told this case had slipped into the premeditative murder realm and arson of my own home?" If the arson is part of this I'm going to be thrown off the case because I'm the victim. Sneaky.

"Ms. Gelbert, are you prepared to speak to these charges today or not?"

"When was that filed?"

She puts a piece of paper on the judge's bench, and he reads it. "This was filed two days ago and was delivered to your office at 428 Breylan Street, Napa, California."

I seethe as I glare at this woman. "Your honor, that was my home office. Which was burned to the ground and is part of a criminal arson case of which Brick Dunne is not currently a suspect and that charge should be thrown out immediately. It's insulting and pure conjecture, there's not one tiny bit of proof to substantiate that claim and was only tacked on to make him seem more ominous."

The judge says to the prosecution. "I concur with Ms. Gelbert. Strike the arson from the charge. But we will need to hear on the other charges."

"I was not given sufficient time to prepare to this premeditative addition. Your honor, there's nothing there but burnt debris. Did they leave it on the charred remains of my home or on the blackened lawn?" The opposing counsel looks smug, and I know I'm sunk.

"Ms. Gelbert, I will overlook that outburst in light of your recent tragedy. Nevertheless, that is the address on record for your practice and therefore if you neglected to refile an address with the court, this remains a legal document, and you were informed in a timely manner for preparation. We will proceed." Fuck.

"Ms. Gelbert, or is it Mrs. Dunne?" Snipes the new prosecutor

I wave my hand as if giving over the floor to her. "Gelbert is fine since I haven't refiled for a new name in a timely manner. Cut to the chase, counselor."

"Between you and me and this judge here, who won't be the sitting judge for the trial if I have anything to do with it." Not sure why the balls on this one. I got the smack down for showing emotion over my burned-down home.

The judge bangs the gavel. "In my court, you will respect the robe, if not the man. I will allow you a little latitude, but this stops now. Argue your reason for this arrest and reissue of a bench warrant, which even I thought was overkill? He's sick, not a flight risk."

I sit back down, and she launches into some kind of bullshit.

"I have Ms. Gelbert's client dead to rights. It's open and shut. There are witnesses to the blood on his clothes even though the knife has yet to be recovered."

"You keep saying things, but none of this is proof. You don't have depositions with these witnesses who, let's not forget, were missing as of two days ago. But if they're miraculously back, where's their sworn testimony? You have no motive, no proof, and no case."

I'm pedaling fast now. I should have added taste. Her suit is a flashy royal blue with a hot-pink blouse. She looks lovely, if she were showing real estate and not in court.

"This is a stall tactic from a clearly addled and disorganized attorney who is going to fail her client and her new husband. Perhaps if she'd been working on her case instead of getting quickie nuptials, we'd all be in a better place in these proceedings."

That's it. I switch off all the warm fuzzy floaty mojo feelings—I'm going full Rebecca on this bitch.

"Letter of the law, sir. Let's stick to the law and leave the personal judgements of my character and abilities out of the courtroom. Mr. Dunne is neither a flight risk"—first lie I've ever told in court, but he's coming back—"nor a violent criminal. He has no prior record, he's a highly decorated member of our armed forces, and holds long employment records as well as strong ties to the community."

The asshole to my right scoffs. I ignore her. "Again, my home was criminally burned to the ground. It was ruled arson. At this point if I handed this case to anyone else, it would take three times as long to gather evidence, and for them to start from scratch, we'll have to begin all over with the presenting of physical evidence, which would be a disservice to my client, regardless of who he's married to."

Bring it, bitches, I'm ready.

"All of that's lovely, your honor, but the facts are on my side." She's quick to quip.

I roll forward, "Furthermore, I have presented enough evidence pointing to the real suspect, that the police have opened an investigation into. I've actively tried to solve this case. I have proof Brick Dunne couldn't have been the one to do this based on the timeline submitted."

"Smoke and mirrors, Ms. Gelbert." She's so dismissive. I grin at her and stare. She breaks the glare first, flustered and rifling through papers.

I say loud enough for her to hear but not loud enough

for the court reporter to hear. "Who's the disorganized one now?"

She didn't know about Chase, but the new police report landed on the judge's desk a couple of hours ago. I don't have to tell her jack shit if it's an open police investigation. That alone gives Brick reasonable doubt; they're investigating someone else.

"But here we are once again, forgetting in this particular matter, none of this is my responsibility."

"She's right, Counselor. You've proven nothing new to conjure up doubt of Mr. Dunne's innocence. You don't have enough. Show me the body, a motive, a witness, or proof other than the retread of the blood-stained clothing. You're wasting taxpayers' money and my time, Ms. Abbot. So happy the assistant state's attorney felt the need to grace our little court, but you wasted your trip and failed to prove burden. All charges in the case are once again dropped against Brick Dunne. Let the record reflect this case was dismissed for a second time because of the prosecution's failure to make their burden."

I add, "Also, on a personal note, for the record I'd like to add, you have a piece of toilet paper on your shoe, Ms. Abbot."

She flips around in a circle trying to grab the piece. She can't get it and glares at one of her underlings who drops to his knees and crawls after her trying to dislodge it.

"Case dismissed." He hurries to chambers and I see him stifling a laugh. Me too.

"Thank you, your honor," I call after him, and he waves me off. I collect my things and see the State's prosecutor scurrying out of the building. She's madly texting. I pull out my phone to text Mel and Ms. Abbot pulls my elbow and spins me to face her. My camera slides open, I push record on the video. Brick and Mel will want to see this woman or hear what she has to say.

Her skin is pale, her lips are contorted. She's aged a decade in the last minute and half.

"You know nothing of what's about to happen."

The phone in her hand rings and her eyes fill with tears. He owns her, that's why Sacramento is down here.

I say, "Is the money worth it? Jumping every time he calls. You're trapped, aren't you?"

"Fuck you, Mrs. Dunne. I'm nothing compared to what's about to be fucking unleashed. You should've taken the dive. Mr. Cady will end this now."

Confirmation.

I lift my phone and stop recording. Her face is even paler as she sees what I've done.

"Oh shit, I hate when I record things and don't even know it."

"That won't do anything." She pushes past me and I'm shaking as I put my phone into my bag. Holy shit. I'm grateful he doesn't own my local judges but I know he's not done trying to stop me.

No one's home, they're all out living lives, and I'm staring at nothing in front of me. Murray's outside but he's not the company I crave. I'm getting ready to fly to LA and bang on warehouse doors until I find him. Mark told me I did well with the recording. They're going to seek her out and see if she'll become an asset in exchange for protection.

I'm itchy all the time, I don't know how Poppy and Sal

have built a relationship like this. How is she apart from him when he's in danger? I don't care for it. I'm not cut out to be a mob wife.

I'm doing laps around the blue couches in my parent's living room trying to calm down after a victory I can't share with him.

The front door creaks open and startles the hell out of me. I'm so nervous all the time. I jump and when I land Lil' Bit stares at me while I put my hands out in a catlike pose. I look behind me to see if there's a weapon I could use, but it's hopeless. I could grab some of my mother's St. Patrick's Day fucking bric-a-brac and hurl a pot of gold pillow at whoever is here to kill me, but instead I flatten myself to the floor and curl up as close to the couch that will shield me if someone glances in this room.

I've got my hands tucked up under my chin and of course I don't have my phone. The cat is staring at me, and I can see black boots under the couch approaching. The fucking cat is going to give me away. I knew I was right not to name that little minx. I hold my breath as the floorboards squeak under the weight of this man. LOOK AWAY, CALICO! You're dooming both of us. I can't breathe as I curl up and squint. The boots round the couch.

"Lemme guess, you got a new yoga routine since I've been gone."

I pop up and stare at the eyes I crave. My entire body is a loose wire dancing on a wet street. I don't think, I leap into his giant arms, screaming as he laughs at me.

"HOW ARE YOU HERE? I LOVE YOU. I LOVE YOU SO BRIGHT AND BIG AND TO THE END OF THE FUCKING EARTH. OH MY GOD, I LOVE YOU. I LOVE YOU BEYOND." I kiss every part of his face. He stops me and puts his forehead to mine.

"Darling, that's honey to my ears. I have two hours. Stop talking, there are other things I need that mouth to be doing."

"YES!"

"Also, take the volume down."

I put my feet on the ground. "Was I yelling?'

"Nah, my eardrums will be fine."

"Fuck me," I say and grin.

"How many times do you think we can get it done in the next couple hours? I have a hard out."

I grab his dick. "Not hard enough. Here let me help." I go to my knees and unzip, and he threads his hands into my hair. I love it when he does this. Then he lets go as I'm about to get his cock out.

"Perhaps we don't do it in the living room of your parents' house. Got a room in this joint?"

I take off running and he follows close behind me. I can't get there fast enough. I unbutton my shirt and toss it at him at the top of the back staircase.

I turn towards him as he takes in my new mesh bra. "By the way, you're innocent and free."

"Free? Sure. Innocent, not even fucking close." He rips my pants down in the hallway and scoops me up.

# CHAPTER 42
## BRICK

bite my woman's neck and she shrieks again. Then I inhale her soft scent and it sets my soul right and my cock on fire. I'm a rocket ready to launch. She can pull the trigger at any time, and I'd spill on the spot. I toss her onto her bed and shed my clothes faster than ever. I'm stroking my dick as she gets up on her knees and pulls off her bra, and I take the liberty of shredding her underwear in one swipe.

She lies back down, and I get to stare at the prettiest pussy. I lay down on top of her, holding myself up with my hands, and I dip to take her lips suddenly. It's hard and pushing forth everything I'm trying to pack into this brief window of time. I grunt and moan as her nails scratch down my back and her tongue tells me the wicked things she could do to me.

"I'll be right back, there's someone else I need to give my greetings and salutations." I force her hands over her head, and she arches underneath me. Then the loudest loveliest groan erupts from her as I clamp down on a nipple, swirling my tongue around the edges of her areola without touching the hard tip. I keep circling and teasing her until she moves her breast into my mouth. I suck hard, pulling that stiff peak as far as I can until she groans, and I suck harder. Fuck I love her tits. They're big and perfectly shaped with nipples the same color as her perfect lips.

I mind the other one, mirroring my treatment until her needy pelvis bucks into me, seeking friction to relieve all that real good pressure I'm building. She keeps pulling against my grip and it makes me double down so she can use the leverage. I slide down further and finally set her hands free. I hover over her clit, breathing heavily, anticipating her reaction, and trying to keep mine under control.

"Mrs. Dunne," I whisper, my lips barely touching that happy little bundle of fun. She gasps just like I want her to.

"Brick. Oh my fucking God. We only have an hour and forty-one minutes left, make me come."

I remove myself from her body. "Have you forgotten how this works while I've been away?"

"Play with me after. I need you. Fuck foreplay. I need you inside of me."

I stand up and stroke as she watches and licks her lips, then I walk around to the side of the bed.

"Begging is always appreciated, but I want you desperate. I've missed every inch of your body and I'm going to take it all in. Like a good tour of a national park, you don't want to miss nothing."

She sits up. "The extended tour is over. Can we skip to the gift shop?" I laugh at her, then thrust my tongue in her mouth. And she grabs my dick as I drift my hand down to her pussy. I run my finger down the very needy part of her, and she's dripping for me.

We're all tongues, teeth, lips, and groans as I part her

and thrust a finger inside. I get back onto the bed, rolling her under me.

"I love you beyond reason and light. Beyond the way the trees grow, and life moves on. At the end of world and universe when I start talking to the mighty one about how things went on earth, it's your face and heart I'll conjure to teach him a thing or two about love."

Her eyes glaze over with sweet tears, and I find myself fighting them off. She kisses me in a way that joins the last remaining pieces we were both holding back. Brick Dunne and Becca Gelbert cease to exist in this moment right here. This is the one when we're reborn as better than the sum of parts. We're both on a new level. When we break the kiss, I wipe a tear from her cheek.

I may need to finish up with us being wild and crazed in all sorts of tangled positions, but now I need to look at her when we connect.

I reach down and notch myself up. She bucks her pelvis and I slide into paradise.

"Brick, fuck."

"Hold on, darling, open up for me, sugar. Surely, your body hasn't forgotten me." And then she acclimates, and I slide deeper. I pull out and slowly ease back in and it's a tight blissful torture.

"Oh. Jesus, my cock won't last long, darling. You've tightened up without me pounding this slit on the regular."

We stare at each other, taking in every tiny detail. She's holding me so taut inside her.

I thrust into her a little deeper and remind us that although that was all sweet tea on a porch, now it's time to add a lil' whiskey in the frisky.

"This is what I dream of, this connection, how deep you are."

"Do you touch yourself when you're having this dream?" She pushes on my ass and licks her lips. I attack them, sucking on her tongue and biting down on her lip.

She whispers as I kiss and suck down her jawline to her collarbone, "Harder."

"Yes, ma'am." I pull out and slam into her and her body bows upwards at the intrusion.

"Harder." I kiss her with a passion reserved for strangers and teenagers. Wild and unskilled. I piston in and out with abandon. Her tits are dancing with each thrust and hypnotizing me.

I gasp out, "You're so fucking gorgeous. Come for me. I want to watch. Climb that fucking hill, take my dick with you." Her hips gyrate in a circle, and I thank the heavens this woman can move like this. Christ it's like she's twirling around my cock. Our bodies slick from sweat are gliding into each other and as fantastic as that feels, I need hard fucking. And from the look in her eyes, so does she. I pull out and she groans. But it's only a second until I'm standing at the end of the bed pulling her to the edge. I impale her instantly, and she screams. Her legs on my shoulders and my hands controlling her hips, I pull her down as I push into her.

"Yes. Fuck. This. That spot. Hit it again."

I let go of a hip, move my fingers to her clit, and pinch while I thrust back in. She's close I can feel it and I need to coat the inside of my woman. My balls are drawn up and there's an ache at the base of my spine that needs to be unknotted. I need to fucking come, in and on her. Gonna be a wild two hours.

"Oh. God. Oh, Jesus." She takes her tits in her hands and kneads then moans loudly. That's it. I press down on her clit and rub her in a counterclockwise direction while watching my dick enter her. I'm so out of my fucking head.

"Come. Come now, you hear. Fuck, you're so tight. You're so hot. Fucking you is so hot."

"I'm coming. Now. I have to."

"Tumble, darling."

And she does, she lifts off the fucking bed, trembling all over as she lets it wash over her. I can't look away, it's so breathtaking. I thrust into her, easing her through this, and she's got a stranglehold on my cock. It's so warm I can't take it and before she's even done, I lurch forward, letting her legs fall to the side and slam into her until I freeze and so much pleasure shoots through my body as I shoot into her.

"CHRIST. Becca. Fuck. Fuck. Fuck. Fuck."

"Yes. I feel you. So good. Fuck me." I can't speak as I have the longest, hardest orgasm of my fucking life. My dick doesn't even know how to handle it, vibrating a little and twitching on its own uncontrollably. I'm along for the ride, it's his show.

I groan her name with what I think is the last burst of cum and fall on top of her, laying my head on her chest as I try to catch my breath. Her fingernails swirl through my hair and I shiver a little. As if she's set off another set of aftershocks.

## CHAPTER 43
# BECCA

'm still aglow with nerve endings that are popping and raw. And my body wants more from him.

He sits up and we both groan as he pulls out. The loss of connection. There's a hollow feeling when he exits that I don't care for. He returns from the bathroom, kneels at the edge of the bed, and wipes me down with such reverence and care. I sit up and break our spell by speaking.

"That was some epic fucking. Are you sure you don't want to go to jail? I can only imagine how good conjugal visit sex could be."

He grins at me. "Are you telling me you're into taboo shit?"

It astonishes me, but he might be right. "Holy shit. Maybe."

He lies down next to me and pulls me onto my side. Then he smacks my backside and my eyes light up.

"I'm not joining the priesthood for you."

I laugh very hard and he does too as he pulls me closer to him. "No, not taboo, just you. I'm into you."

He kisses my forehead. "That's the right answer, Hummingbird." My whole body gets another kick of endorphins as he calls me the name that means so much to the two of us. I kiss his chest and snuggle deeper. We doze off in the cuddle, not a full sleep but a moment of pure us.

Suddenly, it occurs to me we're still in danger. I sit up quickly, and he jumps to his feet, instantly alert. His beautiful dick swinging and making me laugh.

"Don't do that to a man. What?" He drags me to him and kisses the hell out of me. I'm a ragdoll in his arms, but I need to pull back.

"Where's Chase?"

He furrows his brow and kisses me deeply. "Before we get into all that, is that the fucking time?"

I glance over and we have about twenty minutes left. "As much as I desperately want for you to spend the next twenty minutes between my thighs..." He groans and it's lovely. "You have to tell me what's going on. I'm not good without the facts. In the dark is not a place I like to be, and it's real dim around here. Poppy seems to be fine with it, me, I'm crawling out of my ever-loving skin."

"You talking like me now?"

I say in my best Southern accent, "Sure. Sit a spell, pour you a cuppa courage, and let all them words dangle outcha mouth."

"Pretty good. But I like you the other way better."

"Cranky?"

He puts me back on the bed. "I like to view it from the top. I call it persistent or aggressively annoyed. It's cute. I'll tell you what you want to know on one condition."

"What?"

"Spread those legs." He pulls them apart and I gasp. His

311

hand is low and possessive on my stomach as he swipes his tongue over my already sensitive clit. I shudder but he holds me in place. And then like a dream, he thrusts his tongue into me while pinching my clit.

He sits up, his face glistening. "Mark has a plan."

"Make me come first, and fast." His lips curl up into a nasty smile and he spears me again. I can't take it, I'm already so close. He circles my wet clit and when he gives a tiny smack, I detonate unexpectedly.

"Oh. Brick. Brick. Fuuuuck." He's in my face and kissing me hard. I taste me and I don't care. I want his tongue everywhere.

"That was one delicious snack. Now get your fanny in gear and meet me downstairs."

I FIND HIM IN THE KITCHEN SUCKING DOWN COFFEE and shoveling yogurt into his mouth. He pops some blueberries as I watch him.

"Husband."

"Wife." That word sends me to another place.

"What the hell is going on?"

"I'm meeting Mark in a couple of hours to take down Chase. He's been holed up at a place in LA. We grabbed the address from a text Enzo sent. Sal has plans for the nephew but needs to give him some rope, if you get the meaning."

"You know you could say things like, 'Sal's giving him time to lead us to Phil Cady.' I don't need the metaphors."

He takes me in his arms. "You're awful cantankerous for someone who just got fucked properly."

I smile. "Why you? Can't Mark do this?"

"Where's the fun in that? I already don't get to kill him. I have to turn him over to the government. I want him to know it was me."

I run my hands through his hair, then scrape my nails down his stubbly jaw.

"Sorry about the scruff."

"Don't be. I like it."

He kisses me. "Do you, now? I love you, Becca Gelbert."

"Dunne."

He grins. "You really want to be Dunne?'

"There's too many Gelberts in the world and not enough Dunnes."

"Interesting prospect." He puts his forehead to mine. "I have to go, Beauty."

"I know. Can I come with you?"

"You know I'm never going put you near danger on purpose." I exhale. "Now, tell me my pretty words without shouting at me."

I smile. "I love you."

"Good." He kisses me quickly and moves towards the edge of the kitchen. I follow him to the front door where Murray opens the door.

"Thank you, sir. I don't know you and you don't know me, but the service you're providing will never be forgotten. For our peace of mind, we owe you a debt."

He shakes Brick's hand and nods to me.

"The debt is mine to Mr. Pietro. He's done good in this life despite what people think. I proudly serve that man."

I say to Brick, "See, it helps to have friends in high places."

He grips my face. "You be careful, dream of me, and I'll be right back."

My eyes flood with tears. "Promise."

"I promise. It's time to get to the other side. Remember, beyond."

He walks away and the tears fall as I whisper, "Beyond."

# CHAPTER 44
## BRICK

've put her away to get through this shit. Mark and I have been staking out this fucking rat hole for close to three days. The state's attorney has agreed to cooperate and she's in a safe house currently, but she won't tell us shit until she feels ok. Meanwhile, the poor men of Mark's team are simply her slaves. She's a peach you leave on the ground because it never got ripe, so it never got sweet.

"You don't have a family?"

Mark looks up from his phone. "Not really, no room in my life for things that can die. No pets, plants, women, children, parents, siblings—nothing."

"Your career suits ya."

"As did yours," he says with conviction and respect.

"I ain't had a career, I've fallen into a series of things that either gave me money or were part of a scheme. Nothing I'd say I loved."

"Except Becca."

I lean back and stretch my arms high. I lace my fingers to get a good pull on my upper back. "She showed me maybe there's a life beyond waiting to fix something."

"Hallelujah to that." He walks to the back of the van.

The radio in the middle of us squawks to life. "Two blocks."

"Copy. In motion." He turns the box off, secures his earpiece, and flips the safety off.

Mark picks it up and hitches up his vest as do I. I mirror all these moves, ready for this shit to be done. I pull my hoodie over my gear and Mark disappears around the back of the building. The point of this isn't to take him but put him on the run and watch who the hell reaches out a helping hand.

He strolls around the corner and tosses his cigarette to the street. He used to hate smoking. His body was a temple but right now it looks more like a shack. He spies me about thirty feet away, and I put my hands up. I have small piece of equipment taped on the inside of my palm.

"What the fuck you want?"

"Closure, you cocksucking dirty muthafucker."

He pats his side to let me know he's packing his knife and probably several guns. He's paranoid and that can't be because of us. He didn't know I was hunting him.

"My brother, my kin. I'm not here to kill you, so drop your fucking guard."

He stops about ten feet from me, and my hands are still in the air. He won't hurt me on the street. He knows I can take him in a fair fight, and he doesn't have a dirty advantage right now.

"And why the hell would I believe that shit coming out of your mouth?"

I step to him quickly, and I'm in his face in a flash before he has time to react. I clamp his wrists to the side of his body.

"Because I'm not the one who's lied to you."

"Flora Timmons." He spits out.

"Sure, but that was girls." I grin.

"You knew I liked her."

"And you couldn't pull her, so I did. That's why you killed my grandmother? Because some chick gave me a blow job in high school and not you?"

His jaw hardens and doesn't answer me right away.

"Let's get off the street," he says. I follow him to the back porch of an old broken-down apartment.

"I can help you." I remark.

"No one can. But I know you think you can because that's who the fuck you are. The one that can do anything and come out of it smelling like fucking roses. Bitch, you're Teflon and everyone loves you. A backwoods redneck like you pulled an uptight, hot-as-hell lawyer for a wife. How you do that shit? It ain't fair."

He's leaning against a railing. I feel the fight coming. My back is ready if I can only pull off the one thing I'm supposed to. I put my hands into the pocket of the hoodie and encourage him to keep spouting off his bullshit.

"What's not fair is that I worked my ass off in school while you charmed your way through. Charm runs out. How deep are you?"

"Deep. But that don't matter. You had every fucking thing, so when the job came up and it could stop the beat-ings, all I had to do was make her sip sumptum." I struggle not to rip him apart. I move my hands slowly under cover of the sweatshirt.

I shut away that part of me that wants to react to what he's saying, but I do let in a smidgen of relief that the dear woman just went to sleep. Maybe she didn't know the level of betrayal. And she didn't hurt. That was haunting me most nights. Aside from missing the fuck out of Becca, it's the thought she suffered, and it was my fault.

"And you feel good about your soul? I don't have to judge ya. Karma and apparently bookies are gonna take care of your shit real soon. But I do thank you for the details. You know what hurts?"

Chase shuffles his feet. "Besides you being fucking bested by me for once?"

My voice crackles with anger, I can't fucking contain it, and I've done my job here, but I think I might need to see a smidge of fucking blood.

I put my arm across his throat and toss him against the brick wall. He's defiantly smug, and that's the look that's got him into so much trouble it spills out of his pores.

"Look, asshole, you killed an innocent woman so you could keep gambling." All I have to do is push and I choke the life out of him. "You can think you're the big man, but you didn't take a fucking thing from me. Her love will always be around, and you still have goddamned nothing." I step back and he falls to the ground, and I should have known better than to let him out for even a second. He sweeps my legs and I go down.

He's on me and on my throat now. I punch him so hard in the stomach he loses his breath and grip. Then I pick him up just so I can knock him the fuck down. He headbutts me, move of a fucking chump but effective. Blood is down the front of my face as I stumble backward. I see the blade come out and avoid his charge and force it away from me. He's stronger, probably hopped up on something. Mark keeps his distance and I'm grateful for that.

I get the blade tip into the wooden railing, and it's stuck. I seize the moment to wail on his face until he falls backward. I pull my sleeve down and toss the knife into the rubble of the backyard. I don't want my fingerprints on it. He staggers over to me, and I jab him in the solar plexus, and he goes down. He stays down. I kick his ribs, just for fun. His chest is moving, and I finish my mission.

I pull his phone from my pocket. I've already planted the tracker between the phone and the case. I shove it back into his jacket pocket where I picked it from earlier and trade out for mine. I switched them so he wouldn't notice the lack of weight of his phone. Mark had me practice this sleight of hand for weeks. I've picked everyone's pocket at Sal's office and the warehouse.

Mark's behind the steering wheel holding his phone up as I jump in.

"Active and ready. Excellent work. Did it feel good?"

"No."

"Why not? You beat the shit out of him."

"He's still breathing." I remove the hoodie and hold it to my head where I'm bleeding.

"Understood," Mark interrupts my thoughts.

"Understood what?"

"That he's still breathing is a problem. Phillip Cady still breathes."

If he wanted to tell me a tale of why this is personal, well, that's the man's business and none of mine. But I sure am curious.

Mark parks and sacks out while I clutch his phone and wait for Chase to wake up so we can follow this piece of shit.

I startle as Mark nudges me, "He's on the move. He's close to LAX. I have a plane ready to go once we figure out where the fuck he's going. They're scanning for a ticket."

We're on our way to a plane as fast as humanly possible. Hopefully he's on the run and meeting with someone higher on his nasty food chain. Mark pulls directly onto the tarmac, and we hustle onto the jet and wait for the destination.

Mark has locals he could call on but, we're too close to this shit. I can smell the end of this. While we wait for our destination Mark paces.

Mark says, "Mel called earlier."

"Is everything ok?'

"Everything's fine. She and I are convinced there's something with the wife, but she can't find a thing."

I walk up and down the aisle trying to calm myself down about this flight. I hope it's not long. I don't want to be even further from Sonoma or from figuring all this shit out. I try to calm my brain by focusing on the things Mark is saying.

"I thought she wasn't allowed to work."

Mark turns in his chair. "Even Tommi can't stop her. She's latched onto this obsession."

I put my hands on either side of the plane and lean forward. "I'll reach out to some people I know inside the company who I trust. Someone must have gone to their wedding."

"Good call—oh, hold on." He picks up his phone, then hangs up without a word. "Let's go." Then he turns to me and says, "Portland."

"Yee-Haw!"

"He booked a ticket under Brick Dunne."

"Fucker."

"We've got him now."

"We better."

# CHAPTER 45
## BECCA

t's been three days without a word. This is the last time I'm not a part of this shit. I can learn to shoot and cut people. Ok, maybe not, but I don't panic in tight situations. Says the girl who curled up on the floor in front of a couch to hide from someone when I have a bodyguard. Maybe I'm more a 'wait in the car' sidekick, while he exacts revenge.

Poppy told me not to worry, that Sal told her there would be a moment before they could be in touch. All we know is that Sal's nephew is at large, but word from Mark is he's no longer in this country and it's another agency's matter now.

But there seems to be an uptick in beefy, quiet men around town and our friends lately. I wave to Murray and head into my mom's house. I not looking forward to lectures from father about my missing husband or my poor taste in wedding cakes.

There's no one in the house and Elle and Jims Langerford are supposed to come over later so we can cake taste, again. No one respected my first choice. Honestly, I just pointed to one. My dad tried it, thought it was gross, and tossed it across our lawn. So now, I'll try the freaking cakes, the day could be worse. The only thing I insisted on was that Sadie come and help out this time. The girl loves her cake, and it makes me the coolest aunt. I know I have lots of competition, given Sadie's extended family of women, but I like to work a little harder.

"MOM!" I yell and grab a pear. I toss my purse on the kitchen table next to all the cake boxes. I chomp my fruit and walk through the house. David comes around the corner.

"Sup, baby bro."

"That was way too nice. Brick home? Get laid?"

"Ew. Not talking about that with you. And no."

"You've def had an orgasm since I've seen you. Nat and I just finished while the kid napped. Pro tip: don't rest while the kids nap like they all say, that's when you can get some real hard work done."

David comes closer and I try to walk away. "You do get that I'm talking about penis work?"

"Stop. Why are you here?"

"Mom said she'd watch Sadie while Nat and I get an ultrasound. Where is she?"

David shoves a cookie into his mouth, then spits it out in the sink. I sit down at the kitchen island and enjoy him scraping his tongue.

"What the fuck is that?"

"Mom's making dad give up sugar."

"Jesus, that was like an assault. Any word from Mission Impossible?"

"Is that what you assholes are calling him?"

He peeks in the cake box and takes a swipe of icing. I leap up and smack his hand.

"That's what we call that crew of Sal, Brick, and Mark. Like a ragtag team of experts in their field brought together for an unlikely mission."

I glare at him as he drinks milk from the carton. He's never progressed past six years old. How is he a good father?

"You do know that my husband is in danger, right? That I'm out of my fucking head with worry, and I don't know what's happening. That we're all dealing with men tailing us with guns and orders to shoot to kill if anyone attacks us. You know that right?" He stops drinking, puts the milk back, and steps behind me. Then he holds me.

"Sorry. Seriously. If we don't joke, then we don't know what to do. We're in this with you, I promise." I hold his hands to my chest. "Where's Mom?"

"No clue. Where's Sadie? I need her to eat cake with me." I ask.

"Upstairs with Dad watching *The Lehrer Hour*." David gestures to the second floor.

"By choice?"

"She'd do anything for our father, unlike us. I'm baffled but somehow, she's truly interested in the financial analysis program. The only two things she really settles down for are Warriors games and *The Lehrer Hour*."

"Whatever. I'm going to look for Mom."

"Try the hut and tell her Sadie's here." He pulls me into his arms and holds me more than he needs to, but it's not enough for me. But I push down my worry once again. Cake. Sadie. That's the mission for today. Then I can stress about not sleeping, having no home, no clients or career trajectory all night.

I wipe my face, then he smirks at me. "Go away, David."

"You need that man to give you a little naptime loving. You're nicer when you're getting serviced." I roll my eyes and toss a nasty cookie at his head. He ducks and heads out the door.

I yell after him, "I'll tell him when I see him. You guys still have your goons, right?" I follow him to the door.

"Yeah. Sadie's is outside and we're taking our 'not mafia' protection with us to the doctor. How long do we have to walk around like we're the Kennedys?"

I laugh, my father always wanted to be one of the great American families that built this country. It's like his personal cosplay.

"Good." David puts his hand out to slap mine in his strange high five. I put the remnants of my pear in his hand.

"Oh God, I hate you."

"Mutual."

David flips me off and runs out the front door while I walk out the back door. I stare at the patio furniture and it's a fucking mess. It's all wonky. I spend ten minutes moving the chairs back where they should go and lining up the tables, so everyone has a place to put a glass. It really is the optimal positioning. I've even gone so far as to make them a diagram, but they never use it.

I head to my mom's art shack. It's her oasis. She uses it to paint, create stained glass, and other assorted arts and crafts. I never liked doing any of that with her. It all seemed like a silly waste of time. Endless hours resulting in something less than perfect and often not very attractive. Very few of those crafts have practical real-world value. Potholders, ok, I can see that, but when you randomly wrap yarn around things, I don't get that.

But it was David's salvation from the warring parts of his ADHD brain. He was either putting weird shit together or throwing a basketball to straighten out his thoughts. My brain runs more linear. I'm not watching where I'm going and trip over something in the grass.

I look down and it's a smashed phone. Shit. I hope I didn't do this. I pick it up and it looks like it's been punctured by something. I don't see Murray or anyone else around. I shove it in my pocket. I'll apologize when I find the owner. As I get closer, I see that the lights are on in the art shack but only on one side. I run towards it and there's something eerie, she always has music on, and it's quiet. I fling the door open, and my mother is sitting in front of an easel and as I register she's gagged, things go dark.

# CHAPTER 46
## BRICK

**M**ark and I sprint through Portland's airport. Sal's tucked back in Los Angeles negotiating the docks. But this fucker is mine. If an agent of the law weren't tracking him with me, he'd meet his maker here in the airport.

I need all this to come to a fucking end so I can follow through with every single thing I promised her, and myself. Our smart watches are synced with Chase's tracker. He's trapped at one of those cul-de-sacs of gates at the end of a hallway.

He's sitting at a gate bound for Toronto and there's no fucking way we can get to him if he's out of the country. The new plan is to get him, fly him to Toronto, and see who's waiting. I won't go on that leg, but I get to end my part of it all right here. And I do know a few people in that part of the world that might take matters into their own hands if he doesn't behave.

I'm strapped and hyped, but I don't need a piece to take him down. My blood is pumping like a fast-moving stream

KELLY KAY

on a hot day. Cold as hell and crashing up on some rocks. Mark nods to me.

I go to the left, and he flanks to the right. It's crowded and my eyes are pinging between a myriad of faces and expressions. Most of them look bored or annoyed, but none of them are Chase. Mark points to the watch. I walk toward the signal and stop two feet from a woman scrolling her phone. I look around and it dawns on us at the same time. I breathe out, "Sumbitch. That fucking snake." Mark's next to me in an instant.

I kneel in front of the woman. "Ma'am, were you in Los Angeles this morning?"

"What's it to you?" It's like she's trying on a tough girl persona.

"Life or death. I believe a lowlife put a tracker on your phone. I need to confirm it." I don't have time to dance around, because if he's not here, then I will rip open time to get to him. I don't want to think where he is, I can't go there yet. I'm seeing red and this twenty-year-old is between me and the truth.

The faux renegade of a woman freaks out. "Someone's tracking me. Like I'm under surveillance." She flings her phone and breaks into hysterics. I pull the case as fast as I can load and cock a gun. There's a note inside her phone.

*"You should have left it alone. There's no choice now. I did like her —C"*

I toss a wad of cash at the woman and sprint towards Mark who's on the phone and the move.

As security comes flying down the hallway, after all the screaming and I realize we both have guns drawn. Mark and I slip onto a jetway. We escape onto the tarmac while flashing his FBI badge and joining the other agents. I crumple the note in Mark's hand and bolt away from the engines and machinery.

I'm screaming into the phone. I will burn the world to the ground to fucking bury Chase Carlyle. I don't give a shit who gave the order, or that he's going to die for his debts or for killing the only person that ever truly loved me, until her. And now he thinks he gets to fucking touch Becca. There's no more clemency. I'll run if the frame up happens. I'll take that woman and live in the fucking Maldives for the rest of my life as long as I have her.

Finally clear from noise, I scream into the phone. I feel useless but it's all I can do right now. He's got the jump on us.

"MEL. He's there. GET HER! Get in touch with all of them. Chase is hunting Becca. And he has no more fucks to give, he's plum out of reason to keep her or anyone else alive."

I'm shouting into a voicemail, hoping she's on the other line with Mark. I duck inside a hanger and dial Becca. Mark is quick on my heels.

"I have Mel."

I screech in a voice I've never heard from my body before, "Get her. Save her. Don't let that monster cut her up. Find her. Call every fucking person." I get back to my phone and hear Mark say a name that brings on a little faith.

"Sal..."

Fuck, where is everyone? "Becca. He's coming for you. Stay with Murray. Get in your car and go somewhere no one knows. Go to that place Tabi and Poppy ended up running around for Christmas. Go to that place. Do not go with anyone. Get out of wherever you are, my precious reason. You're all my fucking reasons and Chase wants to take that away from me again. I love you more than you can fucking process. Please get this. I'm coming as fast as I can. Run away and I'll find you. I know where you'll be. Go to that place you told me about that's ridiculous and is a friend of a friends. Go now and I'll fix it so that you can get inside. Go. Please be alright." I hang up the phone resigned.

Mark puts his hand on my shoulder. "Sal knows and is working things on his end. The Sheriff has been alerted."

"I sent her to Sal's warehouse in Jingletown."

"Brick, listen to me, Sal said there are multiple people not answering the call."

"What the fuck are you saying to me?"

"Mel's alerting the families. We'll find her. Come." I jump into a cart with him.

"Sal's plane is faster than the FBI one available."

"You and the mobster really are a package deal."

He grins at me. "Alleged."

"Alleged." He takes off and I stick my ear pod back in and call David. It goes to voicemail. I thought these fucking people were told to pick up this number if it rings.

"David. Brick. Find your sister NOW. Chase Carlyle is in town and threatening her. Please be careful. Get to her if you can."

I call again.

Mark is talking. I catch a word or two but the wind and the noises on the tarmac muffle it. And suddenly I get a voice.

"Who is this?"

"Thank fucking God. David. It's Brick. Where are you?"

"Why are the phones popping off?"

"Chase is coming for Becca. Where is she?" I scrub my face and hold on as Mark drives this cart like it's an Indy racer. Fucking swerving around corners and people like a professional, but it's still not fucking fast enough for me.

"WHAT? She's at my parents' house and Sadie's there. We can't get in touch with my dad or Sadie's goon. Fuck. I'm headed there now. Nat, call my mom, now!"

I yell, "Back to me. Hurry and report back and fucking take someone with you."

"We have Gianni with us, and I'll get Josh and Sam."

"GO. Please save her. I'll be as quick as I fucking can, but we're in Portland."

"Why? Really, Portland?"

"Shut the fuck up and go save her."

"On it, man."

As the phone goes dead, I'm filled with relief he's doing something and dread it's not enough. We pull up to the plane, and we're on it and moving in an instant.

I sit down and buckle up, but I'm ready to jump out of my skin.

Mark says, "This is a Cessna Citation X, fastest we can get. We'll be on the ground in under an hour."

"And it only takes a fucking minute to die."

Mark breathes in and out for a second, taking in my words. "I'm going to say something that's going to upset you but might ease your mind."

"What the fuck is that about? I'm not upset, I'm fucking bereft and pure fury. I'm a bull in the red zone, and I will cut down anyone in my fucking way to get to her. So, it doesn't matter what the hell you have to say."

He grips the armrests. "He'd want to make her suffer. Prove to you he's in control. He won't shoot her, you know that. But that ego might keep her alive longer."

"You're saying he'll cut her slowly." He nods. "You don't think I know that? You don't think that's the fucking thing that will haunt me forever, the pain and suffering she's about to endure. Don't say anything else to me. Have the world ready to move out of my way when we land."

"Yes, sir."

I may be crazed out of my head, but this is a good man beside me.

# CHAPTER 47
## BECCA

My eyes lift and I see my mom. She's fuzzy but has tears streaming down her face. Her makeup is usually absolutely perfect on her light skin, but it's streaked black from her mascara. Her petal pink lipstick is smeared on the dirty painting rag in her mouth. I squint and try to reach up to clear my eyes and realize I'm bound to a chair. Her eyes are pleading. With great effort I flop my head over to the front door. The daylight is bright, how can something horrible happen to me in the light? I'm confused and trying to put my brain back online. My head hurts a lot, but I'm baffled as to why.

"Well, there you are, chere." I know that voice, but everything is muddled. My mom's sobbing, and I wake from my fog and assess if she's hurt. I try and say something, but it's terribly muffled. Then the snake I've been avoiding rips my gag down.

"Where's my warm welcome? I mean I rolled out the fucking red carpet for you."

She's a fierce defender of her children so it must be killing her she can't protect me.

"Chase," I gasp out.

"Well, Becca, sweetheart, you do remember. Consider me touched."

"How long was I out?" I need to know what time it is. I need to put this all back into a timeline of some sort.

"Over a half an hour or so, but you pay no mind to time, it don't matter no more." He rubs his knuckle down my cheek and I recoil. My mother screams the best she can through her gag.

Chase turns to her. "Now, now, Mama. I told you to mind your place and tongue or there's going to be more cutting tonight."

"More?!" I frantically swivel my head around and see blood seeping towards the drain in the center of the art shack. There's a large heap in a shiny suit in the corner and my heart breaks for Murray. My parents' guard must be watching the house.

I scream his name to see if he reacts. Chase only laughs as the man stays still. Oh God. He died defending my mom to no avail. I won't be afraid. I have to solve this.

I'll go procedural. He wants something, I just have to figure out what it is. That's how I win cases, figure out the package to deliver the news. How does this judge want this evidence presented? How do I get under the prosecutor's skin? What does each juror want and how can I exploit and manipulate them? What does Chase want from me?

I analyze what my brain has capacity for. I can't let panic overtake me and mom needs to stay calm. I nod slowly at her to indicate we're going to be fine, even though we're far from fucking fine.

Chase circles me, then kneels. I don't react as I see his favorite toy in his right hand, and he splays his left out on my knee.

"You're not happy or surprised to see me." I'm shocked as fuck, but I won't let him know.

"Just can't muster the excitement."

He smacks my face and my mother screams again.

I look straight on at him and say, "I hope you plan to disappear forever because when he sees what you just did—"

"Oh, but that's where you're making a whole lot of assumptions, Ms. Rebecca. He won't see much of anything for quite a while. He's on what I like to call a snipe hunt."

"Where did you send him?"

"Don't know, can't be sure. Could be close, but I hope it's far. I'm a man of many talents, even though some have been overlooked in the past. I'm not as stupid as you fucking people think."

That's the hook, flattery.

I say, "No one thinks you're stupid."

"Brick does."

He needs ego stroking. "No, he doesn't." I try and correct him.

He needs to be better than Brick.

He smacks me again.

"Shut the fuck up. What you know about it? He was the one all them girls wanted. He was the one to get the grades, the college scholarships, the accolades, and the pussy. Fucking Brick could do no wrong. That ain't no kind of fair. I got a fucking raw deal and when his mama left, there was Mimi Tinker being all sweet and perfect. The whole world bends like a willow in a hurricane to whatever the hell Brick wants."

The more I can keep him talking the more I can come up with a plan.

"What is it you want?" I goad him.

"Well, Brick got himself in trouble." He has a sick grin. "But he got himself a fucking hot-ass lawyer wifey out of the deal, at least for a little while. And how the fuck that happen? I'm here to fix the shit you pulled."

My mom's whimpering, but I can also see she's almost worked her hands free. Jana's badass.

I pull his attention.

"Brick told me the only thing he wanted to be in high school, was you."

There's a flicker on his lip. He's standing in front of me. "You fucked up. You got Brick off and gave my name to authorities and now my fucking boss is ready to tie up my loose end. So, you fix it to get my name out their mouths. You fix it so as I didn't kill that girl. That I didn't kill no one. You're a good lawyer, you do it."

He doesn't even know it's the FBI, that's good. That means that no matter what happens to me, Cady still thinks he's protected, which means they have a shot at getting to him.

"I'm good, but I'm not that good."

He squeezes my mouth hard. "Be the kind of good I need. You write something up on that piece of paper saying you fucking lied and it's Brick who done all the killing. That you is a shit-all lawyer and he done it and the two of you go to fucking jail. You in it together like cahoots."

I don't react because I've gone numb. I cock my head at him, and he gestures to paper and pencil on the table. I don't move, just glare. He moves like a snake, fast and slick. Before I even know it, my arm flares red in a stripe. I'm dripping from a cut that's deep enough to pool but not deep enough to incapacitate me. And it's not the hand I write with. It stings and I grit my teeth, much to my dismay.

He grins wide. He wants to inflict pain. Not on me but

on anyone. He gets off on it. Shit. That's not something I think I can cater to.

I say as steely as possible, "Then give me the chance to make it right. I'll need a pen not a pencil. And I'll need to get it notarized, but I'll write you a confession letter. I'll admit to how we did it. But first I need to know how you pulled it off. We couldn't find anything that pins you to the murder of that girl." I need him to keep talking. I don't want that blade near my mother.

"And if you don't, first I'm going to carve up that pretty mama of yours. Then I'm going to slowly take pieces out of you while keeping you awake enough to see how good I am with this blade. Maybe I'll keep your mama awake just long enough to see you suffer if you don't get to fucking fixin' this mess. Then it will be your dear hus—"

We all freeze in place as the voice sweetly singing outside gets closer. Oh God no.

"Mhamo! Mhamo, clay!" And she's pulling on the doors. Oh God. Sadie, don't come in here. My mask, decorum, and any control over the situation have all slipped down the blood-spattered drain. I don't think, I react.

"SADIE, GO AWAY!!!! NO! GET OUT OF HERE. RUN. FIND DHAMO! RUUUUUUN!"

"Aunt BECCA. Beck!?"

"RUN away, SADIE!!! GO AWAY NOW. I DON'T WANT TO SEE YOU." She pulls at the doors and wails about clay. Chase smacks me across the face again.

"Shut the fuck up."

He sees my panic. He knows I can play with him all day, but that little girl is the key to getting me to do anything he wants. He moves like a feral cat, quickly scattering down an ally towards the door.

We react just as quickly when he turns his back on us. I

attempt to stand and my chair falls back. I crash to the floor, breaking the chair legs and freeing my feet. I'm rolling over on to my knees to pop up and get to him, but my arm is bleeding a lot and the blood is making things slippery as I try to roll over.

I glance up and like a cartoon, my mother smashes a large canvas over Chase's head. She traps his arms inside the painting. He's wildly spinning but can't get his arms free enough to use his weapon. I finally get up and my mother smashes Chase's head with her heavy wooden easel.

I'm almost to her when she yells, "No one fucks with my family." He falls in a heap but he's still awake. He's forming words and when he fell, the frame of the painting broke, giving him a little more freedom.

Sadie's wails turn into a chant of "no."

I'm next to my mother as she watches Chase to see if she needs to hit him again. And the screeching child descant of "no" grows faint. I kick him in the stomach. And I realize Sadie isn't at the door. My body floods with relief that someone's got her. There's a loud creak and the doors to my mother's art shack splinter as bodies rush in, smashing the wood to bits. The first face I see is Sam, the second is Josh. There's a wall of men in suits on their heels all with guns pulled.

Sam doesn't hesitate in smashing Chase's face into the concrete with one blow and he stays down. Josh scoops up my mother and carries her out of the shack to the waiting arms of my father. Sam's on me and cutting the bindings off my hands, and I collapse against him. David runs in, I know it was David that rallied everyone somehow. My eyes search the crowd, my head swiveling wildly, and my gaze lands on David. I see all my family and friends, but my thoughts are only in one place.

"Brick?"

David pulls me close and holds me like he actually likes me. I sob because he's not saying anything. I need him to tell me he's ok.

"He's almost here. Brick's on his way to you."

Sam holds a towel to my arm and crowds me with concern. "He sent us. All of us with the edict, 'save my world.'"

"Sal sent him away from me, you all did. I don't like that. Is Sadie ok? Does she hate me now? I yelled at her."

David pulls me tighter. "If my daughter hates you for saving her life, I'll be sure to ground her." I laugh and sob. I let go as everything whooshes through my body at once. I don't do this in public but on my brother's shoulder while my father and my mother surround us, it's my only option. My mother's stroking my hair and my father keeps muttering, "Proud of you, all of you." He never lets go of my mother's hand.

And then there's a crowd of people and hugs. Sadie's at my legs.

I see Tabi throw her arm around Sheriff Robert's shoulder and say, "Well, we solved another one for you." Then she smacks him on his back and walks towards Natalie who's sobbing and putting her hand over her heart when we lock eyes.

There's a blur of love and relief and then the only voice I ever want to hear for the rest of my life.

# CHAPTER 48
# BRICK

"MOVE!"

I'm tearing through people to get to her. I'm like a loose hog on the run, ripping down fences. Physically moving people, picking them up, and moving them out of my way. Some I recognize and others are simply giant obstacles in my way of getting to the only thing that matters.

Poppy points, but she doesn't need to, I can sense where she is, she's the one surrounded by people making sure she's ok. She's the one probably flabbergasted by all these people caring about her. My hummingbird is full of personal self-doubt, not professional, mind you, but after today when the rug got pulled out from under us, she should never doubt again. She's loved more than she was aware. And probably loved the most. All the good she's done for them and the world, and in return, she just slunk away to be alone and wait. Turns out she was waiting for me so we could have a full life.

I move Arthur to the side and at first, he's reluctant, then he pays me mind and sees he's in my spot. I nod sharply at David, thankful as hell he picked up his fucking phone. I don't know what happened here, but I see Chase being pulled away and everyone seems to be accounted for. I rip my girl out of her brother's arms and smother her with mine.

She gasps and cries like the gentle little bird I know she is. My sweet hummingbird, so fast, so strong, and so fragile. Her body is racked with sobs, and I just keep thanking the sweet lord or Mimi Tinker or the mojo or whatever it is that she's mine, she's safe, and she's forever.

"Hummingbird, I got you. And sit in the comfort that you have quite the collection of folks watching out for you and caring for you."

She sputters out, "Where were you?"

"Portland."

"No. Not now. My whole life. Where have you been?"

"Waiting on you, darling. Always waiting on you."

# EPILOGUE

## BECCA

"Well, well, well."

"I don't want to hear it, Tabi." I sway my hips and the satin swirls around me like foam in a cappuccino or the white cap of a Gulfport wave.

Tabi says simply, "You look really beautiful." My head whips around and my hair clouds my vision because it's so damn big. I let them do what Brick wanted. He said he wanted my hair wild like in Mississippi.

"I brought you something old." Tabi smirks, then all hell breaks loose.

"Who in the blazes you calling old? You is bloated." The feisty little woman smacks Tabi's arm.

"Fair." Tabi nods and rubs her growing belly. She's almost eight months.

Lucille pushes her way past my friend, who happens to be my maid of honor, and who the hell knows how that happened, but my cousin demanded I have one. Poppy insisted on officiating the ceremony. She needed something special to look forward to. Sal's been gone for a while now. He came to see her and say hello to us just after the Chase thing. But he's been gone ever since. She's a bit deflated and hollow, so I let her do anything she wanted for this wedding. No one knows where Enzo went either. But today's for us, the '5', and the man who's beyond.

Elle and Natalie will be up there with me too. The only one I really wanted is the one in the over-the-top pink sparkly dress who keeps spinning so the dress is floaty. Sadie's been practicing for a week and the streets of Sonoma are littered with real flower petals. My mom bought in bulk, of course. And our houses are covered with the silk variety. Michael's Crafts strikes again.

Jana behaved and out in the vineyard there are only the five families and of course our various bodyguards. Murray's brother, Morty, stepped in and felt it was his duty to protect us. We tried to pay for all the arrangements, but Sal took care of it. As long as Cady's still out there and Brick's not in jail, we'll probably have a Morty of some sort around.

"Now, rude one, go tend to your youngins and leave us be." The only family Brick has makes her way across the room to me.

I lean over and kiss her papery cheek and she smiles. "Child, have yourself a sit."

I do, I don't care if the satin wrinkles. It's long and simple cream satin with a streak of dark green trim on the hem that Elle found. She said it looked like me, deceptively beautiful and deep. The pop of color at the hem hinting there's something fun lurking underneath. Somehow as I fall more in love with Brick, the rest of my extended family see more of me. Like he unearthed the secret Rebecca that only my mom and brother knew existed. I guess Poppy did as well, but now I feel as if they see all of me.

I was always a background player in my own life until Brick made me step up, and I'm never going back. I should probably use those as vows, but no matter what I say, he'll have something more meaningful and eloquent.

Lucille sits beside me and takes my hand. "That boy is all I got in the world beside my favorite pots back on the burners. You can have those if you want them."

"Like a dowery?" We laugh and she squeezes my hand and arranges my ring.

"Sure, ain't glad you wearing this."

I turn to her, confused, and she smiles big and bright. "No, child, you misrepresent me. It means she ain't here."

"Who?"

"My best friend. This was hers and on the occasion of you having it means she don't. I like that it has a new life and all, but I sure do miss her."

I can't breathe or speak. I am trying not to cry because I have too much fucking makeup on, and Poppy will kill me if she has to do it again. I had no idea this ring was Mimi Tinker's. I've been wearing her real fucking diamond this whole time. I'm going to kill him for not telling me. I put my arm around Lucille and pull her a little closer to me.

"He gonna be good to you. But you know that boy's heart is bigger and brighter than a magnolia in bloom. He a hundred-year kind of fella. Just like his grandpappy Tinker was. Devoted to the only thing they know, love."

"Mojo."

She slaps my arm. "Exactly."

"You don't have to worry about his heart. I am and will forever be the caretaker of his heart. Long after we're both dust, we'll still be written in the stars. I am but nothing except his."

She stands up and I glance to the doorway and my brother is leaning in the doorframe. He wipes his eyes and stares at me.

Lucille gets up turns to me and says, "Good. Now get out there so the boozing and dancin' can start."

David grabs her cane and helps her out of the room, then turns back to me.

I say, "You have something on you." I walk over and stand in front of him. He starts feeling around on his face. "No, on your shirt." He looks down and I take the opportunity to flick the end of his nose.

"Made you look."

He groans, then pulls me into a hug. "You're such a fucking pain in the ass."

"Thank you." Is all I say. I don't know why, but I do know I am grateful for his dumb ass.

"No, Becks, thank you."

I pull out of the hug and ask, "For what?"

"For showing me how to love a strong woman. And for being an epic assface to me all the time so I never forgot who I am for real. Even if others couldn't see it. I see you too."

"I was just thinking about that. How it's nicer on this side of things. Right?"

"And what's on this side of things?" David laughs and offers his arm to me, and I take it.

"Happiness."

He puts his hand over mine and escorts me out the door to deliver me to my father. Just before I get to him, Elle turns around and pops open a gloss.

"I'm fine."

Tabi says, "Let her do it. It's her thing."

Arthur gruffs, "We're late. Is this important?"

Elle pushes him aside. "Of course, it is. Now hold still and slightly part your lips." She paints gloss on top and I try not to hate it.

Natalie coos, "It's perfect."

Elle says, "I know. It's Ilia *Waking Up*."

Everyone smiles at me, and Tabi asks, "How the hell do you do that? Perfect shade and mood every time."

She shrugs. "It's a gift."

And words flow out of my mouth without my permission, "No, you all are."

Arthur takes my hand and places it on his arm as Elle squeezes my shoulder. "Perfect. Let's go pretend to get you married, so your mom can cry. Fair warning. All the Aunties are already crying." Everyone laughs.

Music starts, it's a jangly old piano and a violin. Took me forever to find people who would play a slightly out-of-tune piano.

The girls move out of the tent and into our vineyard, and I wait with my dad.

"I assume you expect something poignant from me right now."

I look over to my dad and roll my eyes. "Because that's who we are. Save the mushy shit for David and Mom. You told me you're proud of me. That will work."

And then tears flood his eyes and his words come out in almost sobs. I wish David were here to see this.

"So. Very. Proud. My. Girl." I hug him and blink back my own tears as my father tries to hold back a lifetime of emotion.

I whisper to him, "I'm proud of you too."

We stand holding each other for a moment and we're a

bit late for our music cue. I hear a very loud and welcoming voice rise above everything.

"Woman! Get your ass out here and marry me in front of God and this cast of thousands that you call your family."

And then he starts singing. We peek out and he's the one at the piano playing, "Good Day for Marrying You." My brother and other "brothers" and Mel are all standing up for him.

His face is beaming. I can't get to him fast enough, but my father keeps a steady pace. He always has.

He walks me to the piano. Brick's in an actual tuxedo and I might die. The black and white is stunning on his broad shoulders, and there's only one pop of color. The green of the hummingbird wing matches the green on my dress. Elle really is good.

He shakes my dad's hand, then gathers me in his arms and carries me to the front of everyone among hooting and hollering, as he'd say.

He puts me down in front of Poppy and she's already sobbing. Who thought this was a good idea for her to officiate?

Brick leans to me and his lips are gentle on the shell of my ear as he says, "I love you beyond everything."

I whisper, "Beyond."

"Beyond."

The world might be full of magic but right now all of it, all of the damn magic in the world, is in his eyes and the way he's looking at me.

## BRICK

The parents have all danced their asses off and are tucked up in their respective houses. And now it's just my bride and all fourteen of her immediate "kin" at the giant fire pit her mama and I created just for her. I knew she'd want and need this moment. Just her cousin, brother, and the others, sitting around cutting up and sipping something divine that one of them had a hand in crafting.

I'm currently drinking one of Josh's father's, Will Whittier, crazy homemade blends. He doesn't send them out with the rest of his wines but hands them out to family and friends. This one is called, "Mosey On Down The Aisle." He named it special for us and his lovely wife, Sarah, painted the bottle with hummingbirds and vines. I was told he's the heart of the crew and he's shown me nothing but kindness. And he's funny as all hell.

Ian, Ingrid's man, looks over at me and shows me a flower tattoo. I smile and point at it. He's a confusing fella.

"No, dude. This is Ingrid. I did the same fucking thing you did. I ran out and got a tattoo so I could hold onto her."

Becca looks to Ingrid. "Really, Omega?"

She shrugs. "Yeah. We have a similar story, Alpha." I love that they call each other that. It's cute as hell, them being the oldest and the youngest of this brood.

Becca cocks her head. "He did that, and you didn't marry him or say yes to any of his million proposals?"

"Nope."

Ian yells, "SEE. Becca was so charmed by it she leapt into marriage. Look how damn happy she is."

Ingrid curls into Ian and say, "I'm also pretty damn happy, and the answer is still no."

Bax hoots, "Keep him in his place, Little Bell."

Everyone laughs as he calls his sister by her former nickname.

I sip again and David looks over at me and I see my brother. Brother. That feels damn good. I might like marrying into a big family since I came from such a tiny one. I squeeze my bride a little closer. I know she's squirmy and wants a chair of her own, but tonight she only sits on my lap or my face. Those are her choices for this second wedding night of ours.

David says, "What are you going to do now?"

"Besides watch our backs and wait for Cady to pop up again? No clue."

I hadn't thought about that at all. I laugh a little, look at these people who have accepted me in their lives, and say, "I guess stay by this one's side. I've been in the revenge business so long, now that it's over, I don't rightly know what to make of the rest of my life." I grin.

Sam doesn't miss a beat and says, "Have you ever considered piracy? You'd make a wonderful Dread Pirate Roberts."

Everyone laughs, then Josh is serious. "There's not a damn thing you won't be able to do if it's what you want. We're here if you want to pick our brains or need something to do. We're all fucking swamped with work. Ever prune a vine?"

They all laugh a bit too hard.

"Wine isn't quite my thing. And I have a house to build."

Josh doesn't miss a beat, "Good luck keeping Elle out of that process."

"I welcome the help, and I also know how to redirect a strong woman, should things get off the rails."

We picked a spot on the back half of Gelbert's property

that's secluded and a ten-minute drive from her parents. Her father sold it to me. I was compensated for Mimi Tinker's land and although I don't want the blood money, I do like that it's a thorn in Mr. Cady's side.

It's fallow but picturesque as hell and will make a perfect homestead someday. It even has a giant old tree that will have to substitute for a live oak. But I guess she's already got all the cottonwood branch she can handle. We've been going at it like rabbits who are out to set a record.

The big tree is perfect for a swing for her or possibly others that might come along. We haven't exactly been careful and neither of us seems to be too concerned should she get pregnant. More family to love is never a bad thing.

Becca turns to me and puts her hand on my cheek. "First, you build me a house."

"That I can do." I kiss her to punctuate the point.

Elle just starts paying attention. She yawns and says, "I can help with that." That little babe in her arms is sweet as hell.

"Ms. Elle, you ever gonna name that babe?" It's been over three months and that poor darling is still called "Four."

"When the name hits me, I'll know. Then we'll call her that. Right now, we're blobs to her." She kisses the sweet girl and even though she's as nameless as Lil' Bit used to be, she knows she's loved.

Josh has the twins asleep on his lap and the other one seems to be walking around bossing people around and dancing with all the uncles.

"I appreciate you kindly, but I think I'll figure out what my next step is by myself."

"Fair enough, but you'll learn."

"Learn what?"

Tabi shifts Nick to her other shoulder and says, "This one doesn't take no for an answer. She already has blueprints in motion."

Sam pipes up with, "And there is no 'by yourself' anymore."

They all laugh, and David adds, "If she's not knocked up again."

She passes the baby to Bax. Then looks each one of us in the eye, ending with her baby daddy.

"NO! I'm done. That one is the last of the great Whittier sperm."

Josh pats her knee. "We'll see." I'm sure that phrase just earned her another pregnancy because he's going to want to try for a boy to carry on that name.

"Joshua Lucien LaChappelle Whittier, I am DONE birthing babies. Done, do you hear me? I don't know what it's like not be pregnant. My entire life is gone, replaced with nothing but memories of being pregnant and nursing and little girls. I love them so much, but I'm throwing out all the pregnancy crap, and we're going to love the hell out of the four little girls we have."

David adds, "Five makes a basketball team and you still don't have a boy." Elle tosses her empty glass at him, and he catches it midair.

I sip my whiskey and grin at their exchange. Then Evan, Jims Langerford's husband, sits forward in his chair. He and Elle used to work together and now he runs a design firm or something.

"I could help with decor if you want. And as for work, take advice from an outsider, find something alongside them, not with them, and you'll thrive."

Nat, Elle, Ian and Ms. Mel all nod at me. I realize I've

just become one of the inside outsiders. I grin at them one by one as if we're a secret club.

Becca leans back and puts her head on my shoulder. And whispers in my ear, "What if you played, just for you? Poppy could learn to do a boil and you bring your world to ours."

Whiskey and oysters with a dash of honky-tonk piano might just be what this town needs. Now that we're building here in Sonoma, perhaps I will find a little spot that needs a jukebox and some decent food.

"No secrets! That's not fair," Ingrid says from the other side of the fire. She's sitting next her world famous musician who, when he's in town, seems to pop up playing all over town. He could play at my place, if I had one. Perhaps there's something in Becca's good idea. I pull her snug and kiss her neck.

"They're not secrets, simply private, Ms. Ingrid." She nods and everyone begins to talk amongst themselves.

Sam stands up. "I'm out." I get it, he and Poppy are the only ones here without partners.

David chastises him, "Where the hell you going?"

"To get laid, and it's certainly not happening here."

Tabi sits up, she was dozing. "Are you fucking kidding me? It's all of us together. That never freaking happens."

He keeps moving away from us and then turns, "You're fucking kidding, right? It always happens. I have to go. Becca, Brick, congrats. Thanks for a lovely time."

Becca nods and Tabi yells at Sam some more.

"Fuck off."

He flips her off and walks away, saying, "That's the plan."

Once he's out of earshot everyone shares a look. Jims,

his brother, says, "I'm not sure how much more of his pain over losing Sammy I can take."

Tabi high-fives him. "I hate new Sam." Everyone starts jawing away about Sam, but I don't care. He'll find his own way.

I run my finger over Mimi Tinker's ring.

I speak so only she can hear, "There's nothing I need to do in this life but honor you and this thing between us. Thanks for bringing me back to life. My whole being seems to be here now, lots of me went missing but it turns out, you had all the pieces of my soul tucked away in that good heart of yours just waiting for me to come a calling."

She turns to me, and her eyes are glassy.

"I will never understand why I get to be this happy, but I do know I'm done questioning it. I love you to the ends of the earth."

"And beyond that, my hummingbird, beyond that. My love knows no boundaries and limitations. And that's completely legal, I looked it up in the California Bar Association penal code of conduct. As long as I honor, love, and cherish you, I think I'll be within the legal limits of our union."

"Case closed." She smiles at me with her whole heart and it's just about too much to bear.

Her lips touch mine, and the group groans, but I don't pay them no mind. It's time to part company for the night. I simply stand and keep my bride in my arms and walk towards our forever.

## BECCA

I'm tracing my hummingbird, the only thing he's wearing right now. We'll have to leave the hotel soon.

"Do you really want to open a whiskey bar?"

"After my research is done."

I grin and climb on top of him. I pull the sheet around me, and I feel that cottonwood start to twitch. "Mrs. Dunne, what do you have up your sleeve?" He puts his hands on my ass and holds on while kneading it. I grin at him.

"I'm serious. What research?"

"Hear me out. You don't have any more clients. I don't need you no more in a lawyerly capacity. And I can tell you as much as I adore your parents, we need out of that house."

I bend down and kiss him deeply, our tongues fighting for dominance. Then I pepper his jaw with more kisses while he speaks.

"Your brother said something about some relatives that might know a thing or two about some good whiskey."

Ireland. He's talking about going away. This makes no sense. We're at a place where we can start to build a normal life, and I can put the pieces of my career back together. I try to shift off him, but he holds me in place with those big powerful hands and thrusts up.

"You want to travel?"

He shifts under me and hits me with some perfect friction. I toss my head back for a second, then snap back to his gaze.

He says, "I want to disappear. With you. Then when we've had our fill of disappearing, we figure out next steps."

"You want to hide until he's caught." I raise an eyebrow and grind down on his now very apparent tree branch.

"How do you know I don't just want to keep you naked for an extended amount of time?"

I've come this far away from who I used to be, why not keep falling into this life? "I'll send Sadie a message and tell her we're coming."

He looks at me funny.

"The other one. Her namesake, my great-aunt's widow. She lives by herself with side-by-side cottages outside of Cork. One has always been a ruse, so no one knew she was living there with my great-aunt. She's a pretty incredible person and as family as one can get."

"Family sure means a hell of a lot to you people."

"Hope that's okay." I move to face him, side by side. I look into his face, and I'm as transformed now as I was the first time I saw it.

"More than, I'll just need to adjust my scope, is all. The family I clung to, other than my grandparents and Lucille, aren't quite worth hanging onto."

I forget that there's a loss; he's so brave.

"Family is all there is."

He grins and kisses me. "And magic."

I respond with our lips still touching, "And mojo."

The End

"THANK YOU SO MUCH FOR COMING ON THE JOURNEY with Becca & Brick. They're return in Poppy & Sal's story Bottled Up: Pietro Family Estate story along with the entire 5 . ——>https://mybook.to/PietroFamily Bottled Up releases mid March 2024.

**A wine country romance with a dash of mafia.**
"It's time you knew the whole story. And I don't trust the wifey to get it totally right."
-Sal

IF YOU'RE NEW TO THE 5 YOU CAN GET ALL THE DETAILS on the next page. Each winery or family can be read as a standalone.

THANK YOU AGAIN FOR READING RS! - KELLY K